Meg Henderson

was born in Glasgow, spending part of her childhood in Drum-chapel, on the outskirts of Clydebank. She is a journalist and the author of *Finding Peggy*, a memoir of her Glasgow childhood, and two novels, *The Holy City* and *Bloody Mary*.

Praise for Meg Henderson:

THE HOLY CITY

'*The Holy City* is a novel about growing up in the close-knit blue-collar community of Clydeside from the Twenties through to the present day... The overall effect is of being at your auntie's, of listening to an enthusiastic storyteller, of the fascination of taking a microscope to seemingly ordinary lives and bringing them into dramatic focus.'   *Scotland on Sunday*

'A hugely absorbing story. Henderson brings the horror and pain of these wartime experiences vividly to life with vigorous humour, common-sense wisdom and vitality.'   *Observer*

'A novel of exceptional warmth and optimism'   *Options*

BLOODY MARY

'*Bloody Mary* reveals the desperate reality of Glasgow's "boarded-outs", unwanted children who were sent to live with surrogate parents as virtual slaves. Henderson has a real feel for the history she revels in and the knack of bringing it to realistic light as she gets behind the bare facts of life in Glasgow and the Western Isles over the last century.'   *The List*

'At once familiar and freshly seen... This is a novel full of the rich detail of domestic lives, told with humour and sharpness.'
                                    Scotland on Sunday

'Henderson's strengths are her ear for idiom, her eye for itemizing, and her love of the local, her generosity of spirit shining through.'   *Glasgow Sunday Herald*

Also by Meg Henderson:

FINDING PEGGY: A GLASGOW CHILDHOOD
THE HOLY CITY
BLOODY MARY

MEG HENDERSON

Chasing Angels

Flamingo
An Imprint of HarperCollins*Publishers*

Flamingo
An imprint of HarperCollins*Publishers*
77–85 Fulham Palace Road,
Hammersmith, London W6 8JB

Flamingo is a registered trade mark of
HarperCollins*Publishers* Limited

www.**fire**and**water**.com

Published by Flamingo 2001
9 8 7 6 5 4 3 2 1

First published in Great Britain by Flamingo 2000

The Author and Publisher are grateful to Scotland In Focus for
permission to reproduce the photograph of the Glenfinnan Monument
on p.189, to the National Trust for Scotland for allowing us to use a
photograph of 'A Highlander of the '45', and to Rab Henderson for
his photographs of the entrance to the Barras Market (p.x), Kathy's
Cottage (p.122) and of 'Rory' the Highlander himself on p.294. Thanks
also go to Macmillan Publishers for their permission to use the poem
'Questions about Angels' by Billy Collins, from his collection *Taking
Off Emily Dickinson's Clothes*.

Photograph of Meg Henderson © Scotsman Publications Limited

ISBN 0 00 655026 6

Set in Bembo by Rowland Phototypesetting Ltd, Bury St Edmunds,
Suffolk

Printed and bound in Great Britain by Clays Ltd, St Ives plc

For Susie,
who nurtures all the Curtis Brown Scotland egos,
in the hope that she might forgive me for killing Helen.

ACKNOWLEDGEMENTS

I find the older I get the bolshier I get too, so this may very well be my last ever batch of acknowledgements in a book. There are those, however, who supplied factual information, like Lillias Grant and her fine body of women at the National Trust for Scotland's Glenfinnan Monument Centre, who gave of their time, and unbeknown to at least one of them, her personality. And the Barras people deserve a mention, the vast army of Pearsons who contributed snippets here and there, and the Barras Enterprise Trust. Most of it, though, the streets, the stories and characters I remember from childhood expeditions to the Barras on a Sunday afternoon, a ritual for many Glasgow children of the time. And there was no particular Father Frank McCabe: he didn't exist. He is an amalgam of all the priests I ever knew. Parts of his personality can be traced back to the many tyrants who tried to impose themselves, unwanted and uninvited on my childhood, so I suppose it's only fair that they should now take a bow. At a public appearance years ago I was ambushed by a coven of rabid nuns complaining that in an earlier book I had used the real names of the nuns who scarred the schooldays of many children, my own included. I pointed out then that those women had enjoyed a great deal of power – which they abused – over little swine like me and the price they had to pay for that power was the risk that one of the little swine would grow up to be a big swine who one day might tell the world about them and name them. However, I enjoyed the Battle of the Rabid Nuns so much that I thought I'd go for the priests this time.

Questions About Angels

Of all the questions you might want to ask
about angels, the only one you ever hear
is how many can dance on the head of a pin.

No curiosity about how they pass the eternal time
besides circling the Throne chanting in Latin
or delivering a crust of bread to a hermit on earth
or guiding a boy and girl across a rickety wooden bridge.

Do they fly through God's body and come out singing?
Do they swing like children from the hinges
of the spirit world saying their names backwards and
    forwards?
Do they sit alone in a little garden changing colours?

What about their sleeping habits, the fabric of their robes,
their diet of unfiltered divine light?
What goes on inside their luminous heads? Is there a wall
these tall presences can look over and see hell?

If an angel fell off a cloud would he leave a hole
in a river and would the hole float along endlessly
filled with the silent letters of every angelic word?

If an angel delivered the mail would he arrive
in a blinding rush of wings or would he just assume
the appearance of the regular mailman and
whistle up the driveway reading the postcards?

No, the medieval theologians control the court.
The only question you ever hear is about
the little dance floor on the head of a pin
where halos are meant to converge and drift invisibly.

It is designed to make us think in millions,
billions, to make us run out of numbers and collapse
into infinity, but perhaps the answer is simply one:
one female angel dancing alone in her stocking feet,
a small jazz combo working in the background.

She sways like a branch in the wind, her beautiful
eyes closed, and the tall thin bassist leans over
to glance at his watch because she has been dancing
forever, and now it is very late, even for musicians.

Billy Collins
from his collection *Taking Off Emily Dickinson's Clothes*

Chasing Angels

The entrance to the Barras Market, and to generations of Glaswegians especially, gateway to exotica. There's not much you can't get there, from candyfloss to snake oil and beyond. For me as a child the real delight was in watching the people, like Chief Abadu and Cockney Jock, and my now famous one-legged Uncle Hughie, who lived in nearby Stevenston Street.

1

She had never much liked her brother, that was what it amounted to. In her hand was a snap of the two of them, taken many years ago when she was a child. She turned it over and saw her mother's small, careful handwriting: 'Peter and Kathleen,' it said, '1956.' She traced the letters with her finger, listening to Lily's voice in her head as she did so. Funny how deeply touching someone's handwriting was when they'd gone, she thought, a link more personal and lasting than anything else she could imagine. No chance of that with her father then; she doubted if Old Con's fingers had ever been free of a glass or a bottle long enough to learn to write. She tried to control the smile flickering around the corners of her mouth. She didn't understand why, but she had been laughing a lot in the last few days, and she was beginning to wonder if it was perhaps getting out of control. She looked again at the studio-posed photo of herself aged three and her fourteen-year-old brother. The child Kathleen was sitting in a wicker chair, her best dress decorously arranged around her, and that peculiar ribbon bow Lily always tied in her hair that made her look as though she had a budgie sitting on her head. She looked at Peter, standing well to the side and looking uncomfortable, as though he didn't want to be there; how significant was that? The distance between the two frozen images was almost palpable, she thought, even on a piece of paper. And it wasn't caused by the eleven-year age difference; they would have disliked each other even if they had been twins.

She disliked everything about him. The way he whistled 'Pedro the Fisherman' as he came up the stairs, in the sure and certain knowledge that whoever heard it would rush to the door to let him in, which, of course, they always did. Who else but Peter would have his own theme song? There was a sureness, an arrogance about him that made you either adore him or loathe him. He always knew everything better than anyone else, and he didn't hesitate to tell them so; Peter Kelly was the arbiter of the universe, and what Peter Kelly said went. That was the odd thing, other people were only too happy to accept his version of their lives, grateful even. Even if they were older and more battle-scarred in life, they accepted that Peter was more knowledgeable than they were themselves, and they revered him for it, honoured almost that he had taken the trouble to involve himself in their humble little existences. For Kathy, though, it had always been like the King's New Clothes, and she was the boy who had noticed he was naked; her brother had never fooled her for an instant, and she sensed that he knew it too. Watching him, listening as he pontificated, she felt his unease at her scrutiny, almost to the point where he couldn't stop himself glancing at her from the corner of his eye, knowing what was in her mind and wondering if she would put her thoughts into words. His sarcasm could be cruel, but it never made any impression on her, even when she was a child and he an adult. There was that one time, that defining moment, when she had seen through him. As a child she had loved reading and writing little stories, and she was good at art during her schooldays, so naturally Peter had to find a way of putting her down. 'You are,' he once said scathingly to her, 'interested only in yourself. All your pastimes are solitary, which proves that you have no interest in other people.' And even as she listened to him declaiming from on high, the thoughts that sprang into her mind weren't of hurt or anger, she felt no impulse to argue her corner. Instead, she suddenly thought, *'He's jealous! The great Peter Kelly is jealous of his wee sister!'* He didn't return her smile in response, but then he knew why she was smiling. *'What an arse!'* she thought, her usual insult towards her brother, and everyone else who annoyed her, come to that. Lily used to chide her for it, but it wasn't as bad as some of the things you heard on the streets every day, it was quite ladylike in fact. 'Ye shouldnae call yer brother that, Kathy!' Lily would say. 'But he *is* an arse!' Kathy would repeat joyously. Blood may well be thicker than water, but it wasn't glue, certainly not in their case, and the fact remained that she had never really warmed to him and, in truth, a truth furthermore that bothered her not at all, he had never really warmed to her.

She was sitting on the floor of her father's home in Stevenston Street, sifting through the detritus of the life Old Con had shared with her mother and beyond, sorting through the papers and family photos, deciding which she would keep. It had been a feature of her nature since her teens, this need to tidy up, to tie off every loose end. Even when whoever held the other end wasn't bothered or wasn't there to be bothered, when arguments were gone and forgotten, to Kathy there was always something more to say, a final comment to *really* finish it off, and only then could she file it away in one of the many compartments of her mind. The tendency had been there already, of course. 'It doesn't matter!' Lily would say. 'Let it be!' She smiled, thinking of the number of times she had heard that, and still she couldn't do it. It wasn't as if she wanted to pursue things to the bitter end, it wasn't really something she could control, that was what even Lily never understood, and after Lily had, well, when Lily was no longer there, the tendency had taken a real grip. She could never forget anything, unfinished business of any kind worried her. It was how she coped, how she stayed in control, which was why she was here, she thought, looking around Con's house, going through the meagre goods and chattels of a dead man. There was little in the entire house she wanted, and that was a fact, maybe because she had never lived here, apart from these last months, and she didn't see that as living, more like boarding or just passing through. Even so the usual nightmares had gathered in intensity while she had been here. Since the day she had left, all those years ago, she had been constantly waiting for a giant hand to reach down from the sky and drag her back to the East End of Glasgow where she had grown up, and where so many of her worst memories lay in wait for her, not to mention the recurring nightmare that was rooted here. That was how she thought of it, as though her life in Glasgow wasn't so much in the past as dormant, waiting for her to stray near enough to lay claim to her once again. Her life in these streets lay some twenty years or more in the past, but it was as though she couldn't believe that her escape was permanent; the hand was ever-present, ever hovering above her, just waiting for an opportunity. In those black dreams she was always back here, and even though she would protest throughout that she didn't belong here, whoever was directing the dream would ignore her, till she woke, sobbing and drenched in sweat, in her cottage all those miles and years away, her legs twisting the bedclothes in a desperate attempt to get away.

When she was a child she had lived with her family in Moncur Street, beside the Barras market. The Barras had been part of her life, the noise, the bustle and the characters. She only had to think back to hear the gramophone records of the Fifties playing in her head as loud as they were all through her childhood, echoing and reverberating through the market to the streets beyond. Patsy Cline, Hank Williams, Connie Francis, Guy Mitchell and Perry Como formed the backdrop to her early life, with their booming laments to lost and crossed love. People now enshrined in Glasgow folklore were part of her daily existence, the McIver clan who started the Barras and still controlled it, Freddie Benedetti, Chief Abadu with his cure-all snake oil that would blow your head off before it cured whatever ills you might have, Curt Cook who sold jewellery, though he wore more on his hands than he had on his stall, and the entire Pearson dynasty in Moncur Street itself. They were as much part of her life as her own family, and the old Moncur Street tenement was where she still placed her mother in her memory; it wasn't until Con was on his own that he had moved into the new house, just round the corner. They had lived two up on the right in Moncur Street, with Lily's mother, Aggie, above them, and the Crawfords next door, across the landing. Jamie Crawford had been her childhood companion; even though he was two years older, an enormous gap to children, Jamie had been closer than a brother. In the bags of photos spread around her, there were lots of snaps of herself and Jamie because they were never apart. They walked to the Sacred Heart Primary School in Reid Street together, met up at playtimes, then after school they walked home, dumped their bags and went out to play together. Lily used to shake her head and smile. If you saw one, she used to say, the other one wouldn't be far behind; they had been inseparable in those days. In her secondary years Kathy had been sent to Our Lady and St Francis Convent School in Charlotte Street, though strictly speaking Moncur Street fell out of the catchment area. But Old Con, who felt that nuns were holier than mortals without habits, had asked Father McCabe to plead his case and Kathy went to the convent. Not that it bothered her, one school was as good as another. Jamie went to St Mungo's Academy in Crownpoint Street, but they would still walk together along London Road till their paths diverged at the junction of the Saltmarket and High Street, and meet up again at the same spot every afternoon for the return journey. Looking at the snaps she was struck by how familiar he still was, it might all have been yesterday. Jamie was always a solid boy, solid in looks and solid in nature. He stood there, foursquare in the photos and in her life, looking the camera straight in the eye, a shock of dark fair hair falling over his forehead. She hadn't seen him in over twenty years now, not since, oh well, it didn't matter; it was all so long ago. Everyone had to grow up, grow older, she hadn't been alone in that at least.

She looked around Old Con's domain and wished she could find a bin liner big enough to hold it and all its contents, and a hole in the ground big enough to throw it into. That had been her instinct about Old Con Kelly himself come to that; it always had been, she thought wryly. But it was in hand now, she thought, good things come to those who wait, though it would be a box instead of a bin liner, and he wouldn't so much be dropped into a hole as scattered to the four winds, much to Father McCabe's irritation, which of course was an added bonus. She had irritated

Frank McCabe all through her childhood and teenage years and he had always let it show, believing that his position was unassailable, that no one knew the secret that could destroy him. And why not? After all, there wasn't another person alive on the planet who did know; what a sigh of relief he must've let go when that funeral was over. But Kathy knew, and that little secret would keep, she thought, smiling quietly to herself, till the time was right.

Earlier they had taken Con to St Alphonsus's. He would lie in the chapel overnight, a ritual she had never understood, but then it was Con's funeral and Con's religion, and now that the battle was over she didn't feel strongly enough to go against either. Con had been one of those loose ends she found it so hard to put up with, and now she just wanted the whole business over, finally, completely, permanently over. The undertaker had asked what she wanted him dressed in, as if she cared. She'd looked out a few things, feeling almost giddy with the nonsense of what she was doing. Eventually she decided on the blazer with the Highland Light Infantry badge on the pocket, the grey flannels he wore with it, and the white shirt and regimental tie that he donned faithfully for every reunion. At least that would get rid of all the irritations at once. She remembered the tears springing to his eyes and his chest swelling with pride every time he wore his civilian uniform. He was useless at family life, but he felt a real sense of belonging to the HLI, though he'd only spent the Second World War years within its ranks. 'The Germans called the HLI "The Ladies from Hell",' he'd say proudly, 'because of oor kilts.' Kathy would stare at him. 'Ye've no' much in yer life if that's wanna the highlights,' she'd reply. Her mother had tried to excuse his emotional attachment; he must, she would say, have gone through some terrible times with his comrades during those years, so it wasn't really surprising that he felt the way he did, probably they all did. 'We've been through some terrible times wi' him,' Kathy would reply, 'but *Ah* don't feel sentimental when Ah see *him* fa'in' through the door, dae you?' and Lily would laugh. Poor Lily. She had no love for her husband, and the guilt of that drove her to defend him, to indulge him more than he deserved, but Kathy had never really accepted his tears as purely sentimental, though God or whoever knew, sentimentality was a mainstay of whatever personality he had. Everyone knew that reunions were excuses for boozing; Old Con was just filled with joy at the prospect of being filled with booze, that was all. Still, she had gone through the motions for this last time, picking out the blazer, flannels, shirt, tie and socks; burning them was a satisfying thought, it would be the end of them as well as him. She drew the line at underwear, it seemed too bizarre somehow, and besides, where he was going the last consideration would be keeping him warm, and he wasn't likely to get knocked down by a bus now either. Then she'd laughed at the thought; as if any of it made sense. Finally she'd looked at his various pairs of shoes, then deliberately picked the ones that had blistered his feet. By that time he was paralysed and couldn't feel his feet, so the blisters had burst and become infected before anyone had known they were there. Eventually gangrene had set in and the doctors had wanted to amputate his leg, but they tried skin grafts over his heels instead as a last gasp, harvesting healthy skin from inside his thigh, and somehow it had been a success. She handed the shoes to the undertaker. 'Put them on the old bastard,' she said.

Later, as she followed the coffin into the church, where it would lie on the night before the funeral, she had caught sight of a notice advertising the Christmas Dance only a few weeks away. 'Come and dance the night away!!!' some enthusiastic believer had painted freehand; three exclamation marks conveying, she supposed, that three times the pleasure was to be had. Then she'd thought of the shoes old Con was wearing in his box and she'd laughed out loud. 'No' in *they* shoes he won't!' she giggled. The undertaker's men carrying the coffin ahead of her turned their heads slightly and looked at her, but made no reply. For some reason she found it hard to control her laughter, her mind seeking out amusement and finding it, whether it was there or not. Before the undertaker had taken Old Con out of the house for the last time, he had asked if she wanted to place anything in the coffin. She stared at him blankly.

'Some people put in a note,' he had suggested helpfully.

'Whit for?' she had asked. 'Sayin' "Haste ye back" or somethin'? That's the last thing Ah want noo that Ah've got the upper hand at last!' Then, as she'd looked around the house, her eyes had fallen on Old Con's collection of religious tat. He had been devoted all his life to the Child of Prague, a figure of the child Jesus wearing an ornate scarlet and gold robe, a crown on his head, his right hand raised in blessing and an orb in his left hand. There were pictures and cards of it everywhere, and statues of every size, Con being unable to pass up the chance of buying yet another, including her favourite little ones inside clear, hard plastic shells, like preserved birds or wedding cake tiers in Victorian times, only in miniature. When she was much younger she'd twist their heads off, replace the tiny mutilated figures inside the plastic tubes and leave them lying around for Old Con to find. He used to go berserk, screeching, yelling and falling on his knees to offer up prayers for forgiveness. Then she had perfected the ultimate blasphemy in his eyes, by performing the Papal blessing over him as he prayed. 'Whit's up wi' ye?' she'd ask innocently. 'Ah'm giein' a blessin', an' Ah'm wearin' a dress just like the boy there! A' Ah need is the crown and the tennis ba' in ma hand tae finish it!' It was the only revenge she was able to get, in those days at least, and it raised her spirits greatly. Beheading the plastic figures had been a vent, she supposed, and performing the blessing was simply enjoyable vengeance.

She had never really got her head round the Child of Prague. A fascination with angels she could understand. They had this ability she had always envied; whenever they felt like it they could flap their wings and take off into the wide, blue yonder. The times she wished she could just close her eyes and wake up somewhere else, somewhere Con wasn't. In the cold winters, with the ice forming inside the windows and the air so cold in her unheated bedroom that she could see her breath, she would close her eyes and pretend to be somewhere warm. She would lie sandwiched between patched sheets, with a couple of ex-army blankets on top and a coat or two in an attempt to generate enough heat to make sleep possible. But in her mind she was somewhere else, sunbathing in some hot country, swimming in a warm, sparkling blue ocean, walking along a deserted beach at sunset, being washed by a balmy breeze. She had no clear notion of where this magical land might be, that didn't matter, just as long as it was hot, the kind of place where she'd need calamine lotion to soothe her pale, freckled skin as it turned red, as it always did – Sunnyland, that would do. And, gradually, as she inhabited her fantasy, she'd make herself relax, muscle by muscle, limb by limb, till her teeth stopped chattering, under the gently waving palm trees in deepest Moncur Street. And getting to Sunnyland wouldn't be a problem, she had already worked that out. The journey wouldn't involve an aircraft, because no one she knew had ever been on one, so it simply didn't figure in her Moncur Street life or her Sunnyland one either. Planes were tiny dots you saw in the sky, leaving white trails behind them, or they were props for film stars to be pictured waving from. So it seemed to the young Kathy that sprouting a pair of functional, as well as aesthetically pleasing, wings from the shoulder blades was infinitely more realistic, more interesting, too, than the possibility of flying on an aeroplane anyway. She would've given anything to have wings, to be able to fly away to Sunnyland, to anywhere, and disappear. She would look at the angels on the statues in St Alphonsus's or at school, where the main subject was always someone supposedly bigger, better and, more importantly, holy, with the angels kind of tacked on at their feet almost as an afterthought, gazing upwards in adoration. Why, she wondered, didn't they realise that their wings gave them an advantage, a skill the holy people didn't have, something she'd have made better use of if she'd had them? But her angelic days would have to be on a strictly freelance, independent basis, she knew that; there was no way she would consider sitting by the feet of saints, waiting for orders to take to the sky. Winged or wingless, Kathy Kelly had never taken kindly to being ordered about. So she had always liked angels, she could see the point of them, and there was a certain kind of logic to liking them that was entirely missing from Con's thing about the Child of Prague, for instance. Why would a boy be wearing a dress? And Jesus was Jesus, wasn't he, the lad from the Holy Land, so where did Prague come into the story? While she was still at school she had discovered that Old Con had no idea who the figure was or what it represented, he simply liked it, and Kathy had taunted him about it for as long as she could remember. Being unable, as usual, to leave the thing alone, she had gone to her favourite place, the local library, to find out about it, and discovered that the original wax statue had been made for a Spanish royal family, who passed it on to some count and countess at their seventeenth-century wedding in Prague. Then the count had died – so much for the figure bringing good luck – and the countess had got rid of it by gifting it to the Carmelites. Over the years it had been destroyed and re-built several times, before being put on permanent display at the Church of Our Lady of Victory in Prague, complete with different robes for different seasons. It reminded her of the dressing-up dolls she had played with as a child, cardboard figures of impossibly beautiful children with shining cherubic faces and mops of irritatingly golden curls. They had paper wardrobes of equally impossibly beautiful clothes, with little tabs at strategic positions that you had to cut round very carefully. The folded tabs held the clothes onto the doll figure and you could change outfits as the mood took you till they fell apart. She couldn't see the difference between the dolls – who at least promised nothing more than a few hours of harmless fun and dreaming – and the Child of Prague, who demanded adoration in exchange for possibly enriching his followers' lives in some way, or possibly not, depending on his mood. When she told Old Con that his revered icon was nothing more than a wax dressing-up doll, he rewarded her tenfold by becoming even more beside himself with rage. He screeched that she was making it all up to mock God, the Child, the Pope and all Roman Catholics across the globe, especially himself; well, at least he was right with the last one. He refused to believe the true story she had recounted to him, but when she'd challenged him to come up with an alternative he couldn't. That was when she realised that Old Con had never had any idea of the figure's meaning, such as it was, or its background, he just liked it, and it had given her a weapon to use against him for the rest of his life. 'Ye've got a thing aboot blokes in dresses, haven't ye?' she'd taunt him scathingly, as Con raged with injured pride. 'First your HLI kilties, an' noo this wee guy, the transvestite frae Prague. There has to be somethin' wrong wi' somebody who likes statues an' pictures o' boys dressed in frocks!' Knowledge was indeed power, and her knowledge of the Child of Prague drove Old Con wild whenever she aired it, as it was intended to. It was a means of evening up the score for Kathy, or as near as she would ever get, and having it at her disposal, she often thought, had probably stopped her many times from lifting a hammer and bringing it down on Old Con's head. She still wasn't sure if that had been a good or a bad thing. 'Here,' she said to the undertaker on impulse, gathering up Old Con's Child of Prague collection, 'stuff his gay icon in beside him. Then him an' the boy in the frock will burn thegither.'

And so, as he was carried into St Alphonsus's, in his HLI regalia and wearing the shoes that hurt his feet, she laughed again, listening for clunks and knocks as the collection rolled around inside. She laughed too when two large candles were placed at either end of the coffin.

'They won't last a minute!' she said.

'They will last for twenty-four hours,' Father McCabe intoned solemnly.

'Ah doubt it!' she giggled.

Father McCabe shook his head, his face a mask of distaste. What he didn't know was that Old Con had pinched candles from the chapel all his life for the next time the family's electricity got cut off, and it often did, because Con had better things to spend their money on, all of them alcoholic. He didn't see purloining the candles as theft, even if he never went out of his way to inform his parish priest; he was one of the faithful, one of the family, so it was probably a kind of honour among thieves as far as Old Con had been concerned, she thought. So she had a mental picture of a hand emerging from the coffin in the quiet silence of the night, clutching the candles and dragging them, one by one, into the dark recesses with him and the Child.

Later, in the vestry, where the priest had wanted to discuss the finer details of the funeral service the following morning, a man had knocked on the door and come in.

'It's you, John,' Father McCabe had said. 'Thanks for coming. We'll need the usual people tomorrow for the service. Could you round them up and be here for ten o'clock?'

John's silent nod veered dangerously near to a bow as he left, and Kathy asked who he was.

'We have a faithful band of parishioners we can call on to attend services like this,' Father McCabe explained; he meant funerals where there might be few mourners, or where the faithful might be in the minority. Couldn't have heathens taking up pew space. If he had his own back-up troupe, then the niceties of the service would be performed as they should, with the congregation giving their responses on time, getting up, kneeling and sitting down on cue and knowing all the words of the hymns.

Kathy laughed at that too. 'You've hired "Rent a crowd"?' she asked. 'That's terrific!' She mopped at her eyes, once again unable to hold in the laughter, unwilling to even try, come to that.

'For God's sake behave yourself,' the priest said, 'and show some respect.'

Well, that was good, coming from him; respect indeed, given what she knew about him. Still, she'd hold her fire on that, for the moment anyhow. 'Look, wee man,' she replied, still laughing, 'Ah'm the wan doin' the decent thing here. Ah'm havin' Auld Con done as a Catholic, but Ah don't havtae, ye know. Ah could just as easy get him done withoot a' the mumbo jumbo. Ah could just stand up at the crematorium, announce "Game over" an' press the button.'

Father McCabe glowered silently at her. He was a portly little man with wild, bushy white hair that seemed to be only just contained by the pom-pommed biretta he wore at all times. One of his habits, when he was thinking, was to hold the biretta aloft with his thumb, and scratch his head with the fingers of the same hand, revealing the shiny, pink dome of his bald head underneath. It always came as a shock, because the vigorous white growth that was visible ear-to-ear gave the illusion of a full and luxuriant head of hair. The whites of his watery blue eyes had a glistening hint of yellow, the result, she had always suspected, of giving the communion wine a fair whacking when no one was about, and they were completely surrounded by heavy folds of skin, so that from a distance he seemed to be wearing thick-framed, legless spectacles. He was never without a cigarette, held downwards between the thumb and first finger of his right hand, with the lit point towards the palm, as though he was trying to hide it. It was, she thought for some reason, the way gangsters she'd seen in films held their cigarettes. In moments of deep conversation, when regular drags at the cigarette weren't possible, he would reluctantly nip it out and place it behind his right ear, half-hidden in the white hair, and over the years a little reddish patch had grown, coloured by the smoke and the nicotine. As far as she could tell his appearance hadn't altered in all the years she had known him. He hadn't so much aged as gradually faded somehow, but you'd still know it was him, even if you hadn't seen him for years. Whatever modernising ploys had been tried by the spin doctors in Rome, he had remained untouched; he still wore his long black robe and biretta and on his feet a pair of beige boot slippers, with zips up the front. She had never known him to wear shoes, and no matter when she saw him the slippers seemed to be exactly the same as the last time, with no more or less apparent wear, even if, like now, decades had passed. If she were any judge he still muttered the mass in Latin under his breath too, like in the good old days.

'The least you could do was to let him be buried in St Kentigern's with the rest of his family, with his mother and sisters, with his *wife*,' he said, establishing his credentials as an intimate of her family, and emphasising the last word, in an attempt to bodyswerve her question by provoking an argument on something else. An old ploy, that one.

St Kentigern's; she hadn't been there since the day before she had escaped. The memories flooded her mind and she shook her head to banish them, turning her attention back to Father McCabe.

'Aye, well,' she smiled at his disapproval, 'if anybody knows aboot ma family, wee man, it's you, Ah'll gie ye that. Ma Granny always said ye were a great help tae her when she was married tae the Orangeman. Accordin' tae Aggie, whit she woulda done withoot your support a' they years didnae bear thinkin' aboot. She said it often.'

'*Easy, Kathy,*' she chided herself silently. '*The time will come!*'

Frank McCabe looked at her. 'Your grandmother was a fine woman,' he stated. 'She was loyal to her faith and kept it alive even after she made her mistake and, when she could be, she was reconciled with the Church.'

'Ye mean when the Orangeman died? That's ma Granda, ye know, an' that's a helluva nice way tae put it, "her mistake".' she shot back at him, feigning hurt. 'But then, him bein' a heathen, no' bein' really human, like, he wouldnae matter that much, would he? Ah don't know why ye didnae just set the dogs oan him. But Ah'm sure yer God blessed yer Christian charity in waitin' tae he died a' by hissel', a few plenary indulgences marked up there, surely!' She'd never met her grandfather, known to one and all as 'the Orangeman', as though even mentioning his name would incur the wrath of Rome, he'd died long before she was born. For all she knew he could've been a monster, and neither had she any time for his kind of bigotry, but it always annoyed the good Father to hear her defend him, so she did.

Frank McCabe didn't answer her, but instead continued with his usual lecture. 'You, on the other hand, never had to fight for your faith, you had it handed to you on a plate, and you turned your back on it!' he accused, stabbing a stubby, nicotine-stained finger in her direction. He hated having his authority either challenged or demystified, even after all the years she had been doing it to him.

'Put that finger doon or Ah'll bite it aff at the knuckle!' she replied tartly, smiling to herself at the priest's angry expression. 'Dae ye no' get bored sayin' the same things ower and ower? Ah mean, Ah don't think either wanna us will ever convince the other. Surely *you* don't, dae ye? The difference is that Ah don't really care a mad monkey's fart aboot convertin' you, so that's you lost the argument before it's even started, because you *dae* care, daen't ye?'

Father McCabe made no reply.

'*Checkmate!*' she thought gleefully. 'But as for buryin' the auld sod beside wee Lily, you're not on. Ah think my mother deserves no' tae have him lyin' beside her,' she said quietly. Then she raised her voice again. 'Besides, for a' you know,' she said merrily, 'it might be time for another miracle. Y'know, wi' the trouble ye're havin' these days tryin' tae force folk intae yer wee club, an' tryin' tae keep them there even if they've been born intae it. At this very minute some big daft angel might be scoutin' aboot, tryin' tae find some way o' reversin' the trend, so tae speak, an' he could see Con lyin' there, an' decide he's the very man tae restore the numbers of yesteryear! He might decide Con's unfortunate demise is the very dab, an' afore ye know it he'll have Con risin' frae the grave! This dump could become the next Lourdes, wi' bus loads o' people comin' tae see the place where Lazarus Kelly jumped tae his feet! Noo, dae you think that's a chance Ah'd be prepared tae take?' She didn't wait for an answer. 'Naw, naw, there'll be nae burial for Con. Ah've never been sure about angels, so it's the burny fire at the Linn Crematorium for him, just in case!'

'Blasphemy is a sin!' Father McCabe said, taking another puff from his cigarette and peering at her through the smoke.

'Christ, is that the best ye can come up wi'? Besides, as Ah say, it would suit me a damned sight better tae cut the proceedin's tae the minimum. Ah'm quite prepared tae let ye aff the hook, an' Rent-a-crowd tae for that matter. A quick trot in an' oot wi' a pause tae press the button, an' then Ah'll go back tae my ain life. Whit d'ye say?'

The little priest glared at her in silence.

'Aye, Ah thought so,' she said. 'Ye aye hing oan in there, frae the cradle tae the grave, daen't ye? He'll be yours till his ashes grow cauld. Ye'd climb in the urn wi' him for wan last look just tae make sure if ye could. But just grit your teeth, efter this Ah'll be oota your life, an' merr tae the point, you'll be oota mine.

Noo is that no' somethin' worth shuttin' your mooth for?'

Later, as she sat on the floor of Old Con's house, going through the pictures, birth certificates and insurance policies, laughing again at the evening's events, she knew that Father McCabe had been right, though; she really would have to get a grip. After all, in the morning, after the final act took place, she would be free at last. After three months of camping in Con's house, nursing him out of life, she would be able to return to her cottage and her real life on the West Coast. '*But there again*,' she thought, feeling another burst of giggles approaching, '*that's likely why Ah'm laughin' in the first place!*'

Her brother Peter hadn't been there when Con died, in fact the beloved son hadn't been there for many a year, but his name was still the last word on the old man's lips. Father McCabe was in at the kill, of course, he'd almost kept vigil by Old Con for months, in case, she'd mused to herself, he really had taken up his bed and walked instead of doing the decent thing and pegging out. During that last week especially he'd hardly been away; the whole place reeked of his cigarette smoke.

'Just as well my auld man is dyin' already,' she said, pointedly sticking another ashtray under the priest's nose, 'or ye'd dae him in wi' fag fumes! Have ye nothin' better tae dae than hing aboot here a' day clutterin' the place up anyway? Is there no' a statue somewhere ye could be noddin' at?'

'My place is with your father,' he intoned mysteriously, 'as you well know.'

'Ach, yer arse!' Kathy retorted. 'Ye'd have thought ye'd have merr tae dae wi' Christ's birthday coming up. This no' wanna yer busy times? Ye've gied the auld man the Last Rites that many times Ah'm beginning tae wonder if ye're oan piecework.'

Father McCabe glared at her. There was once a more respectful age when that glare alone could control his most errant parishioner, though never, it had to be said, Kathy, and it was still the first weapon in his arsenal, long, long after that time had passed. 'Will you never learn to show respect, Kathleen Agnes Kelly?' he demanded, mentioning her grandmother's name as a jibe.

Kathy smiled to herself, flicking cigarette ash off the surfaces with a tea towel, refusing to take the bait. 'Ah shouldnae think so,' she replied coolly. 'Whit aboot you?'

'Even at your christening you were the same,' he said, shaking his head. That was his other weapon, a headshake of disapproval guaranteed to keep the most defiant, rebellious child awake for a week with fear, though once again, never Kathy. 'I've never known a child struggle so, screaming and squirming and refusing to lie quietly.'

Kathy shook her head, laughing at the priest. 'It was probably the Orange blood in me,' she replied, 'but ye still held on though, didn't ye? There's nae chance o' escape wance ye get yer hands on somebody, even if it's a wean wi' nae say in the matter, eh, wee man?'

'Your father was a good, faithful Catholic —' the priest said wearily, going through a litany he had delivered to her remorselessly throughout her life without it ever having any effect.

Right on cue Kathy interrupted. 'He was a useless auld drunk as well! See when ye started dolin' oot the wee drink o' communion wine, ye made his day, he was never away frae the chapel efter that! Drinkin' was his real religion, believe you me, but Ah don't recall ye ever recommendin' Ah follow him in that tae.'

'— so,' he continued, ignoring her intervention, 'you should have been one too.'

'Ye know, that's wanna my highest achievements in life,' she said. 'It bothers the hell oota you that Ah got away. Go oan, admit it, it's only us here and we know it's true anyway. It does, doesn't it? An' Ah see ye havnae changed your tactics ower the years either,' she laughed. 'Still very selective aboot what questions ye answer, ye shoulda been a bloody politician! It must drive ye daft, though, seein' that you really believe your religion is passed on through the bloodline, only wi' wee Lily an' me there's that other bloodline frae her faither. Whit a helluva problem ma Orange Granda has been tae ye, auld man!'

'Just once in your life, at this time of all times, you could call me "Father"!'

'Christ, Ah don't know,' Kathy sighed. 'You know fine whit ma experiences o' the real thing have been like, an' ye really *want* me to call you "Father", dae ye? Ye're a sad case right enough, wee man!'

'You'll never change, Kathleen Agnes Kelly,' he said bitterly.

'Aye, an' neither will you,' she retorted. 'As long as Ah can remember ye've been a mean-minded wee sod, an' a devious wan tae. An' just like the good faithful Catholic in the bed there, ye'll die that way. Get somebody tae tip me the wink when *your* time comes, an' nae matter whit Ah'm daein', if Ah havtae come frae the ends o' the earth, Ah'll be there tae remind ye o' yer biggest failure! Rest assured, wee man, you'll feel me dancin' oan your grave when ye dae!'

But Con's final moment was always going to come first and, when it did, Father McCabe asked if he wanted his daughter. The dying man shook his head. 'Peter!' he gasped, turned his face to the wall and exhaled his last breath. 'Ye're merr like auld Aggie's son than her son-in-law!' she spat loudly, inches from him. 'You miserable auld sod!' She laughed bitterly, hoping it would be the last sound he heard. The priest glared at her disapprovingly. 'An' *you* can shut it!' she told him. 'Ye're only here under sufferance as it is, an' yer only supporter has gone tae meet his maker noo. So wan word frae you an' yer arse will bounce aff the edge o' every step on the way doon! Comprendez, pal?' Father McCabe turned away, busying himself in performing his magic once again, presumably in case Con had managed to squeeze in a silent response to her jibe on his way out.

Then the doctor arrived to certify Con dead as well as saved. 'He's gone,' he announced solemnly. A pleasant enough young man she thought, though she didn't know him. He was probably whichever anonymous name on the health centre notice board had been available, or else some equally anonymous locum. These days it was hard to tell; you saw them once then never again. She wondered if it was a defensive ploy in case something went wrong; in these more writ-conscious days it would be harder to apportion blame if it was shared out among so many instantly forgettable faces. If she had to pick this young man out of a police line-up, could she, she wondered. She looked at Con, now visibly stiffening, his face an ashen grey. 'Ye're sure?' she asked him, sarcastically.

'I'm terribly sorry, dear, but yes, I'm afraid he has,' the young man replied with quiet sympathy.

'*Ah'm obviously an auld biddy*,' she thought, '*bein' called "dear" by a wean like him.*' 'What Ah'm askin' ye,' she replied coolly, 'is to be certain. Can ye no' hold a mirror under his nose tae be sure, like? Ah don't want ye raisin' ma hopes.' She immediately regretted it. The lad was doing his best. He knew nothing about her, the family or even his patient, except that he was dead and the daughter was a bit odd; he was probably putting it down to her time of life and making allowances.

'You are the next of kin?' he asked. 'Mrs . . . ?'

'Kathy Kelly, originally spinster o' this parish, but against ma will. An' aye, Ah'm his daughter, son,' she replied. 'Ah've tried a' roads tae find a way oota that wan, but Ah'm sad tae say Ah canny. Ah'm thinkin' o' applyin' tae the European Court for a definition of "Father" that doesnae just depend oan a quick fumble under the blankets, but Ah don't hold oot much hope, dae you?'

The young doctor looked pained.

'It's a' right, son,' she smiled, 'just sign the certificate an' ye can go.'

He smiled tightly, in a vain attempt to persuade her that he wasn't offended by her manner, or confused at being dismissed. 'Will it be cremation or burial?' he asked, in a determinedly businesslike tone.

'Oh, definitely cremation!' she smiled. 'No' that Ah doubt yer word or anythin', but knowin' ma faither there's still an outside chance he's fakin' it. He spent his life playin' the martyr for a bitta attention, an' noo that Ah seem tae have the whip hand, Ah don't want tae gie him a way back! Though Ah think we should warn the crematorium. Wi' a' the booze he's soaked up doon the years it might be a case o' lightin' the blue touch paper an' standin' well back, wi' the fire brigade in attendance, just in case.'

'In that case you'll need another doctor to see the body and give a second signature,' the young doctor replied diplomatically, obviously deciding to do what had to be done without risking entering into lingering family conflicts by offering more sympathy. 'I'll arrange for someone else to call as soon as possible.' He spoke on his mobile phone and within fifteen minutes another doctor, possibly even younger than the first, arrived and confirmed that Cornelius Patrick Kelly had died from the complications of a long-standing condition of the nervous system. No mention was made of the part booze had played in compromising his nervous system, but it hung in the air anyhow.

Old Con, as everyone knew, had spent a lifetime literally pickling his nerves in alcohol, and for the five years leading up to his death he had been paralysed from the waist down. She had been at home in her cottage just outside Glenfinnan in Inverness-shire when he first became ill, and she was not at all amused. As far as she had been concerned he was part of a life she had left behind and would never return to, even if he had remained, against her will, in the back of her mind. She'd told the doctors this five years ago, when the long, final act had started. She'd do the necessary when the time came, and that was more to do with her own need to round things off than affection for Con, but she would not devote her life to caring for him indefinitely. It seemed that Old Con had set out for the Barras market as usual that day. It was how he had always earned his drinking money, doing odd jobs for the market traders. Then he had settled into the next part of his routine, propping up the bar of the Saracen's Head pub across the road in the Gallowgate. Occasionally, in the weeks leading up to the great collapse, his legs had felt tingly, as though he had pins and needles, he said later, but if he sat down to rest for a while the feeling went away. And on this particular day the tingly feeling had happened again, so he'd sat down for a moment, but this time, when he tried to stand again, he couldn't. From that moment on he was paralysed, it was as quick as that, though the gradual pickling of his nervous system had been underway for many years beforehand.

There had been all sorts of tests done, and at one point he had been transferred in the middle of the night from the Royal Infirmary to the Neurosurgical Unit at the Southern General, by an overenthusiastic medic who thought Con had a brain tumour. That's when Kathy had been summoned from Glenfinnan, the first of several summonings in the years to come, because in the absence of the adored son and heir she was the next of kin, and she felt the touch of the hovering hand as it grazed her life. In time the tumour had been ruled out, as had various other exotic conditions, until the consultant asked to see her.

'Tell me,' he had said tactfully, 'does your father drink much?'

'Only as much as he can get down his throat,' she'd replied, 'and believe me, his throat is wider than the Clyde.'

In that case, the consultant had told her with the deepest regret, it was his considered opinion that Old Con was suffering from a form of polyneuritis, brought on by years of alcohol abuse. He would never regain the ability to walk, he would have to depend on a catheter to drain urine from his bladder into an externally-worn plastic bag, and for the rest of his life his bowel movements would be, as they coyly put it, assisted. As he had no feeling, and therefore no control, over the muscles from the waist down, the nurses would administer suppositories to evacuate his bowel when necessary, and if that didn't work, as happened from time to time, they would perform manual evacuations, a process that didn't bear thinking about as far as Kathy was concerned, but better them than her. She had often thought of poking her finger in his eye, but it was the only part of his anatomy she had ever considered, and she wasn't about to change her mind now, so let the nurses get on with it.

'Ah always knew he was dead frae the neck up,' Kathy had replied, when his condition and future care requirements were outlined by the consultant that day, in the vain expectation that she would take them on. 'Noo he's dead frae the waist doon as well. Doesnae leave much, does it?'

The consultant didn't reply.

She had served her time looking after her father, her apprenticeship had started the moment she was born, and when Lily died she had taken over completely. His entire life had been spent in the care of women. His own father had been a merchant seaman who died on a voyage and was buried at sea, leaving his widow with two daughters and one son, Con. When his mother decided she couldn't cope, it was her daughters she had sent to the nuns at Nazareth House, and Con she had kept. That decision had set the pattern Con would live by; for the rest of his life he had to be the centre of attention for every woman he encountered. His two sisters had died in the care of the nuns, one of TB, the other after falling three storeys while cleaning windows. Quite why it should have been thought safe or appropriate for a nine-year-old girl to be cleaning windows so far from the ground, said much about the standard of care destitute children received from the good Sisters, but in a way their early deaths at least saved the two Kelly girls from the worst excesses of the nuns. Old Con, being as he was, decided to embrace both deaths with his usual Celtic sentimentality. In his mind he had been specially selected by some cosmic influence to suffer greatly; Con Kelly, being an Irish Catholic, was a martyr, born to be persecuted and discriminated against, as Irish Catholics were in turn-of-the-century Glasgow. The deaths of his sisters were part of his lot in life, but he would bear it bravely, if not in silence. Kathy doubted if he had any clear memory of the unfortunate Kelly girls, but he indulged himself in the fantasy that their deaths were somehow targeted at him alone, his tragedy to carry and weep over whenever he'd had a few, and he had a few often, to forget, he said. Not that it stopped at the people in his life, Con was prepared to accept any sad event as his and his alone. In 1962, when Glasgow finally got rid of its 'caurs', its legendary tramcar system, the old vehicles had been driven in one last procession through the city, and great crowds of people had turned out on a rainy Monday night to bid the 'caurs' farewell and to put coins on the rails for the trams to run over as mementoes. Con, overwhelmed by his loss, had lined up twelve brown pennies on the rail and then arrived home bearing the deeply dented coins and sobbing; what no one seemed to realise was that the tramcars were being withdrawn from service to cause distress to Con Kelly alone. 'He's only greetin' because he's realised he canny use the pennies tae buy booze,' Kathy snorted. 'That's an entire bob that'll never find its way doon his throat!' And so to sentiment was added cruelty, prompting Con to subside once again in another rush of tears, for the beloved trams he would never see again and the insensitivity of his daughter. Later, when he had been carted off to bed and was safely if loudly snoring, Kathy picked up the twelve ruined pennies that had slipped from his grasp. Then she made her way across London Road and down to Glasgow Green where she scattered them into the air. Next morning Con asked if anyone had seen his souvenirs, and she replied caustically, 'Mibbe the caur fairy took them!'

'It was you!' he accused, tearfully.

'Whit a thing tae say!' Kathy replied with gleeful innocence. 'Ah'm cut tae the quick! As if Ah would dae that!' It was amazing how childish you could be, what silly ways you could find to extract revenge when there was nothing more substantial available. She had been a child of less than ten years, and already so angry, so bitter. At the time she had thought she was in control, that she was handling her situation, but sometimes Kathy would think back to those years and look at that child she had been, and she would almost weep with pity.

Even from her earliest days, listening to her father's ramblings and his tears, Kathy would exchange looks with Lily, angry looks in Kathy's case, always answered with pleading looks from Lily that her daughter had been reading all her life. 'Please, don't say anything,' they said. 'He'll go to sleep soon if you leave it.' Anything for a quiet life, anything to appease him and avoid upsetting him. It was an image of her mother she would never get out of her mind, and the memory increased her anger against Con. The slight figure of Lily, her reddish hair caught back in an untidy ponytail from her tired face, a functional arrangement rather than a hairstyle, her brown eyes silently begging her daughter to keep silent, to let it pass, though she knew that Kathy was unable to leave any business unfinished. When had she developed that resigned expression, Kathy wondered, like a trapped animal that knows there's no escape? Had her involvement with Con done that, or had she always been one of nature's victims? But Kathy could never hold back, even though there was no real satisfaction in fighting with a drunk man, especially one she could have tied in knots mentally even if he'd been stone cold sober. Fat chance of that, though. 'Ye don't gie a bugger aboot yer sisters!' she'd shout at the sobbing Con. 'Six months it took ye tae find oot they were even deid. Ye hadnae seen them in a' that time, so that shows ye how much they mattered tae ye. But still we get the crocodile tears aboot the tragedies in yer life. Did ye ever think it was a bigger tragedy for they two weans?' And he'd shout and yell his protests – oh what it was to be so misunderstood, abused and put upon by your own daughter, even though you sheltered the cruel creature under your roof! How much more sorrow was one man supposed to shoulder? He would throw his arms about in all directions till he overbalanced and fell down, still sobbing about how Fate had so badly mistreated him, before launching into his party piece, an uplifting ditty that started 'Into each life some rain must fall, but too much is falling in mine.'

'Ah wish it would build up intae a bloody flood,' Kathy would yell above his heartbreaking warblings, 'an' mibbe it would droon ye, ya auld swine!' Finally, beset on all sides by life, fate and the ungrateful fruit of his loins, Con would fall asleep on the floor, snoring loudly. Kathy's anger when she looked back on those useless, pointless battles was always against Con, but she knew she was really angry with herself for increasing the pressure on Lily. After all, it achieved nothing; each time it ended in Lily and Kathy carrying Con to bed, as they had so many times that it was as routine as breathing. The memory of it still disgusted her all these years later. The stink of stale booze and cigarette fumes, the peculiar way the body of a comatose drunk fell in all directions; it was like trying to grasp water, or in his case, alcohol.

She had often wondered why Lily had put up with it as long as she had, because it was clear she would have been better off on her own, without this dead weight ruining and ruling her life. That the marriage was a mistake was obvious, no one tried to pretend otherwise. Lily had been a young girl who had 'got into trouble', and in those days, 1942, there was only one respectable course of action for the truly innocent – marriage. For the more streetwise there were always backstreet abortionists, everyone knew where to find them, but Lily had been sixteen when she had committed her act of folly, no more than a child. So Peter had made his unplanned appearance, though God alone knew how Lily had conceived a second time eleven years later. Kathy always secretly suspected that her own birth had been the result of Lily being overpowered by Con in one of his drunken rampages, but in case that were true she didn't ask, she couldn't have lived with having it confirmed. Lily's punishment for her lapse at sixteen had been a life sentence, she was sentenced to live with Con for the mere twenty-six years she had left, until she died in the James Watt Street Fire in 1968, at the age of forty-two.

It was somehow symbolic of her married life that as she was dying, her husband was in a pub somewhere. Kathy had been at school, in the middle of an Art lesson, when someone came into the class and asked her to report to the headmistress, Sister Felicitous. There had been a fire at Stern's, the upholstery warehouse where her mother worked. Mrs Kelly might be safe, but she might not, and had she any idea where her father might be? It was the wrong way round, she was only a child for God's sake; it was one of the many things she would never forgive him for. For years she would go over it in her mind, much to her annoyance, because she knew it was pointless, that she should've been getting on with her life instead of looking back and trying to correct the uncorrectable. If Old Con had died that day instead, Lily would've heard first and broken the news to her daughter, her mother would've been there to comfort her, had she had a decent father at any rate. Instead, there she was, at the age of fifteen, being dealt the worst blow of her life and in the same breath being asked to help locate her father. Did she know where he might be? Yes, she knew where he was; hadn't she done the rounds of all his haunts so many times that she could do it blindfold? Maybe not the exact pub, but she knew he was in a pub somewhere, and she'd been right. Not that he was any good to her when he was found, he was out of his mind as usual, and the only thing he'd taken from Lily's death was that once again Fate had singled him out for tragedy. It gave him something else to sob about in the years afterwards. Oh, but he'd had a hard life, taken many knocks, and just why it should happen to him he had no idea! That, she thought, was the single aspect of his character that she hated most, his morbid, self-indulgent belief that every event in the universe was aimed at him personally, and the enthusiasm with which he embraced every opportunity to play the martyr. The worst disasters were intended to affect Con Kelly; add a liberal application of booze, as he always did, and the picture was complete in all its nauseating horror. Sometimes, when he wasn't to be found in any of his habitual locations, he would finally be tracked down to St Kentigern's, sitting with his back against the white marble headstone shaped like a heart – what else? – erected for his sisters and his mother, a bottle of Old Tawny cheap wine, usually empty, in his hands, and tears rolling down his cheeks. He would be singing 'I'll Take You Home Again, Kathleen', the name of one of his sisters and his mother, the name Kathy had been given along with Aggie's, her other grandmother. Ironic when you thought about it, seeing as it was always Kathleen taking *him* home, carrying him home.

The maudlin melancholy of it repulsed her, so that from a very young age she became resistant to showing any emotion lest she remind herself of Con. She had mistrusted feelings all her life because she couldn't tell the real from the phoney; look where feelings had got her mother after all. The young Lily's feelings for Con had been genuine at the time, she had no reason to doubt that, but they were wrong; true but false, so how could you tell the difference? It was in the aftermath of Lily's life that her need to be in control took a firmer grip, it was then that she truly learned to compartmentalise her life. You kept the various strands totally separate, tied them off as quickly and tightly as you could without dwelling too much on any one part, then you stored them in their allotted parts of your mind and got on with your life. That was it. Safe. If you thought about things too deeply you might let go, and who knew what would happen? Even Lily's death had remained inside a mental file, on its own all these years, accepted but never analysed for fear of the emotions analysis might release. She had died, that was all, don't go any further, don't ask questions for fear of what the answers would be and how you might react. It went against her nature not to force every detail from wherever it hid, it threatened her need for completeness, but her fear of falling to pieces was even greater, and what good would it do to fall to pieces? So in situations where other people expressed affection, for instance, Kathy Kelly was glib and brittle; she perfected a self-preserving shield of hard cynicism that was never lowered. Well, not never, she thought, casting her mind back as she sat going through the family photos that night, then abruptly shaking her head to banish the memory that appeared. That was another file, another compartment. But that memory was itself proof, surely? Lower your guard, even with someone you trusted as much as you did yourself, and look what could happen, what did happen. She thought of Con once again, lying against the white marble heart and crying, and how her loathing for him at moments like that almost made her feel physically sick. The times she had found him lying by the grave and had wanted to take the bottle from his hand and crash it down over his head, the recurring fantasy of digging a hole as far away from the unfortunate Kelly females as she could drag him and quietly dropping him into it. No one would know – who would care?

2

It had taken a few years for her to wake up after Lily's death, and even then it took another crisis in her life. Looking back, she had probably still been in shock; even though the crisis came along five years later, it was why it had happened. She had always been able to look out for herself, she had no other choice, so it stood to reason that if she hadn't been knocked off course by Lily's death there would have been no crisis. But there was no use thinking about that; it had happened. Funnily enough, Lily's mother, Aggie, her grandmother, had died around the same time, 1973, though that was no more than a coincidence, but it was one less tie to bind too. She had fought with her grandmother all her life, neither one of them having a civil, let alone pleasant word to say to or about the other. Those battles had probably kept Aggie going, though Kathy didn't think of that till years later, and during one of those exchanges the old woman had handed her the single most amusing and valuable piece of information she could ever have hoped for. She had just told Aggie that she was going away, and Aggie was telling her that she was a selfish bitch for leaving Con, for leaving her, come to that, and of course, God would strike her dead. It was always that; seemed to Kathy that Aggie's God was forever in the throes of indecision, caught between striking her dead or forgiving her. Then Aggie would cross herself with theatrical ceremony, as if that sealed the bargain. It was in the middle of that argument she'd let it slip, in the heat of a particularly frank exchange of views, but Kathy was in no fit state to do anything about it then, she had more pressing problems to deal with and so she had filed it away for future use. And the next day, before Kathy could execute her planned disappearance, Aggie had beaten her to it and gone herself, and Father McCabe had rushed to her side, as he always had done. It wasn't entirely unexpected really; any time she was refused what she wanted, usually by Kathy it had to be said, Aggie would threaten to go. 'That lassie will put me in ma grave!' she'd shriek, her hand clasped over her eyes for effect, and Kathy would shout 'Where's the shovel? Ah'll dae it right noo!' So when Kathy finally did what her brother had done many years before, but in Peter's case with considerably less criticism, Con was left to his own devices, this time without even Aggie to fight for him. Now Kathy's leaving *had* been targeted at him, but as is often the way with those supposedly helpless and dependent, Con had survived perfectly well on his own, and in the twenty years or so since, contact had been, now what could she say? Minimal, that was it, as little as she could get away with, of the 'call me when you're dead' variety. But instead of going quickly and cleanly he'd opted to play out his final scenes as slowly as possible, by the progressive destruction of the nerves in his spine from the waist down with booze. She was dragged back for the first time five years ago, but not permanently, it would never be permanent, she'd made sure his doctors understood that. Having already escaped and made a life for herself she was determined that she wouldn't go back and spend what was left of Con's life at his beck and call, and she made it clear that she gave not a fig what anyone thought. Old Aggie would've had a field day if she'd still been alive. Kathy remembered how Aggie had defended Con at every turn, he was a good man, a man who needed to be looked after, one of nature's victims.

'Yer arse in parsley!' Kathy had replied. 'He's an alkie, that's a'. Wance ye've said that ye've said everythin' aboot ma Da!'

'May God forgive you!' Aggie shouted, crossing herself. 'He's a heavy drinker, but he's no' an alkie!'

'Ye've nae need tae tell me how heavy he is, Aggie,' Kathy replied bitterly. 'Ah've had tae lift him aff the floor an' carry him tae his bed often enough. Naebody hastae tell me how heavy a drinker he is!'

But Aggie was long gone when Con at last made his exit, the name of his long-lost son on his lips, though Kathy had no doubt she would be hovering about somewhere, celestially investing her son-in-law's final tragedy with as much saccharine sympathy as he would himself. Kathy had looked after him during those last months, but she had refused to leave her life in Glenfinnan when he first became ill, so, as his ungrateful daughter had declined to become involved, a battery of carers took over Old Con's life. He had a home help every day, district nurses to attend to his needs and check his skin daily for bedsores, because having no feeling he didn't know when it was time to move from one buttock to the other. Doctors arrived regularly to check on his urinary catheter and to treat the frequent infections that flared up, and over the next five years he would be admitted to hospital as and when various bugs became resistant to his usual antibiotics. He quickly adapted to being looked after – why not? He'd been looked after all his life – and soon he had become mentally institutionalised, his entire world revolving around his condition and his little band of helpers. He played the role of the feisty little man to perfection, the plucky little martyr singled out for yet more terrible suffering, and humbly prepared to accept his lot, as long as everyone understood how feisty, plucky and humble he was being. He became a great favourite with the Royal Infirmary staff. They said he wouldn't walk again, but he had hoisted himself to his feet and learned to throw his weight from numb leg to numb leg with the aid of a zimmer, which was why they didn't want to amputate his leg if it could be avoided. Such spirit in adversity, they said, and when he was treated for the inevitable urine then kidney infections, they were touched by his gratitude for all they did for him. And that sense of humour! He must be a joy, a right card to live with!

Kathy made sure she couldn't confirm or deny either opinion, keeping in touch by phone and the odd visit from the West Coast. She'd had enough of caring for Old Con, she'd done it almost all her life in one way or another, and having once departed there was no way she would go back. And the medical people caring for him made their displeasure very clear in a hundred different little ways, all of which Kathy ignored. Much of the criticism being voiced behind her back centred, she knew, on the fact that she had no other family responsibilities. She was the spinster daughter with no one and nothing else in her life, and therefore little to do but care for her ailing father, who had, as far as they were concerned, provided for her all her life. They couldn't understand how anyone, least of all his own daughter, could be ambivalent about such a resilient, grateful old soul, and somehow the cause of his condition was quietly laid to one side, out of reach of their critical faculties or their imaginations. Drink had caused his condition, a lifetime of heavy and constant boozing, but the judgemental medical people had contrived not to think beyond Old Con's apparent good humour with them, and so they didn't try to imagine what life with him must have been like for his family. Kathy kept her own counsel, but she had her answer ready for the first one unwise enough to openly suggest she should do her duty by her ailing father. No one did of course, they just hinted and looked, but she knew what they were saying to each other once she'd gone. The poor man, and him so cheerful and grateful for everything that was done for him, and his daughter was so hard. His son was different of course. They knew about Peter, Con saw to that, even though no attempt had been made to contact him, because, well, he was obviously out there in the world 'doing things', and probably *important* things. He had a life of some merit, whereas the spinster daughter couldn't have any life worth bothering about, certainly not one that she couldn't, shouldn't, give up to nurse her wonderful old father. And inevitably she had given it up, though only for these last three months before his death. Now at last he had succumbed to all the debilitating infections that can hit the paralysed; the bugs had gradually gained the upper hand against the frequently used antibiotics, and the card had finally been trumped. Just a few more things to attend to and in a matter of days she would leave this place and never come back, all loose ends finally and firmly tied, all duties performed. Please, the God that doesn't exist, let it go quickly and without a hitch so that I can be free!

As if on cue, just as the medico-legal formalities had been completed, the undertaker had arrived. He immediately reached up to the bedroom window and released the catch to open the small top pane.

'Whit on earth are you doin'?' she asked, amazed, because

everybody knew that letting air in was the worst thing you could do with a newly dead body in the room; it made them go off all the sooner.

'There is a tradition of letting the soul go free,' he replied, in a voice he must have practised for years to get the deeply sad, and yet mysterious, tone just right.

'Well if that's the case, let's open a' the windaes an' the front door as well, tae make sure the old bastard really goes free! Or,' she continued, 'on second thoughts, don't bother, son. If Ah know Auld Con, an' believe me, Ah know him better than most, he was oot the keyhole wi' his last gasp an' on his way tae the nearest boozer while Sanctimonious Joe was still doing the business with the oil an' the mutterin'. Take my word for it, if ye care tae visit the Sarrie Heid ye'll find "the soul" propping up the bar, soaking up the bevvy like a sponge! Wan thing the business o' dyin' did,' she laughed bitterly again, 'was keep him anchored tae his bed an' away frae the water of life. Noo that he's "free", he'll be makin' up for lost time. Talk aboot the final revenge! When his legs gied oot wi' the booze it was the first time in a' my life Ah'd seen him sober, the only time in fact!'

It wasn't, though. 1968; that was the first and only time he had temporarily seen the world as others did, non-drinking others anyway. When he had eventually been traced on the day Lily died he had been shocked into sobriety for a brief moment. And that was when she realised that she had never seen him without a drink in him ever before; even if he hadn't been falling down drunk he had always had enough in his system to keep him permanently inebriated. For that one, fleeting second he had been sober, and she had nothing to say to him, or he to her; they were total strangers. She didn't know him any way but drunk, not the *real* him anyway, if indeed the real him existed or ever had. Peter, the prodigal son, hadn't turned up then either, come to think of it. He'd sent a message that he was involved in some extremely important but unspecified work and was therefore unable to arrange his mother's funeral, but he hoped to make it for the event on the day. When he didn't make that either, Aggie had been sympathetic. 'Poor Peter,' the old harridan had said, 'it would likely have been too much for the poor boy. He did the right thing stayin' away, so he did.'

Kathy had been, what, fifteen? So 'the poor boy' had been around twenty-six. Outrage almost overcame her grief. 'Christ, aye, Aggie,' she spat at the old woman, 'that's right! It's too much for poor bloody Peter, an' here's me, right enough, havin' the time o' my life at my mother's funeral!'

'Peter's different,' Aggie replied savagely. 'Oor Peter's sensitive, he's no' a callous wee swine like you! Allowances havtae be made for the sensitive!'

'Well Ah guarantee he'll be just as sensitive when your time comes, Aggie!' Kathy spat back. 'He won't be here tae see you away, Ah'd lay money oan it! There won't be anythin' different then either!'

And she'd been right about that as well. She only hoped Aggie was hovering about at her own funeral a few years later, as Father McCabe did the business. When Aggie went the priest had been right there, ready and desperate to administer the Last Rites, however belatedly, just as he had been in the background all through Aggie's marriage to her late husband, the much reviled stalwart of the Orange Lodge. Not that Aggie could be received back into the one true church while her husband was alive, because having married in a Protestant church she was living in sin as far as the Catholic Church had been concerned, but as soon as Aggie became a widow it was as if the unfortunate, unspeakable marriage to the evil Henry Bryson had never been. Aggie was a Catholic once again, and that was at least one reason why Father McCabe had pulled out all the stops to give the reclaimed one a feature-length send-off when she died, even if it perhaps wasn't the only reason. And if she was around, supported by her new wings, she would've seen her granddaughter's smug expression and heard her mutter as the coffin passed, 'Ah told ye, Aggie! Nae Peter for you either!'

'Different,' that's what Aggie had said, Peter wasn't like Kathy, and funnily enough, 'different' was how her mother had always described her and Peter. 'The two o' ye are the same,' Lily used to say, as Kathy wondered which of them should feel more insulted by the description, 'but different.' 'But a helluva lot different, well!' Kathy would protest. In many ways it was true though. Peter was a lot older than her, ten, no, eleven years, and handsome all of his life. He had Old Con's thick black hair, grey eyes and sallow complexion, whereas his much younger sister had auburn hair, brown eyes and pale, freckled skin, just like Lily and the long-gone Orangeman, Henry Bryson. But different as their colouring was, there were similarities. For instance, they both had skin so easily irritated that the softest wool brought it out in a rash, and their features had an undeniable look of kinship about them, despite the different colour schemes. But there was something about Peter, something that had been there since he was a child by all accounts, an air almost of not belonging to his own family, of being too good for them and their station in life. It was something they almost admitted themselves in a guilty, apologetic way, as though it was their fault for landing him with his own background. Peter was, from the very beginning, on his way up and out, and he had a confidence that left no one in any doubt that he was meant for better things. Part of what Kathy disliked so much about him was his easy rapport with everyone he met, he was all things to all men but he stood for nothing, except his precious self, of course. 'He can talk to prince or pauper,' Aggie used to say proudly of her 'sensitive' grandson, and it was true, but Kathy knew he was always well aware of which was which. She didn't understand why no one else objected to Peter's clear agenda, his clear image of a destiny that didn't include the pauper, or any of the family either, come to that. She had worked out long ago why she knew this. It was because they had similar characters too, however much she hated to admit it to herself, but at a certain point they had diverged. They saw things in much the same way, but the roads they decided to take as a result, their priorities, were widely different. It was as if they looked through the same eyes on the same scenes, she had always thought, then made opposite choices based on the identical views they saw. Who, after all, has a clearer picture of what is in the mirror than its reflection? Lily, her daughter knew, was more right than even she realised; Peter and Kathy were indeed the same, but different. *Very* different.

Peter was the reason, Kathy knew without asking, that eighteen-year-old Con Kelly had married sixteen-year-old Lily Bryson all those years ago, and even then Aggie, Lily's mother, had taken her new son-in-law's side. It was her daughter's fault alone that Con had got her pregnant, and for the rest of her life Aggie had continued to take his side. The bond between Con and Aggie was their religion, which Aggie had to lose temporarily during her marriage but had never quite forgotten, and it mattered more to her than her daughter, her elder daughter at any rate. Lily had no time for religion of any kind, a neutral stance that was interpreted as a vote against Catholicism as far as Aggie was concerned, whereas Lily's younger sister, Jessie, shrewdly sided with their mother on this and all other issues. Lily it was who ran after her, danced attendance on her, and Jessie it was she adored – and Con too, of course. It was as if Con and Jessie were her children and Lily the unwanted in-law. 'Oor Jessica shoulda married Con,' Aggie would say openly. 'An' if Lily hadnae got herself in the family way, he woulda.'

'Aye, Aggie,' Kathy would reply darkly, 'it was a' doon tae Lily. Ah thought ye'd have approved o' a virgin birth in the family. Any virgin ower the age o' ten in your family would've been an achievement for that matter. An' the Virgin Lily even gi'ed birth tae Peter the Messiah – Christ, Aggie, Ah think ye might be on tae somethin' here y'know! But ye're right, it was a' Lily's doin'. That an' the fact that my Da was a randy auld swine who didnae care where he put it, of course! Him an' Jessie are well-met in that department tae!'

'You keep yer dirty tongue aff oor Jessica!' Aggie would argue back. 'You mind yer ain business!'

'Ah'd rather mind *ma* business than *hers*, Ah'll tell ye that! But right enough, Aggie,' her granddaughter would say with a grin, 'Ah've likely got your Jessie a' wrang. Ah havtae admit, though, Ah still wouldnae want to get too close tae her business. Ye're a blessed wumman right enough, the Virgin Lily, Peter the Messiah and Jessie Magdalen, plus whoever the hell ma auld man is, a' in wan family, must be a record that! But come tae think o' it, Jessie Magdalen would never have done business wi' ma auld man anyway, seein' as she's rarely been known tae gie it away free, has she? An' Ah don't think ma Da could've afforded her *an'* the booze!'

'Ye're an evil wee swine!' Aggie would screech. 'Ye know fine that oor Jessica works in Stobhill Hospital as a secretary!'

'Naw she doesnae, Aggie!' Kathy would reply sweetly, as though talking to a particularly dim child. 'Has naebody tellt ye? That's just where the VD clinic is! Jessie doesnae *work* there, she *provides* work there. They're that grateful tae her for keepin' them in business that she's even got her ain chair . . . Mind you, naebody else would sit in it anyway, she's likely got her ain cludgie seat tae for the same reason.'

'Ya filthy-moothed wee midden ye!'

'She's their best customer, Ah'm tellin' ye, Aggie, withoot Jessie the VD clinic would've shut doon years ago. If she's no' in for a bitta cleanin' up hersel' she's providin' patients tae keep the place goin'. Ah'm tellin' ye, ye should be proud o' her, keepin' a' they hospital folk in jobs. Every advance in the treatment o' the clap that's been made has been doon tae your lovely Jessica. She's been a godsend tae medical science so she has, an' Ah'm proud o' her, even if you're no'!'

While Lily worked to keep old Con in booze money, and Peter and Kathy fed and clothed, she had also slaved for her mother. She did the old woman's washing, did her shopping, took her turn at scrubbing the stairs and generally made sure she was fed, watered and healthy. Lily was regarded as 'a good wumman', by everyone who knew her, but it was Jessie who provided Aggie with cash, and cash was much closer to Aggie's heart than goodness or devotion. And everyone knew too how Jessie earned the cash, though, of course, only those outside the family gave it a name and never when talking to those inside. Kathy remembered Lily's response whenever the subject of her sister was raised, a quick sniff, and 'Aye, well. We a' know oor Jessie's problem. She's got this affliction that means she can only see the world frae her back!' Everyone knew it too, and the tales of Jessie Bryson's adventures were part of the folklore of the East End. But you had to admire her, the way she affected not to acknowledge her reputation; looking at her and listening to her, you'd think being on the game was like attending a particularly expensive finishing school. Not that Jessie suffered from low self-esteem; there was no chance of her doing it for a couple of pounds to keep the wolf from the door, for instance, she performed her skills only for and with those who could reward her well. Jessie was no common slapper, but Kathy used to wonder what it was that she could possibly do that was different enough to keep her in the style to which she had become accustomed. For the life of her she couldn't think of any variation on the norm, or the perverted either, that could be worth the money, and even Jessie's best friend, if she had one, couldn't say she was a great beauty. Jessie took after Aggie in looks, and as everyone knew, Aggie had a face like a bag of tatties, and knobbly ones at that, she looked like Sid James in drag. Jessie was probably what Aggie looked like when she was young, a small, thin woman with dark, straight hair, though her dark eyes, just the right side and no more of bulbous, were all her own, as was the sallow complexion that produced dark circles under her almost bulbous eyes years before they would've shown on anyone else. But there again, she was literally a lady of the dark, so her physical appearance could've been down to her lifestyle rather than her genes, because a good night's sleep didn't quite fit in with her line of work. Still, whatever wonders Jessie performed on the libidos of her customers, it kept her in luxury. Jessie it was who wore the first mink coat Kathy had ever seen.

'It's true then,' Lily had whispered to Kathy, watching her sister swanning around in her latest acquisition.

'What?' Kathy had asked, and Lily had laughed so hard that she'd almost choked. 'Fur coat an' nae knickers!' she had squealed. 'In Jessie's case it's definitely true!'

'My, Jessie,' Kathy had said, feeling the silky, luxurious pelt, 'Ah bet a few cats laid doon their lives tae make that!' Behind her she could hear Lily stifling a giggle.

'It's mink,' replied the insulted Jessie. 'It's no' catskin.'

'Well don't you worry, Jessie,' she said sympathetically, 'naebody'll know it's no' cat unless ye tell them. It looks just like the real thing tae me.'

And the be-furred, half-naked Jessie's earnings were enough to keep her two children, Harry and Claire, at the best private schools in Glasgow. Kathy had been jealous of her cousin Claire when she was a child, not because Claire was darkly beautiful, which she was, but because while Kathy went to the local primary school then on to Our Lady and St Francis Convent School, Claire had attended the up-market, fee-paying Notre Dame Primary and then the High School, the top Catholic girls' school in Glasgow. Harry had gone to St Aloysius, but that had bothered her less because unlike his sister he had a brain, and Kathy liked him too, but education was, she always felt, wasted on Claire, who seemed to get from one breath to the next without any conscious effort or aim. 'A bit fey,' was how Lily had described her, while 'Daft as a brush,' was Kathy's more accurate opinion.

And Jessie's two children had no visible father, though she had been married briefly to a man called Sammy Nicholson, whom everyone thought of as a decent enough bloke, until he fell down a flight of stairs and broke his neck. 'Fell or was pushed?' Kathy used to ask Lily, and Lily would laugh, 'Kathleen! That's terrible!' 'Well, he'd served his purpose, hadn't he? He'd supplied Jessie wi' an alternative name tae make her respectable, or as respectable as a name change alone could ever make her.' In the curious way of things, she was known locally all her life as Jessie Bryson, even if legally she was Mrs Nicholson, while both Harry and Claire, who had no relationship, either biological or legal, to the unfortunate Sammy, had taken his name, though Harry had been there many years before his mother's brief marriage, and Claire didn't appear till much longer than nine months after Sammy's death. What always fascinated Kathy was what explanations Jessie could possibly have given her children about their origins, or were they unaware of the time scales involved in their births and the demise of their 'father'? The rest of the family knew of Harry's origins, but Kathy was never sure if he did. His father was Eddie Harris, a notorious Glasgow gangster, and for however long the relationship lasted he would visit

Jessie in her home in nearby Broad Street on a regular basis, while his two bodyguards waited outside. Thus, anyone passing knew that Jessie and Eddie Harris were inside, attending to 'business'. There was a suspicion that Eddie Harris was the only punter who didn't actually pay for Jessie's services, though for some years afterwards he contributed to the upkeep of the product, known for the first few years of his life as Harry Harris. 'D'ye no' remember him comin' tae see Harry when he was a wee boy?' Lily would ask Kathy, but Kathy had been even wee-er than Harry at the time and she was never sure if she could remember, or if her mother had told her so often that she thought she could remember. 'D'ye no' mind the time ye asked why Harry wasnae comin' oot tae play an' Aggie said his Daddy was visitin' him, an' you said, "But Harry's Daddy's deid"? Ye coulda heard a pin drap!' Kathy wasn't sure whose memory that story came from either, but from somewhere there was an image of a tall, thin man wearing a tight, double-breasted suit and a hat, and black suede shoes with thick crepe soles. But then that was everyone's image of a gangster and Kathy could have lifted it straight from a comic or a film, even if her vision of Eddie Harris was taller than either George Raft or Edward G. Robinson.

In time, though, the visits had stopped and Jessie had married the ill-fated Sammy Nicholson, and from then Harry was known as Harry Nicholson. If he was aware of having changed names he gave no indication of it, but certainly Father McCabe had been aware of that and all the other intricacies of Jessie's life story, not that it stopped him accepting cash from her and welcoming her into the faith. Kathy supposed that Jessie just trotted along to confession once a week in her mink coat, repented of that week's liaisons, took her penance and emerged clean as a whistle and ready to liaise again. And oh, by the way, Father, here's a couple of bob for the new roof. Was that how it worked, she wondered? Claire's father had come from climes further afield, as was evident from her exotic features. That two such handsome children, one blond and blue-eyed, the other darkly beautiful, should have come from Jessie, was a thing of wonder to Kathy. How was it, she mused, that they had been lucky enough to take their looks so entirely and obviously from their fathers, when Jessie's plainness was so strong? No one knew for sure who Claire's father had been, but around the time of her conception and birth there were increasing numbers of immigrants arriving from the Indian subcontinent. As it was always assumed that Jessie's skills did not lie in her brain power, she would probably have had more difficulty than most telling one of her dusky customers from another, if, indeed, she was ever able to distinguish the features of any of them, regardless of their colour. The price was all that interested Jessie, so whoever had fathered Claire one thing was certain, he must've been one of the wealthier new arrivals, because Jessie had her standards, or her tariffs at least.

In time, though, Jessie's line of work got to her, and it was a great sorrow to Kathy that Lily hadn't lived to see it. Jessie developed a phobia about germs, though, as Kathy wryly noted, not until her physical charms, such as they were, had faded and presumably – but who knew for certain? – business had dropped off. Wherever she went Jessie held a handkerchief over her mouth and nose with white gloved hands, in an attempt to avoid whatever bugs were seeping out of passers-by and making their way directly to her. It didn't help that Kathy was always overcome with sneezing and coughing attacks whenever Auntie Jessica appeared, or that she was so happy to see her that she insisted on hugging Auntie Jessica whenever they met either. Then Jessie began washing her hands so often that the skin was permanently red and weeping, and instead of attending the VD clinic she transferred to the Dermatology clinic, where various unguents and lotions were tried over the years; in vain, of course, the problem being in her mind, not her hands. Where once she was instantly recognisable by her expensive clothes and potato-like, young Sid James features, together with the treasured mink coat and her lack of nether garments, everyone's perception of Jessie Bryson was changed in later years, and she was reduced in their minds to two weeping, red, raw hands, enclosed in white cotton gloves, clutching a handkerchief against her nose and mouth.

'Poor Jessica,' Aggie sympathised, 'her hands is that bad she's had tae gie up her work.'

'Nae wonder,' replied Kathy. 'Ah know men don't care too much where they put their willies, but even a scabby auld horse would think twice about lettin' Jessie touch them wi' her hands in that state! Efter a', if the ootside's like that, there's nae tellin' whit the inside's like!'

'Ah'll swing for you, lady!' Aggie screeched, rising menacingly from her chair beside the fire.

'Aye, well, make sure ye wear a wee sparkly costume when ye dae, Aggie. The effect is everything when it comes tae pleasin' the public. Just ask your Jessica.'

'As God is my witness, may you be struck deid for whit comes oota that mootha yours!' Aggie screamed, spittle flying in all directions, and her hands performing a blessing across her body to seal her granddaughter's fate.

'Christ, Aggie,' Kathy responded conversationally, 'if ye don't go a bit easier wi' yer sign o' the cross ye'll dislocate yer shoulders wanna these days. An' anyway, if yer God hasnae struck Jessie deid for what he's witnessed hur daein', Ah don't think he'll bother too much wi' me, Aggie. Dae you, really?'

Jessie and her children moved from Broad Street after the demise of the unfortunate Sammy. With business booming she, Harry and Claire moved to Newton Mearns, on the affluent southern fringes of the city, the natural home of Fifties yuppies, where she bought a 1920s bungalow with double bay windows. Family visits to Jessie were not frequent, so Kathy only saw her house once, and was struck by how respectable it looked, with its net curtains and neat garden. Jessie didn't exactly ban the family from her home, she just didn't issue invitations, and in a strange, but civil, way there was a feeling of polite discouragement. Kathy's great friend, apart from Jamie, had always been her cousin Harry. Jamie was her soulmate, but she knew he had no interest in the things that interested her; they were so close because their personalities complemented each other. Jamie's dreams for the future were simple and commendable, if dull. He would serve his time as an engineer then settle into married life and have two children. He wanted a better life for his children than he had had himself, a better house in a better area, better clothes, better schools, in fact in the future he envisaged life would be much the same, only every aspect would be better. She had always known that his horizons didn't stretch as far as her own. He had no interest in books for instance, and books were her great solace. They would go to the library together, he to study for his City and Guilds, she to read poetry, though she never told him that; he had assumed she was doing homework and she didn't deny it, that was all. But it was different with Harry, because Harry had been educated, and out of the entire family he was the only one on her wavelength. He was a cheerful, good-natured boy, always with a welcoming smile, happy to talk books with her, the only one she could ever divulge her deepest ambitions to. Harry didn't laugh because she wanted to be a writer, though the dream was so far away that she knew it was indeed laughable, and from her very earliest days she felt an unspoken understanding between them. She was proud of Harry, he was clever, he was pleasant, and one day he would, she was convinced, be somebody, he would succeed. And when that day came, she could imagine him being the same open, pleasant chap, unlike her brother Peter, who wanted nothing to do with his background or the people he came from, who was ashamed of them, regardless of the adoration they all felt for him, well, almost all. Peter too would make it big, of that she had no doubt, he would have it all one day and he'd keep it, whereas their cousin Harry's success wouldn't stop him being one of the family. Peter was a phoney, she thought, but Harry was the real thing.

When she asked Harry about his mother it was as if he knew why she was asking but wasn't offended, in fact he was so easy about it that she often wondered if he really knew what Jessie did for a living. Until the later days of her germ phobia, Jessie always presented an immaculate figure to the world. Kathy would see her at Aggie's house, the only place she ever did see her, and she never tired of examining the vision that was Jessie. Everything was a little overdone. The black of the eyebrows was too strong, the face powder too heavy, and too pink. Her rouge was just a hint too rosy red, and applied as a precisely defined circle of colour on each cheek. Her habitual scarlet lipstick was too red and too thick, so that it overran her lips, bleeding into the tiny lines leading from her mouth. She looked to Kathy like one of those women you saw in the big stores being taught how to apply make-up, but over time she had remembered the impression while becoming hazy about the detail, so that the result became increasingly imprecise, and her face more like a mask. Then there was the mink coat, of course, and an ever-present, black velvet concoction of a hat, like a little saucer with a saucy bow on top, sitting on her head. Two open triangles of velvet-covered wire held it tightly in place at both sides, and a delicate black veil with little dots, like a spider's web full of dead flies, fell from her forehead, ending at the tip of her nose. She wore plain, black suede shoes with pointed toes and high stiletto heels, the most oddly sophisticated yet questionable shoes Kathy had ever seen. Around the edges, where each shoe met the foot, a thin, white leather lining was just tantalisingly visible against the sheer black of her stockings. In ancient Greece prostitutes wore shoes with 'Follow me' imprinted in the soles, leaving an invitation to potential male customers with every step. Jessie's shoes, Kathy always thought, were the modern Glasgow version, they were twentieth-century 'fuck me' shoes. They were decadent and slightly kinky, in their oddly sophisticated way, a way you instinctively understood without knowing how or why, whore's shoes without a doubt. With her decadent shoes, Jessie wore fully-fashioned stockings with a design of little graduated steps climbing upwards and getting smaller from the heel, fading to a black line up her calf so straight and precise that it looked painted on her leg. Even when fashions changed and women everywhere gave thanks for the invention of tights, Jessie wore her fully-fashioned stockings, but then it was understood that men hated tights and loved suspender belts and stockings, because they didn't have to wear them, so maybe it was less to do with choice than Jessie's ability to look after business. Her clothes under the mink were always black and simple, no frills or flounces, and over her left arm she carried a plain black handbag that fastened with a gold clasp. On the third finger of her left hand she wore a slim gold band under a black leather glove, in which she carried the right hand glove, so that she could smoke a cigarette. The cigarette was held in an elegant pose between two fingers, the other two fingers gently curved towards her palm, the pose set off by scarlet painted nails like talons. It was, Kathy knew, the way Rita Hayworth held a cigarette, because she'd seen it in a film. Yet Kathy never actually saw Jessie put the cigarette to her lips, the cigarette just sat in position, the smoke curling high into the air until the glowing tip finally burned so low that it was in danger of scorching her fingers, then it was stubbed out. Apart from her wedding band, the only jewellery she wore was a gold watch, and on her ear-lobes, single pearl studs, white and virginal, the traditional choice of white brides everywhere. Instead of having her ears pierced, Jessie wore earrings with a loop of gold running from the pearl and under the lobes, where it was held in position by a tiny screw arrangement. The whole picture was one of determined sophistication, which, apart from the shoes, never really rang true as far as Kathy was concerned. Despite the expense of this carefully cultivated image she still looked like Jessie Bryson trying to look sophisticated, and Kathy often wondered if she lived her life in that mode. She couldn't, for instance, imagine her aunt in a wraparound pinny, ankle socks and slippers, her hair in curlers and pins and a fag hanging from her lips, as she did the dusting in Newton Mearns, listening to 'Mrs Dale's Diary' on the wireless. And Harry confirmed this. A woman came in twice a week to do the cleaning, he said, and a man appeared every fortnight to tidy the garden. And did Jessie do the shopping? No, Jessie did not; the same woman who did the housework also did the shopping. So what exactly did Jessie do with her time then? Well, she worked in the hospital, didn't she, said her son. Kathy never did work out if Harry was saying this tongue in cheek, or if he believed it. For a start, didn't he ever wonder how she could type with those nails? But in case he did believe it, she left it alone and said no more.

'Does she ever just laze aboot the hoose, though?' she asked instead.

Harry looked perplexed. 'What d'you mean?'

'Well, sometimes, when ma Mammy has a bath, she puts on her pyjamas an' lies on the couch wi' her hair in curlers, readin' a magazine. Does Auntie Jessie dae that kinda thing?'

Harry looked lost. 'I've never seen her like that,' he said with a smile. 'She gets her hair and her nails done every week.'

'Her nails?' Kathy asked, raising her voice. 'Ye mean somebody does her nails for her?'

Harry nodded. 'She goes to a beauty parlour and has a manicure, her hair, the lot, all done at once every week.'

Kathy was amazed. It was all done with mirrors after all then; Jessie regularly got herself professionally refurbished, inside and out.

'Whit else does she dae, when ye're at school, or when ye go hame?'

'Well, she has her work during the day, hasn't she?' Harry asked. 'Then someone comes in and sits with me and Claire most evenings, so that my mother can go out.'

Ah ha! 'Where?'

'I don't know,' he shrugged. 'Clubs or somewhere, I suppose. Or to her dressmaker, because she's too busy working at the hospital during the day to see her then, isn't she?'

Was Harry having her on? Didn't he know that Jessie's 'work' took place at night? Kathy never found the answer to that one, because, being fond of her cousin, she didn't have the nerve to say, 'Look, Harry. Your mother's on the game, she always has been. Everybody knows she's a slapper.' Neither did she feel comfortable hinting at what he should know, that not many hospital secretaries could fund the lifestyle Mrs Nicholson and her children enjoyed, and damn few could afford weekly trips to beauty parlours and dressmakers. But Harry was a clever lad, she thought, surely he must've thought of all this himself and wondered? And if he had done, he had obviously decided to keep such musings to himself, so just like the confused topic of Harry and Claire's true parentage, Kathy stopped asking her cousin questions, though she never did stop wondering just what he did know, and how much he had decided not to know.

3

Her first taste of life outside the East End had been on a school trip when she was thirteen. Somehow Lily had scraped together a few shillings and, even more amazingly, had successfully kept them hidden from Con, so that Kathy could go on a coach trip to Fort William with her class. She remembered Lily seeing her off that morning, her stomach in knots of anticipation and fear, because however excited she was at the prospect of the trip, the Highlands were another world away. She had never been that far from her mother before, there hadn't been a second of their lives when they hadn't known exactly where the other was, and though she felt embarrassed about it, there was a very childish fear deep inside that she might vanish off the edge of the earth and never see her again. As she boarded the coach Lily had pressed more money into her hand, all of it in pennies and silver sixpences, telling her 'Mind, noo, ye've no' tae bring back presents. That's for you tae spend.' She'd felt guilty, though, knowing that Lily would have done without herself to finance the trip, and she made up her mind there and then that of course she would buy Lily a present. It was a cheap enamel brooch of a bunch of heather held together with a tartan ribbon, and Lily had worn it from that day on; it was still pinned to the scrap of charred cloth that had been her coat, recovered from the fire a couple of years later.

The trip seemed to last for days, though it could only have taken two or three hours to get there, but as far as Kathy had been concerned it didn't last long enough. As they left the built-up centre of Glasgow the buildings gradually thinned out, and there was a feeling of light and space that she had never experienced before. Everyone else was singing, or eating too much and being sick, or chattering to each other in high excited voices, but Kathy Kelly sat with her face pressed against the window, soaking up the scenery in silence. Glencoe completely overawed her. In the background a teacher's voice tried to penetrate the garble of the girls, and even when she knew she had lost the battle, she kept trying valiantly; this trip *would* be educational, whether or not it was also enjoyable. To many of the girls it was neither. Born and bred in the city, they had no liking for this vastly different landscape, finding it alien and almost threatening. Anxious voices kept asking 'When will we be there, Miss?', desperate to reach Fort William, where there would be streets and pavements and people once again. 'Many people,' the teacher screeched over the noise, 'find Glencoe a brooding, dark place,' but Kathy didn't. She turned her head from side to side, desperate not to miss the mountains rising high on both sides of the narrow, winding road, and thought of them standing here for millions of years, not brooding or dark, but magnificent. It probably hadn't changed in *trillions* of years, and if you blotted the road out of your mind, you could imagine that the ancient people of Glencoe were still alive, just over that hill, round the next bend in the road. 'Many of the Redcoat soldiers,' preached the teacher, 'searching for the remnants of the 1745 Jacobite Rebellion, had never seen scenery like this before, and they suffered badly from vertigo as they hunted through these mountains.' But you didn't have to be English to be affected, many of the Glasgow girls on the bus, coming from just as flat a landscape, clearly felt exactly the same as the Redcoats. Kathy didn't find it frightening or disorientating, though, it was a fascinating place, a magical, glorious place, and with each new ridge that appeared her imagination soared. She spent that day in silence, so full of the place that she couldn't have described it or given an opinion, her throat tight, transfixed by the grandeur.

At Fort William they had stopped to have their packed lunches, then they had gone round the shops in the small main street, but even as she bought Lily's brooch Kathy was anxious to get back on the road again, to travel through Glencoe. These days she knew the names of all the mountains, she could tell Buachaille

Etive Mor from Buachaille Etive Beag, point out the difference between the Chancellor and the Study, if you could see them for people that was. There wasn't a lay-by on the winding road that wasn't crammed with Volvos and Mercs, and you'd a better chance of meeting your nextdoor neighbour trying to walk up Aonach Eagach in trainers, than in the local supermarket. But the feeling of awe never lessened. Every time she went through the Pass of Glencoe, the power, the raw beauty of the place hit her again just as strongly, and tears would spring to her eyes. She would get annoyed at herself, horrified at the thought of Old Con's sentimentality creeping up on her as she got older, so she would blink in an attempt to banish them. And though she would never have admitted it out loud, and furthermore, would have denied it ferociously had anyone suggested it, the Western Highlands had entered her soul that first day, never to leave again; there was an immediate sense of belonging to a place she hadn't known existed till then. When she'd returned from the school trip all those years ago, exhausted emotionally rather than physically, she had tried to describe to Lily what she had seen, but all she could do was wordlessly hold her hands wide and high in the air. What words were there that could do justice to the feeling of space, to the light, to the ever-changing shadows dancing across the mountains, to how it all made you feel? It was like trying to describe colour to the blind and music to the deaf all at once, it filled your senses on so many levels and in so many directions that you couldn't verbalise one sensation without taking off at a tangent on another, and another after that. She had tried to explain it to Jamie, knowing deep in her heart that it was outside Jamie's understanding. His world consisted of where he lived and what he was doing, or knew for a fact he would do, he wasn't the type to take flights of emotional or imaginative fancy. Jamie wasn't stupid, but he was intensely practical, and one of the things she always liked about him, had relied upon in fact, was how grounded he was, because she knew she wasn't. He was safe, sure and dependable, whereas she was prone to acting on impulse, to saying and doing what was in her mind. It was why she argued so much with Aggie and Con, she knew that, she lived on her emotions, terrified all the time that she was showing signs of Con's greatest weakness, and desperately trying to rein herself in. But Jamie balanced her with his down-to-earth view of life, reflecting reality on to her fantasies and evening them out, and given their lives that was a valuable quality to have, or to have access to. Even so, she couldn't contain herself over Glencoe, and Jamie had indulgently smiled his solid smile as she described it.

'But there's nothing there, is there?' he asked kindly.

'Whit dae ye mean?'

'Well, there's nae shops an' streets, nae buses, nae people, is there?'

'Why does there havtae be?' she had demanded, annoyed that he was putting down her great adventure.

'But ye canny live up a mountain, can ye?' Jamie persisted. 'Ah mean, it's mibbe OK for a trip, but ye wouldnae want to live there, would ye? Ye *couldnae* live there, noo could ye?'

She was almost angry now. 'Naebody says ye havtae live up a mountain,' she scowled at him. 'There are hooses no' far frae the mountains, Ah saw them, an' people *dae* live there.'

Jamie shook his head slightly and smiled affectionately at her. 'But there's no' a lotta work in they places, is there?' he stated, rather than asked. 'If ye wanted tae be an engineer, ye wouldnae go tae the back o' beyond tae dae it, would ye? An' ye wouldnae want tae live in a place where there's only grass, an' sheep an' things.'

She said nothing, but she was almost crying, and at the time she couldn't understand exactly why. She was talking to him of beauty and feelings, of flights of fancy and dreams, of almost seeing in your mind the defeated Highlanders making their way home through the glens and mountain passes after the defeat of the Jacobites at the Battle of Culloden, and he was dashing it all with casual, cruel insensitivity, because he hadn't the slightest glimmering of an understanding that such notions existed or should. But the tears prickling at the corners of her eyes, making her blink furiously to stop them escaping over her cheeks, were caused by something deeper than Jamie's lack of imagination. All her life she had valued his outlook, it was part of what had made her feel safe, but suddenly she felt that she was talking to a stranger who didn't understand the language. Her tears marked the first time she had felt *disappointed* in Jamie, let down almost, by his inability to see with her eyes, even though she knew that was unfair, because it was precisely the quality in him that she had so loved. She had felt the earth stir under her feet, that was what it had amounted to, a fissure had unexpectedly opened up on solid ground, exposing in someone she loved a weakness that she had always regarded as a strength. And that in turn made her feel disloyal to Jamie. He was who he was, who he had always been, and his qualities were the ones she had depended on all her life. If the value she now placed on them had changed, well, then, that must be her fault, not Jamie's. Confused, she turned to her cousin Harry, and to her great joy and relief Harry understood; she could always rely on Harry. He sat listening as she described what she had seen, what she had felt, what she had imagined, nodding and smiling at her enthusiasm. There were times when she didn't know what she would do without her cousin, he was the only one in her entire family, in her entire life, come to that, who understood her completely, the only person in the universe who treated her dreams as not only possible, but sane. Harry saw beyond the lives they were forced to lead by the circumstances of their birth, he had imagination and intelligence, and above all, unlike her brother, Peter, Harry was kind.

Nothing much had been heard of Peter since he had finished his National Service. His intake had been the last to be called up, after that conscription into the British Army ended. He had gone happily enough by all accounts, but then it was some sort of move away from the East End, if not the ideal one, and after serving two years in Germany he was asked to train as an officer. He didn't though, instead he had remained in London after being demobbed, though no one seemed very sure what he was doing there. He worked as a barman in an Irish pub in Kilburn until he found his feet, and the next anyone heard he was training to be a teacher. Everything was a stepping stone for Peter, even if he had no interest in teaching children, and Kathy knew instinctively that he hadn't, it was that much farther away from Moncur Street. There had been one, fleeting, miserable visit home shortly before Lily's death, when Kathy had resented his being there almost as much as he had resented it himself. Nothing pleased him, everything disgusted him. It was as if he had come back one last time to prove to himself that he didn't belong there, and when he had gone Kathy felt as much happiness as he did himself. She didn't know then why he had bothered to come back if everything and everyone displeased him so much, and she hoped he wouldn't repeat the exercise ever again. And he didn't, even for Lily's funeral. A few years later a postcard arrived from Canada, saying he was working there, and then a local man who was in the Merchant Navy reported meeting him in Alaska. In his absence his frontier spirit was held up to be admired by Con and Aggie, and he was much praised. 'Ah always knew he would make somethin' o' himself,' Aggie would say, her voice cracking with pride and emotion, re-reading the few lines on the postcard, until it became so creased with handling and age that the writing was illegible. Even so, it would be produced for the admiration of everyone who entered the house, regardless of how many times they had been forced to admire it in the past, and for some reason it didn't seem to occur to her, or perhaps it didn't matter, that the gaps between future postcards, with their few noncommittal lines, stretched for years, and there were never any letters. During the frequent deification ceremonies of Peter and his postcards, Kathy would catch Harry's eye and they'd smile like conspirators. She had never heard Harry say anything critical of anyone, not even Peter, but she always knew what he thought because of the bond between them. Peter never came home again, but he was forever announcing himself as being on the verge of doing so, and that was enough for Aggie and Con. Kathy, though, knew better. 'Liar!' she would mutter, and wonder what Lily would've thought, had she been alive. But Lily had never said much about Peter. Kathy had thought about her mother's silence on the subject of the prodigal son many times over the years, wondering why she never volunteered an opinion or a thought about him. It was because she knew him, Kathy thought. Lily took no offence at what amounted to Peter's rejection of his entire family, whether his father and grandmother recognised it or not, because she knew it was how he was and that there was nothing anyone could do to change him. Peter, like Jamie, was as he was, that, Kathy imagined, was how Lily thought of her son, but even so, she wondered, would she have felt hurt or disappointed if she'd known he would never come back? Well, she would never know now, the fire at Stern's made sure of that.

It was November, a cold Monday. She remembered that so clearly because the next day was Lily's birthday and Kathy had a present for her that she knew her mother would love. She had come upon it weeks before on one of her hunts for Con. When he went missing there was no doubt that he would be in some drinking howff, and finding the right one was a simple case of following his trail from one to another until he was found in his usual slumped condition. With Jamie in tow as usual, she had been going round the Barras stallholders asking if anyone had seen her Da, when she had spotted it on Cockney Jock's stall. A Londoner called Dick Lee, he had been renamed 'Cockney Jock' and ran a 'swag', or fancy goods stall. The unsuspecting customer could buy any number of treasures from Jock, 'Roldini gold brooches', 'South Sea Island Pearls', all of them one hundred per cent counterfeit, and Kathy was especially fond of him because he got away with the most blatantly dishonest claims. She had been in his audience one day when he'd been selling paint and found himself being constantly interrupted mid-spiel by a heckler. 'It's no' paint at a'!' yelled the heckler merrily, trying to take over the attention of Jock's punters. 'Pull the other wan, it's even cheaper!' At each jibe Jock would stop politely and assure the large man and the potential customers in the crowd that it was indeed the finest paint. And not just any paint at that, but of the very best quality, surplus from a job that had just been done at Buckingham Palace and, being a Cockney, by birth at any rate, he had been given the chance to buy, at a knockdown price which he was about to pass on to the lucky punters, what was clearly the Château La Fitte, if you took his meaning, of home decorating materials. Still the large chap shouted him down, till Jock could take no more. 'It's merr water than paint!' came the taunt, at which Jock had tipped a canful over him. 'What's up with you?' Jock demanded as the heckler protested. 'It's no' paint, it's water, you said so yourself. I'll do you a good price on a towel to dry yourself off with!'

That day, Kathy's eyes had fallen on something in the corner of Jock's stall and as soon as she had seen it she knew Lily must have it. It was a rectangular box about ten inches long, covered in bright red, padded satin with a heart design woven into it, and finished around the edges with gold cord. She asked if she could see it and Jock handed it to her, muttering with hurt pride that it had been left over from Valentine's Day, and it wasn't his fault that Glaswegians had no romance in their souls, was it? The inside of the box was lined with mock red velvet, and a removable shelf had been fitted with various compartments so that it could be used for anything the owner required. Leave the shelf intact and it could be a jewellery or a sewing box, remove it and you could store photographs or papers or whatever you wanted. She asked Jock how much he wanted and unable to do a deal without at least the pretence of haggling, he grinned and asked her how much she had on her. Kathy had rifled in her pockets and come up with 2/6d, gleaned coin-by-coin from her lunch money over several weeks, and a further search of Jamie's pockets turned up another 2/-. 'Take it,' Jock said happily. He'd sold it, a couple of months late, but still, honour had been restored. 'It's only taking up room anyway.' So she carried it home wrapped in brown paper and hid it carefully in her bedroom, knowing how delighted Lily would be, anxious for her birthday to arrive. Lily's world was completely devoid of anything feminine or frilly, there was no satin and lace about life with Con, but now she would have something pretty, and more to the point, it wasn't worth enough at the pawn shop for Con to hawk it for booze money, so Lily had a chance of keeping it.

So it was Monday, the day before Lily's birthday, and Con was doing whatever Con always did, probably helping around the market for ready cash after the busy weekend trading, then making for the Sarrie Heid, as Lily worked in Stern's warehouse. She had been so happy to get a full-time job at last, after years of doing three or four jobs a day, working herself to death for a collective pittance that never amounted to a full-time wage. Working herself to death; now there was an ironic phrase. B. Stern & Co Ltd was an upholstery firm, housed in an old whisky bond built in 1850 in James Watt Street, in the warren of narrow streets down by the River Clyde. It hadn't been used as a bond since 1961, but the wooden interior staircases were still there, and every window had remained protected by iron bars, even though these days anyone breaking in to the three-storey building would find only sofas and armchairs to steal. Stern's neighbours were mainly just as far removed from the old days of whisky bonding: a tobacco warehouse, the local branch of the Seamen's Union, a glassware warehouse, and just 400 yards away was Cheapside Street, where nineteen men from the Fire Service had died fighting a blaze eight years before. Lily had enjoyed working at Stern's, the other workers were a good lot, she said, a mixture of around twenty-seven men and women, from teenagers to sixty-somethings. She liked the companionship and the easy friendships with people like herself, and before long families had been shared. Kathy knew all about Nancy, whose daughter had given birth to a profoundly handicapped baby girl a couple of years before, only Nancy couldn't accept that there was anything wrong with her grand-daughter. She would come in to work with pictures of a toddler who, though beautiful, was clearly 'no' right', who had to be held in a sitting position for the camera. She was, said a desperately upbeat Nancy, who deep inside knew the truth, 'a wee bit slow', but she was improving every day, and sometimes the other women would feel her pain so strongly that they would hit out at her. 'She's no' right, Nancy! Will ye stop kiddin' yersel'?' they'd say, and Nancy would rush to the toilet in tears, locking the door behind her and refusing all entreaties to come out till she had composed herself. By that time the women would feel guilty about what they had said and once again look at the latest clutch of photos, announcing that 'Ye're right, Nancy, the wee yin's gettin' oan fine, so she is!', all the while exchanging sad glances behind the delighted Nancy's back. And Kathy knew from Lily whose daughter was having a baby soon, whose son was doing well at school and, she supposed, the other women had also glimpsed something of the difficulties in Lily's life. It was how women were in those days. It was an era when they accepted that their lives were devoted to their families, and that included having to take low-paid work outside the home. The money they more than earned went towards providing for their children, and there was no thought given to their own career structures, competitiveness or promotion. They did dull, boring, repetitive jobs for little money, and found whatever satisfaction they could in being together, in having a laugh and a gossip and sharing their family worries and joys with each other. Being working class it was all they had been conditioned to expect of life, and regardless of how intelligent they were, or what heights they might have reached had they been given an even playing field, it was a situation they had to accept for themselves, even in the Sixties. They knew they had been short-changed, that they were being used, but what was new in that? But one day, they hoped, it would be better for their daughters, and that was very often why they accepted their own lot. Many of the women were saving every penny to put their children, girls as well as boys, through university, so that they wouldn't have to work in places like Stern's.

Suddenly on that Monday the fire alarm had sounded. The secretary had tried to dial 999, but an incoming call prevented her, so the Seamen's Union next door summoned the fire brigade. The fire started on the first floor, where the showrooms were situated, and the building very quickly 'went up like a box of fireworks', according to a survivor. For a few moments a man was seen inside, frantically trying to force the iron bars covering the only escape route, with several women behind him. Then, as the attempt failed, the desperate faces behind the barred windows were lost in the smoke. The only doorway to freedom and safety was locked, the key that would have opened it locked in a downstairs office. People working in other warehouses came running, alerted first by the screams, and repeatedly tried to force their way through the smoke and flames, choking with the heat and the fumes. Two men were seen inside the warehouse, trapped in a lift that had become stuck between floors, the flames licking around it, as the wooden staircases, then the roof, collapsed, bringing down the floors below. Twenty fire units rushed to the blaze, and three foam units, as the thick smoke rose hundreds of feet into the air above the city, the firemen helplessly trying to find an exit route for the twenty-two terrified souls who clawed at the barred windows. Then the screaming stopped and the faces disappeared from the windows, leaving only outstretched, charred arms visible through the smoke.

At Our Lady and St Francis Convent School in Charlotte Street Kathy's class was doing a double period of Art that afternoon, and as Art was one of Kathy's favourite subjects, she was happily engrossed in what she was doing. She was distantly aware of the door opening and someone entering the Art Room and whispering to the teacher, who looked up quickly at Kathy Kelly. She felt the hairs standing up on her neck. It must be Con. How many times had she imagined this scenario in her mind? He had either been found drunk somewhere and they wanted to know where Lily was, or he'd fallen in front of a bus; oh, please, let it be the bus! She felt her cheeks flush red with embarrassment. Funny to think there was a time when she'd been so innocent that she actually believed there were some folk who didn't know what he was like, and how desperately she had wanted to keep the knowledge secret. Now everyone would know her father was a drunk, she would be shamed in front of them, even if, deep down, she had always known it would only be a matter of time anyhow. 'Kathleen,' said the teacher quietly, 'you're to report to the Headmistress.' Everyone in the class looked at her as she left her desk and walked to the door. Walking along the corridor she had whispered to the messenger, 'Whit is it? D'ye know whit she wants me for?' The girl shrugged and ran back to her own class-room, leaving Kathy to do the long walk on her own. She knocked on the door and entered, looking quickly at the Sister's expression, trying to guess what was wrong. A black look; yes, this was the day. From now on everyone would know. Even looking back from nearly thirty years the impression of slow motion persisted. She sat down and the kindly Sister told her gently that there had been a fire. Even then Kathy had wondered if Con had burned the house down, and if he had, where would she and Lily live now? Well it certainly wouldn't be with Aggie, even if Aggie's house had escaped unscathed, there was no chance of that! She was still working out the logistics, hoping Jamie's house wasn't damaged, when she heard Stern's being mentioned. The Sister must be asking if her mother was working at Stern's. Kathy nodded; yes, she was. It took an interminable time for her to understand that the fire hadn't been at Moncur Street, but at Stern's, that Lily was involved, not Con.

They took her to a Seamen's Hostel down by the Broomielaw, where other relatives were gathering, hoping against hope for good news. They looked at each other only briefly and spoke little. An instinct was at work. By then it was clear that the fire had been a major one, that many had died, and some of the people in the room would undoubtedly be told that their relatives were dead. So there was a feeling, a tacit agreement, that you didn't want to speak to one of the potentially bereaved, in case the bad luck that had already settled on them would somehow rub off on you. It was stupid, but it was there. If you kept to yourself then it wasn't happening to you, it was happening to those other people, and as you weren't one of them, you should keep your distance. It took a long time, days in fact, and they were all thinking the same thing. Even though you knew there was no chance, until you were told, officially and irrevocably, you just didn't believe it. Lily could be anywhere, Kathy decided. Maybe she hadn't been inside the warehouse when the fire broke out, what if she'd nipped out to a nearby shop for something? And even if she had been inside, in the confusion she could've got out without anyone noticing and gone into shock. She could, at this very minute and two days later, be wandering the streets, cold, hungry and lost, but alive. It *was* possible, there were even stranger stories than that in the *Weekly News* every Friday. The day after the fire Con and Aggie, accompanied as ever by Father McCabe, had gone to James Watt Street where, much to Kathy's fury, they had knelt in the street and prayed. Kathy had broken away, she was having no part of this, and instead she had run through the streets, still heavy with the acrid, choking smell of burning, shouting Lily's name till her throat ached and her legs gave way. There was no answer.

Twenty-two people died in the fire, spanning the same cross section of men and women that Lily had described, aged from seventeen to sixty-four, all of them so badly burned that identification took days. The number of corpses was too much for the city mortuary to cope with, so the gym of the Western Infirmary was used as a temporary mortuary, and years later those who had worked in the hospital, all fairly unshockable folk, could still recall, with a shudder, the smell of burnt flesh that permeated the corridors from the basement, upwards and outwards. They talked in hushed tones of how the arms of the blackened bodies still stretched out in death, as if in a last desperate attempt to escape through the barred windows. Lying on their backs, warped and twisted by the flames, each one indistinguishable from the others, their arms reached straight upwards, an image that would stay with those who saw it, as indelibly as the sight of their terrified faces would remain in the memories of those who had tried to rescue them.

It didn't do to dwell on it, Kathy decided. If you thought about it too deeply it might drive you mad. Better to keep your emotions locked away inside yourself, and your feelings beside them. It didn't help to think about the barred windows, the terror of the dying and the thoughts that ran through their minds as they looked out to safety only feet away. Sometimes, if she wasn't on her guard, she would find herself wondering what went through Lily's mind as she fought for her life. Did she think of Peter, or Con,

Aggie even? Did she send a last frantic message to her, and if she did, why had she been unaware of it? How could she have been unaware as Lily died? How was it possible that she didn't feel something? She had been painting in the school Art Room, happy, enjoying herself, while Lily was dying. How could that be? Then she'd catch up with her mind, drag it back and lock it up again. Art became a trigger, though, all thoughts of Art reminded her of Lily's dying. One of her greatest escapes from life at Moncur Street had been to visit the Art Galleries near Kelvin Hall, where she would wander round the vast, usually quiet rooms, the squeaking of her shoes on the polished floors the only sound, lost in the canvases, and sometimes there would be an exhibition at the McLellan Galleries in Sauchiehall Street. She was always careful to keep her interest in Art to herself, barely mentioning her Gallery jaunts even to Harry, and never mentioning them to Jamie, because she knew he would think it odd. Had the word got round it would've given Aggie in particular ammunition against her, but even in the wider community where she lived, an artistic bent would've been regarded as deeply suspicious. Lily's death put an end to all that anyway. All Art became inextricably linked to that day, so she never visited the Galleries again, and she never painted again either. Reminders were dangerous; they prompted thinking, which brought feelings to the surface, and what use was that?

Neither was it of any use to those who died or those who mourned them that questions were asked about the fire in the House of Commons, or that Scottish Secretary Willie Ross was called on to make a statement in the House about Glasgow's worst fire disaster. What did all the speeches by the civic leaders achieve, when the dead remained dead? After the James Watt Street fire there was public outrage about the lack of safety in warehouses like Stern's, and bars were removed from similar buildings later, but that was no consolation either, because it had come *later*. It was always later. Nothing ever happened before innocent people needlessly died, only after the event, only *ever* later, and it was no use then, because Lily was dead. Kathy finally had to accept that. Lily wasn't lost in a backstreet, Lily was dead. They wouldn't let her see her mother's body once it had finally been identified, but even without that proof she knew that had Lily been alive she would have come home.

They buried her in St Kentigern's, the Catholic burial ground in Springburn, beside Con's mother and his sisters. Father McCabe had even worked a flanker by doing the full business at her funeral and seeing her off as the Catholic she wasn't, because Lily had no time for any religion. Con was in fine form; becoming a widower, especially in such public circumstances, was the pinnacle of his suffering, and his dramatic acting skills raised Lily's funeral to a theatrical event. He cut a splendidly tragic figure and he knew it; this was the performance all his previous smaller roles had been leading up to. Kathy had wanted to stop it, but she couldn't summon the energy; it was all too difficult. She was floating somewhere, detached, not part of it, and so it would continue for years afterwards. She was fifteen years old and her mother was gone, so what did anything matter any longer, least of all how Con was behaving? What sobs he conjured up, whatever words were chanted over her, wherever they buried her and how, one thing was sure: Lily wasn't coming back. The funeral had been like being in a fog, with only the occasional thing getting through. There was the constant flash of cameras, but she couldn't have cared less about the press, they simply didn't matter. She had argued briefly with Aggie over Peter's non-appearance, a touch of normality there at least. When it came to the part of the service for taking Communion Father McCabe had glared directly at her, willing her to walk out and receive the Eucharist, and she'd defiantly stared back at him and remained in her seat. Jessie in her 'fuck me' shoes, her face buried in a handkerchief; shades of things to come, had she only but known it. Harry smiling sadly at her, telling her he was sorry with his beautiful blue eyes, his sister Claire looking blankly, and Jamie standing stiffly to the side, characteristically unable to express anything, because Jamie didn't do emotion. And Aggie, dry-eyed as her first-born was laid to rest at the age of forty-two. No mother should have been that composed at outliving her child. She knew then what she had always suspected, that Aggie had never really liked Lily, though it would take her a few years more to find out why. None of it felt real, though, and next day she fully expected to see Lily again. It was as though in her mind she thought, '*Right, that's that over. Now I wonder when Lily's coming home?*' And even all these years later, locked away in her mind, fifteen-year-old Kathy Kelly was still waiting.

The only possession of Lily's retrieved from the fire was a charred scrap of material from the coat she had been wearing that November morning, identifiable only by the cheap heather brooch Kathy had bought for her in Fort William two years before. And, of course, there was the bright red satin box from Cockney Jock's stall, that would've been her birthday present from her daughter on the Tuesday Lily never saw. For years it lay untouched, still in its brown paper wrapping, inside a big, tan, papier-mâché suitcase under her bed. But Kathy didn't have the box or the brooch any longer, she had given them to someone long ago.

4

It had taken everyone at school a while to get back to normal after Lily's death. The other girls would talk quietly as she passed and look at her from the corners of their eyes, but it was meant kindly; they were treating her with kid gloves. She noticed it, but like everything else, it didn't matter. She dropped Art, much to her teacher's annoyance. Art, like home economics and shorthand and typing, was usually given to the idiots, to fill the gaps in their timetables left when they were withdrawn from more academic subjects, but Kathy was actually good at it. 'But why, Kathy?' the Art teacher asked. 'You're good at Art, and you enjoy it so much. Why would you drop it just like that?' Kathy shrugged. 'Because I want to,' she replied. 'I never really liked it anyway.' The teacher didn't understand and there was no way Kathy could explain, not that she wanted to. What no one seemed to realise was that there was no purpose to anything any longer, not to Art, not to life. They had been such a close partnership; Lily and Kathy against Old Con, against Aggie, against the world. Not only had it ended, but it had done so without a proper, neat ending, without a finale. It remained in Kathy's life like a loose tie and, having no idea how to deal with it and proceed, she didn't. Old Con had settled in to his role as a very public widower with ease, the general air of sympathy being translated into as many free drinks as even he could manage. Having had no marriage for many years, if ever, his only need was to be looked after, and Kathy had already been doing that for years along with Lily anyway. Only now she was alone.

When she was sixteen she left Our Lady and St Francis. The Careers Officer had got her an interview for a job with William

Hodge, a printing firm in the centre of the city. He had looked at her previous school record, noted her artistic ability and decided this was just what she was looking for. She wasn't looking for anything as it happened, she was going with the flow. She entered Hodge's through the impressive frontage in Frederick Street, all glass and polished marble, to be interviewed by Mrs Smith, a woman of indeterminate age that the teenage Kathy had mentally classified as 'old'. Mrs Smith had very black, very neat hair and thick glasses with rhinestone-studded frames that swept up outrageously at the corners. She spoke sweetly and quietly. There was room for career advancement with the firm, she said, for the right sort of girl, and an interest in Art was essential, because the high-quality work was of a demanding nature. The starting wage would be £3 1/11d per week. When Kathy started she discovered that Mrs Smith was in fact Miss Smith, the married title having been awarded to deflect attention from the fact that she was a bitter spinster. If it had been intended as an honour it had achieved the opposite, and when the other women said her name you could hear the quiet sarcasm in their voices. It was, to their shame, their only sign of rebellion against her unnecessary harassment of them. Mrs Smith hated women who were married, and perhaps hated those who still had a chance of marrying more than those who already had. Despite her sweetness at the interview, it was very clear from the first morning that she had Kathy Kelly in her sights. There would be no more entering through the Frederick Street portals, from now on she would arrive for work at the business end, the dingy back door in John Street; she wasn't a visitor now, she quickly realised, she was a worthless drone. The job involved sitting at a long table in a cramped, dull workroom from 8 a.m. to 5 p.m. with ten or twelve other women. Requests to visit the toilet were carefully considered by Mrs Smith, and permission was often refused for no reason other than her mood. Kathy was amazed to see that the women accepted these arbitrary refusals calmly and without protest. There were no tea breaks, and the half-hour allowed for lunch was spent at the worktable eating sandwiches, or, as in Kathy's case, standing outside, whatever the

63

weather, to escape what was inside. The artistic skills required were put to good use assembling calendars, the mainstay of the firm's production. There were four different pictures that had to be first glued on to cardboard. One was of an idyllic farmhouse set beside a sparkling clean yard, despite flocks of hens and ducks running around in brilliant sunshine, another showed a country cottage set in a garden overflowing with flowers in full pastel bloom. The last but one was a portrait of a pink-crinolined lady, wearing a wide straw hat tied under her perfect chin with broad pink ribbons, and carrying a basket of roses and, finally, two white Highland terriers wearing stupid grins and tartan bonnets. Pots of thick, brown glue sat in the middle of the table, and the revolting smell hung heavy in the air. Mrs Smith checked the levels in the pots regularly, glaring at the women as she passed, and any request for a fresh supply from a stone flagon kept in the corner was greeted with abuse. What were they doing with it? Did they think the firm was made of money? It would come out of their wages, and not just the one asking for more, but all of them would be penalised for making free with the glue. The stink of the stuff was everywhere, the smell attached itself to their clothing and hair and irritated their eyes and nasal passages, and after the first hour she spent in the place Kathy had a headache. At the end of the table the pictures were glued to their backings and passed down to another group, who glued on two pieces of ribbon at the centre on the back, and finally they were passed down to where Kathy sat, ready to glue the small calendar booklet precisely to the ribbons, so that it hung below the picture. She could see immediately where the art came into the procedure, and as for career advancement, that consisted of the possibility of moving up the table, from glueing on the calendar to glueing on the ribbons, and perhaps in twenty years' time she might reach the pinnacle and be trusted to glue the pictures to pieces of cardboard. But not if Mrs Smith could help it she wouldn't. Five hundred of these works of art had to be completed each day, though God alone knew where five hundred people with sufficiently bad taste were to be found willing to buy them, and Mrs Smith took great delight in harrying the new girl into, she hoped, some form of abasement. The other women whispered to her not to cry, that Mrs Smith was an old bitch, and just to ignore her, but Kathy was completely unconcerned, she'd dealt with worse in her time. Day after day they sat there together, either talking or not as they worked, depending on Mrs Smith's humour at any given moment, sticking things on to other things. If talking had been allowed that day they would try to brighten the tedium with the odd short burst of conversation, which Mrs Smith took pleasure in slapping down after a couple of sentences as her mood altered. They talked of the professional wrestling on TV, of what bad buggers that Mick McManus and Jackie Pallo were, and how somebody should give them a doing. Once, to relieve the boredom, Kathy interrupted in an aggrieved tone of voice to say that Mick McManus was her favourite uncle, and she objected to him being called a bad bugger. This was greeted with silence. Sometimes, to vary the conversation, they talked of what they had on their sandwiches, or what they might have tomorrow, but regardless of the topic of permitted conversation, Mrs Smith, her mean little face twisted with bitterness, kept on at Kathy. The others told her it would stop when another girl arrived, then Mrs Smith's malevolent attention would pass to her instead. They had all gone through it, they said, and Kathy was amazed that they hadn't left years ago, or that they were all so easily browbeaten that not one voice had ever been raised in support of each new girl.

The end came one Monday morning, when faced with another pile of artistic calendars, an exciting new range showing spaniels wearing outsized glasses this time, Kathy knew she couldn't stand another day there. She had taken her coat off, Mrs Smith snapping at her heels the minute she walked in the door, and then she had moved to her stool. She looked at the waiting pile of rubbish, then at the others, women who had spent their entire working lives in this room, doing the same worthless tasks, being verbally abused by the old biddy who had never snared a man and hated them all because they had or might. She turned again and put on her coat without a word.

'Where dae ye think you're goin', lady?' Mrs Smith demanded.

'Ah'm off, *Miss* Smith,' Kathy replied calmly.

Mrs Smith bounded across the workroom and grabbed her by the arm, propelling her back to her stool. 'You'll sit oan your arse!' she shouted.

Kathy said nothing. Leaning forward she lifted a pot of thick, brown glue from the table, turned to where Mrs Smith was still holding her by the arm, and slowly poured the glue over her head. There wasn't a movement or a sound in the room as the women watched the glue coating Mrs Smith's carefully coiffed hair, then run over her glasses to her face before dripping down her cardigan in thick, brown stripes. Then an intake of breath broke the silence, closely followed by Mrs Smith's screams of rage. Her hands flew to her perfect hair, which lifted off her head; she had been wearing a wig. Kathy wondered in a detached way if there was anything real about the woman; would she claw at her now two-tone cardigan and blouse to reveal a robot underneath? Mrs Smith lifted a pair of scissors from the workbench and came at her, screeching like a banshee, but Kathy sidestepped the assault and neatly put her foot out, tripping her, so that she landed in a heap on the floor and lay yelling on her back. Before she could get up again, Kathy put her foot on top of the older woman's stomach and pressed hard enough to discourage her. 'If you know whit's good for ye, ye'll stay there, ya miserable auld bitch!' she said very quietly. She reached for another pot of glue. 'Wan move, wan merr noise oota ye, an' ye'll be drinkin' this!' She moved the pot menacingly in the direction of Mrs Smith's mouth, and smiled as it was promptly shut. 'Right, fine,' she said brightly, smiling at the other women, all of them standing back, their eyes wide with shock. 'Ah'll be off now,' she said conversationally. 'Y'know, if wan o' youse lot had had the guts tae take her oan years ago, ye wouldnae have hadtae put up wi' a' this –' she threw her arms wide to take in the workroom and Mrs Smith, the glue pot still in her hand, and the glue from the pot flew out, landing in a long, lazy arc against the wall, 'a' this *shite!* Ye should think black burnin' shame o' yersel's that she's been treatin' ye a' like this, ye deserve everythin' ye got, every wanno ye!' And with that she removed her foot from Mrs Smith's stomach, carefully replaced the glue pot on the table, and walked out, never to return.

At the Employment Exchange the following day she was asked why she had left Hodge's. She said the smell of glue made her sick and was immediately sent after a job in Wilson's chemist's shop in Govan, across from Fairfield's shipyard, which she got. The staff were all female, apart from the two pharmacists, a pleasant man of about sixty, Mr Liddell, whom she liked, and another in his thirties, Mr Dewar, who regarded himself as a cut above everyone else. The women were addressed by their Christian names regardless of age, while the two pharmacists were 'Mr Liddell' and 'Mr Dewar' to the women, and Desmond and Nigel to each other. Mr Liddell was very tall and slim, with what was left of his white hair carefully slicked down with Brylcreem, which he bought every week with his staff discount. Looking up at him from below, as everyone had to, there was an illusion of his body gradually tapering to a point, with the sheen of the Brylcreem adding to the way the light reflected off his shiny bald head beyond. A little way short of that he had horn-rimmed, half-moon specs perched on a long sharp nose, with a little bump at the end that seemed to have been put there specifically to keep his glasses in place. He wore a white coat at all times and was polite but distant, and he gave the impression of being a man serving out his last few years before retirement, keeping his head down and putting in the time, all the while discreetly itching to be gone to the little boat he kept off Largs and sailed whenever he had a free moment. It was his idea that Kathy should become a trainee dispenser in the little pharmacy, filling prescriptions that then had to be checked by whichever pharmacist was on duty. She was aware that Nigel Dewar checked everything she did with what seemed like undue thoroughness, and she felt slightly uneasy with him. He moved around the pharmacy and the outer shop with a kind of deliberate energy, as though now that he was here, everything would work as it should. He was a small man with a ferretlike face, receding mousy hair and a wispy goatee beard and moustache, and he had a liking for wearing corduroy; he seemed to have trousers and jackets in every colour. Everything about him seemed to have been carefully and precisely worked out to convey some picture of perfection he held in his mind of what a wonderfully offbeat character he was, from his velvet waistcoats, his collection of bow ties, the ever-present desert boots, and the contrived way what was left of his hair was carefully arranged to fall over his brow. For some reason he thought it added to his self-constructed eccentricity that he drove an elderly red BMW that was forever breaking down and was his pride and joy. Pompous, that was the description of him that came most easily to mind, and she disliked him on the spot. She noticed the way he always seemed to undermine Mr Liddell in very subtle ways, and his almost imperceptible impatience with the older man, even in front of others. He didn't ever say anything out loud, but he treated Mr Liddell with an exaggerated deference that the older man didn't seek, somehow calculated to give the impression that he did.

His great collaborator in the shop was Ida Stewart, a woman in her late fifties who had worked at Wilson's for many years, and Kathy was sure that she wasn't the only one who caught the little sarcastic, amused 'what can you do with him?' looks concerning Mr Liddell that passed between them. Though Ida was on her feet all day she wore stiletto heels, if not the kind Jessie wore with such aplomb, and her girlishly golden hair was piled high on her head in an impossible confection of curls, framing a too perfectly made-up face. She was forever nipping to the loo to refurbish the overall effect, and seemed to spend most of her wages, albeit with her staff discount, on the latest cream guaranteeing to reduce wrinkles, or make-up claiming to disguise them. She was clearly enamoured of the much younger Mr Dewar in an oddly coquettish kind of way, forever smiling overmuch when she spoke to him, her eyes bright and her cheeks flushing with pleasure when he spoke to her. Kathy could imagine her going home and mentally replaying her conversations with the bearded one over and over again till they were permanently committed to memory. It wasn't so much a sexual attraction to the man as to his lofty position as pharmacist, an expression of Ida's lack of self-esteem. She was flattered by being on close terms with someone she saw as an educated, important man, even if she had to call him Mr Dewar while he called her Ida, and she protected her association with him, deliberately placing herself between him and any of the other women he had cause to speak to. But mostly he spoke to Ida, and Kathy formed the opinion that Ida kept Mr Dewar fully informed of everything that happened in the shop, and she felt also that Ida's opinions were sure to be those expressed first by Mr Dewar. And Mr Dewar, who hadn't interviewed Kathy for the job, she felt equally sure, didn't like her, whereas Mr Liddell did, which in turn meant she wasn't Ida's favourite person either, though there was no telling which came first. Nothing was said, but there was a slight atmosphere, and she was always glad when her shifts with Mr Dewar were over, whereas she liked working with Mr Liddell. It seemed that Nigel Dewar always had some niggly thing to say, and always with a slight, patient smile that she instinctively distrusted. He would comment on how she wrote out prescription labels – 'It's clearer if you do it this way, Miss Kelly' – or how she lifted the gallon glass containers of the common cough linctuses – 'If you drop it, you see, we lose that much profit', whereas Mr Liddell rarely found fault, and when he did there was no feeling that he enjoyed it. Their shifts together passed easily, either in companionable silence, or with him giving her details of the conditions the prescriptions were supposed to cure, and she never felt on probation with him in the way that she felt sure Wee Nigel wanted her to feel with him.

The other thing she liked was that the shifts, from 9 a.m. till 5 p.m., or from 2 p.m. till 9 p.m., kept her away from ordinary life in Moncur Street, and from her relatives, for longer than the hours alone suggested. Working shifts involved different living arrangements from other people, so it was possible to avoid Con for weeks on end. She would hear him go out or come in, but as they were inhabiting different time scales there was no necessity to actually meet. At nine o'clock, when the pubs closed, he would make his way unsteadily homewards as she was leaving the shop, and by the time she got home around 11 p.m. he would be in bed, sprawled in an armchair or, depending on how drunk he was, lying on the floor fast asleep. There were no arguments, no fights and no sobbing, well, none that she was present to hear, and she had decided long ago that her days of lifting his dead, sodden weight off the floor and into bed were over. So she locked the door behind her, stepped over the deeply snoring heap on the floor and went to bed. Even without her shifts their lives had gradually separated, but they certainly helped to confirm the arrangement. From her meagre wages as a trainee dispenser, plus whatever she found going through Con's pockets, she made sure the rent and electricity were paid, and what was left over after she had fed and clothed herself and paid her fares, was carefully hoarded away for come the day. She had no idea what the day was, maybe it was just a habit she had learned from her mother, but either way, she somehow believed that the day would come when her hoard would be needed.

The other welcome spin-off from working in Wilson the Chemist's was that she had a legitimate excuse for seeing less of Jamie Crawford, her childhood companion. He had achieved his first ambition in life and was an engineering apprentice at the Albion Motor Works in Scotstoun, now he had only to settle down into married life and produce a couple of children and his dream existence would be complete. She had no idea how it had happened, but without being asked she somehow found herself eased into the frame as his future wife. It was so taken for granted, not just by Jamie himself, but by everyone in the neighbourhood, that she would wonder if there had been a discussion that had been erased from her memory by some kind of blackout. She hadn't entered their marriage into whatever internal plan she held in her mind for her future, but even so, she didn't tell Jamie this either; something would evolve, she thought, it would all work out without hurting him, though she had no idea what or how. She'd been a coward, she knew that. She should've told him right at the start, nipped it in the bud, but the start had been so insidious that she didn't know when it had occurred, and besides, he was

Jamie, he'd been there all her life, stalwart, loyal; how could she deliberately hurt him? The thought of causing him any kind of pain made her feel physically sick, so she played for time, while waiting for the something that would help her to escape the future Jamie had mapped out for them both, something painless. She lied to him, that was how she had handled it, and she knew she was doing it at the time too, it wasn't just in 20–20 hindsight; all she could think of was buying time and lying was the easiest way of doing it. Working different hours across the Clyde from each other meant that inevitably they saw less of each other, so feeling insecure, or perhaps sensing her increasing distance, even if she thought she had it contained within her own mind, he kept pushing for some sort of commitment. It wouldn't be for ever, she told him, and the money she was making was going into the bank. She had a tendency to blush when she told a barefaced lie to a decent person, so she trained herself to completely empty her mind during these conversations, and Jamie's face beamed with delight, believing, she knew perfectly well, that the money was going towards their future together. She didn't actually say that, but she phrased it in such a way that he would take that meaning; it was a deliberate lie, she couldn't pretend otherwise. But after reassuring him in this dishonest way, his demands would stop, though not for long. Soon he would be back with the same complaints, that she was never there, not even on Saturday nights, that they never saw each other. It was as though she was administering a verbal painkiller that wore off after a while, and so she force-fed him another, higher dose, then another. He wanted to get engaged, a measure of his desperation, she sensed, he needed her to wear his ring, his brand, to be sure he had her. It was a simple, blameless enough request, but instinctively she fended him off. They were saving, weren't they? Why spend hard-earned cash on something they didn't need? They didn't really need a ring, did they? And reluctantly he gave way. It was only because he wanted everyone to know that they would end up married, he said, and all the time she knew it was because Jamie wanted to know, yet she refused him even that. And she didn't know why, that was the odd thing. He was a good man, he didn't drink or smoke, he was reliable, devoted, and once his apprenticeship was over he would earn good money and be able to provide for his family. Looking at the families she had grown up around and still lived among, Jamie was a catch, everyone told her so. 'That Jamie o' yours is a good man,' that was the general opinion. 'He'll no' gie ye ony trouble,' and knowing female looks would be exchanged; every woman knew what was meant by 'trouble'. And it was true, all true, and yet, well she didn't know, but thinking ahead to their projected life together one question kept repeating in her head no matter how much she reminded herself of her luck: '*Is that all there is?*'

'That Crawford boy willnae wait for ever!' Aggie would tell her with glee whenever she saw her granddaughter. 'Ye don't know when ye're well aff, that's your trouble!'

'Aye, well, Aggie,' Kathy would reply coolly, 'it's no' as if we're bad at attractin' men in this family, is it? Ah mean, a' Ah havtae dae is follow ma Auntie Jessie's lead, she has merr through her hands than she can cope wi', hasn't she?'

Aggie spluttered with rage from her chair beside the fire.

'An' no' just her hands either, eh?' she winked theatrically at her grandmother for effect. 'In fact, wi' they scabby mitts she darenae touch them withoot rubber gloves, an' that's no' awfy erotic, is it? Ah must see if we've no' got somethin' in the shop that would help her, mibbe Ah could get her usual double dose o' penicillin, or bulk orders o' rubber gloves, oan ma staff discount!'

'Ah'll tell ye this!' Aggie yelled, rising from her chair and crossing herself. 'Ah'll tell ye this!'

'Aw for Godsake get oan wi' it an' tell me, Aggie! Ma shift starts in four hours!'

'That Crawford boy is too damn good for ye! There y'are! Whit dae ye thinka that then? Ah've a good mind tae have a serious talk tae him an' tell him whit ye're like, so Ah have, ya black-hearted wee swine that ye are!'

'Aye, you dae that, Aggie. Tell ye whit. If ye really want tae put him aff, take alang exhibit A, your scabby Jessie, show him whit he'll be marryin' intae. If that doesnae put him aff, nothin' will!'

She could still hear Aggie screaming as she walked down the stairs and made for Govan.

But the Jamie dilemma remained and deepened, until the evening of her nineteenth birthday, when he presented her with a small, mock-leather box bearing the name of H. Samuel's the jeweller's. They were sitting in Dino's café in Sauchiehall Street, a place Jamie had decided was sophisticated, when he presented his gift. Taking the little box in her hands and opening the lid she truly knew what it meant to have her heart in her mouth, or her throat to be exact. She knew what was inside, and she didn't want it, but she knew with equal certainty that she would have to accept it; she had been trapped. Sitting in a slot in the velvet interior of the box was a solitaire diamond ring, the very one that Jamie had pointed out to her on past missions to persuade her into an official engagement. It wasn't a big diamond, in fact it was hard to distinguish where the setting finished and the diamond began, and she knew exactly how much it had cost, because she had been forced to look at it so often in H. Samuel's window in Argyle Street: £66. It wasn't the size of the stone that she disliked, and she knew how hard Jamie must have saved to afford £66, the problem was that she wouldn't have wanted even a ten carat diamond from him. That was it. The truth was that she didn't want Jamie. She could feel a rush of tears to her eyes and knew they were born of shame; this was Jamie, who had been by her side all her life, who had been loyal and loving, and she neither loved him nor wanted him. The impulse to throw the box on the floor and run away was hard to resist, her legs actually trembled with the urge, and her face muscles seemed frozen when she desperately needed to compose them into a smile. Her mind was racing though, before she had even uttered a word her mind was thinking forward to how she could get out of this. She would have to feign surprise and delight of course, but a plan of escape was already being formulated. Thus reassured that she could ultimately escape the trap, she allowed the beaming Jamie to put the ring on her engagement finger. *For now*, a voice in her mind said.

'There!' he said. 'That's it official!'

'*For now*,' the voice repeated.

'There's nae escapin' *noo*!'

'*For now, for now . . .*'

She wore Jamie's ring when she knew she would see him, but at all other times she left it in its box in her room, vaguely hoping in fact that Old Con would find it and pawn it for drinking money. Naturally, the one time when she needed his thieving ways they deserted him. Once she had forgotten to put the ring on before she saw Jamie and seeing the panic and hurt in his eyes, she came up with an instant explanation. 'Ah forgot it!' she said brightly. 'Imagine that! Ah don't wear it at work, ye see, because o' the chemicals an' things.' She looked up at him and was relieved to see him nod in agreement. 'An' Ah was that late gettin' here that Ah must've left it oan the chesta drawers! Oh, Ah feel that lost withoot it tae!' '*An' a total fraud intae the bargain!*' she said to herself. And so the awkward moment had been salved, but though he seemed to accept the explanation, Jamie's anxieties were activated once again by the incident. And that was why she had slept with him, or so she told herself. The truth was that she didn't know why she had done it. At the time it had been like the next step in a long progression of pacifiers, a means of keeping at bay the day when she would have to tell him she wouldn't marry him, she had simply been buying more time. She knew it was stupid and that she was doing something totally illogical. She wanted rid of this nice but boring man whom she didn't love, so she became engaged to him, then started sleeping with him as a means of getting away? Where was the sense in that? What the hell was she doing, what was she thinking? Sex as a bargaining ploy, sex without love. Dear God, the older she got the more she resembled Auntie Jessie! Her mind was full of 'maybes'. Maybe if her mother had been there it wouldn't have reached this stage, maybe with Lily's support she could've told Jamie much earlier that she didn't want him, extricated herself with some dignity. But she couldn't escape as easily as that, and she couldn't blame anyone or any situation, it was down to her, the whole sorry mess. Maybe it was in the genes after all. Not that the latest concession worked long anyway; the supreme sacrifice had only heightened Jamie's desire to be married. He was a deeply conventional man, he needed security, not some halfway measure, however enjoyable, for him at any rate. Mentally and verbally she ran from him, until the day came when he wanted to set a definite date and she couldn't run any longer, she had to admit that she wasn't ready to get married. It still wasn't the truth, of course, the perfect opportunity had presented itself and she had messed it up. She didn't want to marry Jamie, now or ever, and that was what she should've told him, but she used the 'not quite ready' excuse instead.

'Look, Kathy,' he said, looking so desperately hurt that she almost caved in and hugged him, 'ye canny keep puttin' it aff like this.'

'Jamie, Ah'm no' puttin' it aff!' she lied. 'But we're baith young, Ah'm no' even twenty yet. Whit's the hurry tae tie oorselves doon?'

'Whit's the pointa waitin' when we know we're gonny get married? Ah've finished ma apprenticeship, Ah'm earnin' good money. It's time tae get married.' He shrugged his shoulders; for him the evidence was overwhelming and unarguable. For a long time there was silence. 'Kathy, Ah know Ah'm no' excitin',' he said sadly, 'but we've known each other a' oor lives, you knew it when we got engaged. Ah don't see whit else you want, unless there's somebody else, of course?'

'There's naebody else, Jamie.'

He cleared his throat. 'Kathy, Ah just want tae settle doon. Ah'd rather dae it wi' you, but if you don't want that, Ah'll find somebody else tae be ma wife.'

Looking back, she remembered feeling sorry for him at that moment, she had thought it was a kind of ultimatum born of Jamie's desperation, and Jamie being a solid man without a rich imagination, it had been the best he could come up with at the time. And she'd been wrong, of course. They had continued seeing each other over the next six weeks or so, the subject of his need for marriage sooner rather than later lying in the air, but unspoken between them, while she scrupulously remembered to wear his ring. They were in a booth at Dino's when he once again asked her to name a date, and when she hedged he told her about Angela. Angela was a nurse, she worked in the medical unit at the Albion, and Angela wanted him, apparently. Desperation again, Kathy thought. He wanted to marry Kathy, he always had, he said, but if she wouldn't then he would settle for Angela. Kathy, still trying to work out what was true and what was panic, didn't reply. He got up and stood fidgeting beside the table. 'She's pregnant,' he said quietly.

'Yours?' Kathy asked, sounding considerably calmer than she felt.

Jamie nodded, his head down.

'So ye've been seein' her while ye've been seein' me?' she asked incredulously.

Jamie nodded again.

'Sleepin' wi' the baitha us?' she demanded, her voice rising.

'Shh!' Jamie said, looking around the other diners. 'Keep yer voice doon!'

'Bugger ma voice! Ye've been sleepin' wi' this lassie as well as me?'

He nodded miserably again.

'Then why the hell are ye askin' me tae marry ye?' she demanded. 'Ye've got this lassie pregnant already an' ye're sayin' ye want tae marry somebody else?'

'Ah'm no' prouda it!' he said defensively.

'Oh, well then!' Kathy said sarcastically. 'You're no' prouda it, so that makes it OK, then!'

'It wouldnae have happened if you hadnae kept puttin' it aff!' Jamie replied accusingly.

'So it's *ma* fault, is it? You've got this poor lassie pregnant while ye're engaged tae somebody else, an' it's *ma* fault?'

'In a way,' he said unconvincingly.

'Don't talk such shite, Jamie! A' these years Ah've known ye, an' Ah didnae believe ye were that kinda man, tae treat any wumman like that!'

'Ah've been tryin' tae get ye tae marry me for years noo –'

'No' *me*, ya numpty! The other lassie! Whit's her name?'

'Angela.'

'Angela. An' this Angela, does she know ye're engaged tae me?' Jamie shook his head, looking away.

'Ah canny hear ye, big man,' she said harshly. 'Speak up!'

'Naw, she doesnae know aboot me an' you.'

Kathy stared blankly at the uneaten meals on the table in front of her. 'Ah canny believe it, Jamie, Ah really canny! Ye never told me aboot her or her aboot me, so she doesnae know ye're here, askin' me tae name the day either. An' there she is, expectin' your wean, an' somehow it's a' *ma* fault! Whit kinda man are ye?' She took the solitaire ring off her finger and handed it to him without looking at him, taking care as she did so that her fingers didn't touch his. 'Away an' marry the lassie,' she said. 'She's probably too good for ye, but she's carryin' yer wean, so she's stuck wi' ye!'

Jamie put the ring in his jacket pocket and stood uneasily by the table.

'Whit ye waitin' for?' she asked.

'Ah thought we'd go hame thegither,' he said innocently.

'Away tae buggery, Jamie,' Kathy said sourly. 'Even the sight o' ye would make me sick!'

She remembered a whole flood of feelings from that night. Relief at getting rid of the burden of the H. Samuel's ring and all it threatened, there was that, of course, but there was also anger, and she never did work out all the levels of her anger. There was her injured pride, she couldn't deny that. All that time when she had been agonising over how to let him down as gently as possible, and Jamie already had his escape route not only planned, but well broken in! And the indignity of it, sleeping with both of them at the same time and neither knowing of the other, when she had expected him to observe a decent period of purdah after she had dumped him. Well, it was only right, after all. He would have been dumped by the love of his life, and though she didn't want it to blight his life for ever, she did expect it to blight it just a little. Surely some temporary heartache was in order, for God's sake! Christ, but it was just like a man when you thought about it, absolutely par for the course, but this was *Jamie. Jamie!* Jamie who was solid, dependable and, by the say-so of everyone who had known the two of them all their lives, he was a good, non-smoking, non-drinking man who wouldn't give her 'ony trouble'. When he had said that he wouldn't wait for ever she had thought it a sad bluff, an attempt to make her come to heel. Presumably, then, this Angela was already on the scene as he delivered his ultimatum, so why didn't he tell her outright instead of hinting discreetly, the creep? Now there was a new concept, Jamie Crawford as a creep. She would've staked her life on her reading of Jamie's character, she would've trusted him with her life, come to that. As well as solid and dependable he had always been open and honest, there wasn't one thing he had ever said or done, no matter how boring, that she had cause to doubt. He was Jamie; what more was there to say? Or at least he had been.

And now she would have to brave the gossip and the stares. She had always known that day would come, but she had planned it to be on *her* terms, so that they would stare and talk about how Kathy Kelly had dumped poor Jamie Crawford, hard, callous bitch that she was, after all the years they'd been together. Jamie's worth and suitability as a husband and father would've been gone over till they achieved heroic proportions, and as the injured party all available sympathy and support would've gone to him. She had long been prepared for that, but now the dynamics had changed irrevocably. Everyone knew what a saint Jamie was and how quick Kathy Kelly was with that tongue of hers, so it would be accepted that she had in some way let him down, that if he had found someone else then it must be her fault, because Jamie was flawless, always had been. They'd laugh at her. She didn't mind them condemning her for dumping him, but she hated the idea of being laughed at because Jamie had someone else and she didn't. And she didn't have long to wait. In the spirit of family solidarity, Old Aggie was first up.

'Ah tellt ye that Crawford laddie wouldnae wait for ever!' she announced gleefully. She was sitting in her usual armchair by the fire, looking like a malignant troll and wallowing in her joyous task of taunting her granddaughter. 'Miss High and Mighty! Ah aye said ye thought ye were somethin' an' a' the time ye were nothin',' she said happily, 'Ah never did know whit that laddie saw in ye, when it was quite clear ye didnae gie him the time o' day, or anythin' else for that matter!' she cackled heartily.

'Noo Aggie, he couldnae have been that perfect, he got another lassie pregnant after all,' Kathy replied pleasantly.

'Well mibbe if you'd been a bit merr understandin' o' his needs he wouldnae have hadtae go lookin' elsewhere!'

'Christ, Aggie, ye're that pleased wi' yersel' ye could die happy right this minute, couldn't ye? It's the only reason Ah come tae see ye, ye know. Wanna these days ye'll be so drooned in yer ain malice an' spite that ye'll drap deid right here at ma feet. If it wasnae for that thought Ah'd have abandoned ye years ago, miserable auld sod that ye are!'

'Ah wouldnae gie ye the pleasure!' Aggie spat at her. 'Ah'd haud ma dyin' breath tae Ah heard the door slammin' behind ye!'

Kathy smiled. 'Oh, ye've got class, Ah'll say that for ye, Aggie! But ye see, an' Ah know this isnae somethin' the females in this family are known for, so it might be askin' a bit mucha ye tae understand, but there's really nothin' wrang wi' keepin' yer legs thegither when a man passes within a hundred yards. Some o' us like tae keep a bit in reserve, no gie it away or sell it.' She paused for the slightest moment. 'An' by the way, how's your Jessie daein' these days?' she asked sweetly.

'Don't you think Ah don't know whit ye mean by that, lady!' Aggie screeched, rising from her chair, her hands preparing for the obligatory sign of the cross.

'Oh, Ah'm sure ye dae,' Kathy continued. 'Ah'm bloody sure ye dae, that's ma point!'

'Wait you a minute –'

'Y'see, it seems tae me that the men aboot here get married tae the first wumman they get pregnant, nae doubt that brings back a few memories tae yersel', Aggie, though Ah havtae confess that it's hard to understand you ever bein' anybody's object o' desire, an' Ah decided it might be interestin' tae find oot if there was another way. No' Jessie's way, of course, but Ah just wondered if there was somethin' different frae giein' it away or sellin' it, and if mibbe Ah should be the first wanna this family tae find oot.'

'Ya evil-minded bitch!' Aggie yelled, as Kathy slowly walked towards the door. 'That somebody should say such things aboot their ain family, showin' nae respect wi' their filthy tongue –'

'Aw for God's sake cross yersel' an' have done wi' it, Aggie!' Kathy cut in. 'The only reason ye're rantin' an' spittin' a' ower the place is because ye know it's true. There's no' wanna ye that isnae a slag, an' Ah'd lay odds it a' started wi' you. Sit doon and shut up, ya stupid auld bugger, Ah'm off.'

It was a fine display of bravado, of course, but that's all it was, because Kathy already knew that she had a lot in common with those other women in her family, the slags. That nice Crawford laddie was about to become a father not once, but twice over. She was sure that if she told him the glad tidings he would in turn dump Angela, which was another reason why he would never know. This problem was hers alone, caused by using sex to appease Jamie rather than tell him the truth, so this one of his bastard weans he would never know about. And neither would Aggie, Con, or anyone else in the East End, Kathy would see to that.

Sitting on the floor of Con's house all these years later, looking at the snaps of herself with Jamie all through their childhoods, she was aware of her mind playing a kind of conjuring trick. Somehow he looked dead in the photos; it was like looking at someone who was no longer in existence, when she knew he was very much alive. She couldn't quite figure out how long he had seemed like that to her, though she suspected his demise dated from that night in Dino's, when the Jamie she knew had indeed died before her very eyes.

5

The plan formed so slowly in her mind that it couldn't really be called a plan. She knew her current predicament dictated that she couldn't stay in Moncur Street, which in turn meant that she would have to go elsewhere, but beyond that was a blur. Then circumstances took a hand. She had turned up for her shift in Wilson's to find both Mr Liddell and Mr Dewar in the pharmacy. For a brief, happy moment she hoped this meant that Mr Dewar, with whom she was due to share the shift, had been called away and Mr Liddell was taking over. Nigel Dewar broke off from whatever he was saying to Mr Liddell as soon as she appeared and quickly busied himself about the pharmacy. Mr Liddell asked her to step into his tiny cupboard of an office off the pharmacy. There was, he said, something he had to discuss with her. It soon became clear that, in her absence, a casual conversation between the women had escalated into a major conflict, and poor Mr Liddell had been charged with facing her about it. She could hardly remember what it had all been about. Down in the basement there was a room the women used at lunchtime, and a week or so before there had been the usual conversation about what had been on TV the previous night. It had been a documentary about religion, made and intended for the south of England, as everything seemed to be, with no inkling whatever of how it might be viewed in other areas. The role of the churches in modern-day life had been questioned, and the women, all of them at least middle-aged and of different religious persuasions, were united in condemning it. Kathy had been asked for her opinion and had replied, 'Didnae see it, Ah was oan the back shift an' it was eleven when Ah got hame. No that it matters,' she had added, 'as far as Ah'm concerned Ah wouldnae shed a tear if every church in the world was boarded up.' There had been a hush, then someone had asked, 'Dae you no' believe in God, well?' Kathy hadn't looked up from the magazine she was reading. 'Naw,' she had said; that was all. Not that the conversation had stuck in her mind, in fact she'd had to fight hard to dredge it up from her memory when Mr Liddell broached the subject.

'The thing about working with people,' he said gently, coughing a little with obvious embarrassment before going on, 'is that you have to be careful of their feelings.'

Kathy looked at him blankly.

'Religion is a sensitive issue,' he continued, looking deeply pained, 'and you have to be careful what you say, especially in Glasgow, as I'm sure you know, Kathleen.'

'Mr Liddell,' she said in calm, perfect English, 'I have no idea what this is about. I'm sorry, but you'll have to spell it out.'

Mr Liddell looked even more pained. He took a deep breath. 'It seems there was an occasion recently when you strongly volunteered the view that there is no God.'

It took Kathy several minutes of silence to locate anything approximating what he had described. 'Oh, wait a minute now!' she said, suddenly remembering the discussion in the basement lunch room. It couldn't possibly be that – could it? 'I was asked a question and I replied, that was what happened, I did not volunteer a strong opinion. As I remember it I was actually reading a magazine at the time and had taken no part in the discussion.'

'Well, I'm sorry, Kathleen, but I was asked to have a few words with you, to remind you that other people's feelings can be offended.'

'And mine can't? And just out of interest, Mr Liddell, who asked you "to have a few words"?'

Mr Liddell looked flustered. 'It was only because I am the senior man,' he said, trying to make light of it. 'I think it's one of the penalties of age, Kathleen, but ticking off employees is not something I enjoy, especially when I have no means of judging what actually took place.'

'So it was that wee skunk Dewar then.'

Mr Liddell looked away, trying, Kathy sensed, not to laugh. 'I don't think he'd welcome that description, you know,' he said.

'And if it was that wee skunk Dewar,' Kathy continued, 'Ida Stewart must've clyped to him.' She went into the pharmacy, where Nigel Dewar was dancing about in his desperately bright and efficient manner, and briefly sensed in passing that he was more than usually pleased with himself. She looked through the tiny hatchway into the shop, but Ida was nowhere to be seen, so turning on her heel she made her way downstairs and found her in the lunch room. 'Just the auld bitch Ah was lookin' for!' she said, standing against the door to block any escape Ida might try to make. 'Listen, you,' she said menacingly, 'Ah hear you've been whisperin' in Lover Boy's lugs aboot me.'

Ida looked up and then away again. 'I have no idea what you're talking about,' she replied, in the kind of false modulated tone that set Kathy's teeth on edge.

'An' ye can drap the Kelvinside accent,' Kathy told her. 'Everybody here knows ye're a common auld cow frae Govan.'

The other women in the room smiled, trying to pretend they were doing other things and taking no interest while every ear was cocked, and Kathy knew this scene would be repeated to those who hadn't witnessed it. She could almost hear them saying to each other, 'Oh, aye, Kathy gave *her* her character!'

'Ye told yer wee pal that Ah'd been moothing aff about religion when, as Ah recall, you were the wan askin' the questions.'

Ida shuffled in her seat and tried to look unconcerned. 'As you ask,' she said, smiling primly and trying to include the others with a glance around the room, 'I did mention to Mr Dewar that you had offended some people here by questioning the existence of God, and he thought that it might be in your own interests to learn not to upset folk.'

'Anybody here offended because Ah'm a pagan?' Kathy asked. There was silence. 'Anybody here remember me askin' them tae join me in Devil worship?'

The other women laughed quietly. 'We'd be hard pushed in

here tae find a virgin tae sacrifice, Kathy!' one remarked. 'Don't take it so seriously, hen.'

'But Ah dae!' Kathy replied, 'because thanks tae Ida pal here, Ah've just been reprimanded upstairs by Mr Liddell.'

'Ach, Ida!' another woman said. 'There was nae cause for that!'

Ida, suddenly beleaguered, rose to her feet, and as she did so she appeared to lose her Kelvinside accent. 'Listen you tae me, Kathy Kelly,' she spat furiously. 'You're the kinda Fenian shite that thinks ye're better than anybody else! Ye just walk in here an' next thing we know ye're made trainee dispenser, while the resta us are still stuck behind the counter sellin' shampoo! Ye're fulla yersel', ye act as though ye're due it, an' ye say things because ye like tae cause a fuss. A' Ah did was shut ye up an' get ye reminded o' yer place.'

'Well, no' that Ah know much aboot the theology, Ida, no' bein' a Fenian masel' despite the name, but Ah don't think ye'll find many o' them that don't believe in God, Ah think it's kinda mandatory. An' it seems tae me that you're the wan that caused the fuss, a' Ah did was tae answer a question. But it's no' aboot that, is it?' Kathy laughed. 'It's because you're tossin' an' turnin' in yer bed a' night, thinkin' me an' Lover Boy are at it like rabbits in the pharmacy when ye're no' there tae stoap us, isn't it?'

A chuckle ran round the room.

'Christ, Ida, ye must see that he's a wee nyaff! You're the only wan would gie him the time o' day, the resta us wouldnae spit oan him if he was oan fire!'

'An' Ah'll be reportin' that tae!' Ida shouted furiously.

'Away tae hell, Ida,' Kathy laughed. 'Ah'll tell him masel'.'

With that she raced back upstairs, Ida puffing hard behind her, her stilettoes clicking furiously on the steps as she tried to get in front to present a united front, her and Lover Boy against Kathy Kelly, and all the 'Fenian shite' in the universe, or in Govan at least.

'I'd like a word with you, Mr Dewar,' Kathy said, and looking round at Ida behind her, her face flushed and the pile of hair on her head falling over to one side with exertion, she said, 'In private, please, not in front of the floor staff.' Then she waved a hand in Ida's direction. 'Ida,' she said kindly, 'you'd better away and do something about your hair. When it collapses like that your roots show something awful.' Then she led the way into Mr Liddell's office, with Nigel Dewar so taken unawares that he followed behind.

'I suppose,' she said, looking round the tiny space, 'that this wee kingdom will be yours when Mr Liddell finally goes?'

'Yes, I suppose it will,' he replied.

'Not much of an achievement, is it?' she asked. 'A cupboard pretending it's an office. No wonder you're a bitter, twisted wee get!' He opened his mouth to speak but she silenced him with a raised hand. 'Shut it!' she said quietly. 'You've never liked me, I know that, and I've never liked you. The difference is that I've done my job here, never once tried to undermine your position, such as it is, while you've done everything you could to make me uncomfortable, haven't you?'

Nigel Dewar didn't know how to reply, he was the kind of man who did his dirty work through other people and rarely took the blame for anything. 'I think you're unsuited for this job, Miss Kelly,' he replied, choosing his words with care, 'and it was always going to be difficult to assimilate a Catholic into this business. Not that I'm biased, you understand, but as I said to Mr Liddell at the time, there's never been a Catholic employed here before and some people could make it unworkable. Not that I approve, of course, but that's the reality.'

'I hate to rob you of one of your perfectly reasonable objections, Mr Dewar, but I'm not a Catholic.'

He quickly turned his attention to his other objections. 'And you have a kind of inappropriate over-confidence.'

'You mean I don't bow and scrape to you? I say what I think instead of trying to work out what you think and say? I'm not like daft old Ida there, I don't wait for you to drip-feed me your golden thoughts?'

'You see, that's what I mean,' he said, smiling tightly. He tried to ease past her to sit on Mr Liddell's chair to give him some authority, but Kathy didn't move and he was forced to say 'Excuse me.' She took a step back and sat on the chair herself, leaving him no option but to sit on the other, less well-upholstered chair meant for whoever Mr Liddell was talking to.

'Again,' he said, 'you demonstrate the problem. You have absolutely no respect.'

'Respect isn't the same as fawning,' she said, returning his smile. 'And considering that I think you're an arse, I think I do pretty well covering up and treating you civilly.' He opened his mouth to speak again and Kathy raised her hand once more. 'The difference is, Mr Dewar, that I'm saying this to your face, I haven't sneaked around and put Mr Liddell in the embarrassing position of saying it for me. But that's part of the plan, isn't it? He's only got a short time to go before he retires from here, and as for your good friend Ida – does your wife know you're having an affair with someone from work, by the way?' His eyebrows shot up and his mouth fell open. 'Obviously not,' Kathy said. 'Maybe somebody should tell her, poor woman. Does she know you're, if you'll pardon the expression, into older women? No doubt she's sitting at home raising your weans while you're knocking off old Ida in the basement at every opportunity. I'd be prepared to swear on a pile of Bibles that it's common knowledge, by the way. As I was saying, this little empire will be all yours when Mr Liddell goes, won't it? How wonderful if he should just go now and leave you to it, instead of hanging around, eh? But I'll tell you something, he's more of a man, more of a gentleman than you'll ever be. You might sit in his seat one day, but I'll tell you this, you'll never fill his shoes.'

With that she left Mr Liddell's cupboard, headed back to the pharmacy and started working as though nothing had happened. Nigel Dewar had been left in an unusual position, he had been faced with the consequences of his own dirty work and would need time to work out what to do next. Once he had collected his thoughts he would, she knew, find a more effective way of getting rid of her than the pathetic nonsense about offending other people's religious beliefs, but she would beat him to it by leaving. Her instinct was to walk out in a blaze of glory, but she decided instead to see out her shift, as a courtesy to Mr Liddell, who had stood against Nigel Dewar to give an overconfident Fenian shite a chance. The opportunity arose just before nine o'clock that evening. An agitated girl, younger than Kathy, had come in asking for something for a burn and, as was the custom, the counter assistant asked the duty pharmacist to advise her. Listening to the conversation, Kathy heard with mounting horror that the girl was a new first-time mother who had accidentally placed her two-month-old baby in a bath of water that had been too hot. The child had screamed before she had fully lowered him into the water, but both buttocks and part of his back were scalded. In a panic she had replaced him in his cot, and leaving him alone in her home in nearby Carmichael Street, ran to her local friendly chemist to seek help. Mr Dewar listened, bristling with pomposity, and then recommended several brands of ointment she could purchase.

'Mr Dewar,' Kathy called, 'can I speak with you for a moment?'

He came back into the pharmacy looking annoyed. 'I'm with a customer, Miss Kelly.'

'Look, you,' she said, 'why aren't you telling that woman to dial 999 and get her baby to hospital right away?'

'You've got to give them advice and sell them something,' he replied, 'or else they lose confidence in you, and if they lose confidence you lose future sales.'

'She could lose her wean!' Kathy said. She had never thought much of him, but now she thought considerably less. She went out into the shop. 'I'm a doctor, dear,' she calmly lied to the girl. 'I'm overseeing the training of Mr Dewar here.' He tried to interrupt but she rushed on. 'Now he's given you the wrong advice I'm afraid. It's not really his fault, he's recovering from a nervous breakdown and he's not long out of a mental hospital, that's why I'm here, to supervise him as he gets back on his feet. I don't want to frighten you, but burns are very serious and small children can die from them.'

The girl's shocked eyes went from Kathy to Nigel Dewar, who was looking flustered in the background. 'You just wanted me tae buy somethin', didn't ye?' she demanded.

'Your baby needs to be taken to hospital as soon as possible,' Kathy continued. 'If you give me your address I'll call 999 and get an ambulance to take him to the Sick Kids.' The woman quickly reeled off her address which Kathy repeated on the phone. 'Now you dash off home to your baby and the ambulance will be there almost before you are.'

The woman immediately burst into tears and thanked her, then turning to Nigel Dewar she spat at him, 'An' you, buster, you should've stayed in the funny farm. Ma man an' ma da'll be doon lookin' for you the morra. If Ah was you, Ah wouldnae be here!'

Kathy collected her coat and bag from the pharmacy and as she walked out for the last time she smiled sweetly at Nigel Dewar and his good friend Ida standing behind him.

'Just do me one final favour,' she said. 'Don't listen to her – *be here* when her man and her da come looking for you, contemptible wee swine that you are!'

In different circumstances she would've been bereft at having to leave her job, but she at least would've known why it had happened. She did, as the besotted Ida and her hero had said, have an air of confidence about her; she had never felt unequal to anyone and, whatever the circumstances, she always seemed self-assured, though she rarely felt it. Her mother, Lily, had been a gentle soul, her father, Con, a useless one, and her brother Peter had long ago abandoned everyone to save himself. Kathy had always had to be the strong one. Even when she felt neither sure nor strong she had to pretend to be able to fend for herself; it was how she had got by all her life and that protective veneer had become part of her. But youngsters were supposed to be unsure, everyone knew that, they were expected to be overawed by older people, especially those in authority, and if the people in authority were unsure of themselves they preferred youngsters to be even more so. It was why the old harridan at Hodge's Printworks had picked on her, because she was young, female and new, and harassing that combination of individual had made Miss Smith feel superior and more secure in her position of very little power. Only Kathy didn't react as Miss Smith expected, as all the others before her had reacted, and the only thing the woman could think of doing was to pile on more of the same until Kathy called it a day in her own inimitable style. That same quality, or failing, depending on your point of view, had irritated

Nigel and his follower Ida, because they too were very little people with very little power, and they resented anyone who didn't help them enhance it by cowering. Even at the age of twenty Kathy knew, or at least sensed, that this was how she annoyed insignificant people, but there was nothing she could do about it; she was who she was. Had her present circumstances been different she would perhaps have fought for her job at Wilson's, but she had to leave anyway, just as before too long she would have to leave Moncur Street too, and at least there had been some unexpected satisfaction in departing in the way she had.

Often she thought back to those days and tried to work out what had been going on in her mind. Somehow she had closed off any thoughts of the developing child inside her; she would have to leave the life she had and find another, that was her all-consuming obsession, without admitting the reason even to herself. At no time did she give a conscious thought to the child, she dealt with that reality by simply ignoring it, by almost going on to autopilot. Jamie Crawford was now safely married to his Angela and living elsewhere, so there was thankfully little chance of bumping into him on the stairs as they went to and from their homes. The only embarrassment was meeting his mother and feeling sorry for the older woman, because she knew old Mrs Crawford didn't know what to say to her. She had been fond of Kathy all of her life, and she had no knowledge of what had happened between her and Jamie, but being his mother she naturally sided with him, so when they met face to face Mrs Crawford became flustered. Kathy wanted to put her arms round her and tell her it was OK, but she feared that might open up dialogue between them and that was the last thing she needed or wanted. But even though she was in a predicament and had no idea how she would get out of it, she still knew that getting rid of Jamie and his H. Samuel ring was a great relief. If only she had managed to extricate herself before – well, just before.

She couldn't wait much longer, though. Four months had passed and she would have to go soon. But go where? Just go, that's all; that would do for the time being. It was as if she had a mental check list of loose ends to be tied up, with the most important and pressing items way down at the very end, along with the reason, the child. She had finished with her job. Tick. She had a tidy sum in the bank, with her bankbook safely hidden away under the lino in her bedroom, beneath the tan case containing the red satin workbox she had bought for her mother's birthday, the birthday Lily had never reached. The bankbook had to be safely hidden lest Con get his hands on it, because he would've found a way of releasing the cash. Tick. He had sold and pawned everything in his time to get booze money, even Lily's wedding ring had been hawked so many times during her brief life that she probably lost track of when it was on her finger and when it wasn't. And Kathy knew there had been money around after Lily's death, donations from a shocked public that was shared between the families of the dead, and compensation too, but she had left her knowledge of it vague because she wasn't interested in it. However kind the intentions, it was blood money and it wouldn't bring Lily back, the only thing she wanted. So Con was just as well pissing it against various walls as far as she had been concerned. The next task on the list was to tell Aggie she was going away.

She sat in a chair at one side of Aggie's hearth and as she looked around the familiar sitting room it struck her that it could be the last time she would ever see it. She didn't know whether to dance or sing. The old beast was sitting in her usual chair, glowering at her granddaughter, waiting for the onslaught.

'Yer ship's come in, Aggie,' Kathy said brightly. 'Ah'm goin' away.'

'Away?' Aggie asked, as though Kathy was speaking a foreign language. 'Whit dae ye mean "away"?'

'Gone, vamoosed, left, shot the craw,' Kathy smiled. 'That "away".'

'Away frae Moncur Street?'

'Christ, ye're fast!'

'This you gettin' yer ain place, like?'

'Aye, Ah suppose so. Ah don't know where it is yet, Ah've just decided to get away frae here. An' before ye ask, aye. Ah'm brokenhearted ower Jamie Crawford an' Ah'm runnin' away tae sea. Ah'm happy for ye tae spread that aroon', a'right?'

Aggie glared at her. 'Ye'd havtae find a heart first for that,' she said with sour glee. 'If ye'd had a heart ye wouldnae've lost him in the first place. A' they years ye put in wi' him an' ye let somebody else have the benefit! Ye'll rue the day, lady, mark ma words, ye'll rue the day!'

'Ah canny help markin' them, Aggie, ye've said them often enough.'

'Ye're a hard wee bitch!' Aggie spat with feeling.

'An' ye've said that afore tae,' Kathy replied amiably. 'Ye should hoist yer arse oota that chair an' get oot wance every ten years, Aggie, it might gie ye merr tae talk aboot. It's like listenin' tae a gramophone that only plays wan record, haudin' a conversation wi' you. Aye the same borin' tune.'

'So where are ye gaun', then?' Aggie sniffed.

'Dunno. Thought Ah'd travel the world for a while.'

'Away tae hell! Who d'ye think ye are?' Aggie chuckled.

'How aboot ma brother's sister?' Kathy replied slyly.

'Oor Peter's different,' Aggie said with pride. 'Oor Peter was made for better things.'

'An' Ah'm no'?'

'Coorse ye're no'!' Aggie laughed. 'Ye only think ye are! He was the real thing, you're only copyin' him. Ye've aye thought ye were somethin', an' Ah've tellt ye afore this –'

'Aye, aye, Ah know,' Kathy replied. 'Ah'm nothin'.'

'Exactly!' Aggie stated with utter conviction. 'Besides, ye're flyin' a kite, Ah know that fine. You'll no' go away, ye're tryin' tae wind me up. Think Ah don't see that?'

'Dear Sweet Jesus, Aggie!' Kathy said with mock surprise, knowing how much Aggie hated her to use the expression. 'So there's a key somewhere that winds ye up? Ah never knew that! So does some bugger come in here every mornin' and get ye workin', then? The dirty swine! Tell me who it is an' Ah'll slap his ear!'

'Oh, aye, very clever. An' Ah've tellt ye afore, don't take the Lord's name in vain in ma hoose!' She blessed herself.

Kathy grinned. 'Well, anyway, Aggie, whether ye believe it or no', Ah'm off.'

Aggie studied her for a moment. 'Jesus Christ! —'

'Aggie!' Kathy reprimanded her. 'Is that you takin' the Lord's name in vain? Noo, Ah'll no' have that!'

'Ye're serious, aren't ye?' Aggie demanded. 'Ye're just gonny bugger aff an' leave yer poor faither behind like some auld used rag!'

'Aye, Ah'm serious! An' ma Da isnae some auld used rag, he's a permanently wet wan, as well you know. Ah've no' seen him conscious for years noo, he won't even know Ah'm no' there.'

'Selfish!' Aggie roared, rising from her chair.

'Oh, Christ, here we go,' Kathy moaned. 'Get the holy watter oot, she's gonny curse me again.'

'Selfish an' rotten tae the core, just like yer mother!'

'Whit?' Kathy asked in amazement.

'She was just the same! She left poor Con tae!'

Kathy laughed. 'Aggie, listen tae me, hen,' she said kindly, 'an' try tae concentrate whit brain cells ye have oan this, it's kinda important. Ma Mammy *died*. Dae ye know whit that means? Is nae merr, doesnae exist, *deid* for God's sake! She's lyin' up in Springburn. Mind when we put that box doon the big hole an' covered it wi' dirt? Well, she was inside the box, hen. Did ye no realise that? Have you been waitin' a' this time for her to come an' dae yer washin' an' go for yer messages? Did naebody explain it tae ye?'

'Shut yer mooth, you!' Aggie yelled back, all control gone. 'Ah never wanted her in the first place!'

'Ah know that, Aggie,' Kathy said. 'Ah always knew it. But Ah never knew why. Why did ye no' like ma Mammy? She was yer ain wean, an' she couldnae dae enough for ye!'

'She was like *him*!' Aggie said darkly.

'Him?'

'Her faither, that bastard, the Orangeman! He got me pregnant an' Ah hadtae marry him!'

'Wait a minute, Aggie,' Kathy chuckled. 'Ah think there's a wee discrepancy here. When Auld Con knocked ma mother up, it was *her* fault, accordin' tae you, but when ma Granda knocked *you* up, it was *his* fault. Somethin' no' strike ye as odd there, Aggie?'

Aggie swayed on her feet with rage, frantically blessing herself over and over again, like a tic-tac bookie gone mad.

'An' he married ye tae, didn't he?' Kathy reminded her. 'Ye were never any oil paintin', but he didnae hop it an' leave ye wi' his wean.'

'They like daein' that,' Aggie replied, her eyes blazing. 'It's a' parta their plan tae get rid o' the Catholic religion! They get respectable Catholic lassies pregnant an' marry them so that their weans willnae be Catholics!'

'Yer arse, Aggie!'

'Wis him called yer mother Lily!' Aggie responded with passion. '*Orange Lily*! An' she looked like him tae, right frae the start.' She looked at her granddaughter laughing at her. 'An' so dae you!' She pointed an accusing finger at Kathy. 'Peter looks like his faither, but you an' yer mother were aye the double o' the Orangeman. Ah'll never forgive ye for that!'

Kathy had always accepted Aggie's daftness, but she was exceeding all boundaries. 'An' whit aboot yer precious Jessie then? She was his as well. Why was she aye the favourite?'

'Because she *wasnae his*!' Aggie shouted. 'She was special!'

'Special?' Kathy asked, delighted with this turn of events. 'Was she conceived by Jesus Christ himself then?'

'Naw, but nearly!' Aggie replied, her face suffused with ecstasy as she blundered on. 'Her faither was a priest!'

Kathy nearly fell off her chair with surprise. 'Ach, ye're makin' it up, Aggie,' she laughed. 'It's a' wishful thinkin', ya daft auld bugger! Next ye'll be tellin' me wee McCabe's her faither!'

There was a sudden and total silence, as Aggie realised how far she had gone and knew that all roads of retreat were blocked.

'Are you serious?' Kathy asked quietly, her eyes fixed on Aggie's face. Aggie nodded and sat down again, almost disappearing into her chair. 'You an' wee Frank McCabe, Parish Priest o' St Alphonsus, a'-roon' saint and saviour o' the wan true faith? *That* Frank McCabe, Aggie?'

Aggie nodded again and started weeping quietly. 'No' a livin' soul knows that apart frae me an' him!' she said. 'No' even oor Jessica.'

'An' yer God tae, surely, Aggie!' Kathy thought, her mind spinning. And she was further confused by the Aggie she saw before her; she had never seen her grandmother this vulnerable. She almost felt sorry for her, and being unused to feeling anything but combative towards Aggie, the emotions she was now going through confused her still further. 'Ah'll no' say anythin', Aggie,' she said seriously. 'But how the hell did that come aboot?'

'It was when Ah wanted back tae the Church,' she wept. 'When the Orangeman went tae work Father McCabe would come tae see me an' we'd pray thegither.'

'Sounds like ye did merr than pray thegither, the randy wee bastard!'

'Naw, it wasnae like that!' Aggie pleaded. 'He was only a boy, a few years younger than me, just oota the seminary. He'd been there since he was just twelve year auld. He didnae know nothin'. It was ma fault, no' his.'

'Aggie,' Kathy said gently, 'ye canny hae it a' roads. It was the Orangeman's fault for gettin' ye pregnant wi' ma Mammy, but no' McCabe's fault for gettin' ye pregnant wi' Jessie. Does that make sense, hen?'

'But it *was* ma fault!' Aggie insisted. 'Ah knew merr than him, he had never had anythin' tae dae wi' women afore.'

'He musta learned bloody fast, then! So who decided tae cover it up an' pass Jessie aff oan the Orangeman?' Kathy asked suspiciously.

'He didnae know whit tae dae,' Aggie explained.

'Up tae a point!' Kathy interrupted.

'Ah said we should leave things as they were. There was nae point gettin' the boy intae trouble, he had God's work tae dae. An' Ah was right, because he's been a good priest, he's got a hearta gold an' there's many folk aroon' here he's helped ower the years. An' yer grandfaither never knew the difference, he thought Jessica was his ain. Ah just decided God had been good tae me, giein' me this special wean, it was a sign that he'd forgiven me, an' that wan day Ah'd get back intae the faith.'

Kathy had no doubt that young Father McCabe had been only too happy to go along with that interpretation, but what the hell, if it hadn't occurred to Aggie in all these years, why force her to see it now?

'He always kept in touch, though,' Aggie said, her face beaming. 'Never abandoned me in a' that time.'

'*He was just protectin' his interests, ya daft auld bugger!*' Kathy thought furiously. '*Makin' sure ye kept quiet!*' but she said nothing.

The two women sat in the first silence there had ever been between them, each lost in their own thoughts. They were some crowd, the women in her family, Kathy thought wryly, nobody could ever accuse them of not being sociable, and their fertility was every bit as notable as their morals. The Orangeman had married Aggie in a 'havtae' situation because she had been pregnant with Lily, then Frank McCabe had bestowed Jessica, the 'special' child on her. Lily had been pregnant with Peter when she married Con, while Jessie had never married the gangster who was Harry's father, and her other child was certainly not the offspring of her legal union to the unfortunate and long-deceased Sammy Nicholson either. And now here Kathy Kelly was herself, the fiercest critic of all of them, with another bastard child growing inside her and the father already married to someone else.

When Kathy got up to go Aggie pleaded with her again not to say anything about Jessie's holy, if not immaculate conception, and Kathy repeated her promise that she wouldn't. 'Christ, Aggie,' she said kindly, feeling the only affection she ever felt for her grandmother, 'we're family, hen! Even if Ah dae look like the auld Orangeman, the wan thing Ah know for sure in this mess o' a family is that ye're ma Mammy's mammy, an' that makes you an' me related!' Aggie smiled and reached out to Kathy as though to embrace her. 'Noo wait a minute!' Kathy said, laughing. 'Don't go overboard, Aggie! Ye're still an evil auld bugger, an' Ah'm still me tae!' But as she made her way back to her own home it occurred to her that even without the laying on of hands, the atmosphere between them had been like an embrace anyway.

Next morning Aggie was found dead in bed, she had indeed held her last breath till the door had closed behind Kathy.

6

She had bitterly resented coming back to Glasgow to nurse Con through his last months; it had been an odd experience. On that first evening she had walked up London Road, wondering at how small the place seemed; once it took for ever to walk from Glasgow Cross and along London Road. Glickman's Candy Shop was still there, where the famous Glickman's cough sweets came from. The shop front, with its long, low windows, was painted in black gloss, framing the crammed displays of every sweet you could imagine. The years of her life she must've spent with her nose crammed against the glass. It was a ritual that she had never questioned. At the end of the school day she would meet up with Jamie and they would walk home together, and always stopping to stare in Glickman's window, though they rarely had money to buy anything; it was just something they did. Arranged on glass stands were thick bars of coconut ice, fudge, peppermint fondant, nougat, all coated with chocolate, and they would examine everything on display, wave to Frances, Anne and Max Glickman as they served inside, then continue the walk home. It was almost an arrival ritual; when you saw the Candy Shop you knew the school day had gone and you were home again, and staring in the window was the way to mark the passage from one part of their lives to the other. There was something comforting about seeing it there after all these years, even if Frances, Anne and Max must be long gone. And a little further on, before you turned into Kent Street, was where Maggie Davidson's fruit stall stood. Maggie was the tiniest woman Kathy had ever seen in a city of small people. She had fair hair, though she had never been seen without her headscarf, and friendly blue eyes all crinkled at the corners, and she always wore a long coat held close to her by an apron with two deep pockets along the hem for keeping change, and heavy, zip-up, suede boots with thick crepe soles. Her stall was a wonder to behold. It was narrow, with a small passageway to the side giving Maggie access to the back to construct her display, and there was a stool there where she supposedly sat at slack times, though Kathy could never recall seeing her sitting down. From the front of the stall the fruit was displayed on a carefully constructed and incredibly high slope, boxes of immaculate oranges, apples, bananas and whatever else was available, all beautifully presented in their shining, glossy glory. Maggie did a roaring trade, yet the display was rarely seen with an apple or an orange missing, because Maggie always had a ready supply of equally perfect, identically glossy fruit ready at the back to replenish her stock. If anyone could pass Maggie's stall without buying something they had no heart, because more artistically appealing fruit could not be found anywhere. She was a friendly soul too, never letting a child pass without throwing them an apple, and she always kept sugar lumps in an apron pocket for the delivery horses.

Kathy had been there when the horse fell down; she had only been about five years old and it became the day when her hatred of Father McCabe had taken firm root. Maggie had been getting a delivery by horse and cart from the fruit market in Candleriggs, and the horse had slipped on the cobbles and fallen, scattering the cartload across London Road. It wasn't an unusual occurrence in those days, so there was never any shortage of passing males giving advice, and soon a crowd had gathered. The horse had tried to get up a few times, urged on by the efforts of the carter who dug the toe of his boot into the animal's side and beat it with a strap. But every time it tried to struggle up its hoofs would slip again, sending it crashing once more on to the road, and each failed attempt made it that much less keen to try again. The animal was scared, and the gathering crowd was scaring it even more, and soon it decided to stay where it was no matter how much

97

encouragement the carter gave it. It lay there, a great, huge, tragic creature, beaten by the cobbles and the crowd, neighing pathetically on the ground. St Alphonsus's was only yards away, and Father McCabe was soon on the scene. 'Nae show withoot Punch!' a voice muttered from the crowd, and everyone laughed.

'Right, that's enough commotion!' he cried authoritatively. 'Get a vet to put it down!'

'An' who the hell might you be, pal?' the carter demanded. 'It's ma hoarse an' ma livelihood, Ah'll decide whit's tae be done.'

'You don't come from around here,' Father McCabe remarked, as though that entitled him to take control of the situation. 'The whole road's blocked by this, we need to get it cleared.'

'Take wan step near ma hoarse an' Ah'll clear you!' said the carter menacingly.

'Well, I'll call the vet if you won't,' responded Father McCabe, and made to walk off, but the carter grabbed him by the back of his collar and held him fast with a huge, grubby hand.

'Whit does he want tae dae?' Kathy had asked Jamie.

'He wants tae get somebody tae shoot the hoarse,' replied Jamie, and Kathy was aghast. Horses were noble beasts, she'd never met one she didn't like, yet this priest, revered in the area, wanted to kill it *because it had fallen down!* The scene was frozen in her mind like a tableau, the distressed, demoralized animal on the ground, its eyes rolling with fear behind the blinkers, the carter holding Father McCabe by the collar, and the crowd framing the picture, all shouting and laughing. And totally unseen into this mêlée had stepped the tiny Maggie with a handful of sugar lumps and a quartered apple, and began stroking the horse's huge head. Kathy had only been aware of her because she was so small herself, it had seemed to her that there were two scenes going on at different levels, and she was part of the lower one, together with Maggie and the horse. Maggie crooned softly to the animal as though to a baby, and when she'd got its attention she began feeding it sugar lumps, then she coaxed it from its defeated place on its side on the cold, hard cobbles, its great hoofs scraping and sparking for purchase as it rose, as the rest of the performance took place above and around. Finally it stood there, shaking slightly from its ordeal but happily accepting Maggie's apples and sugar lumps, until someone shouted, 'Jesus Christ! Wee Maggie's got it up!' The delighted carter promptly forgot about thumping Father McCabe and returned to his task of unloading the fruit, and the crowd, having witnessed good entertainment, went back to what they had been doing before the drama began. It became part of the folklore of the place, though, that people telling old Barras stories would start off with: 'D'ye mind the day Wee Maggie saved the hoarse?' But Kathy remembered something else about the event, something she didn't think anyone else had heard. As Father McCabe tried to beat a hasty retreat to reclaim his dignity, Maggie had said in a low, dark, dismissive voice, laden with disgust, 'So your God doesnae love dumb animals, does he no'? Or was the poor auld hoarse a Proddy? That why ye wur so helluva fast to see it deid?' Father McCabe hesitated for a second then headed back to his chapel without looking at Maggie, far less replying. From that day on Maggie had been Kathy's absolute heroine and Frank McCabe her enemy. In years to come she would have many more reasons for despising him, but the first had happened on the day that Maggie had saved the horse.

Walking past the closed market that evening, and coming to the very spot where Maggie's stall had been, it suddenly struck her that Maggie must be long gone now too, even if her horse-saving tale would live for ever, and she felt tears prickling her eyes. Then she laughed at herself. If anyone had asked why she was upset and she'd replied it was because Maggie Davidson was dead, they would've thought she was daft, as indeed she thought herself, because Maggie had died many years ago. But she had never seen the place without Maggie, hadn't become used to her absence by witnessing the day-to-day changes as Barras life closed around her loss and went on without her, so to Kathy it was as if it had just happened that evening, as she was walking towards Con's home in Stevenston Street. And along London Road was the glowering red sandstone heap that was St Alphonsus's, where Aggie had been accorded every rite known to Rome at her funeral. Kathy remembered watching Frank McCabe going through it all, making sure no prayer was missed out, not a drop of holy water unsprinkled, no incense unburned, and wondering what could be going through his mind. Here he was, seeing off with due ceremony and more the mother of his child, as that 'special' child, Jessie the whore, sat, stood and knelt as required, her handkerchief clutched to her face, watching her father officiate at her mother's sending off! It was a bizarre scene, and how relieved he must've been that with Aggie finally silenced, there was no longer any danger of their secret leaking out, the only wonder was that he didn't break into an Irish jig midway through the rites he was so enthusiastically performing. No one else knew, not even Jessie, that was what Aggie had said the night before she died, another twelve hours and he would've been as safe as he already thought he was. Only he wasn't. Kathy knew, and she was the last person on earth he would've wanted to know, because he had no control over her. His God had forgiven him, no problem about that. One of his comrades would've absolved him of his sin, or more likely he would've gone in mufti to some strange priest for his absolution all those years ago, but either way, the secrecy of the confessional was sacrosanct – how terribly convenient *that* was – and then he had left the cuckolded Orangeman to rear his illicit child. Well, what could you expect of a man who would shoot an innocent horse because it was blocking the road?

And there were other dark secrets. She had hardly noticed the backache at first, and even when she did she put it down to the effort of clearing out Aggie's house. How a woman who had hardly moved from that chair beside the fire, except to regularly call down the wrath of her God on her granddaughter, could've collected so much stuff was beyond Kathy. Frank McCabe had been in attendance at various times throughout the day, just in case, she mused, there might be something in writing about the little secret he had been only too glad to let Aggie carry all her life. Well, *nearly* all her life. There were rosaries everywhere, made from various materials, each one more ornate than the one before, all of them, she was sure, specially blessed for her by the wee man himself. When you thought about it, Aggie's demands must have run him ragged, blessing statues of the Virgin Mary – how he must've blushed a bit while doing the business over that one – pictures of the Sacred Heart, holy medals of every description, and providing holy water for the tatty plastic shrines all over the house with little wells at the base for moist sponges. Every time Aggie passed one she would dip her hand to wet her fingers before blessing herself. 'Christ, Aggie,' Kathy would remark, 'if ye threw some Fairy liquid in there ye'd never needtae climb intae the bath again.'

'An' nothin' would clean that soul o' yours,' Aggie would counter. 'It's as black as the Earl o' Hell's waistcoat, so it is! Ye'll burn in Hell for yer blasphemy, you mark ma words!'

'Is that how the Earl o' Hell's waistcoat got so black, then? Was he wearin' it while he burned?'

'Ye know fine whit Ah mean, lady! You're no' kiddin' me!'

'Christ, Aggie, Ah've never understood a word ye've ever said, an' you know *that* fine. Ah think ye make it a' up as ye go alang. Either that or ye've got a special line tae yer God.' And all the time she had, that was the funny thing. She had her own direct line through McCabe and their 'special' child.

If she had admitted her pregnancy to herself she would've at least suspected that the backache was connected to the child she was carrying, but she had kept it filed away in the back of her mind. No one knew, and at around five months she had still managed to cover it up, but deep down she had been making some sort of provision for the fact that she couldn't hide it for ever. There was nothing focused about it, just a quiet acknowledgement that, as she had told Aggie, she would have to go away from here soon. She had no thought for the child growing inside her, in fact she didn't even think of it as a child. It was an inconvenience, a situation she would rather have been without, but she had never imagined it as a human being, a small, living, growing human being. So there was nothing in her mind about what would happen, how she would cope with the birth or what would become of the child, because it wasn't a child, it was something that she dealt with moment by moment. The pain wasn't severe, a dragging discomfort more than anything, and with Con out on his usual round of the pubs in the area, parading his grief about the late, lamented Aggie to anyone who would stand him a half, she was alone in the house. She decided to have a bath to ease the aches of the day, and then, after she pulled the plug from the bath and started to get out, the world became blurred. Suddenly there was a tiny thing lying there and blood everywhere. The universe contracted and time stood still as she tried to make sense of what was happening. She had been getting out of the bath, then somehow the tiny thing was lying there in front of her, and she had no idea if it had happened minutes or hours ago. Her mind was trying and, so far, failing to function. She wondered where the thing on the floor had come from; it simply didn't occur to her at first that it had come from her, and when she gradually realised that she was bleeding she still didn't see any connection. There was nothing beyond what was going on in the bathroom, where time was moving at a snail's pace, with huge delays between thought and action. Slowly she reached for a towel, clamped it between her thighs and sat down on the bathroom floor again, her back against the wall, staring at the thing. There was no plan of action, one thing simply led to another without any real reason or thought. Somewhere in her mind she knew she would have to *do* something, but she didn't know what, so she sat against the wall for another uncertain aeon and did nothing. Eventually she looked at the thing on the floor. It was a baby. Dear God, it was a baby! It didn't look exactly like other babies she had seen, its head was out of proportion to its body, as it lay there, unmoving, curved in a fetal position, the cord and the placenta still attached to it. But it was undeniably human, a little person, pale and dead, but a person, and as there was no one else around she surmised that it must've come from her. She reached out and lifted it from the floor, cradling it on her knees for a long time, looking at it, examining it. It was a girl. It felt waxy and looked like a newly hatched chicken, not quite complete, not ready, covered all over in a fine hair. Its large, bulging eyes were shut and veins were clearly visible through its translucent skin, but everything was where it should be. She couldn't stop looking at the smallest details, the fingers with their fingernails, the toes, the way it curved inwards as if to protect itself. It looked so pathetically small and defenceless. There was no world outside the bloodstained bathroom; the only reality was her and her dead child. Feeling cold, she reached for her thin, flower-patterned dressing gown and gently wrapped it around the child. She put it back on the floor before stepping once more into the bath and removing the bloodsoaked towel from between her thighs. The bleeding had eased and was no longer gushing down her legs. She ran the water till it was lukewarm and sponged herself off, watching it, tinted orangey-red, disappearing down the plughole till it became clearer. Stepping out once more she took a towel and ripped it, placing half between her thighs again and slowly, carefully, drying herself with the other half. Then she brushed her hair, and finding it nearly dry, she wondered how long she had been in here. Lifting the flower-patterned bundle, she made her way calmly back to her bedroom and sat on the bed, then she left the bundle on the bed and looked in her chest of drawers for a sanitary belt, a Dr White's towel and a pair of pants. She put them on in an unhurried manner, one thing at a time, then she reached for the suitcase under her bed and took from it the brown paper parcel containing the red satin box with the woven hearts that she had bought for Lily all those years ago. Inside, in one of the compartments of the red mock velvet shelf, she saw the charred enamel brooch she had brought back for her mother from that long-ago school trip to Fort William, three sprigs of white heather tied together with a tartan ribbon. She was gripped by the need to give the dead child something precious and the brooch, the only link she had between herself and Lily, was there, so she eased the pin through the thin material, taking care not to hurt the child underneath. Lily would want her to have it. Then she removed the shelf, before lifting the bundle and gently fitting it inside the box and closing the lid, trailing her fingers along the gold cord at the edges. Finally, she lifted the covers on the bed and slipped between the sheets, taking the box with her, to lie at her right side. She was more exhausted than she thought possible.

She had no idea how long she slept, a deep, dreamless sleep, all she knew was that it had been dark as she lay down and was lighter as she awoke. Covering the red satin box with the bedclothes she took a fresh Dr White's towel from the drawer and made her way to the bathroom again where she changed it for the soiled one before returning to the bedroom to get dressed. In the bedroom she gathered together all the bloodstained towels, put them inside a carrier bag and placed it in the case under her bed. Outside the Sunday market would soon be stirring, and looking at the clock she saw the hands at nearly 7 a.m. She dressed, straightened herself before the mirror on the inside of the room door, and lifted the satin box from her bed. In the kitchen she found a shopping bag that had belonged to Lily, placed the box inside and pulled the zip, put on her coat and let herself out. Then she stopped for a moment outside the door, turned and let herself back in. In the kitchen she rummaged through the cutlery drawer till she found a broad-bladed knife that she wrapped in a copy of the *Evening Times* and placed inside the bag before letting herself out again. The last thing she could cope with was conversation, so in case there were people at the bus stops in London Road or Gallowgate, she walked instead the short distance to Glasgow Cross, firmly holding the precious cargo. There she waited for a number 37 bus to Springburn, and once aboard sat in detached silence till it arrived outside St Kentigern's. At a nearby shop she bought a bunch of flowers and then made her way to the grave of the Kelly women, with its white, heart-shaped headstone. It was oddly quiet in the early morning, the sparse Sunday traffic noises fading into the distance. Kneeling down she unzipped the bag and, leaving the newspaper wrapping behind, began cutting through the dew-heavy turf with the knife till she reached the earth below. She dug into it with her hands and, when the hole was big enough, she took the box from the bag and carefully lowered it into the hole. After covering the small grave with the disturbed earth, she replaced the rectangle of turf, laid the flowers on top and replaced the knife in the bag. She didn't realise that her hands were covered in thick earth, made muddy by the dew, till she stood up again and tried to zip the bag, so she took the newspaper out and rubbed off as much of the mud as she could from her hands and her knees; there was little she could do about the hem of her coat. Before she left she gently re-arranged the flowers covering the spot where her child was buried. 'Her name's Lily,' she said quietly. 'Take care of her, Mammy,' the first words she had spoken in many hours, and then she turned and walked back through the gates. Sitting on the bus going back to Glasgow Cross, the conductor looked at her. 'Did ye fa' or somethin', hen?' he asked.

'Aye, that's right,' she replied flatly, 'Ah fell.'

He grinned at her. 'Ah bet ye canny remember how! That's whit happens when ye go oan the skite oan Setterday night an' don't waken till the mornin'!' he replied cheerily.

'You're tellin' me!' she said quietly, smiling wanly.

'Ye look as if ye've got a heid like the inside o' a badger's arse that'd been well kicked wi' a tacketty boot!' he said. 'Bet yer maw gies ye a tankin' when ye get hame!'

'Aye,' she said, 'likely enough.'

As she got off the bus at the Cross he called after her, 'Maws is queer things, hen. Take ma advice, tell her ye were abducted by wee green men. She'll likely believe that easier than the truth!'

'OK,' she smiled, 'Ah'll remember that!' Then she walked back along London Road, past Glickman's, past Maggie's perfect fruit stall, the wooden bones of her display still having the flesh put on them as Maggie set up for another day's trading.

Maggie looked her up and down as she passed. 'Whit happened tae you?' she asked.

'Ah fell, Maggie. Makes ye feel that daft!' she replied and kept walking. Back inside the house she went straight to her bedroom, feeling consumed with weariness once again, but there were things to be done, loose ends that had to be attended to, before she could rest. She felt as if she was being directed by some outside force, as though she wasn't really there. It was like sleepwalking, only she was conscious and aware of what she was doing, if not why; decisions were being dictated to her, and she was obeying them to the letter without the slightest question or pause. She sat on her bed, her head down and her hands crossed in her lap, till she heard Con in the background getting ready to leave for the Barras to pay for his next drink, and as he closed the door behind him she took the suitcase from under her bed. In the living room she removed the bloody towels and ripped them up into as small pieces as she could. Then she burned them, bit by bit, in the fireplace, as she was used to doing every month, only this time the pile seemed endless. When the more saturated pieces wouldn't burn she looked around for Con's lighter fuel and dripped it on to the material till it caught fire, sitting alone by the hearth for what seemed an endless time, making sure there was nothing left in the grate but sticky, black ash. When it was finished she returned to her bedroom and emptied her possessions into the case, retrieved her bank book from its hiding place under the faded lino and placed it safely under her pillow, only then gratefully lying down and slipping once more into the deep, dreamless sleep of the night before.

When she woke she heard a child crying somewhere in the distance; it must be morning. After dressing she wrote a note and left it on the kitchen table for Old Con. It simply said, 'I'm off.' He was still lying inside the front door snoring loudly, he'd had such a skinful that he hadn't made it to bed. Kathy moved him by repeatedly opening the door against his back, pushing it a bit more each time. Somewhere in his drunken stupor each nudge of the door registered, and he muttered petulantly in his sleep, but eventually the shapeless heap on the floor had shifted enough for her to open the door and let herself out before closing it quietly behind her. As a final gesture she pushed the key through the letter box and heard it land with a crack on the lino; she would never be back here, so she would never again have need of a key. It was quiet outside, the Barras was recovering after the weekend trading, and there were only a few non-market people queuing at the bus stops on their way to work, all wearing their Monday morning depression like an extra coat. She looked at her watch: 5 a.m. She had no idea it was that early, but still, there was no reason to delay her departure. Looking around she felt an unexpected stab of sorrow at the thought of never seeing again people she had grown up among. She was saying goodbye to everyone she had known throughout her life, to Maggie, Chief Abadu, Cockney Jock, the McIvers and the Pearsons, only they didn't know it. Still, they all knew she had been planning on leaving, so no one would think it strange that she had simply gone. They would assume that being heartbroken about Jamie Crawford's betrayal she had deliberately opted to slip away quietly. She smiled wryly and glanced at St Alphonsus, thinking of Frank McCabe inside, hugging his secret safely to himself; there were some she felt no sorrow at never seeing again. She knew exactly where she was going now, though she had made no conscious decision. She was going to Queen Street Station to catch the train to Fort William. She would leave behind her everything that had ever made her unhappy or caused her grief, and that included what had befallen her in these last months and days. Once she was clear of this place her life would start anew and nothing that had happened in the past would count. It would be like completing a circle. With her escape from the East End to the West Coast the slate would be wiped clean, no pain, no suffering, no disappointment or loneliness. She would head for the Western Highlands to heal it all, to do what or for how long, she had no idea, but that was where she was headed on that crisp March Monday in 1973, and she was never coming back to this place ever again.

7

Only, of course, she did come back. Against her will, to be sure, and many years later, first when Con was ill and then when he was dying, and now here she was, sitting in his house, sifting through what was left of him before she escaped again. Since she had arrived three months ago she had slept on a fold-down bed in the living room. There was only one bedroom, and Con had that, but even if there had been five she would still have used the fold-down; it was a statement of the temporary nature of her stay. He had died thirty hours ago, though who was counting, and in another twenty-four she wanted to be gone from here, so she was in a rush to get as much done as she could, to get the thing finished. He was lying in St Alphonsus's, a candle at each end of his box, and hopefully with the communion wine safely locked away, just in case. In the morning there would be a funeral mass, followed by the long trek to the Linn Crematorium to have Con cremated, then back to the East End for the traditional reception. And as soon after that as she could manage, she would be on her way back to the West Coast, this time for ever. This place would have no further claims on her, no ties of duty or emotion, and with all the loose ends finally tied up, maybe the dreams would disappear too.

When she awoke for that last time in the Moncur Street house all those years ago, the first sound she heard was a child crying. She had paid no particular heed to it, there were many children in the area, all with reasons to cry. What she didn't know then was the crying child would haunt her for the rest of her life; it hadn't been *a* child, it had been *her* child. Sometimes the dream would disappear for months at a time, but it would always return, triggered by something that reminded her or by nothing that she could identify, but it always returned. She would hear a child crying, and in the dream she would run through streets she had long since left, searching for her child, frantic with worry, shouting that she was coming, that she would be there soon. But wherever she ran, however hard she searched, she could never find the child, and she would wake drenched in sweat, sobbing and panic-stricken, with the child's cry fading into the background, till the next time. And in the months of Con's dying the child cried longer, stronger and more often. The East End was where she had last seen the tiny, dead form, it was where the nightmare had started, and it was as if the ghost of the daughter she had failed still waited here. And the aftermath was always the same. She would sit in the twisted bedclothes, hitting her head rhythmically with her fists, sobbing 'Useless! Useless!' over and over again. She hadn't wanted the baby, it had been a mistake and a huge inconvenience, but once it was gone she would've done anything to bring it back to life again. Those months of her hidden pregnancy when she had desperately detached herself so successfully from what was happening inside her body that she had barely felt the pain of labour, and the months before when she had safely concealed her gradually swelling belly, yet what had it all been for? Given that time over again she would have been happy to brazen it out, to display her illegitimate daughter to the world, if only she could hold her again and see her breathe, see her pink and smiling. She felt less than a woman, she was *useless*. Anyone could grow a child, a glance down any street confirmed that, it was easy, it was normal and natural, but Kathy Kelly couldn't do it. Kathy Kelly who had always thought herself so smart, so clever, Kathy Kelly who judged all the women in her family and found them wanting, who always had the last word, and she couldn't do a simple thing like have a baby. Well, Aggie could, the Aggie she had regarded as stupid and had baited all of her life, and even Jessie the whore could, yet *she* couldn't, so she must be something less than a woman. She had never given a thought to being female before, she just was, that was all, but any real woman could have a child. What kind of abnormal specimen couldn't even reproduce? A failure, that kind. Her, Kathy Kelly. She had failed at the most basic, fundamental task, and she had failed her tiny, dead daughter. All the baby had needed was somewhere safe to grow, any child had a right to that, and any other woman could have provided it. *Only she couldn't.* She had turned her own helpless, defenceless daughter out of the safety of her womb to die, little wonder that she cried in revenge all those years.

Lost in thought, tears streaming down her cheeks, she barely noticed the knock at the door. Probably that wee swine Frank McCabe with another entreaty to have Con buried in St Kentigern's, she thought. She wasn't worried about being found out, about the grave with the white heart-shaped headstone being opened and the red box containing the remains of the child being discovered. What had happened that night in Moncur Street was private, it had been between her and the child and Lily, it was no one else's business. Even as she was burying the box with the Kelly women, her thoughts hadn't been on the fear of discovery, but on placing her dead baby in Lily's care. Her refusal to bury Con there was based simply on the belief that they were all free of him, his tragic sisters, his mother and his wife, and now the baby she had called Lily, and she didn't want Con near any of them even in death. There was another, louder, knock. 'Ah'm comin',' she shouted wearily, and took her time wiping her eyes before she opened the door. She was shocked to find Jessie standing there, though she didn't show it. 'Come in, Jessie,' she said calmly. She had only vaguely registered Jessie's face in the chapel earlier, or what had been visible above the ever-present handkerchief covering the lower half, and had silently nodded to her in passing. Now Jessie passed her with a small but detectable body-swerve, you could never be sure about germs, and headed for Con's living room. She still held the handkerchief to her nose and mouth with gloved hands, and the mink coat, her proud acquisition of long years ago, hung absurdly over her emaciated frame. Jessie looked around the living room, taking in the scattered pieces of paper and photos on the floor, then she glanced at Kathy.

'Ye shouldnae let this upset ye, hen,' she said briskly.

'It doesnae,' Kathy replied.

Jessie gave her a disbelieving look. 'So that's why ye've been greetin', is it?'

'Aye, well, mibbe a bit,' Kathy grinned. 'There's stuff here aboot ma Mammy,' she sighed quietly, 'things Ah havnae seen for years. God knows why she married the auld bastard!'

'Because she was up the duff!' Jessie said simply. 'Ye surely didnae think it was love!' Jessie rolled her eyes as she said it. 'He was nae catch, ye know. Naebody but an innocent lassie like oor Lily woulda been taken in by Auld Con!'

'Christ, that's good!' Kathy laughed. 'Yer mad auld mother wanted *you* tae marry him, reckoned Lily had stolen him frae ye!'

Jessie snorted. 'Wouldnae've spat oan him if he'd been on fire!' she said calmly. 'An' aye, Ah'm here at his funeral, Ah know, but ye've got tae go through wi' these things, haven't ye? At least ye can satisfy yersel' that the auld sod is really deid an' gone if ye've seen the lid screwed doon oan him.'

'Sit doon, Jessie,' Kathy said. 'Ah've a feelin' Ah've mibbe misjudged ye a' these years!'

Jessie looked around for the smallest surface she could risk sitting on, her gaze settling on a kitchen stool with a plastic seat. She took an antiseptic wipe from a packet in her bag, wiped down the plastic and perched on the stool. 'Aye, ye have,' she returned eventually, 'but it wasnae really your fault, hen. Ye never really liked me, did ye?'

'Ah didnae really *know* ye, Jessie.'

'But ye looked doon oan me, thought Ah was a slut.'

'Aye, well, Ah was young then. Ah've learned no' tae make that kinda judgement.'

'Och, ye were *right*!' Jessie laughed. 'Ah aye liked that aboot ye, Kathy, hen! Ye were the only wan that was open aboot it, everybody else kept up this pretence tae ma face that Ah earned ma money daein' somethin' respectable while they talked behind ma back, but you were aye open aboot it. Ye were a nasty wee swine, mind ye, many's the time Ah felt like giein' ye a dirl aboot the ears for yer cheek, but as Ah say, ye were aye honest.'

Kathy took in the thin frame, the hankie held in the gloved hands, the skeletal legs so tightly crossed that they almost twisted around each other. It was as if Jessie was trying to make herself small and insignificant enough to almost not exist; blink as she passed and you would miss her.

'Have ye never tried tae get treatment for a' this?' she asked, her hands forming a circle in the air in an attempt to take in Jessie's affliction in its entirety.

'Ye mean go tae wanna they psychiatrists?' Jessie asked. 'Ah'd probably find Ah'd done the business wi' them or their faithers hen. Awfy hard tae have confidence in somebody when ye've seen them doon oan a' fours in the buff, askin' tae have their arse slapped for bein' bad. Besides, Ah don't think there is a cure. Ye'd be askin' for a cure for ma life, efter a'.'

'Is that no' whit wee Frank McCabe specialises in?' Kathy laughed. 'A couppla Hail Marys an' yer life's cured?'

'Aye, that'll be bloody right!' Jessie said sourly. There was a moment's silence. 'He's ma faither, did ye know that?' She said it so casually that Kathy wondered if she'd heard her properly. She was so surprised that if she'd been perched on the stool instead of Jessie she'd have fallen off, and as it was it was all she could do not to land with a thump on the floor.

'Well!' she said uncertainly. 'Ah knew, but Ah didnae think you did!'

'Known since Ah was a wean,' Jessie smiled smugly. 'Was sent hame frae school early wi' a dose o' the lurgy wan day an' heard the two o' them talkin', so Ah waited ootside the door – y'know the sleekit way ye dae when ye're a wean. It was just before ma confirmation an' they were discussin' names. Ye could tell he'd rather no' have been consulted, but Auld Aggie was determined. She wanted me tae take the name Francesca an' he was sayin' there wasnae a St Francesca. Auld Aggie said it would look like it was efter St Francis o' Assisi, but they'd baith know it was really efter him, an' it bein' kinda Italian insteada just Frances, it would put folk even merr aff the scent. The wee man wasnae happy, ye could tell, went oan tae say it still might make folk wonder, like, which was really stupid when ye thinka it. Who the hell would put two an' two thegither – especially they two – an' realise he really was *Father* McCabe? He said they had made a pact wi' God tae keep it secret an' she hadtae keep tae that, she couldnae gie anybody the slightest idea that Ah was his.'

'Musta gied ye a helluva shock, did it no'?'

'Well, aye and naw really,' Jessie replied with a chuckle. 'Ah'd always known Ah was different, Ah just didnae know how till then. Ah was always treated different frae oor Lily, the auld yin was aye helluva hard oan her, an' Ah didnae know why. So then Ah understood.'

'An' ye never told them? Her an' him, Ah mean? Ah know ma mother never knew.'

'Naw, Ah never let dab tae Lily or tae them,' Jessie replied. 'The wan Ah felt sorry for was the Orangeman.'

'Ma Granda? Dae ye think he knew?'

Jessie shook her head. 'Ah'm sure he didnae. Poor auld bugger. He just worked tae keep us a' an' was never considered by anybody.'

'That's no' the picture Aggie painted,' Kathy said. 'Accordin' tae her he was some kinda monster, a deflowerer o' Catholic maidens!'

'Ach, her!' Jessie said dismissively. 'She put it aboot merr than a bit, Ah can tell ye! Gied it away. The Sailor's Friend, that's what they used tae call her when she was young, would let anybody park their boat in her harbour! If Lily hadnae looked so much like the Orangeman Ah wouldnae've believed he was her faither, it coulda been anybody. The poor auld sod got caught, that was a', he did the decent thing insteada denyin' it or bungin' her a few bob tae get ridda it. He was a decent auld man, the Orangeman, Ah always liked him, even if he was a sap. Ah aye thought marchin' aboot wi' his sash was a' he could dae tae fight back, his last rebellion against her.' She thought for a minute. 'Ah took care o' his funeral, by the way, did ye know that?'

Kathy shook her head.

'Oh, aye!' Jessie said with relish. 'Ah was only aboot twenty year auld, at ma earnin' peak so tae speak. Ah told the undertaker tae make his coffin long enough for him tae wear his bowler hat as well as his sash! Aggie never knew! See when they carried him oot tae bury him, Ah could hardly keep frae laughin', him being carried past his Fenian widow wearin' his sash!'

Kathy thought of Con wearing his Highland Light Infantry gear, with his Child of Prague collection rolling around inside his coffin, and laughed. 'Christ, Jessie! We're helluva alike, you an' me! How did Ah never notice that afore?'

'Ye were too busy gettin' by the best way ye knew how, hen,' Jessie said quietly. 'Ah know how that feels.'

'But ye didnae needtae go oan the game, Jessie, did ye? There musta been an element o' choice there, surely?'

'Ach, well, mibbe they psychiatrists would have an answer tae that wan,' Jessie smiled. 'Low self-esteem or somethin' they'd likely say, or because Ah'd had a bad childhood, only Ah didnae, or a way o' hittin' back at Aggie an' dear auld Dad. Wasnae that either, though Ah havtae admit it was a treat confessin' tae him, knowin' that Ah knew who he was, an' him no' knowin' Ah knew, if ye follow me! Ah aye gied him a' the gory details tae, "Bless me Father, for I have sinned. This is *exactly* whit yer daughter did wi' every trick she had last week." Ah kept imaginin' his toes curlin' inside his wee boots!' Jessie stopped and chuckled loudly before continuing. 'But it was nane o' that lot, it just happened, an' that's the truth. When it did Ah realised Ah was good at it, an' the money was bloody good tae! It was efter Harry's faither got killed.'

'Uncle Sammy?' Kathy asked.

'Come oan noo!' Jessie laughed. 'Ye know bloody fine Sammy Nicholson wasnae Harry's faither! Naw, Big Eddie Harris, he was Harry's faither. Well, he was only big *here*, in Glesca, but he wasnae big anywhere else, or in the brain department. Y'know how a lotta men keep their socks oan? Well Big Eddie never took his soft hat aff durin' proceedin's or efter. I used to look at him an' wonder whit he kept under it. Bollock naked except for his soft hat! But he got it intae his heid that he was a top rankin' hard man, went doon tae conquer London, only they knew rightaway whit an arse he really was. He was found knifed ootside a night club somewhere doon there, they probably just got fed-up tellin' him tae bugger aff. An' efter him, well, ma reputation was kinda sealed. It was wan thing bein' Eddie Harris's tramp, but take Eddie away an' ye're just left wi' a tramp, a tramp wi' a wean come tae that. It was always assumed that Ah only went wi' him for the money anyway, so efter he was oot the game it was assumed that Ah'd dae it for anybody's money. An' they quite liked the idea o' daein' it wi' Big Eddie Harris's moll, didnae take me long to realise that. Seemed tae make them feel kinda dangerous theirsels for some reason. Funny things men, brains in their willies every wan!'

'Ye make it sound that simple!' Kathy said.

'It was! A' Ah hadtae dae was think a bit. If Ah was gonny dae it for money tae support wee Harry, Ah wasnae gonny dae it for pennies. Ah decided tae go upmarket, where the real money was. Made sense tae me then, still does.'

'But whit can ye possibly have done wi' them that was worth big money, Jessie? Ah never understood that.'

'Och, hen, it's got nothin' tae dae wi' *whit* ye dae, it's *who* ye dae it *wi'*, that's a'!'

'How d'ye mean?'

'Christ, ye're helluva innocent for a wumman o' yer age, hen! Look, men're a' the same, they're a' useless buggers, they never grow up. The secret is in knowin' that ye're dealin' wi' weans, so ye treat them like weans. The only difference worth a mention is how much money they've got. The wans wi' nae money dae it in backcourts or up closes for tuppence, ye don't havtae spend any time oan them. The wans wi' money are used tae better things, a bitta comfort an' consideration, so ye restrict yersel' tae them, gie them a comfy place tae perform, put oan the polite accent, an' there ye are. Ye tell them anythin' they want tae hear, an' men're no' big oan imagination so it doesnae vary much.

Ye've never seen anythin' that big, never had a better time, "My, but ye're Rudolph Valentino tae the life!" – that works a treat the wee-er and clumsier they are, but any auld lie will dae. Men will believe anythin' ye tell them when it comes tae gettin' their end away, the merr ye tell them the merr they're willin' tae pay, so the merr ye tell them. See?'

'An' that's it?'

'Och, well, Ah'm bein' modest here,' Jessie smiled to herself. 'Ah was bloody good at it tae, mind ye. Ah musta got some o' ma talent frae Aggie, only Ah polished it up a bit, an' insteada giein' it away like her Ah made a decent livin' at it. If the daft sods had any wee special requests they couldnae ask the wife for, Ah was always happy to oblige. The trick was in no' laughin' tae they'd disappeared doon the road.'

'Like whit?'

'Well, if they wanted tae lick apple crumble an' custard aff ma tits, or tae have me dressed up in a gym slip an' prancin' aboot wi' a perra they navy-blue school knickers showin', well, Christ, it was better than workin', wasn't it? Look at yer poor Mammy, puttin' up wi' Auld Con, daein' a' they wee jobs a' they years an' just gettin' by if she was lucky, then dyin' behind they barred windaes. Think for a minute, hen. If she'd been wi' me, changin' some daft auld bugger's nappy, or leadin' him aboot oan a dog leash on the best Axminster carpet for an hour, she'd still be here. Would ye no' rather have had that?'

Kathy thought for a moment. Jessie's argument made perfect sense; she would rather have had Lily alive and well and with her all these years, she had no doubts about that, but still there was something that rankled.

'So ye never actually enjoyed it?'

'Whit's there tae enjoy?' Jessie shot back.

'An' ye never liked the men?'

'Whit's there tae like?' she repeated. 'Ye just havtae get it straight in your mind. They're a' useless craiturs, no' wanna them worth the bother, even the best o' them. Can you thinka wan that's worth wastin' yer time oan? Big Eddie Harris? Yer Da? Your brother Peter? By Christ, an' did he no' shake the dust o' this place aff his feet sharpish like! Wee McCabe? The Orangeman? He was a nice man but, as Ah said, a big sap, that's how Aggie managed tae fool him so easy.'

'Whit aboot Sammy Nicholson, well?'

Jessie laughed wryly. 'Aye, well, he was ma last chance before Ah took up ma chosen career. Ah thought Ah'd won a watch wi' Sammy, mug that Ah was. Could Ah pick them, or could Ah pick them?' she asked, shaking her head. 'A' Ah wanted frae him was a name for Harry an' me an' a fresh start, an' whit does he dae? He canny even walk doon his ain stairs withoot fa'in' an' breakin' his neck! Talk aboot daft? That's when Ah decided that Ah'd stick tae the money, the true love game wasnae for me. Only twice Ah tried it, an' baith times Ah latched oan tae daft buggers! An' as for that clown you nearly lumbered yersel' wi', that Crawford boy. Christ, Ah was relieved when ye gave him the elbow, hen! Ah mind thinkin', "She's got merr aboot her, but if she doesnae get oota that her life's goin' doon the Clyde in a banana boat."'

'He was quite a nice boy when he was younger, Jessie,' Kathy replied. 'Ah knew him a' ma life. He was loyal and dependable an' always there.'

'So's a mongrel wi' nae brains,' Jessie replied tartly. 'Just throw it the odd stick an' it'll keep comin' back waggin' its tail, but ye'll never get away frae it, will ye? Ye'll havtae look efter it, because it's daft, it canny look efter itsel'.'

Kathy laughed; it wasn't a million miles from her own reading of Jamie Crawford's character.

'An' did ye never notice that his hairline started hauf an inch above his eyebrows?' Jessie asked. 'Noo Ah was never much good at pickin' long-term men, hen, but even Ah knew that hadtae be a bad sign, that. Ah'm tellin' ye, him gettin' that other lassie up the duff was the best thing that ever happened tae you, ye were just bloody lucky he didnae dae it tae you tae. But ye were aye a sensible lassie that way, naebody could ever point the finger at you.'

Kathy said nothing.

'Ah'm tellin' ye,' Jessie continued, well into her stride, 'wanna these days a scientist will come up wi' a way of makin' weans withoot them, a *wumman* scientist, an' that's the enda them. That's a' they're good for noo, think aboot it. Whit else can they dae that justifies their existence?'

Kathy still said nothing. She had never heard Jessie talk as much as this in her entire life, could never have imagined that the desperately stylish figure Jessie had always cut could have had these thoughts running around her head. Maybe it was the tightness of the metal triangles holding that little velvet hat to her head that had contained them all those years ago.

'Look at ma Harry noo,' Jessie invited. 'Hari-kari hissel'. A bright boy that had the besta education. An' a nice boy, everybody liked him, naebody has ever had a bad word for him. Good-lookin' tae. Remember?'

Kathy nodded; she had always liked her cousin Harry and looked up to him. Harry it was she took her childish scribbling to, Harry it was who discussed books with her. She had had such high hopes for her cousin; he would become successful, he would be somebody, she had never doubted it. One of her biggest disappointments when she came back was to find this oddly vague stranger who almost looked and sounded like him, but somehow wasn't.

'Ah was told tae expect great things o' Harry, but Ah always took that wi' a pincha salt, mind. Ah knew his faither efter a'. Whit's he daein' noo? He tells fortunes!' Jessie bent over, laughing through her handkerchief. 'He goes aboot there wi' his crystal ball, a medallion roond his neck an' a mysterious look in his eye, tellin' fortunes for any numpty daft enough tae hand ower the dosh! They actually listen tae him, they've got him booked a year in advance!'

'Well, he's makin' a livin', isn't he?' Kathy laughed back. 'It's surely better than endin' up a redundant boilermaker!'

'Ye're missin' the point, hen. That's a' Harry's good for, that's a' he's ever been good for. Ye know that auld sayin', "There's merr tae him than meets the eye"? Well, ma Harry's the opposite, there's a damned sight *less* there than meets the eye! He *believes* that shite he tells the numpties, he's no' just makin' easy money. That Ah could live wi', Ah've done it masel' a' these years efter a', but the daft bugger really believes he's got the second sight, that's the difference. Ah was never fooled aboot whit Ah did, because Ah'm a wumman, an' we've got oor heids screwed oan. Harry's just a man, a daft, stupid man, an' as Ah tellt ye, they're that easy tae fool that they dae the job for ye, they fool theirsels.'

'An' whit aboot yer son-in-law, Claire's man? Noo, he's clever, isn't he?'

'He's a *dentist*!' Jessie hooted. 'Whit kinda man's a *dentist*?'

'Wan that makes money, that's for sure!'

'Aye, Ah'll gie ye that,' Jessie conceded. 'But ye havtae bear in mind that he married ma Claire, a lassie that could bore for Britain. How clever can he be? Can ye imagine the conversation in their hoose? Nothin'! Bugger all! Silence! If ma Claire ever had a thought in her heid, an' there's nae proof that she had, it got lost oan the way tae her tongue an' died o' loneliness!'

'Och, Jessie! That's a helluva thing tae say!'

'It's true though. The only way Ah ever knew she was alive was if she was movin'. Never said a word in her life. How the Hell she got through her weddin' vows is a mystery tae me, Ah think she had a special arrangement tae use semaphore. So *of coorse* she married a dentist. They spend their time muckin' aboot in folk's mooths so they canny talk, maybe they prefer them that way, that's how they become dentists. But whit kinda man wants a wife as borin' as ma Claire? Does that no' just prove ma point?'

Finally Jessie brought the conversation round to the reason for her visit. 'Ah'll needtae tell ye this noo, hen, 'cos Ah need a pee an' Ah canny use anybody else's lavvy,' she said conversationally, as though it were the most reasonable thing in the world. 'Did ye know aboot the money?'

Kathy shook her head. 'Naw.'

'McCabe's got it,' Jessie said simply. 'It was money Auld Con got when yer Mammy died, merr than a bob or two it was tae.

Compensation an' money folk donated tae a fund that was shared oot between the families. McCabe took it aff him, said it was because he'd just drink it. Auld Aggie told me aboot it at the time. It was aye ma guess that if naebody brought the subject up, neither would he.'

'The dirty wee swine!' Kathy said, outraged. 'It's the first Ah've ever hearda this!'

'Aye, Ah thought he probably hadnae volunteered that infor-mation tae ye,' Jessie said darkly. 'But don't dae anythin' daft noo, don't go rushin' roon' there and slappin' the sly wee bugger oan the ear. Well, no' unless he pays for it anyway!' She exploded in laughter behind her handkerchief shield. 'Ah just wanted tae make sure ye knew aboot it, we've plenty o' time tae think o' a way tae sort him oot later. Efter a', we know somethin' he doesnae know we know, an' that's real power. Noo Ah'll havtae go, hen, ma bladder won't haud oot for ever. Harry's sittin' doon the stairs in the car waitin' tae drive me hame, he's probably been readin' palms tae while away the time, or recitin' wanna his mantras!' She shook her head. 'An' ye'll no' believe this, but know whit his other skill is? He does conjurin' tricks! Pick a card, that kinda thing, an' the besta it is, *he* canny see the connection between that an' him tellin' fortunes, the daft sod!' Jessie cackled loudly behind her handkerchief and Kathy shivered.

'Whit's the matter? Somebody walk ower yer grave?'

'Just aboot, Jessie,' Kathy replied. 'That mad laugh o' yours there, it sounded just like yer demented auld mother!'

'Aye, well, as Ah've often said masel', parentage will out.' She winked at her niece. 'You an' me'll talk efter the funeral the morra,' she said firmly, turning to go. Then she looked again at the papers and photos on the floor. 'Ah thought ye'd be reddin' the place oot. Ah wanted tae tell ye tae look through it carefully, there might be somethin' oan paper aboot Con gettin' the money. Find it, then get ridda the resta that shite, hen. There's nothin' there worth sheddin' a tear ower. Toodle-oo!' And with that she was gone.

Kathy could hardly believe it. Ever since the day he had wanted to shoot the horse at Maggie's fruit stall her opinion of Frank McCabe had been as low as she'd thought it possible for any human being to go, but there was a depth he would stoop to, *had* stooped to, that was even lower than that. Had that been why he was never away from Con's house in the months before he died, in case the old man spilled the beans to his daughter? She had done everything but bodily lift him and throw him down the stairs, but he had stuck it out well, the insults, the complaints, the abuse. She thought back to the months and years after Lily's death in the fire, of the constant panic she had felt trying to make sure there was enough money to pay for the essentials of life, a child thrown into the adult world of paying bills and keeping one step ahead of Con's drinking. And all the time there had been money. She had always assumed there would be, though she had never asked. If it existed it would be blood money, and the thought that cash could make up for losing her mother was offensive, so she had never asked. Con would have drunk it, she decided, and that would've been fair enough, but the idea of Frank McCabe taking charge of it and never saying a word appalled her. Better that Con had wasted the lot on booze than putting it in McCabe's hands. Well, if he had it, he wouldn't have it for long, she decided. All through the long, weary months of Con's dying her one thought had been to get it over with and to leave this place for ever, but now she knew she would stay here for as long as it took to prise McCabe's mucky little fingers off the cash he had taken into 'safe keeping' all those years ago. So she spent the entire night searching the house for some sort of proof that it had ever existed, but she came up with nothing. Morning came, dawn broke, and the hands of the clock on the mantelpiece were creeping towards ten o'clock, the time of the funeral mass. She had a quick bath, made herself toast and coffee and then dressed again in black. What a joke, she thought, what a hypocritical joke. For this occasion a scarlet flamenco dress would've been more in keeping with her feelings, and she could've been persuaded to dance down the aisle too, castanets going like the clappers till they caught fire in her hands.

From a Glaswegian tenement to this. I first saw this cottage when I was in my early teens. You can't miss it, high up off the road between Fort William and Glenfinnan. I've loved it since the first time I saw it, so where else would I put Kathy?

8

The Glasgow to Mallaig train, stopping at various stations along the way, including Fort William, departed twice daily, at 6 a.m. and 4 p.m. When she arrived at Queen Street at 5.30 that morning she had no idea of this, but she took it as a good omen that she could leave Glasgow so quickly. A short visit to the fancy toilet at the far end of the station was all she had time for. Never having given birth before and being unable to ask for information, she had no means of knowing what would happen in the aftermath. The child had been born on Saturday night and it was now early Monday. It wasn't like a period – should it be? At first there had been small pieces of unidentifiable tissue in the heavy postpartum bleeding, but now that had stopped and the loss had slowed and turned into a brownish discharge. Was that supposed to happen? Was it normal? She smiled wryly to herself. Normal! What did that mean? Nothing about her situation was normal, nothing in her life ever had been. She had felt all her life that other people were living normal lives while she struggled with the absurd, all the while trying to pretend, to the outside world at least, that her life was just as normal as theirs. But what had happened over the last couple of days especially had upset everything and it was as much as she could do to maintain her understanding of which end was up. There had been a certain wonder over these days at the way the rest of the world was going on as usual, as though nothing out of the ordinary had happened. She had given birth to a secret, unfinished child, a dead child, and buried it beside the other Kelly women, her mother in particular, and then she had destroyed every last trace of what had occurred, yet she was walking about, still bleeding, of course, but as if she wasn't any different from the Kathy Kelly she had once been. And every human being she had encountered since, those she knew and those she didn't, treated her so casually that she almost felt they were pretending not to notice. Surely they must suspect something? Surely there was some difference in her that those who knew her must detect, and there had to be something so fundamentally odd about her behaviour that even those she had never met must wonder? And yet they didn't seem to. She had bought her one-way ticket and received a civil smile at the ticket office, along with a friendly comment about the ungodly hour of the train's departure, and she had answered in the same tone. The toilet attendant had taken her 10p, given her a ticket and let her through the little gate at the entrance, apologising that the ticket machine operating the turnstile had broken down again, bloody useless thing. She climbed the two flights of stairs and found her reflection in a long bank of mirrors along the wall on the left, and wondered how she could look so normal. There it was, that word again. Inside the toilet she changed her towel again. The discharge was less, but it was still there; how long would this go on? Could she count on it gradually lessening all the time, or was there a point in this alien process where she would suddenly bleed profusely again? She thought of this happening as she sat on the blue train seat, and imagined her horror as the red flood ran out of control. She sat on the low toilet and took a deep breath. This had happened to other women besides her, she told herself, it had to have, it stood to reason. Stay calm, deal with the crisis when it arrived, that made sense, and maybe there would be no crisis, maybe the worst was over. Still, better find a seat on the train near to the toilet, just to be sure. But no sooner had one problem receded than another demanded to be faced. It had started the morning after the birth, but she had been so preoccupied then that it had barely registered, and besides, she was wet in so many places that she couldn't be sure what was coming from where or why. Her breasts were sore and she was leaking fluid from them, sometimes quite copious amounts of fluid. She had tried not to think about it because she had more than enough to think about, but now that other things were coming under control, the wetness seeping through her bra and down the front of her blouse took on a new importance. In the toilet cubicle she stuffed toilet tissue into each bra cup to soak it up, wincing slightly as it grazed her sensitive nipples, and quickly made her way down to the platform. And that's when the true enormity of what had happened began to assert itself. She was leaking milk, she suddenly realised; her body was providing nourishment for a baby that would never suckle. As the train entered the first of two long tunnels at the exit of the station she felt a cry of the deepest pain trying to escape her throat, and lowered her head to contain it. She had never felt in the least maternal, not once in her life had she looked at a child and hoped that one day she could have one just like it, but the tragedy of producing milk when there was no child to feed over-whelmed her, and sitting in the quiet railway carriage in the early morning she turned her face to the rough material of the seat and sobbed into it. More than anything she had ever wanted, more even than wanting her mother, she wanted her child, the ache in her full breasts matching the pain in her empty arms, her empty heart. The loss of the child seemed to have tapped into a deep part of her that she had had no idea existed, but now it was raw, aching and weeping in sympathy with her uselessly over-full breasts. '*Useless!*' she thought savagely. '*Useless, useless, useless!*'

The train pulled into Fort William four hours later, just before 10 a.m. She had managed to doze back and forth during the journey, which made her feel worse than if she had remained wide awake throughout. Short naps had always done that to her. 'Feast or famine!' Lily used to say with a smile. 'Ye were aye the same as a baby, Kathy. Ye hadtae have a good three or four hours tae be bearable, less than that an' ye were *un*bearable!' She felt her eyes tearing up again. Everything had taken on a new emotional significance. Would her daughter have been like that too, she wondered, and instantly felt the pain of loss again. She would never never know that, would never be able to tell her daughter stories of her babyhood, because the dead child would have none. She shook her head as she got off the train and breathed deeply.

The spring air was cool and clean, her breath like puffs of smoke as she exhaled. The tiny tourist office was inside the train station and she approached a woman putting out leaflets and asked for help in finding somewhere to stay.

'It's just before Easter, lass,' the woman told her. 'If you're looking for a self-catering cottage or something like that, then lettin' doesn't really start till Easter, and most of that will be already fully booked. People tend to come here year after year, you see.'

'I need somewhere for a few days while I look around,' Kathy replied. She had automatically adjusted the way she spoke to something nearer to the English spoken by the woman. The words were the same, but the accent changed the sound, and there was something about her Glasgow vowels that sounded abrasive against the lilting, gentle tones.

'Well, there's the Alexandra Hotel across the road,' the woman replied. 'Unless you want bed and breakfast somewhere smaller. I could call round, I'm sure there would be no problem setting you up with that.'

'No,' Kathy said. 'The hotel sounds fine.' The last thing she could cope with right now was conversation, particularly the friendly sort; the slightest kindness, even from an unsuspecting stranger, and she felt she might collapse in a sobbing heap. She felt like a wounded animal with an instinctive need to be on her own. 'Is there a Royal Bank here?'

'Aye,' the woman smiled brightly, 'just down the High Street there on the left. Beside the church.'

As Kathy picked up her case and turned to leave the woman called after her. 'If something comes up, a cottage that might suit, would you like me to leave a message at the hotel for you? I'm sure I'll find you something. I'll look through the books and even if there's nothing there, there are bound to be cancellations.'

'Aye, that would be good,' Kathy said.

'And it's just for yourself?' the woman asked. 'And for how long?'

Kathy sensed there was more than business in the question, the woman knew perfectly well she was alone and was wondering why. 'Yes, just for me,' she replied. 'My name's Kathy Kelly and I'm hoping to find work here. I know the area from when I was a child.'

A slight exaggeration, but what the hell?

'Aye, well, there's a lot of that about. It's a bit different actually staying here,' the woman smiled gently.

'That's why I want to stay here,' Kathy said, smiling back, 'because it's different.'

'Off you go then, Miss Kelly,' the woman smiled. 'By the time you get across the road I'll have called the hotel and let them know you're on your way. My niece, Kirsty, works on Reception. And the minute I hear of anything suitable I'll be in touch. Don't you worry, we'll get you fixed up!' When Kathy was out of earshot the woman picked up the phone and dialled the number of the Alexandra Hotel. 'Oh, hello, Kirsty,' she said brightly. 'Seona here. I've just sent a lassie over to you, Kathy Kelly's her name. Looking for work and needs somewhere to stay till she finds it. Aye, one of them I'm afraid! Used to come here on her holidays when she was a child, probably won't last more than a month, but there again, she might surprise us I suppose!' There was a pause as she listened to Kirsty's comments. 'Aye, well, looks a nice sort of lassie, but awfy pale. Looks as if she's been ill, needs a good sleep. See what you can do for her, and I'll see you tonight in the bar of the Nevis Bank. Bye!'

The Alexandra Hotel dominated the far end of Fort William, sitting off the road on an elevated position above the main street, looking like a grey granite castle, but Kathy barely noticed how grand it was, it was simply a place to lay her head. And for two weeks after her arrival that's exactly what she did. Her body returned to normal during that time, the bleeding stopped and so did the leaking breast milk, as she began to settle down again after the mental and physical turmoil of the last months. She did little apart from sleep for long spells, taking walks by Loch Linnhe in between. The wind coming off the snow still capping Ben Nevis was cold, or, as the tourist brochures preferred to describe it, 'bracing and refreshing'. Even in March it numbed exposed areas of the body and stung tears to the eyes, so that everyone walked with their hands in their pockets, heads down. At the time she was aware that she was hiding, but looking back it had also been a kind of con-valescence, a necesssary period of withdrawal in order to adjust and regroup, though what would have happened if outside forces hadn't brought it to an end she wasn't sure. As she passed the desk after one of her walks, Kirsty, the receptionist, stopped her. There was a message from Seona in the Tourist Office, she should call straight away. The girl smiled and held out her hand, indicating the phone on the desk. Kathy dialled the number.

'Oh, hello there!' Seona replied, as though she had been waiting for this phone call all of her life. 'I was wondering what kind of work you were after?'

'Anything,' Kathy replied.

'Really? Oh, that sounds good!'

'Not really,' Kathy replied, 'just desperate.' Where in hell did the woman get that cheerfulness from? Were Tourist Officers bred in captivity?

'I bumped into Major Angus on my way in this morning,' Seona rushed on. 'He and his wife live up at Glenfinnan and the old girl's getting over a broken hip, so they're looking for someone to give them a hand round the house, and the very best bit about it is that it's live-in. He was going to advertise it, but I said I might know someone, so he's holding off in case you're interested. There's not much at Glenfinnan, mind, but I thought it might be a good fill-in if nothing else, give you a chance to look around kind of thing. What do you think?'

'Aye,' Kathy said immediately.

'You're sure?'

'Definitely.'

'Och, that's great! Let's see. It's half eleven now, he'll be going back up to Glenfinnan around three o'clock and I told him to call in, so maybe you could meet him here?'

When she came off the phone Kirsty was standing there, eye-brows raised quizzically, waiting for the full details as if she didn't already know.

'Major Angus!' she said, smiling.

'Yes. Do you know him?'

'Och, everybody knows Major Angus,' Kirsty laughed. 'But don't you believe what they say, I've always wondered if he makes half of those stories up himself!'

Kathy was about to ask what stories and which half, when Kirsty continued. 'There's no harm in him, honestly, and his wife is, well, you have to remember that she's been married to Major Angus for a long, long time!' She threw her head back and laughed.

'What is he, a mad rapist or something?' Kathy asked uncertainly, which made Kirsty laugh even harder.

'No, of course not! He's just a bit odd, but in a non-threatening way!'

'You'd better explain,' Kathy suggested.

'Aye, well, maybe you're right, but not here. When're you meeting him? Three o'clock? I'll call Seona and we'll meet her in the Nevis Bank at one. If we meet here I'll be on duty even if it is my lunch hour.' She looked at Kathy's concerned expression. 'Relax, it's not whatever you're thinking!' she laughed.

'You don't know how bad my thoughts can be!' Kathy replied.

When they met at the Nevis Bank Hotel Seona and Kirsty quickly got down to business. The first thing they had to tell her was that Major Angus wasn't a major at all. He was Angus Macdonald, born and bred in Glenfinnan, and when he was a young man he had worked for the original major, a retired Englishman who had inherited his estate from his father. It took in much of the area around Glenfinnan, the hills that Angus had known all his life and considered his own. It was his job to drive the old boy in an ancient Daimler, from his house, a red sandstone mini castle high overlooking those hills, to wherever he wanted to go, and he rowed him out across Loch Shiel when he wanted to do a spot of fishing, and all the time the two of them fought ferociously. And not just verbally either, frequently their disagreements became physical.

'My mother told me about them,' Seona laughed. 'You'd see this boat rocking from side to side in the water with these two daft creatures throwing punches at each other and yelling like bulls. Nobody bothered, they knew it was just the two of them at it as usual. As often as not the boat would capsize and they'd have to swim ashore, stopping on the way to shout a bit more and throw another couple of punches, and when they got out of the water they'd drive home to change, still roaring insults at each other. The next day they'd have bruises and grazes all over their faces, but they were still together.'

'Gran said it was the same when they came into the Fort for their messages,' Kirsty smiled. 'If Angus arrived on his own you knew it was OK, but if the two of them arrived together you knew they were on a binge, and it always ended with them fighting. Never touched anyone else, mind you, perfect gentlemen if you happened to stray within punching distance, stopped right away, bowed and exchanged a few polite words till you were out of the way, then got laid into each other again.'

'What did they fight about?' Kathy asked.

'Och, everything and nothing really,' Seona replied. 'They fought about the shinty, whether Lochaber was better than Camannach, then the other way round. Silly stuff. Or you'd hear Angus cursing the Major for being a Sassenach, an interloper, taking his birthright away, and the Major would call him a typical drunken teuchtar, too fond of the hooch to do a decent day's work, and if it wasnae for the English they'd all starve. But my father always said that was made up, something to keep the fight going rather than the cause. Everybody thought they just liked fighting. When the Major died he left the estate to Angus, on condition that he married the cook, Bunty Campbell.'

'You're joking!' Kathy said.

Kirsty and Seona laughed. 'No, honest! He was in his forties at the time, and Bunty would've been near enough forty herself,' Seona replied. 'I think he was quite sweet on her anyway, but she was a Campbell, for God's sake, and no Macdonald would marry a Campbell without a lot of thought, not up here in those days. That was the Major's parting jab, I suppose, giving him back the land that Angus had always maintained belonged to him anyway, but making him marry a Campbell for it.'

'And she went along with it, this Bunty person?'

'Och, aye. But you have to remember that she'd been patching up their cuts and bruises for years as well as running the house and feeding them. She knew them better than anybody. My mother always said Bunty and Angus would've ended up together anyway, but the Major doing that, it gave Angus the excuse that he'd been forced to marry a Campbell. The other condition of the will was that Angus should personally scatter the Major's ashes across the hills, so that he'd always be there, keeping an eye on him. Angus swears that he still hears the Major shouting at him, drives him mad, so it does. After that Angus was called "Major Angus", because he had taken over the Major's estate. He's a helluva man, you'll like him,' said Seona, exchanging amused glances with Kirsty. 'Wears the kilt all the time, and a Tam-o'-Shanter with a bloody big eagle feather sticking out the top. He's like something from Brigadoon!'

'Why does he go about like that?' Kathy asked. 'I don't think I've seen anyone wearing the kilt since I arrived here.'

'Och, who knows?' Seona said. 'I think he just likes the idea of being a Highlander of years ago. It's as if now that he's got the land he always believed was his anyway, he's reverted to the time before the old Major's people had it, to kind of wipe out the foreign occupation. He's totally harmless though, he's not some kind of nut, he just lives in his own wee world, that's all, and he's not the only one who does that.'

Kathy said nothing. Seona might've been talking about her, after all.

'He still comes into town for groceries and stuff, and to pick up whatever thing he's ordered for his latest obsession. He gets hooked on things, you know the way you do.'

'No,' Kathy said uncertainly.

'Well, he's been like it all his life from what I'm told. He took a helluva interest in pigs once, I think that was the start of it. Somebody gave him a piglet and he bought another and before anyone knew it he'd become an expert on all things pig. He never does things by halves, he really studies his subject. Soon it became a roaring success, people came from miles around to buy his pork, so he gave it up.'

'Why?'

'Because it had become a business, I suppose. He just wanted to find out all there was to know for himself, he didnae want a business. Bunty says it's because he has the concentration span of a midgie, as soon as he gets to grips with something he loses interest and has to move on to something else,' said Seona.

'D'you mind his frogs and newts?' Kirsty laughed.

Seona nodded. 'Became almost a world authority then,' she laughed. 'The house was crawling in frogs, toads and newts and they were popping out of every pocket he had, and his sporran. Wrote papers about them. Bunty went mad that time, newts wernae really her thing, but she just had to hang on till he'd gone off them and hope that he dived into something sensible next time.'

'And did he?'

'Not really. Started to breed Clydesdale horses, won all sorts of awards. Had people who'd been in the business for generations queuing up for his foals. But the trouble with horses is that they have trouble foaling, so he had Bunty sitting up all night with him waiting for the mares to deliver, and their whole lives were dominated by them. I think he went into Highland cattle after that, or did he pick up on Ancient Egypt before that, Kirsty?'

'Aye, I think it was Ancient Egypt before the cattle,' Kirsty said. 'In fact I think tapestry was before the cattle, come to think of it.'

'*Tapestry?*' Kathy asked.

'Aye, and he was great at it too,' Seona replied. 'There's not a church for hundreds of miles, or a university across the country that hasnae lined up to commission a tapestry from Major Angus. I'm telling you, he does nothing by halves, he's an expert in anything he turns his hand to, he just loses interest once he's learned all there is to learn.'

'So what's he into now, then?'

'Not sure,' Seona replied thoughtfully. 'It was orchids for a while there, but he may have gone past that now. I think I heard a rumour that he was building working models of steam trains, but who knows?'

'How old is he?'

'Well into his seventies anyway. Let me think. His Rory went to school with me, so he'll be thirty now, and Bunty had him less than a year after they were married. My father used to say that was another thing he got the hang of before moving on to something else, so there were no more wee Macdonalds after Rory. Mind you, I think it was pretty heroic of Bunty to produce even one at her age. So that would make Angus about seventy-five now, but you'd never think it.'

'And did having a bairn make any difference to Angus?' Kathy asked.

'Och, aye,' Seona replied. 'Of course it did! He did a degree in Child Psychology right away.'

'That's not exactly what I meant,' Kathy laughed. 'So what became of the son?'

'Well, he's nothing like Angus, that's for sure!' Seona replied. 'Took off as soon as he could, he's worked all over the world doing all sorts of jobs. Once he painted white lines on the roads of New York, and he worked on a farm in Australia once, and he did something or other in New Zealand after that, forestry I think it was. He hasnae been home for a few years now, but I suppose he'll come back in due course. Bunty's broken hip is likely the first sign that her and Angus will be needing help to run the estate soon. It's not a huge estate, mind, most of it is rock and scrub, but there's a few sheep and beef cattle, and the fishing of course.'

'So Rory's a bit of an adventurer then?'

'No, I wouldnae really say that,' Seona replied. 'He was always a loner, quite happy in his own company sort of thing, but friendly and easy-going when you talked to him. There was this laddie at school with us, can't remember his real name, but for some reason the other lads called him Guff McGhee. You know what lads are like. They used to form this circle round him and chant "Guff

McGhee! Guff McGhee!" and he'd get that mad he'd take his shoes off and throw them at them, which was what they wanted. They'd throw them on the school roof, a right lot of bullies they were. And it was always Rory Macdonald brought it to an end. He'd climb up and get Guff's shoes for him, and scatter the rest of them with a look. He never had to raise his fists, yet they never annoyed poor old Guff when he was about. I always liked that about Rory, I always thought he was a good sort who just liked his freedom, always did what he wanted to do, still does. He was clever as well, went to Glasgow University for a while, but he gave it up after a year or so, it just wasnae his kind of thing. He liked being outdoors. I mind when he was at school all he wanted to do was be a farmer, but the ground about here isnae exactly green and fertile.'

And then the three women talked of other things. Seona and Kirsty were polite, but they wanted to know where she had come from and why she was here. They had put themselves out to help her after all, they had a right to have their curiosity satisfied in return. She came from Glasgow, she said, and she had been ill recently, following a family bereavement. Seona and Kirsty exchanged knowing looks. 'I knew you'd been ill,' Seona said. 'Didn't I say that the very first day, Kirsty?' Kirsty nodded. Kathy gave no time scale, but she told them that with her mother dead there had been nothing to keep her in Glasgow any longer. True, if not perfectly and completely true, a skill she had learned, she thought ruefully, while dealing with Jamie and fending off his insecurities. Both women listened sympathetically.

'Was it sudden?' Seona asked.

Kathy nodded. 'She died in a fire.'

'That's awful, Kathy. I mind when my mother died,' Seona said. 'Remember when your Gran died, Kirsty?' Kirsty nodded sadly. 'We knew she was going to die, but it didnae make any difference when it happened, it was just as much of a shock. It happens to everyone, I know,' Seona continued, 'but I canny understand how other people manage. I just fell apart, couldnae imagine life without her, still canny.' Her eyes filled with tears.

'Three years,' she said, 'and it feels like yesterday. I still expect to see her every day, still include her in everything as though she was living up the road.' By this time all three of them were dabbing at their eyes, and suddenly Seona looked around and let out a great peal of laughter. 'Look at us sitting here!' she laughed. 'What're we like? Macbeth's witches stirring up a pot of depression! If my mother was here she'd give the three of us a good slapping and tell us to behave ourselves!'

They were back in the Tourist Office inside the station when Major Angus arrived. He wasn't a tall man, but somehow he looked it, he had a presence. He was of medium height, but you could see that once he had been well-built, with wide shoulders and muscular arms. The hair under his Tam-o'-Shanter – and how glad she was that she'd been forewarned about that hat and the feather erupting from it – was snow-white and shoulder length. Merging with it at the front was a full set of whiskers, so that the visible part of his face consisted of a nose, ruddy cheeks and two amazingly bright blue eyes. She had trouble taking her eyes off his, deep-set but sharp and intelligent, almost lit from within. On his feet he had heavy, well-worn brown brogues and thick woollen socks with a *sgiann dhu* tucked into the top of the right one. His kilt was in a muted, dark tartan and quite different from any she had ever seen, but her acquaintance with men in Highland dress had been restricted to TV programmes, where the outfit was refined and brightly coloured. The men wearing those kilts, usually entertainers with no Highland connections, also had frilly jabots underneath delicate jackets with silver buttons, and shoes made of shiny patent leather, but Major Angus was wearing the working variety, the genuine garb. His kilt was held at the waist by a thick, no-nonsense belt, and the only sign of frivolity was the silver edging on the large sporran hanging from the belt. On top he wore a rough, dark green shirt rolled to the elbows and a sleeveless, brown leather jerkin that buttoned up the front, the kind she had seen working soldiers wearing on newsreels of the War. Kathy thought back to her only trip through Glencoe all those years ago, and how she had imagined the road missing and the remnants of the Forty-Five Rebellion making their way homewards from Culloden, being hunted across their own land by the Redcoats. She couldn't make up her mind if Major Angus would fit that bill, or if he was more like an escaped extra from some embarrassing piece of Scotch kitsch. All he needed was a plaid across his shoulder, a studded targe in one hand and a broadsword in the other, but there was no denying that even without them the overall effect was arresting. She wondered if he had a horse waiting outside and would throw her roughly up behind him, then she reminded herself that he had driven a Daimler for the original Major, so she was being stupid. Still, even a Daimler would add to the impression, she thought, until they got outside and found a battered white Mini waiting to convey them to Glenfinnan. He had asked her no questions, he had simply accepted her on Seona's recommendation, in fact he hadn't spoken at all, and within minutes her suitcase had been retrieved from the Alexandra and they were on their way. '*Who'd have believed it?*' she thought gleefully. '*Two weeks ago Ah left the Barras, noo here Ah am, bein' driven through the Highlands in a Mini by Rob Roy's wee brother!*' And being driven fast at that, Major Angus had little time for details like speed restrictions, or any other requirement of the Highway Code either.

Once out of Fort William they passed through Banavie at breakneck speed, with Neptune's Staircase on the right, the series of locks on the Caledonian Canal bringing boats through the short cut from Inverness to Fort William, and Loch Eil on the left. They drove through Corpach, Fassfern and Kinlocheil, names she had never heard of, all of them as exciting and exotic as Zanzibar or Valparaiso, especially if you came from Moncur Street; she only wished she'd had the chance to actually see them. High on the right hand side of the road at Drumsallie, outside Kinlocheil, she noticed a small whitewashed cottage with a bright red door and window surrounds. Though she couldn't get more than a swift glance before it had disappeared in the distance, she could see that it was completely on its own, with sheep grazing nearby. 'Who lives there?' she asked. 'It's Rory's,' said Rob Roy's younger brother, 'but he doesnae live in it. He's away at the minute anyway.' She wondered briefly how he could be sure she knew who Rory was; it would be a few years yet before she understood that everyone in the area knew everything about each other, even the ones who couldn't claim direct or indirect kinship. Major Angus would have known perfectly well that Seona had already fully briefed her, he would've expected nothing less. And then they drove round a corner into a moment she would never forget. That first sight of the Glenfinnan Monument standing at the head of Loch Shiel, the mountains on either side and into the distance rising in perfect symmetry, literally took her breath away. She gave a little involuntary gasp and Angus turned to look at her. 'Aye,' he said simply, smiling at her. 'It is.' A statue stood on top of the sixty-five foot tower, with an octagonal wall around the base, but the car passed too quickly to take a closer look. Even with that brief glimpse the beauty of the thing almost brought tears to her eyes. It was so picturesque, so perfect, that it looked not quite real, as if someone had painted it and let their enthusiasm run away with their brush. And Seona had said there was nothing much at Glenfinnan! That first sight of the tower standing against the landscape, with the hills, the loch and the sky framing it, instantly entered into her memory. She would never forget the first time she saw it and when she was away from it that picture was the one she drew to mind. Even though she would see it again every day for many years in different weather and light, she carried that initial impression in her mind, and later it would sustain her through the months of Con's dying that lay far in the future.

The Mini swept past the monument and lurched to the right up a road that became a hillside track, finally ending outside a large, red sandstone construction. She never settled on what it actually was, a house, a villa or a small castle, with turrets and arches in abundance, but for years it had been the Major's domain, stolen though Angus considered it to be, and now it rightfully belonged to the Macdonalds. Inside the front door, off a long hallway, was a large room that seemed to be built entirely of books. Stacked shelves lined all four walls from floor to ceiling, with interruptions for doors, windows and the fireplace almost there by sufferance. This, she would discover, was Angus's room, where he kept the results of his endless quest for knowledge over the years. Here he would sit most evenings, reading by the big window that looked out over Loch Shiel and the breathtaking monument they had passed earlier. Angus threw his Tam-o'-Shanter in the direction of a wooden hallstand inside the door, where it landed effortlessly on a hook, then he left her with a brief 'She'll be through in a minute.' She had never seen so many books outside a library – Angus had his own library! – and she walked about, touching them, running her fingers down the spines; it was like discovering hidden treasure.

'Is that you back at last then, Macdonald?' a woman's voice called from somewhere inside the house. 'And about time too! Where the hell have you been all this time? Running after those loose women in the Fort no doubt! You're always the same when you get let off the leash! You'll be drunk too, you useless creature!'

'Och, shutup!' Angus replied casually. 'Who are you to call anybody useless? There was never a Campbell anywhere that was any good to man nor beast. And aye, I am drunk, and there's not a loose woman within miles I havenae taken care of in the last few hours, now that you come to mention it, and a bloody good time I gave them too!'

'Then it'll be the first time,' the voice responded, coming nearer. 'There's nothing under that sporran of yours worth tuppence! Am I not the living proof of that, and isnae that the very reason you keep me prisoner in this terrible place, so that I canny tell anybody?'

'No, it's not,' Angus called back, his voice receding as the female voice came nearer. 'It's because you're the ugliest old witch for miles around, and I hate to be pitied by people when they see you with me!'

Kathy was beginning to panic slightly. She had heard many a verbal joust before, had taken her full part in more than a few, but these insults were being bandied around in voices that could've graced a garden party, the words were full of bile but they were delivered in honeyed tones. A fight was a fight, wasn't it? At least it was where she came from.

'Hello there,' said the female voice behind her, in exactly the same friendly tone of voice. 'And who are you then?'

Kathy turned to see an elderly woman, her white hair caught in a lazy bun at the back of her head with strands escaping in every direction. She was leaning heavily on a stick; the fabled cook left to Angus in the Major's will. 'I'm Kathy Kelly,' she said. 'Major Angus brought me here to help you out . . . I think.'

'Och, that's nice!' said the old lady pleasantly, advancing on her as she stood looking out of the window. In view of the equally pleasant conversation that had started as she and Angus had entered the house, Kathy wasn't entirely sure whether she should shake hands or take cover. Bunty made her way over, leaning heavily on her stick, and put out her hand. 'I'm Bunty,' she smiled. Her face was covered in wrinkles, yet she was incredibly beautiful, her soft, pink skin glowing through the lines, and smiling eyes a shade or two of blue deeper than her husband's. 'My, but you're a pale wee thing!' she said. 'Are you all right yourself? Here, sit you down by the fire and we'll get that useless creature to make you a cup of tea. Macdonald!' she shouted. 'Macdonald, whatever you're doing, stop it this minute and get your idle self in here!'

Angus had been unloading the car and was passing with his arms laden, but he threw the large parcels he was carrying on the floor with some force and entered the room.

'What is it, you old beast?' he asked amiably.

'Get the lassie a cup of tea this instant!' Bunty commanded. 'She's frozen cold, so she is!'

Kathy opened her mouth to protest that she was no such thing, but both protagonists ignored her.

'Listen to her!' Angus muttered. 'Thinks she's the lady of the manor! Silly old sow!' but he went out of the door and headed into the depths of the house anyway, picking up the discarded parcels on the way.

'And you can stop acting the big man!' Bunty called after him.

'You're impressing no one here!' She turned to Kathy. 'You've got to treat them rough,' she said gently, 'get them by the scruff of the neck right at the beginning or you'll lose control for ever, mark my words!'

She turned awkwardly, heading for an armchair beside the fire and Kathy instinctively moved to help her by taking her arm.

'Och, that's kind of you, lass,' the old woman said. 'I can see it'll be nice having you here. You'll be from Glasgow by the sound of you? Aye, I thought so. I've always wanted to go there, but that mean old miser keeps me prisoner here without a penny to my name.' Just then Angus came in with a tray, and Bunty continued speaking to Kathy while aiming her comments at him. 'And I'll bet he had nothing to do with picking you either,' she said. 'Left to him we'd have one of his fancy women under my roof!'

'*My* roof,' Angus corrected her, setting the tray down on a table beside his wife.

'Some floozy he'd had his way with so often that she'd be giving him discounts!' Bunty continued.

'Don't be so stupid!' Angus said, pouring tea into three cups. 'I do them so much good that *they* pay *me*. You just canny bear to face the truth, can you?'

'No more than you can tell it!' Bunty replied, and in the same breath and voice she said to Kathy, 'Help yourself to biscuits, lass.'

Kathy wasn't quite sure how to handle the situation, so she started to ask about her duties.

'Just keep her out of my way,' Angus said. 'I don't care if you leave the place like a pigsty, but keep that old woman away from me, that's all.' He lifted the teapot and refilled Bunty's cup, put milk and sugar in, stirred it, then carefully handed it to her.

'You're not married, are you, Kathy?' Bunty asked kindly.

Kathy shook her head.

'Good for you!' Bunty smiled. 'They're not worth it, you know. Men, that's the creatures I'm talking about. Look at the state of *me*, and all because I got in tow with that bundle of uselessness there!'

The bundle of uselessness continued to munch on a biscuit. 'And who else but me would've taken pity on you?' he asked. 'You were only a cook with nowhere to go when I offered you a roof over your head, and a rotten cook at that.'

'I've been the making of you, Angus Macdonald,' Bunty grinned knowingly. 'Everybody for miles around knows what an uncivilized thing you were when I took you on. Everybody knows what a difference I made to your life.'

'Aye, you did that!' he replied. 'You've made it a bloody misery all these years! When the hell are you going to die, woman?'

'Och, I'll see you out, make no mistake about that! I'll dance on your grave, Angus Macdonald, they'll have to drag me away at nightfall the next day, still dancing! Pass me one of those biscuits before you eat the lot.'

Angus passed the biscuits politely, and as he did so he said, 'I'll poison you first! That's my next project, I'm studying poisons.'

'Studying them? Your whole character's full of them!' Bunty said.

'I think you should have a lie down, Bunty,' Angus said. The tone of his voice hadn't altered, Kathy noticed, it could've been just another barb.

'Aye, I think I will,' she replied. 'Give me your arm, Macdonald.'

He carefully bent to help her out of the chair and looked to Kathy, who took Bunty's other arm.

'It's just through here,' he said, indicating with his head as they moved down the corridor. 'I've made the big room at the back into a bedroom for the ungrateful old cripple.'

'Just so that you can sneak out to meet your harlots!' Bunty responded, as they eased her on to the bed. 'I don't know why I've stood it so long, Macdonald, I'm too damned good for you!'

Angus gently put an arm under her legs and swung them on to the bed so that she could lie down. 'Go to sleep, woman,' he said, covering her with a quilt. 'Only this time, don't for God's sake wake up again!' He went to the kitchen and collected the large parcels he'd brought from Fort William. 'You can have the front bedroom upstairs if that's all right,' he said to Kathy. 'It has a fine view across the loch. And if anyone wants me, tell them not to bother looking for me. I've my knitting to do and I don't want to be disturbed.'

She took her courage in both hands, addressing his disappearing back. 'Um, can I ask, I mean, would you mind?'

Major Angus turned and stared at her with those wonderful eyes.

'What I'm trying to say is, would it be all right to maybe read some of your books?'

Angus smiled at her. 'Do you hear that, you ignorant Campbell witch?' he shouted at the closed door. 'At last we've got somebody in this house besides myself who can read!'

'Go you to hell!' Bunty's voice replied conversationally.

Angus laughed softly and turned away without answering Kathy's question, so she presumed he had no objections. He went off to do his solitary knitting, leaving her in his wake feeling more than a little bemused. From the moment she had entered the house the entire conversation between its inhabitants had veered between insults and kindness then back again without a moment's pause, yet there hadn't been any hint of venom throughout. No one had called God's wrath upon anyone else, no one had slumped to the floor sobbing like a child or singing a maudlin song. Was there something in the water up here?

9

It soon became clear that her duties with Bunty and Angus were whatever Kathy wished them to be. As long as she was there to help Bunty get back on both feet she had the run of the house, and she found that she wanted to help Bunty. She was a different person up here, there was no impulse to hit first just in case, no anger. She wasn't sure if it was the place or the people, or a combination of both, she only knew that she felt at home here. Bunty was still mistress of her own house, her mind was active and clear and all she needed was time for her hip to mend. They were in the kitchen and Bunty was baking, with Kathy as her fetcher and carrier.

'You must be fed up with hanging around an old woman!' she said.

'Fed up? No, no,' Kathy protested, 'I love being here with you!'

'My, but you're such a kind lass. Could you get that big sandwich tin out of the cupboard there and grease and flour it? Aye, that's the one, the big shallow affair. Have you done much baking, Kathy? No? Well, this is your chance to learn. I'm the best for hundreds of miles!' She chuckled loudly. 'You'll have to be able to cook and bake or you won't get a man!' she continued.

'Who says I want one?' Kathy replied wryly.

'Ah, so it's like that, is it?' Bunty laughed. 'I thought I sensed a sadness!'

Angus came into the kitchen carrying a piece of knitting with six different coloured balls of wool and several needles attached. 'Dear God!' he said, making himself a mug of coffee. 'Now the daft old woman's got the second sight!'

'I can certainly tell that you're not wanted here!' Bunty

responded quietly. 'So be off with you before this bowl lands on your head, Macdonald!' She turned her attention once again to Kathy. 'We need the mixed spice and the ginger,' she said, and Kathy handed them to her. 'So!' Bunty said happily, adding treacle to the mixture in the bowl. 'You were going to tell me all about this love affair of yours that went wrong. He let you down, I'll bet.' She glanced at Angus as he left the kitchen, shaking his head and grinning. 'And we won't even look at that one, we'll just treat him with the contempt he deserves and ignore him,' she said dismissively. 'Well?'

Kathy laughed. 'It's no big deal,' she said. 'I was engaged and I called it off, that was all.'

'Och, away with you!' Bunty said. 'Anyone can see that you've been badly let down by some man who didnae deserve you in the first place!' She raised her voice. 'The way that one has been letting me down all my married life,' she called down the corridor, then lowering her voice again she said, 'What did he do then, this blaggard of a man?'

'I just didnae want to marry him,' Kathy said, shrugging her shoulders, 'I didnae want to marry anyone, he just took it for granted that I did.'

'Aye, well, they're all good at that! Macdonald himself would've been married sooner if he hadnae assumed that I'd jump at the chance,' she said happily. 'Took it for granted he was the only one interested, so I kept him at arm's length. So this man. You just broke it off? It was that simple?'

Kathy smiled but made no reply.

'Ah, I knew it!' Bunty said smugly. 'He had someone else, didn't he?'

'Well, in a way,' she said. 'He'd got this other lassie pregnant and he told me that if I didnae marry him soon he'd marry her instead.'

'Oh, the swine!' Bunty said in a quiet, shocked tone. 'He would've left the other lassie on her own with his bairn if you'd married him? He really said that?'

Kathy nodded.

'Well, you did the right thing there!' Bunty told her, wiping the sticky gingerbread mixture off her hands with a cloth. 'Even if you had wanted him, you wouldnae've after that, would you? You wouldnae want a man who could do that to any lassie, would you?'

'I didnae want him before that,' Kathy said. 'I kept trying to tell him without hurting him, only I left it too long and everyone got hurt.'

'Not you, surely? You knew you were better off without him?'

'Aye,' Kathy said, 'I knew that for sure.' But she had been hurt, of course she had. She would carry the grief for her lost child for ever, and even in those early days after it had happened she knew it would always scar her. Bunty had managed to get more out of her than she had ever told anyone or intended to and she had no idea how the old woman had done it, so to protect more secrets leaking out she changed the subject and asked how Bunty had hurt her hip.

'I see,' Bunty smiled amiably. 'You don't want to talk about it any more!'

'No, it isnae that . . .'

'Och, it's all right, I'm a nosey old woman!' she chuckled. 'Well, I was standing on the top step of the ladders putting curtains up,' she explained, 'and I fell. Have you ever heard anything so stupid? Only old folk fall off ladders, I felt so angry for making such a fool of myself.'

'Well, you're hardly a teenager, are you?' Kathy laughed.

'What a thing to say to a friend!' Bunty replied severely, feigning hurt. 'That's only on the outside, I'm seventeen years old in the inside, and that's where it counts!'

'I think I'm about ten!' Kathy grimaced.

'There was such a fuss! They had to take me to the Raigmore in Inverness in an ambulance.'

Angus came in again with his now empty mug. 'And despite everything I said, they insisted on bringing her back again,' he said quietly.

'You couldnae have lasted another day without me, and you know it!' Bunty replied.

'I offered them money to keep her for another week,' he said to no one in particular, 'or to send her back here and give me a bed there. But they'd had enough of her too, and as I was the legal owner of the baggage there was nothing I could do about it.'

'Listen to him!' Bunty said. 'Sobbed like a baby all the while I was lying in that hospital bed, the nurses told me, couldnae bear the thought of being without me. "For God's sake get up and take him away with you, the place is awash with his baby tears," that's what they said to me.'

'Tears of happiness,' Angus responded, going out the door once more, 'I don't deny it, that were cruelly turned to tears of sorrow when they told me I had to have her back home or they'd all resign in protest.'

'Och, get away with you! Look, you've dropped a stitch. Away and knit, you great nit!'

Angus wandered off, smiling to himself.

'What's he knitting?' Kathy asked.

'He's teaching himself Fair Isle,' Bunty replied brightly, pushing the gingerbread mixture into the oven. 'We'll be forced to wear things we don't want once he gets the hang of it. But don't you worry, he'll be on to something else soon.' She eased herself into a chair by the kitchen table. 'But at least it's not frogs. I barely managed to get through his frog phase.'

'I heard about that!' Kathy smiled.

'Everyone in Lochaber heard about it!' Bunty replied. 'I know that every living being has a right to life, but I canny abide frogs and things. Everybody's allowed something not to like, aren't they? Well frogs and things is mine. And as for those lizard creatures, scurrying about and turning their heads to look at you!' She shivered theatrically. 'Ugh! My son has told me of a few things he's seen in his travels. Apparently, in India, they have cockroaches four inches long, and they can fly! We have enough trouble with those damned midgies, but can you imagine those things coming at you? He says they turn and look at you too. And there are fishes somewhere that use their fins to walk out of water! Now that's not right, is it? And I bet they turn and look at you too!'

She shivered again. 'Things that do what they're not supposed to give me the grues!'

Kathy laughed with her, but she could see that Bunty was tiring. 'Why don't you have a lie down?' she suggested.

'Oh, I see. It's heave the old woman into her bed, is it?' Bunty asked severely, but she was getting up from the chair, leaning heavily on her stick. 'Well, I'll do it, but just to be polite, you understand! Now remember, don't let my gingerbread burn! Have a look at it in another hour and a half. Stick a knife in the middle, just pretend it's that swine of a man you had!' she chuckled to herself. 'And if it comes out with nothing sticking to it, take the tray out and leave it on the table there to cool.'

Kathy nodded, giving Bunty her arm to lean on.

'Och, I don't know what things have come to,' she said, 'leaving an amateur in charge of my gingerbread that's famous all over the Highlands and Islands! And all because of a pair of curtains too!'

They reached the sitting room that had been converted to a bedroom and Kathy went through the ritual of settling Bunty down for a rest.

'On second thoughts,' Bunty said, 'don't worry about it. I'll likely smell when it's ready myself.'

As Kathy gradually eased herself into whatever the job was meant to be, she and Bunty established a routine. She would take the older woman a cup of tea first thing in the morning and leave her to come awake. It was a matter of pride to Bunty that she should wash and dress herself, though Kathy knew it took her a great deal of effort and time, but what did either matter when she had an abundance of both? It was the way of life in these parts, there was little reason to go tearing around. Time passed slowly and easily, there was no pressure to be super-efficient and to run yourself ragged. Depending on how Bunty was feeling, she either slept through what in other parts would be considered to be lunchtime, or slept in the afternoon. Mealtimes were whenever people felt like eating, the clock wasn't important. And while Bunty slept Kathy would tidy up quietly or explore the house. It was an impressive place, full of oddly-shaped little rooms and others not so little. In one she discovered a collection of musical instruments, violins, violas, mandolins, all beautifully crafted in wood by Angus during that phase of his life. They took up the entire room, lying at various angles against the walls and the furniture, as though they had been delivered by mistake and simply forgotten. Lying at the back of the room were two beautiful dark wooden trunks, their entire surfaces covered in ornate carvings. She looked closer and ran her fingers over the wood, recognising individual scenes on the trunks. She traced carvings of the house she was standing in, the hills behind, boats on the loch and the wildlife, deer, otters, eagles, all exquisitely worked into the wood. In another room she found paintings in every style, delicate water-colours and strong oils, and from every school of art. There were some that were clearly influenced by Picasso, others Turner, all done by skilful artists or, she thought, coming to terms with Angus's ways, possibly by one. She was lost in examining the canvases when Angus entered the room, his knitting in his hands, and she sprang back, blushing to her toes at being discovered, desperately embarrassed at being caught snooping. Angus smiled and shrugged his shoulders.

'It's your home,' he said gently. 'Look where you want.' He walked forward and picked up a canvas that was clearly influenced by the cubists. 'Bunty hates this kind of thing,' he laughed. 'She's a realist, you see, likes things to be as they are supposed to be, hates anything out of place.'

'Like flying cockroaches and walking fish?' Kathy said.

'Aye. She told you that, did she? Our Rory is always writing home with stories he knows will make her grue, she kind of likes it in a funny way!'

'And do you like the cubists?'

'Och, it wasn't about *liking* them,' Angus replied. 'It was about finding out how they did it. Once you know that, there's no point in going on with it, is there?'

Kathy nodded, but she wasn't sure she really understood. To have the time and opportunity to do something you liked and did supremely well, that seemed to her a perfectly happy way to live, but Angus loved the finding out, not the actual doing, and she wondered if there would be a time when his curiosity would have led him in every available direction. What then?

'When I don't have anything to find out,' he said quietly, almost reading her thoughts, 'that's when I'll turn up my toes.'

'But all these things you have, the books, the musical instruments, the paintings, you must like them or you'd have sold them long ago.'

Angus shrugged again, turning his intense blue eyes on her, almost with disappointment.

'Why would I bother?' he asked. 'Why would I waste time selling the damn things when I could be using it learning something else? They don't matter, you see. As you said yourself, they're things, and things only have the value you want to put on them. It's knowledge that's important, the true value is in the knowledge itself.' Then he turned to leave, still knitting.

'The pattern,' Kathy said, indicating the work on his needles, 'it's really beautiful.'

'Och, aye, I suppose it is,' Angus replied, stopping and holding it up for examination. 'It looks much harder than it is, it's all in the tension really, and having an eye for what colours go together. It's not like Aran, mind, you couldnae do this while you were reading a book, you have to keep an eye on it. It's a bit like tapestry in that way.'

As he wandered off, she remembered the two carved trunks in the other room. 'Can I ask you something?'

Angus turned to look at her. 'Well?'

'The two trunks. Did you make them too?'

'Aye,' he smiled. 'Took me a bit of time too. That was one of my hardest jobs, but I have to say I was pleased with them,' he chuckled quietly. 'They're for the Campbell woman and myself when the time comes.'

Kathy stared at him for a long moment before she understood, then she didn't believe she did. 'They're not ... you don't mean ... ?'

'Aye.' He smiled at her kindly. 'They're coffins. Did you not realise that?'

Kathy shook her head. He had made coffins for himself and Bunty!

'Och,' he said softly, 'you're not shocked are you?'

'No, no . . .' she lied, aware that her eyes were wide with shock.

'I see that you are!' he laughed. 'It was something I wanted to try and I had to work so hard that I suppose my pride took over,' he explained. 'It seemed a good way of putting it to use. It's all arranged. When the time comes they're for Bunty and me, we'll be cremated in them.'

Kathy was even more shocked than she had been. 'You're going to *burn* them? But they're beautiful! All that work!'

'Aye, but at the time I was learning an art,' he explained again patiently. 'And as I say, they're only things, aren't they?'

As he was talking she noticed that he was no longer looking as he knitted, and as he wandered off, leaving her to examine his past artistic experiments, she sensed that his Fair Isle period would shortly be drawing to a close too, Angus had already worked it out.

He was the most generous individual she had ever encountered. There she was, a stranger in his home, and a Lowlander at that, not a local, and fair enough, he needed her to keep an eye on Bunty, but he showed none of the irritation the elderly often feel when their routines are disrupted or their familiar territory invaded. In the evenings the three of them would sit together in the big room at the front of the house, Bunty doing a crossword and swearing at it in that gentle accent that sounded like a lullaby for a baby, or sewing, 'Though no Campbell could ever sew as well as me,' as Angus noted.

'Shutup, you great fool!' Bunty would reply.

'If you have any problems with that crossword, just ask,' he'd say. 'You canny expect a Campbell to be literate after all.'

'Hell,' Bunty would say archly, 'will freeze over before I ask for your help, Macdonald!' and Angus would smile and turn back to what he was doing. He would sit by the big window in the gathering dusk, reading, or knitting, looking up contentedly every now and again to gaze over Loch Shiel, and Kathy would sit with him, a small table between them, sharing it all, and still he showed no resentment that she was intruding on his private, quiet moments.

'The books,' she said one night as they sat reading by the window. 'They're not "just things" then?'

It had been weeks since they had had that particular conversation, but Angus answered instantly. 'No, no, of course not!' he replied. 'Books are different from everything else. Every time you read a book you find something new in the very same words, a book is never the same twice. You're always learning with books, you never finish.' He looked at the book open in front of her and smiled. 'Sure, you know that already.'

She was learning from him too, she knew that just as surely. She had never met anyone she was more in tune with, they seemed to be naturally and instantly on the same wavelength. Whenever she encountered him about the house or on the hills outside, whenever they spoke, she felt a pang of excitement in the pit of her stomach. Angus excited her, his mind, his thoughts, the soft, gentle way he spoke to her, the way he looked at her. If she hadn't known him, if she had seen him on the streets of Fort William, she knew she would've laughed at him, however quietly. She would've glanced at his kilt, the Tam-o'-Shanter with the enormous feather sitting on top of the long white hair and beard, and made a swift, superficial judgement that he was a bit weird; people did that all the time, of course, made swift, superficial judgements about each other. But now that she knew him, she realised how much she admired him. No, that wasn't it. She *loved* this man. '*He's nearly eighty!*' her voice echoed in her mind. '*You daft bugger, Kathy Kelly!*' and she laughed.

Angus looked up. 'What?' he asked.

She shook her head, still laughing, then to change the subject she said, 'Nothing. Would you like a cup of tea?'

She loved watching the different lights flit across the loch, with the monument as the focal point. In the early morning there would sometimes be a purple-tinted haze, turning through the spectrum to gold as the sun slowly broke through. When a shaft of sunlight pierced the cloud, it would suddenly illuminate the green of the ferns and trees and the purple of the heather and thistles. Where light found rock high on the mountainsides, the seemingly flat surface would break into facets of light and shade, small crystals being uncovered as bright, silvery, reflective shards. It was like the magic painting books she remembered as a child, where one sweep of a water-laden brush replaced black and white with a few colours. The colours were never as vivid as you expected or wanted them to be, but that wasn't the point, it was the magic of the thing that impressed you. But the magic colours uncovered on the hillsides by the shafts of light exceeded all your expectations, all your hopes, and then they exceeded themselves again next time. In the evening, with the last rays of the sun turning the waters of Loch Shiel orange, the deer would come down from the hills to graze in the silence. And there wasn't a silence like it. It wasn't simply an absence of noise; the silence itself could be heard, it had its own sound. But it was a sound you didn't hear exactly, you felt it somehow. Even when it rained there was a gentle, soft grey light about the place, and now and then a bright rainbow, with colours so vibrant that you couldn't believe they hadn't been painted on, would straddle the waters of the loch. There were times when it seemed too perfect, too picturesque, and then you remembered that Glenfinnan had stood here exactly like this, unchanged for hundreds of years, and even without the monument it had been naturally picturesque for thousands of years.

The monument, though, dated only from 1815. It was commissioned by a local landowner, Alexander Macdonald of Glenaladale, who, it was said, had been irked by the building of a monument to the English Admiral Nelson on Edinburgh's Calton Hill. A man who enjoyed life to excess and had a leaning towards the romantic and the theatrical, Alexander Macdonald decided that the sacrifice of the Highlanders in the Forty-Five should be honoured at Glenfinnan, though, as was his custom, he omitted to pay the architect, James Gillespie Graham, for his work on the tower. The monument commemorated the day when Prince Charles Edward Stuart, 'Bonnie Prince Charlie', first raised the Jacobite banner on mainland soil, and proclaimed his exiled Catholic father James VIII of Scotland and III of England and Ireland. Thus the ill-fated rebellion of 1745 had been started, leading eight months later to Culloden and the decimation of the Highlands and the clan system. Kathy, sitting in companionable silence with Angus and Bunty during those evenings, devoured the books in Angus's private library, discovering a history she hadn't known existed, because Scottish schoolchildren were deliberately force-fed English history, presumably in case learning of the tragedies in their own country's past would incite them to rebel again. And being so near to where it had actually started as she read, with living history just feet away in any direction, intensified the impact of what she was learning. Every day she walked on land the Jacobites had walked on, the Prince and his followers had arrived by boat on the loch she lived beside, and they had probably stopped to gaze at the perfection of the changing light playing on the water and the mountains, just as she did. The Prince and his party were rowed up Loch Shiel from Glenaladale on 19 August 1745, arriving at Glenfinnan after midday, and there the standard had been raised, exactly where, some said, Macdonald's tower would be built seventy years later, or, according to others, on the hillside beyond, below Angus's land, on Torr a Choit, Hill of the Boat, because it looked like an upturned boat.

If there is nothing Scots like better than romantic myth it is romantic myth that turns out tragically; if St Jude was indeed the patron saint of hopeless cases he must've been a Scot. And so the story of Bonnie Prince Charlie's doomed adventure would still be bringing tears to the eyes of Scots exiles across the world for generations, whether they knew the real story or not. Some of the finest Scottish songs were written in honour of Charlie and the Forty-Five, beautiful and haunting, as long as you didn't stop to examine the futility, the tragedy and self-delusion of the events they commemorated. Kathy remembered singing in the school choir when she was a child. The song was 'The Skye Boat Song', much beloved of Catholic schools, since had the Stuart dynasty been re-established, Scotland would've become a Catholic country. There had been, she recalled, a great deal of effort put in to teaching the children to harmonise, and she had sung the descant, which seemed appropriate, given that she had felt out of tune her entire life. The Young Pretender, a tall, slim, handsome, bisexual Frenchman, drew support from the all-powerful clan chiefs, who pledged their subjects to the Jacobite cause, ordinary Highlanders obliged to die for their chiefs. And die they did, in great numbers, though worse was to come. The Prince escaped five months after Culloden, being conducted from one place of safety to another, often barely one step ahead of discovery and certain execution, and though he was a fugitive with the immense bounty of £30,000 on his head, he wasn't betrayed. He returned to France by ship from Loch nan Uamh, Loch of the Caves, where he had landed fourteen months before, leaving 'his' people to face the terrors of the Duke of Cumberland's army as it marched north bent on retribution, 'Butcher Cumberland' as he came to be known. Cumberland's men, the very ones who, as Kathy remembered from her school trip, had suffered from vertigo as they marched through the mountains in search of Highland men, women and children to kill. They systematically pillaged and destroyed every village they came to and those who survived, already poor people, were left to starve. The London government passed laws demanding the surrender of weapons, banning the speaking of Gaelic and 'the wearing of the kilt, tartan, or any part of the Highland garb'. The clan chiefs were stripped of their powers and became ordinary landlords, though they were still strong enough to burn their tenants out of their homes and force them to leave the land some sixty years later, to be replaced by a more prized, lucrative crop: sheep. Generations of families that had survived the endeavours of Prince Charlie and the Jacobites, followed by the attentions of Butcher Cumberland and his men, were herded like cattle on to ships taking them to foreign lands in what became known as the Highland Clearances. 'Bonnie

Charlie's noo awa', Safely ower the friendly main,' went 'The Skye Boat Song'; yup, the royal personage made damned sure of that. 'Mony a heart will break in twa, Should he ne'er come back again.' Aye, but more Highland hearts would've kept beating had he stayed put in Paris in the first place. Had she known all this, she mused, she would've sung quite another descant to the powerful lament to 'the King across the water', she would've rewritten all the verses of the song come to that. Something along the lines of 'Why did ye come here in the first place?' and 'Don't bother comin' back again, We've got troubles of our own, So don't call us, we'll call you.' And of course Charlie didn't come back, he died a syphilitic, drink-sodden death in Italy, without gracing Scotland with his company ever again. He died, it was said, still thinking of his beloved Scotland and feeling sorry for himself. Oh, well, at least it confirmed that the blood running through his royal veins was indeed Scottish, it was probably near enough 100% proof when he died. She wondered if, like another maudlin, sentimental Celt of her acquaintance, Charlie Boy sang about too much rain falling in his life, or whatever tear-jerking ditty had been popular at the time.

Kathy looked up from her book and gazed down on the monument. The stone figure on top was assumed by most people to be a statue of Prince Charlie, but it wasn't; it was a representation of all the Highlanders who had suffered in the Forty-Five, a small enough tribute when you thought about it. And to think Old Con sobbed over the tragedies in his little life, she thought with a wry smile. What weeping, wailing and gnashing of teeth might there have been had he known the history of the Western Highlands? It would've been sackcloth and ashes for life! But Con didn't regard himself as a Scot, he wouldn't even have agreed to be called a Celt, come to that. Con was an Irishman in exile, he didn't belong in Scotland. One day, he knew, he would return 'home to the ould country', his fabled Emerald Isle, though he had never set foot there and never would. She hated his sentimentalism, his phoney emotion, yet something stirred in her as she learned of the Forty-Five and looked around her at where it had happened. Sorrow, pity, fellow-feeling, it was all of those things, and anger too at what had become of the people. She didn't know them, their fates had been played out a couple of hundred years before she had even known they had existed, but the geography had changed little and it was easy to imagine them haunting this place. At least she *hoped* it was imagination, '*Or else, dear God! Ah'm turnin' intae Con!*' she thought with horror.

She rarely thought of her father, or of the rest of the family. Even if Con was a tie, a loose tie that would be there till he died, Glasgow was a long way off, another world away. It was like being reborn; somehow she seemed to belong in Glenfinnan. All through her life in Glasgow she had felt out of place, everything about it was strange, as though she had landed there by mistake. Maybe, she thought, the stork had dropped her down the wrong chimney, and the child destined for Moncur Street had grown up in the Western Highlands instead, foul-mouthed and angry, raging at the stupid teuchters she had been forced to live among, just as Kathy had raged at the family she had been landed with. In Glasgow she had to keep one step ahead just to survive because nothing seemed to work for her, and the exertion kept her short-tempered and miserable. On the West Coast there was no effort, she just lived happily within her surroundings. It was like a time of renewal, too, after the disasters that had come along, one after another, and she grasped the chance to reinvent herself. Her life in the city was carefully filed away in a secret place in her mind that she would try her damnedest to forget existed. She was no longer who she had once been, she was now who she should always have been. A few months after leaving Glasgow she wrote a note to her cousin, Harry, because she and Harry had always shared a special bond. Not that they established a correspondence, that wasn't what she wanted, but she was reluctant to let the special link she had with him die. She told him that she didn't want anyone else to know where she was, that she was never coming back, and had been quite happy when Harry hadn't replied. He didn't have to reply, he was Harry, they understood each other. But he had her address, and one day she would be sorry she had given it to him.

10

In Stevenston Street Kathy was preparing herself for the last couple of acts of Con's departure. Act One was over. After three months that had seemed like three hundred years he had finally died and been carted out of his home, dressed in his HLI regalia and with his Child of Prague collection rumbling about inside his coffin. Act Two had been the Receiving, taking him to lie in St Alphonsus's chapel overnight, and now all she had to do was get through the funeral mass, then the reception afterwards. By that afternoon she would finally be free, even if there was the small matter of facing Frank McCabe about the missing money. So even though the drama was only halfway finished it felt more like being on the home stretch, and this time, when she got home to Glenfinnan, she wouldn't be keeping in touch with Harry. She wouldn't make that mistake again.

She didn't know if she had any real justification for being disappointed in her cousin, but she was. Jessie had laughed at him, at his conjuring tricks and his fortune-telling, and she wondered if her aunt had simply known him better and so had fewer illusions from the start. But Kathy had always adored Harry. If she ever had to re-visit Glasgow – touch wood – she expected to find him happy, healthy and wealthy. It wasn't just his looks, though being so film-star gorgeous certainly helped pad out those illusions, it was everything about him. His good nature, his intelligence, his ability to understand all her confused thoughts throughout her life; there had never been a single thing she'd needed to explain to him, he had understood instinctively. To Harry she had entrusted her dreams of one day being a writer, when she had read a book she liked she had given it to him, bestowed it upon him as a golden gift, and Harry had taken it each time with his generous smile, silently sensitive to the precious treasure he had been given. He knew of her visits to art exhibitions, deep, dark secrets she never told anyone, and when she had discussed the peculiarities of their shared family, he smiled with easy understanding. Throughout her childhood Harry had been the keeper not only of her secrets, but more than that, of her soul. But when she had been forced back to Glasgow by the news of the onset of Con's illness five years before, it was Harry who had contacted her, he had brought this duty to her and laid it upon her. Her own fault, of course, for giving him her address, but still, it rankled that Harry of all people should assume she should know, that she wanted to know. And so she had come back. Why? There was no clear answer to that no matter how many times she had asked herself the question, but she knew that she had always been aware of family ties, even those she would've been happy not to have. She supposed her mother had instilled that into her, and then her own natural instinct to always complete the circle, to always end things properly, had compounded Lily's morality. She had done her best to keep in touch with Aggie after Lily's death because her mother would've wanted her to do so, and probably Con fell into that category too, especially since her brother, Peter, the adored absent son, had never again made contact. Her attendance, she supposed, fell into the duty category, not to Aggie or Con themselves, but to Lily. She did it because Lily would've been disappointed in her if she hadn't; she was fulfilling Lily's duty for her. And it was during that first phase of Con's illness that she met her cousin again after fifteen years. She had been so shocked by the meeting that she had to dig deep to rationalize it. Fifteen years was a long time, she told herself, people change, she had changed. What had she expected? The same fresh-faced boy, his early promise now blossomed into a mature, happy and successful man? Well, yes, that was exactly what she had expected, and no matter how hard she tried to convince herself that she had been expecting too much, the disillusion had found its way into cracks and crevices she didn't know existed in her vision of Harry, and had set there like concrete. Maybe somewhere she had always had her suspicions, but if she had, she had kept them locked away in her own private filing system. What was it Jessie had said of her son? 'Less there than meets the eye.' That was it.

The first time she saw him was at her father's bedside in the Royal Infirmary, just after the nerves in his spinal column had frozen for good. Con was lying on the fresh, crisp bed linen, so delighted with the attention he was receiving that you'd have thought someone had told him he would live for ever, and he barely acknowledged the arrival of the daughter he hadn't seen or heard of in all those years. It was as if, for both of them, they had seen each other hours ago, and neither had been anxious for the time to have passed quickly. 'Why the hell am Ah here?' she asked herself. If she had ever needed proof of the complete absence of affection between her father and herself, it was contained in that passing glance; she only hoped that wherever Lily was, she knew how much she was in her daughter's debt. But there again, Lily had been looking after someone for her all this time too. The man standing at the bed with his back to her looked familiar, but the impression was so *not* Harry that she decided not to recognise him. Then he turned round to face her and she felt a prop giving way somewhere in her life. He wore a white, shiny suit with a royal blue shirt open to mid-chest level, and dangling there – dear God, it *couldn't* be! – was a long gold chain with some sort of medal attached, the size of an old half-crown. She tore her gaze away and looked down to the floor. She had hoped this would stop her from giggling out loud, until she saw his bare feet inside a pair of Indian thong sandals. It must be a way-out doctor, she decided desperately, the medical profession had replaced the traditional white coat with a white suit, and perhaps they were more open these days to alternative outlooks, even to the mysticism of the East. Please, let it be that! Then she looked up at the face beneath the long, shaggy, dark blond hair and all was lost; it was indeed Harry. But still, she reminded herself, swift, superficial judgements were wrong; think of Angus, and how she could've dismissed him as an oddball just because of how he chose to look.

But this was *Harry*, not a stranger she might pass in the street, they had known each other all their lives. If this was the same Harry he should be wearing an understated, handmade suit, with a silk shirt and a discreetly expensive Hermes tie. His carefully coiffed locks should complement the tan he had picked up on a secluded beach somewhere exotic, and he should be carrying a neatly folded cashmere coat, with Gucci shoes on his feet. Instead he looked like the result of some hideous genetic accident. It was as if Mr Whippy the ice cream man, Jesus Christ and Medallion Man had for some reason been in a laboratory while experiments in fragmentation were being conducted. Only things had gone wrong, there had been an explosion and they had all ended up with bits of each other. '*They should sue*,' she thought grimly. But it was Harry. It *was* Harry.

After exchanging a few words with Con, whose attentions were anyway directed towards performing his suffering, humble martyr routine to a new audience, she and Harry had gone to the Women's Voluntary Service cafeteria on the ground floor of the hospital. She would've preferred to go elsewhere, but the thought of walking down Castle Street, of actually being seen with this apparition, was too much. Most people in hospitals, she reasoned, had other things on their minds, so they probably wouldn't notice the odd duo in their midst. Or so she thought. As they sat stirring their coffees she was aware of glances in their direction, and then reverential approaches from what she supposed were normal people with mental problems. They clasped Harry's hand and stared into his eyes, ecstatic smiles suffusing their faces, and on each he bestowed his benign attention and murmured a few words before they backed away, tears in their eyes. Kathy had no idea what to make of this, but her cousin, seeing the look on her face, quietly explained all. He was now a well-known, not to say renowned fortune teller, and he was no longer Harry Nicholson, he wasn't even Harry Harris, he was simply Hari; such was his importance and fame within Glasgow that he needed nothing more to identify him. His appointment book, which he called 'my client audience list', was booked up a year in advance at any given time, and he had been forced to invent a means of not being contacted by phone. He had a series of codes that had to be changed frequently as the wily Glaswegians, hellbent on receiving his forecasts, or perhaps desperate for a card trick, cracked each one. At the moment, if she wanted to speak to him, or his mother, Jessie, he informed her earnestly, she should let the phone ring three times, hang up, redial and let it ring twice, hang up again, and on the third attempt, let it ring four times, and on the fourth ring either he or his mother would know it was safe to answer. She watched in amazement as he took a notebook and pen from his pocket and wrote the sequence down before slipping it across the table to her, making her promise – 'On what?' she thought, suppressing a mad giggle. 'Ma faither's life?' – never to let anyone see it, no matter how much they might plead with her. She took the piece of paper and put it in her coat pocket, scrunching it into a ball as she did so; she thought she could assure Harry that she would neither divulge it, sell it, or use it, for that matter. The citizens of Glasgow, he explained, held him in such high esteem that he could barely venture outside his, or, rather, his mother's door, without being recognised and a few reassuring words requested by those who crossed his path. Harry had become Glasgow's very own guru, sought out by the famous, by footballers even, and for many Glaswegians few came more famous than that. She had felt slightly light-headed; never before had she regarded Glaswegians as being particularly stupid or gullible, but sitting before her, wearing thong sandals on bare feet in the middle of a chilly autumn and sipping coffee that was too hot, too weak and needed more milk, was the living proof that they must be. If she hadn't seen the way total strangers were still approaching him, she would've assumed by his conversation and appearance that he had gone gaga, but she could see the truth with her own eyes: they did worship her oddball cousin. Had this happened, she wondered, after she had gone? The citizens of Glasgow couldn't have been like that while she lived there, she would've noticed, surely? Had some alien species landed and brainwashed them all? Was it like the sci-fi film she remembered from when she was a child, *The*

Bodysnatchers? Had pods containing embryo Doppelgänger Glaswegians been deposited in the backcourts of tenements, waiting for the tenants to fall asleep before being taken over by the physically identical creatures growing inside the pods? She laughed quietly to herself at the thought, then laughed again because it seemed more likely than Harry the Fortune Teller. He showed her the medallion around his neck, given to him by a grateful client, and when he insisted that she look closer, she saw that it had been specially designed for him. It was like a large coin surrounded with a frill of gold filigree, with Harry's profile pressed in to the centre. Harry the Queen, she smiled, then wondered if he was, in more ways than one. He was beaming with happiness. Warming to his theme he described the centre of his operations, a tiny single-end in Maryhill where he granted audiences to his clients; he thought it was important, apparently, to stay close to their roots. '*Aye*,' she thought, '*an' their money tae, Harry!*' The single-end was decked out in dark green chintz and the very best second-hand Victoriana, he had an absolute rule that everything had to be at least second-hand, had to have had a 'past life'. He could, he said very calmly and seriously, spot a reproduction piece by the aura it gave off, and he allowed nothing in the single-end to ever be cleaned, the spiders' webs and the dust were crucial to the aura. Spiders were his 'thing', he explained, they had mystical significance, he even had one on his business cards. He produced a card for her inspection and, sure enough, there it was, the single word 'Hari' with a tiny spider dangling by a thread from the first letter. Kathy tried to concentrate on a blank section of the card, because had she looked up and met her earnest cousin's gaze she knew she would giggle till she collapsed in a heap on the floor. In the middle of the one room in Maryhill, he continued, was a table, an old one, naturally, to avoid causing hell to the all-important aura, and on it was a crystal ball. Looking at him she wondered if he'd seen his psychiatrist lately, and if she could get to the door and take off before he caught her. And around the room were various other items that also held mystical significances. There was, for instance, a piece of stone sacred to Highlanders and, he said, teuchters keen to curse enemies arrived in a steady stream at his door to hold the stone and send its destructive vibes on their way. Kathy nodded seriously; no doubt Harry had discovered the 'sacred stone' in some backcourt, backcourts being particularly abundant in similar 'sacred stones'.

'I foretold your father's illness,' he intoned.

'So did Ah, Harry,' she laughed. Now she was back in Glasgow she found that the harsh accent she had thought lost for ever had re-established itself without a pause, and the thought depressed her almost as much as being there. 'Let's face it,' she said to the guru, 'the drink was aye bound tae get him in the end. No' think so?'

A slightly irritated but tolerant smile played across his lips, but he said nothing.

'Can Ah ask ye somethin', son?' she asked.

Harry nodded.

'Are yer feet no' freezin' cold in they sandals? Would ye no' be better tae just wear them in the summer, like?'

Harry smiled sadly. She didn't understand, he said, his aura kept him warm at all times, he didn't feel things in the same way as other people.

For some reason an old song popped in to Kathy's mind. '*I've got my aura to keep me warm.*' She almost laughed out loud, then she looked at him again and felt like crying.

'When did this happen tae ye?' she asked, her voice full of concern, despair and sympathy, that obviously passed over his head.

He took a deep breath and launched in to what she realised was his standard reply to an oft-asked question, if not the one Kathy had asked. 'I always knew I had the power,' he said, and she knew he could hear the words echoing mysteriously in his mind as he spoke, 'but I had to keep it in check. I had much to learn, I had my art to perfect before I gave it to my people.'

'Away for God's sake!' she said kindly, as if talking to a misguided but basically pleasant child. 'Harry, son, this is *me*! Kathy, remember? We've known each other since we were weans.'

The guru gazed at her sadly; he had been denied once.

'Harry, Ah don't mind ye foolin' a' these folk, except it tends tae be the poorer wans that are easiest fooled, an' they don't have money tae gie tae guys wi' crystal balls!' She laughed at her own double entendre. 'Everybody hastae earn a livin', that's fine, Ah can see that. But Harry, son, you don't really believe a' this, dae ye?'

Harry looked even sadder; denied twice. Then suddenly he screwed up his eyes and squinted at her so intensely that she had a hard time not giggling hysterically. He grasped her wrists in his hands, closed his eyes, breathed so deeply and evenly that he was in serious danger of hyperventilating. Kathy looked up, and all around them were anxious faces, witnesses to an impromptu guru session. 'I see,' Harry intoned, his voice dropping a couple of octaves, 'your future. I see you in a foreign land –'

Kathy yanked her wrists out of his grasp and got up to leave. 'Away tae hell, Harry, son! This is *me*, no' wanna the punters!' she said. 'You're the wan in the foreign land, it's called Nutterville!'

Thrice denied. He sighed; it happened to the best of gurus.

That had been their first meeting in fifteen years and, thereafter, throughout the progression of Con's illness, Kathy had contrived to keep Harry at arm's length. She had thought about it often during her blessed returns to Glenfinnan between crises. There had been no special link between them; it had all been an illusion. Harry was one of those people who are all things to all men, and women too, presumably. What she had thought of as deep and meaningful had in fact been a vacuum, everything, even the dearest dreams she had entrusted to him, went in one ear and out the other. She suspected that everyone he had ever met had thought they had a special relationship with him too, because Harry listened uncritically while smiling that lovely smile. He probably couldn't remember anything she had ever said to him, anything anyone else had ever said to him either for that matter, there was nothing inside that lovely head and never had been. But she had loved him as a child, as she had loved Jamie Crawford, and at least Harry had done her no harm. Well, no conscious harm anyway; it was hardly his fault that she had invested more in her vision of him than actually existed. How could Harry be blamed if people built castles in the air, just because that was all his mind consisted of? So on subsequent visits to Con she had avoided her cousin in order not to hurt the feelings of the Harry she had once thought he was, in case that shining creature should be in there somewhere, locked behind the banal gaze of the guru. Still, you couldn't help laughing when you thought about it. Harry Nicholson, true son of Eddie Harris the gangster, a soothsayer in sandals!

And now, a few years later, here they all were, the ungrieving daughter, Harry, the fortune-telling cousin, Jessie, his ex-whore mother with the germ fixation, sitting in their places in St Alphonsus's, with Con in his box at the front and Rentacrowd a few pews back, ready, willing and anxious to do their stuff but tolerant, if only just, of the family's right to be at the front. Kathy looked at Con's coffin; the twenty-four hour candles were still burning and, more to the point, they were still there, as Frank McCabe had promised. 'The auld bastard must be deid right enough, then,' she smiled to herself. She turned her gaze on Frank McCabe himself, all togged up in his business vestments, though still with the habitual slipper boots on his feet. The little priest had been worried that few people would turn up to see Con away, hence the booking of Rentacrowd, but many old-timers from the Barras had filed in behind what was left of the family. Some were missing, of course, Maggie, the Chief, the older Pearsons. She swallowed hard; the last thing she wanted to do was to start bubbling, that might well be mistaken for tears for Con. Hysterical laughter, dancing down the aisle with those castanets burning holes in her hands, all of that would be acceptable, she mused, but tears were definitely out. Frank McCabe started the mass. She had already decided that she would not be bobbing up and down as required, she would remain seated at all times. She was not of this faith, therefore, she reasoned, it would be patronizing to ape its rituals, which anyway had changed out of all recognition since the last time she'd been at a mass. And apart from that, she knew Frank McCabe would be watching her and her refusal to conform would drive him mad. It was all in English now too. Hadn't it still been in Latin in 1973 when Old Aggie had been seen away? She couldn't remember, but her mind had been full of other thoughts at that time, there had been no room for registering the language of the rituals. There was a shuffling noise behind her and a hand touched her shoulder. She looked round but didn't immediately recognise the man and woman standing there, so she smiled non-committally and faced the front once more. Then it hit her. Jamie Crawford! She felt the hairs on her neck stand up – another cliche that was true – and kept looking to the front rather than turning round again. What was she supposed to say anyway? What exactly was the etiquette for greeting your former lover, the father of the unfinished child you had secretly buried early one Sunday morning a lifetime ago? The woman must be – what was her name again? Angela; that was it. And how was she supposed to make conversation with *her*? Oh, you had the live baby, did you? How nice! Mine was dead. I just put her in a red satin box with hearts on it and stuck her in a muddy hole beside my mother.

Frank McCabe was well into his stride, he must've circled Con's coffin a dozen times, tossing the incense about like there wasn't a budget to consider. The time for Communion came and he stopped and stared at her. Kathy stared back. Behind her Rentacrowd waited for the bereaved daughter to take the host first, but the bereaved daughter returned the priest's stare with one of her own, and then added the sweetest of smiles to her coquettishly batting eyelashes, as the seconds ticked by. Behind her Jamie moved towards the altar, then others followed him, and the moment was over. There was another bizarre episode that she caught from the corner of her eye, when everyone turned to those on each side and shook hands. She couldn't remember anything like that. She was sitting in the front pew with Jessie, who had placed herself far to the left, out of the reach of all but the most determined germs, so she knew she could count on her not to attempt shaking hands, but she couldn't be as sure of the rest of the congregation, so she kept her back firmly turned to them.

'*Just let one of them try it,*' she thought savagely. '*Just let them try it!*' and was almost disappointed when no one did. What she needed at that moment was the chance to take a swing at someone, the feeling of fist on chin, but her lack of enthusiasm for the hand-shaking innovation had doubtless been put down to her deep level of grief, and a communal decision had obviously been taken not to intrude. There was a great deal of hymn singing, which was fair enough when you thought about it; you couldn't book a turn then only let them loose with a few choruses of 'God Save the Pope' to sing, after all. Then Frank McCabe was at it again, this time soaking the entire area as he circled the coffin dispensing holy water held by an altar *girl!* Kathy did a double take and then smiled slyly, catching Frank McCabe's eye. In her day only boys were allowed to assist at mass, but it wasn't, she suspected, as much a case of gender equality, as a lack of lads willing to take part that had let the girls in to this once jealously guarded male closed shop. The girl held a silver bowl into which the priest dipped a metal implement with a wire gauze head, then he vigor-ously shook it in the direction of Con's coffin, chanting as he did so. 'Dear God!' Kathy muttered audibly as he passed close by. 'Throw in some carbolic soap an' we'll gie him a quick scrub! Let it go at that, gie it a rest, wee man!' The priest's stride was broken for the briefest of nanoseconds before he reloaded and defiantly threw yet more water about, but the slight hesitation was enough to cheer her. Then the undertaker's men walked forward, moved the candles, lifted the coffin from the bier and performed a perfect about-turn. This was traditionally the hardest part of any funeral service, when the body was taken away; for genuine mourners it was the beginning of the final act. When they had carried Lily down this same aisle all those years ago, it was as if Kathy suddenly wakened from a trance and instead of following behind she had kept in step with the front pallbearers, desperately fighting the urge to get in front and demand that they stop right now and take her mother back. The moment had come too soon, she wasn't ready, but then she never would be. There was no such feeling about Con being taken away, it had all gone on far too long a time as far as she was concerned, not too short. Still, she went through the motions, falling in step behind the coffin, Frank McCabe in the lead, a prayer book and a rosary held in his hands, and the rest of the congregation following on behind her. Once outside, the undertaker took firm hold of her elbow and tried to guide her into a large, sleek limo behind the hearse. 'Ever broken an arm at a funeral?' she asked in a quiet, pleasant tone of voice, picked up from those masters of the conversational insult, Bunty and Angus Macdonald. The undertaker looked confused. 'Well this could be the day, sunshine!' she hissed, making sudden, savage eye contact with him while pulling her arm free. It was probably her own fault, she mused. She hadn't thought about the details, she had thought in gigantic leaps: Con in his box, Con in the chapel, Con out of the chapel, Con at the crematorium, she simply hadn't thought of protocol, like the big cars and who went in them. Her cousin, the guru, appeared at her elbow. 'My mother says you've to come with us,' he announced. In deference to the occasion he was wearing a crisp white shirt over his medallion, and he had ditched the shiny white suit in favour of an identically shiny one in bright fuchsia, with an all-over pattern of tiny spiders weaving tiny webs. There was no sign of a black tie, but black was represented in a pair of patent leather Doc Martens instead of the usual sandals; Harry, it seemed, preferred to wear his grief on his feet. Still, she was only too happy to follow the apparition to Jessie's Mercedes and sink gratefully into a deep leather backseat beside her aunt. She noticed without the slightest offence that Jessie moved further over in her own seat, all the better to keep bacteria at bay, the ever-present hankie held to her nose and mouth with the white, cotton-gloved hands. They exchanged brief, conspiratorial smiles, or at least Kathy thought Jessie was part of the exchange, though who could tell behind the hankie? As they moved off from outside the chapel, though, Kathy looked back at the defunct limo that had been earmarked for the chief mourner, and she threw back her head and laughed loudly. Beside her, Jessie did the same.

The Linn Crematorium was on the South Side of the city,

which meant that East Enders in the cortege had entered a foreign land. They may spend their holidays trekking the Sahara, ski-ing down Mont Blanc and paddling a canoe down the Orinoco in the 1990s, but for all Glaswegians the other side of their home town would for ever be regarded as truly 'abroad'. But if Con was to be cremated, and Kathy had decided that he was, the Linn in Lainshaw Drive was the nearest place where it could be done, and it gave the mourners a look at the alien landscape as they drove along. Old Con was bound for the St Mungo Chapel, the larger of the two in the Linn, and walking in Kathy was sure it would've met his need for the theatrical. At one end was a huge stained glass window in the shape of a Maltese Cross, bathing the chapel in shades of brilliant blues and yellows as the sun streamed through. There had been some heated discussion beforehand about what should happen to Con's ashes, with Father McCabe insisting that they be buried beside his wife, mother and sisters in St Kentigern's, and Kathy making it very clear to the undertaker that they must be dispersed in the crematorium's garden of remembrance as soon as possible. Even so, the undertaker had called again after receiving yet another demand from Frank McCabe, and Kathy had left him in even less doubt that he would take his orders from the one paying the bill. But she knew Father McCabe well of old, and so when they arrived she had buttonholed the undertaker and sought out the manager of the Linn, who both assured her that no one could countermand her instructions. After the initial cremation Con's remains would be put through a cremulator to grind the larger bones to dust, and by nine o'clock the next morning, his ashes would be dispersed without a priestly hand being laid on the urn. Still, she thought, she'd phone and make sure. She turned to the undertaker.

'Ye heard that, Mac, did ye?' she asked.

'Miss Kelly,' the undertaker protested, 'I had no intention of letting Father McCabe have his way. I'm not a Catholic, if that helps any.'

Kathy smiled. 'Why did ye no' say that at the start?' she asked. 'It woulda saved a' this aggravation, son.'

The undertaker dropped his gaze. 'However,' he said, 'there is the question of who should say a few words before the actual, um, service. He did say you were happy for him to do it. I suppose that is acceptable?'

Kathy nodded. 'No' acceptable exactly, but, aye, Ah said the wee swine could get his oar in.' The undertaker looked relieved. 'But a' the same, Ah think Ah'll make sure he understands the rules.'

Frank McCabe was standing below the lectern, readying himself for his speech, when Kathy grabbed his sleeve.

'Listen, wee man,' she said sternly. 'We'll have nae histrionics up there, understand?'

He glared at her in silence.

'What we're lookin' for on this sad occasion,' she continued glibly, 'is gettin' oota here double quick. Comprendez? Think minimal, that's what Ah'm sayin', nae embroidery. OK?'

He made no reply, but turned and climbed up behind the microphone. Kathy sat in the pew at the front, immediately below the lectern, with Jessie and the guru at the other end, a large gap between them.

'We are here today,' intoned Frank McCabe, 'to bid farewell to our dear friend Cornelius Patrick Kelly, a good man who suffered much in his life.'

'*Christ!*' Kathy thought, '*the auld bastard musta written his ain funeral address in advance!*'

'Widowed in 1968, he bore the loss of his wife, Lily, with all the fortitude that we had come to expect of him, and thereafter he devoted his life to caring for their only daughter.'

Inside Kathy's head alarm bells were ringing furiously as she entered into a frantic conversation with herself. '*Ye knew the wee bastard would double-cross ye! Why did ye let him up there in the first place?*'

'*Well, what dae Ah dae noo, then? If Ah keep ma mooth shut it'll be ower in a coupla minutes, then Ah'll gub him wance we're ootside.*'

'*Aye, well, that's wan option. But listen tae him!*'

'*Does it matter, really? OK, so it's no' the tyin' up o' the loose ends that ye'd prefer, but does it really matter?*'

'Beloved of his family and the community of which he has long been a pillar . . .' the priest droned on.

'Aye,' she said out loud, getting up from her seat and advancing on the lectern. 'It bloody does matter! Right, you, sunshine,' she said, grabbing Father McCabe by the arm. 'Oota there right now!'

There was a short tussle before the priest gave way, and she decided the matter by stamping hard on his slippered feet then pushing him roughly out to the side. Looking down from that position, the stunned faces before her seemed a very long way off, and she had no idea what she was going to say. Would 'The wee priest's a bloody liar!' do, she wondered? She cleared her throat. 'I'm sorry about this,' she smiled uncertainly, then she paused, breathed out, ditched the perfect English and spoke, as some would say, from the heart. 'Look, Ah've looked efter Auld Con these last months, but don't let anybody be under any illusions here. In fact, ye wouldnae be the people Ah think ye are if ye were. Ah didnae come back an' look efter him for *him*, Ah did it because ma Mammy would've wanted me tae dae it. So noo Ah'm gonny dae somethin' else for her, though Ah can hear her voice sayin' "Don't say anythin', Kathy, let it lie!" That's how she spent her life wi' ma Da, trying tae keep the peace, scared o' what he'd be like if any wee thing upset him, an' everybody here that knew her knows she didnae deserve that, she was a good wee wumman, too good for him. Everybody knows tae what ma Da was really like. He wasnae a good man, he was a drunk, an' no' a happy drunk, but a maudlin drunk at that. An' naebody could call him an' wee Lily soulmates either. He gied ma Mammy a life o' hell, her only escape was bein' burned tae death, but Ah bet it was preferable tae spendin' another thirty or forty years wi' him. Her entire life was spent trying to keep me an' ma brother fed and clothed, hidin' every penny frae him, payin' for his booze, payin' his debts, an' payin' the pawn back for everythin' he'd hawked for booze money. He pawned her weddin' ring that many times she had it oan a bitta elastic, though it always beat me why she wanted it back in the first place.'

There was total silence in the chapel.

'He was a rotten faither tae. When Ah was growin' up Ah

thought it was perfectly normal for a wee lassie tae help carry her Daddy tae his bed every night, stinkin' o' booze, then mop up his vomit before she could go tae bed hersel'.' She looked round the congregation. 'No' such a good laugh, no' such a rerr character noo, Auld Con, is he? But that's the truth, an' everybody knows it, everybody's always known it, so let's stop kiddin' on here.'

Again silence.

'So we'll go back tae the beginnin', only the wee man there,' she nodded in Frank McCabe's direction, 'won't be doin' the honours. This,' she said, gesturing towards the coffin, 'is what's left o' ma Da. He was a famous martyr, a victim who never suffered in silence. He caused his family a lotta pain an' misery, but he was true to the Catholic Church. Noo, some o' ye might think that cancels oot everythin' else, but personally, Ah don't. Take frae that what ye want.' She looked around at the undertaker. 'Where's the button on this thing Ah havtae press?' she asked.

The undertaker raced forward and made to press the button sending Con to his cremation.

'Naw, naw, son,' she smiled. 'Ah want tae dae it.' As she pressed the button the coffin began slowly to descend and she looked up, catching Father McCabe's eye. 'Game over,' she said firmly.

'That,' he announced gravely, in a voice that rumbled around the four walls and the pretty glass window, 'was a disgraceful thing to do!'

'*Christ, does he never gie up?*' she thought furiously. She grabbed the microphone again. 'Oh, afore everybody goes,' she said, 'Ah havtae pay tribute tae the priest here. For years noo he's been lookin' efter thousands o' pounds that ma Da got when Lily died, stoppin' him frae drinkin' it. Wasn't that good o' him? An' noo he's gonny gie it back tae the family.' Instantly she regretted it. In one sense it was entirely in character, but in another she had broken one rule of a lifetime, she had let Frank McCabe get to her. She looked across at Jessie, whose eyes above the hankie showed deep disappointment. Kathy shrugged her shoulders in apology, and after a moment Jessie gave an answering 'What the hell? Canny be helped noo' shrug in reply.

Frank McCabe was standing at the lectern, shocked into silence as the mourners began filing out, and as Jessie passed him her muffled voice muttered, 'So me an' the lassie'll be roond tae collect later then, *Father!*'

As they left the chapel Frank McCabe was still standing there, trying to regain his composure. If Kathy had let him get to her, she had certainly returned the compliment. 'And not even a hymn to see him away!' he called out, rallying his spirits.

Kathy turned round. 'Aye, well,' she said. 'We did thinka his usual anthem, "Into Each Life Some Rain Must Fall", or even "Nobody Knows the Troubles I've Seen", but tae be honest, either wan woulda turned ma stomach. But you can sing a wee song o' yer ain if ye like. "Who Wants To Be a Millionaire?" Somethin' like that?' As she turned towards the exit she called after her, 'An' we've got the receipt ye gave Con for the money, by the way. Ah think ye're up shit creek withoot a paddle, son.' Then she swanned out with casual ease and made her way back to the guru's car.

'Is that true?' Jessie asked. 'Did ye find somethin' then?'

'Naw,' Kathy replied with a laugh. 'Turned the place inside oot last night, couldnae find a sausage. But the wee swine doesnae know that, does he?'

11

They had arranged to have the reception at Lynch's Bar, something that would have warmed Old Con's heart; the Sarrie Heid it wasn't, but it was still a local bar that he knew well. On the journey back from the Linn Kathy wondered how many of the original mourners would be there, given her impromptu speech in 'honour' of her father, but then she reasoned that everyone there had either known her, or known of her all of her life. They would just put it down to 'that Kathy Kelly – you know what she's like,' but, of course, she was only 'that Kathy Kelly' when she was in Glasgow. Take her out of the city and she became someone else entirely, someone they wouldn't recognise, just as the people she lived and worked among in Glenfinnan wouldn't recognise 'that Kathy Kelly'. Sitting down at the first table she came to, she beckoned the manager over and asked him to serve up the meal, that there would be no speeches. That way, she thought, the thing could be got over as easily as possible, and anyone who felt offended by what she had said could absent themselves from any further proceedings. It had to be said, though, that there was a reassuring murmur about the place rather than total silence, so it didn't look like many had staged a boycott, apart from the good Father McCabe, that was, and he was no loss. He was probably back in his lair, looking out his passport and sunglasses for a quick trip to Rio, she thought, laughing at the picture that sprang into her mind of wee Frank wearing a sombrero, a gaudy shirt, Bermuda shorts and his boot slippers.

It was somewhere between the Scotch broth and the battered haddock and chips that the first approach was made. She looked up and found herself confronted by Jamie Crawford and the lady she had assumed, rightly, as it turned out, was his good lady wife. No mention was made of her alternative eulogy, Jamie simply wanted to introduce her to Angela. He was slightly heavier than she remembered and there was a hint of grey about his hair. Jessie had been right, though, that hairline definitely did start dangerously close to his eyebrows. He would be in his mid-forties now, a few years older than herself, and he had a smug, satisfied air that wasn't there before. If she didn't know better she would've thought Angela was being paraded to demonstrate what she had lost all those years ago. Angela was a thin, dark woman with nervous eyes, dressed in a neat black suit and high-necked white blouse, and somehow you had the feeling that she'd put a lot of thought into it. As she stood wringing an unfortunate pair of gloves in her hands, Kathy felt instinctively that today's oufit had been carefully put together, and then probably checked several times. She looked so, well, respectable, really.

'I've been so scared of meetin' you!' she said, in a high-pitched, querulous voice. She shook hands a little too enthusiastically. Her hand was hot and sticky. She sat in the chair beside Kathy without waiting to be invited, more from a fear of her knees knocking together if she stood than from familiarity. 'I've been hearin' about you ever since the first day I met James.' Kathy could hear in her shaky voice a strong attempt not to sound too Glasgow, like someone who thinks they've moved on enough to speak proper English but still can't quite stop dropping every 'g' without a lot of effort.

'*Well, that was a damned sight sooner than Ah hearda you!*' Kathy thought, but she said nothing and smiled politely.

'It was Kathy this, an' Kathy that,' Mrs Crawford continued nervously. She looked suddenly deeply sad and dropped her voice accordingly. 'Me an' James are sorry for your loss, by the way,' she intoned solemnly.

'Well, don't be,' Kathy replied, wondering if Angela had actually heard her diatribe in the Linn. 'Ah'm bloody sure Ah'm no'.'

Jamie Crawford, still standing beside her, frowned slightly. 'Why don't you bugger off, Jamie?' she said conversationally. 'Gie me an' Angela here a chance to get acquainted.'

His disapproving expression deepened to one of anxiety, but he went.

'So, Angela,' Kathy said. 'We never got the chance tae meet before you an' Jamie got married, an' Ah wondered what you'd be like tae.'

'I know, I know!' Angela replied. 'I'd heard that much aboot you that I actually suspected there must've been somethin' goin' on between you an' my James! I used to ask him, long before we got married, he had an awfy time tryin' to put my mind at ease. Said you were just pals, children that had grown up together. I've often wondered if that was true, or if I got him on the rebound!' She laughed happily, but she left the question hanging in the air.

'Aye, we were good pals when we were weans,' Kathy replied. 'But ye know how it is, ye don't keep the same pals wance ye get up a bit. So, where do you live these days?'

'We've lived in Moodiesburn since just after we got married,' Angela replied. 'It was all open fields then, our house was one of the first on the estate. But it's better now, there's houses all around, so it's not so isolated.' She smiled nervously. 'The Albion works closed down, of course, but James got a nice wee job with a local engineerin' firm, an' I've always been able to get some kind of work. I was a nursing auxiliary when we got married. Always said I wanted to do the full trainin' to become a nurse, it was a wee ambition of mine, but as James says, what does it matter as long as you're earnin'?'

'*Bastard*!' Kathy thought.

'We've only got the two children,' she continued, delving in her bag and coming out with several snapshots. 'Jane was the first,' she said, handing over a snap of a girl in her twenties.

Kathy felt her insides turn to liquid. This was the child Angela had been expecting at the same time as she had been carrying her own secret, doomed baby. This was what her baby could've looked like today, should've looked like. That tiny, unfinished human being she had placed in the red box all those years ago. She could've been handing around snaps of her and saying proudly, 'An' this is my Lily.' If she hadn't turned her out of her body before the child had a chance to grow to life, to be finished. If she, Kathy Kelly, hadn't been so *useless!* She closed her eyes for a second.

'Then James Junior came along two years later,' Angela trilled on. 'We stopped after two. I'd have liked more, but as James says, you can look after two properly, three might've stretched us financially.'

Jane and James Junior; how very predictable. The lassie should be grateful she didn't end up as Jamesina. The boy looked like his father, down to the low hairline, and Kathy was glad of the distraction. 'He looks just like Jamie,' she smiled, handing the photos back.

'Oh, I know!' Angela cried delightedly. 'I always said to him, "You can't deny *that* one!"'

Kathy wondered if there had been some attempt to deny the first one.

'But he's always been a good man, a good earner,' Angela said, as though trying to wipe out any hint of discord. 'We had our silver weddin' recently, see what he got me.' She held out her left hand to show off an eternity ring. 'It's only a half-hoop,' she said. 'As James says, what's the point of wastin' money on a full hoop when nobody ever sees the diamonds on the inside of your finger!'

'*Bastard!*' Kathy thought again. '*He would!*' Then she looked at the other rings, the plain wedding band below the half-hoop eternity ring, and above it – *it couldn't be!* '*It bloody well is!*' Kathy said to herself. Sitting proudly on top of the other two rings was the £66 solitaire diamond ring from H. Samuel she had once so reluctantly worn herself! She took Angela's hand in her own to look closer.

'They go nicely together, don't they?' Angela asked.

'Aye, aye, they do,' Kathy replied.

'Jamie picked my engagement ring himself, said he wanted it to be a surprise. Took me to Dino's in Sauchiehall Street one night and gave it to me over dinner,' she continued dreamily. 'He's thoughtful that way. It's not what I'd have picked myself, but I was quite pleased with it all the same. Not too flashy, just nice.'

'Aye,' Kathy said absently again, letting go of Angela's hand.

'*What a complete bastard he was,*' she thought, wishing there was a better insult to use. He hadn't even had the decency to buy the girl her own ring, he had simply taken the one he had given to Kathy, placed it back in its box, and presented it to Angela! And in Dino's too! She wondered if he'd arranged to have the remnants of their last meal together re-heated and served to him and Angela, and had a hard time stifling the laughter.

Just then Jamie came back with a tray of drinks; Cokes all round.

'*Tight git!*' Kathy thought. 'Angela's just been showin' me pictures o' yer weans,' she said pleasantly. 'Yer laddie looks awfy like you, Jamie, but yer lassie's had better luck, she looks like her mammy.'

Angela laughed happily, Jamie less so.

'An' she's been lettin' me see that nice ring you got her for her silver weddin', tae,' Kathy continued. 'Lovely ring, an' it goes that well wi' her engagement ring, tae.' She looked directly at him. 'Just as well ye went tae a' that trouble an' got her somethin' she really liked, it woulda been terrible if she didnae want a solitaire, eh, Jamie?'

Jamie busied himself with the terrible responsibility of telling one identical can of Coke from another and making sure they got to their rightful owners.

'To tell the truth,' Angela said beside them, holding her hand out to admire the adornments on her ring finger, 'I aye had a notion of a three in a twist. I used to look in the jewellers' windows, you know the way lassies do, Kathy?'

'Aye,' Kathy replied, still looking at Jamie, 'that big wan at the corner o' Argyle Street was a favourite. What was it called noo?'

'H. Samuel's!' Angela said delightedly. 'Did you look in there too?'

'Oh, a lotta folk looked in there, Angela!' Kathy replied meaningfully.

'Well, I only ever looked at the three in a twists, but if I'd got that it would never have sat right with the half-hoop come the day, would it?'

'Naw, ye're right there, Angela,' Kathy said kindly, still staring at Jamie. 'It wouldnae have sat well at a'. So well done then,

Jamie. When ye chose that nice solitaire specially for Angela, ye certainly chose well.'

Just then her cousin arrived at the table and announced that his mother wished a few words. Kathy looked up at Jessie, sitting by herself, and grinned. 'Don't you go away afore we get a few words thegither, noo, Jamie, son.'

Jamie made no reply.

When they reached Jessie's self-inflicted isolation, she dismissed her son. 'Me an' Kathy has things tae talk about, Harry son, so away you and play. Yer public awaits ye.'

Kathy watched in amusement as Harry was immediately swallowed up by the crowd; it hadn't occurred to her till that moment that most of them had come to Con's funeral to see a public appearance by Hari, rather than to see Con away.

'So,' Jessie said. 'Ye didnae find anythin'?'

Kathy shook her head.

'Well, it woulda been nice, but ye're right, it's no' really a problem. We can wave a bitta paper in the wee swine's face, he'll no' know whether it's the real McCoy or no'. An' we've got bigger guns than that anyway. But that was helluva stupid o' ye blurtin' it oot like that at the Linn! Ye gied him time tae think!'

'Ah know, Ah know, Ah'm sorry aboot that, Jessie, but ye know what Ah'm like –'

'Aye, ye aye ran aff at the mouth, Kathy, hen. Ye aye hadtae have the last word, even if it was a daft wan. But Christ, hen, Ah thought ye might've learned better ower the years! Still, as Ah say, it was never oor main weapon, so tae speak. When dae ye want to go roond and see the wee swine, then?'

'The morra? He'll probably have the place barricaded if we go roond the day, or else he'll have taken care no' tae be there. If we go the morra he'll mibbe have relaxed a bit. Eleven?'

'Aye, OK. Ah'll get Harry tae gie ye a shout at yer Da's place at eleven. Noo, Ah needtae get away frae here, the place is polluted.' She waved her hankie in the smoke-filled air, swiftly covering her nose and mouth with her other gloved hand. 'By the way, have ye heard anythin' frae yer brother?'

'Ah've no' seen or heard o' him since before ma Mammy died, Jessie. Wouldnae have entered ma mind tae try an' find him, but even if it did, Ah would've nae idea where to start lookin'.'

'He's in California, sure,' Jessie replied.

'Noo, how the hell dae you know that?'

'Hari-bloody-Kari, that's how Ah know, ya daft bugger! Everybody keeps in touch wi' him, sure ye did it yersel'.'

'Well, how did ye no' tell me before this?'

Jessie shrugged. 'Well, Ah reasoned that either ye knew or ye didnae want tae know, so it was nane o' ma business. He's in wanna they cult things oot there, or he was the last time Harry mentioned it. They're no' penpals nor nothin', Ah think it's just the odd line here an' there.'

'A *cult*?' Kathy asked incredulously. '*Peter*? Peter the Messiah is in a *cult*?'

'So Harry says. Harry says California's teemin' wi' them.'

Just then there was a great burst of laughter from the other side of the room.

'Oh, Christ!' Jessie moaned. 'Ah bet he's daein' conjurin' tricks! Away an' find oot, hen, tell him Ah'm waitin' here tae be taken hame.'

As Kathy pushed gently through the throng she discovered that Jessie had been right. Harry was sitting at a table, three small, differently coloured plastic cups in front of him, while the mourners tried to guess which cup had a coin concealed underneath. As each one got it wrong there would be another burst of laughter, then Harry's hands would move swiftly to confuse the issue even further.

'Harry, son,' she said quietly, 'yer mother wants ye.'

Harry got up, disentangling himself from the hands of his admirers as they clung to any part of him they could reach, all imploring him to give them an appointment for a reading. Then, with Kathy beside him, he made his way to where his mother was waiting impatiently for him.

'Did Ah no' tell ye no' tae start any o' that daft nonsense the day, Harry? Did Ah no' tell ye no' tae bring a' that magic stuff in yer pockets? Dae ye ever listen to a word Ah say?' Jessie demanded.

'I'm sorry,' said the guru contritely, turning to Kathy. 'It just seemed a bit gloomy to me, I thought the occasion needed to be brightened up.'

'It's a bloody *funeral!*' Jessie hissed at him. 'It's meant tae be bloody gloomy!' Then shaking her head she walked towards the door, leaving Harry to follow behind.

Poor Old Con, Kathy laughed. If ever there was a man who wouldn't have told those left behind not to grieve, it was him. He would've wanted weeping, wailing and tales of his brave yet humble suffering to be endlessly recounted at his wake, and mourners so deeply affected by his demise that they would be unable to lift their heads for weeks at least. And what had he got? He'd got Hari-Kari's magic tricks, performed to an appreciative and highly amused audience, he got giggles instead of grief. He would've wanted to go out in a vale of tears, and he'd gone out instead playing second fiddle to a game of Find the Two Bob Bit!

At the end of the event she made her way back to Con's house, feeling depressed at having to stay another night. She had planned to collect her bags and leave immediately after the close of play, finally go. Even if she couldn't get a train back to the West Coast till the following morning, she would stay in an hotel overnight; she just wanted her business here to be finished. But Jessie's story of the money in Frank McCabe's keeping had changed all that. Even after Jessie had left Con's house the previous evening, Kathy had wondered if the money was worth bothering about. She didn't care how much there was, or had been, she had never cared. When Lily died all those years ago she had vaguely assumed there would be money, but she had wanted no part of it then and wanted no part of it now. It was blood money, and apart from that, she didn't need it, so why disrupt her life for even one more night? Because of Father McCabe, the man who'd wanted to shoot a horse; that was why. She knew that had she shrugged her shoulders and gone it would always annoy her, she couldn't rest while he remained a loose end, while he thought he had success- fully kept not one, but two secrets. She and Jessie would get the money back, even if it was only to burn it in front of his eyes and, as for the other secret, well that was Jessie's business more than hers, so she'd play that one by ear. It wasn't the cash itself that was important, it was removing it from him; that's what made another night in Con's house bearable, if only just. And there was a lot to mull over. There was Peter for a start. She couldn't believe what she'd heard about him, and her spider-obsessed cousin was hardly the most reliable witness after all. But still, what Jessie had said about everyone keeping in touch with Harry was true. She had long ago worked out Harry's allure. He was a blank canvas, he had no thoughts or opinions, no critical faculty, he simply said what others wanted to hear and listened to what they said. Harry made no judgements, put up no arguments, because even that much mental ability was beyond him, and other people mistook this for the opposite of what it was, for something deep and meaningful. Everyone who encountered him thought they had this bond with him, that his smiling response to whatever they told him had as much mystical significance as his spiders had to him. He listened to their troubles and dreams without interrupting or introducing reality, therefore Harry understood them, only, as she had discovered herself, the whole point was that Harry didn't understand anything. So if there was one person in the world Peter would keep in touch with, it was bound to be Harry, that made sense, and being almost brainless, Harry wouldn't have thought of volunteering this contact with Lily and Con's almost forgotten firstborn. He would've told you had you asked, but he wouldn't have thought of telling you otherwise. *Thought?* A thought inside that handsome head would've died of loneliness, she thought, the first time she had ever detected any likeness between him and his lovely, blank sister. Not that it mattered to her what Peter was doing or where he was, she hadn't seen him in over thirty years and had scarcely given him a thought in that time. But she would ask Harry tomorrow, she decided, out of curiosity, just to put the matter to rest.

And then there was Jamie Crawford; he had taken care not to speak to her before he left. She had watched him going round the others, the old neighbours and Barras worthies, and they all smiled upon him. He was the local lad who had made something of himself, a favourite son of the East End who had worked hard and fought his way out of his circumstances to become a respectable member of society, though not of East End society, of course. As he left with the nervy Angela, Kathy noticed that he was holding her firmly by the upper arm, not holding her hand, not with an arm about her shoulders, not even with her arm possessively linked through his. He was holding on to her, propelling her through the door, not escorting or accompanying her. When he reached the door he had turned and glanced briefly at Kathy, then within an instant he was gone. '*An' good riddance tae you tae!*' she thought bitterly, sure that she was reflecting his thoughts. She hadn't really wanted to speak to him, she had only said so as a threat, knowing it was the last thing *he* wanted. But had they managed to have a few words she would've told him a thing or two, given him his character! She thought back to when they were children; she had never noticed that he was tight-fisted. Fair enough, he had very little as a child, but neither had anyone else, they were all in the same boat. Maybe that was why his meanness hadn't registered, maybe he had to get £66 to be able to afford to be mean. But she had no more than him, she probably had less, yet she didn't constantly think of ways not to spend what she now had. And that poor woman he was married to! He wasn't her husband, he was her keeper and she was his possession. That was why she would never be allowed to become a qualified nurse, to stop her straying outwith his control. That wavering, high-pitched voice, the nervous movements and deference to everything 'James says'; she'd probably been on Valium for years. And what had she got in return? A twee little Wimpey house in Moodiesburn with lots more twee houses all around to hem it in, the regulation two kids, one of each, naturally, and a half-hoop eternity ring to go with someone else's engagement ring, as a reward for sticking it out for twenty-five years! But why was she so angry? Angela wasn't a friend, she was just someone who'd turned up at the funeral of someone she never knew – 'Lucky sod!' – as an accessory to her husband, and though she wished the woman no harm, she knew that they could never have been close friends, and that had nothing to do with her marrying Jamie. She was angry because that was what Jamie Crawford had in mind for *her*, she realised. What he had wanted was the exact same captivity, only with Kathy imprisoned in the Wimpey house instead of Angela, and not from any kind of deep love either, but because she had been there, a handy, available female. He hadn't married Angela on the rebound, or as second choice to the love of his life, he married her because the nearest candidate had retired from the contest. Not that she could ever have surrendered as meekly as Angela, but she was angry at herself too for not getting out sooner. What if he hadn't arranged for a pregnant substitute to be waiting in the wings? Would she have been so reluctant to hurt Jamie's feelings that she might even have gone through with it? Everyone wanted it, everyone expected it, so there was certainly pressure to marry him; he was, by popular acclaim, 'a good man', after all, who'd 'never gie her ony trouble'. The thought that she might've settled for that enraged her almost as much as the certainty that he had wanted her to do so. And, of course, there was that other reason for her anger: he had won, and ratfinks had no business winning, it wasn't fair. He had achieved exactly what he had planned all his life and had escaped scot-free. Jamie Crawford hadn't suffered, he had felt no pain, and that just wasn't fair. She cast her mind back to that night in Moncur Street, when the child he would never know about had been born, and she thought of the pain she had carried ever since. Then she thought of the smiling, healthy twenty-something daughter in Angela's family snaps. She thought of her growing up in her family, talking, laughing, going to school, getting up to all sorts of mischief, while her daughter, her tiny scrap of a baby had never even made it to full term. All these years, as Jamie's other daughter had been living and growing, the baby she had called Lily after her mother, had been lying in the cold earth. She lay down on her folding bed and sobbed. That night, in Kathy's dreams, the child cried louder than ever, and who could blame her?

Harry's knock at the door came at ten o'clock the next morning.

He was wearing his everyday suit, the white one, she noticed, as he entered the small flat followed by his mother.

'You look like hell!' Jessie said by way of greeting, and perched once again on the kitchen stool after giving it another wipe-down.

'You try sleepin' on a camp bed an' see how you feel!' Kathy replied.

Jessie looked around and, taking in the two packed suitcases by the door, she said, 'Ah see ye're no' thinkin' o' hangin' aboot?'

'No' a second longer than Ah need tae.'

'Right, well,' she said, looking at Harry, 'tell Kathy aboot Peter then.'

He stared into the distance. 'He's in this commune thing. It's a cult. He's been in it for years. That's all I know.'

'Oh, for Christ's sake, Harry!' Jessie moaned. 'Get oan wi' it! Stop bein' mysterious, there's naebody here tae see ye but us! Noo tell Kathy everythin'!'

'Well I only know what he's told me. He's called Brother Peter now.'

Kathy and Jessie giggled and the guru looked peeved.

'The cult is in California, they kind of keep to themselves. They have their own place in the desert.'

'Whit dae they dae?' Kathy asked.

'They meditate and seek enlightenment,' Harry replied, or perhaps it was Hari.

Kathy and Jessie giggled again.

'I honestly don't know why you think it's so funny!' the guru protested. 'Lots of people seek enlightenment, it's a good thing, they get to know their inner selves better.'

'Harry, son,' Kathy replied gently, 'Ah've known ma brother, inner and outer, *very* well since Ah was a wean. If he wanted to know aboot hissel' he only hadtae ask me! An' as for him bein' in a cult, the only way he'd dae that was if he was the treasurer!'

'The leader,' the distressed guru continued, 'is an angel. His name is Walter.'

This time Jessie laughed uncontrollably for several minutes. 'My God!' she said, mopping her eyes. 'Ah havtae admit, Ah like that!

Jist thinka the effect oan Christianity if *he'd* been sent tae talk tae wee Mary insteeda that Gabriel fella. "Behold, I am the Angel Wally!" She'd have gied him the bum's rush before he got another word oot, so she would!' Jessie collapsed in another fit of laughter that once again sounded eerily like Old Aggie's and Kathy had to admit that it was the funniest thing she'd heard in ages. Peter – sorry – Brother Peter in a cult!

'Harry, son,' she giggled, 'ye must've got the spellin' wrang! Oor Peter never did a thing in his life that didnae have an *angle*, no' an *angel!*'

But though she was laughing she was secretly annoyed that her brother had picked on an angel, that he had access to an angel; angels had always been *her* thing. How dare Peter Kelly, how *like* him, to go chasing angels and find one before her! Was it any wonder she disliked him?

'I think you're both being unfair!' protested the guru with a petulant toss of his golden locks. 'I've often thought of doing the same thing.'

'Aye, son,' Jessie said, still wiping her eyes, 'but a perra wings wouldnae dae anythin' for ye, for wan thing they'd spoil the looka yer nice suits. Besides,' she said, slyly, 'the money's better ower here, isn't it? California is fulla nutters, ye'd be nothin' special ower there, they'd probably think ye were too normal an' send ye back oan the next plane!'

'So, dae ye hear frae Peter regularly?' Kathy asked brightly, trying hard not to upset her sensitive cousin, whose aura was looking severely dented, judging by the sour expression on his beautiful, chiselled features.

He shook his head. 'The odd card,' he said. 'I send him a Hallowe'en card every year.' His face now assumed a superior expression. 'I,' he said, 'do not believe in Christmas cards, you see.'

Jessie raised her eyebrows and threw in a shake of the head for double emphasis.

'Christmas,' continued the guru, 'is an artificial festival, it has nothing to do with the old ways and the old religion.'

'Aw, Harry, son!' Jessie said with feeling. 'Pipe doon for God's sake! Ye're among family here! Ye only spout that kinda crap when the punters are payin' for it!'

'An' he's still there, then?' Kathy asked. 'When did you last hear frae him?'

Harry handed over a postcard dated six months before. It said, 'It's harvest time. We're working hard in the vineyards,' and was signed 'Brother Peter and Sister Rose.'

'Who the hell's Sister Rose?' Kathy asked.

'His wife.'

'His *wife*? When did that happen?'

'Oh, a long time ago,' the guru replied distantly.

'Ye never told *me* that!' Jessie protested.

'You didn't ask,' Harry said, then he smiled smugly. 'You won't believe this,' he said, 'but his wife's mother is a client of mine! She came to me a couple of years ago, worried about her daughter and her son-in-law, thought they were involved in something odd in America.'

'The wumman must be psychic hersel',' Jessie muttered. 'Whit the hell was she daein' wastin' money goin' tae you?'

Harry ignored her. 'She was very impressed when I was able to tell her exactly what they were involved in.'

'An' did ye tell her ye were related tae her son-in-law?' Kathy asked.

Harry shook his head. 'Certainly not! She came to me because she had been guided to me, it was no coincidence. She could've gone to any mystic, but she came to me because I had the knowledge. We were brought together by unseen forces, the source of my knowledge is immaterial.'

Kathy and Jessie looked at each other and smiled. She turned the card over; there were six pictures on the front arranged in sequence, each one showing a different kind of front porch. Some were made of wood, others glass, some had the traditional rocking chair carefully positioned while others were inhabited by exotic foliage, leaving little room for human beings, of whom there were none anywhere. She and Jessie exchanged looks.

'Musta taken him a long time tae find such an interestin' card, no' think so?' Jessie asked scathingly.

'You don't understand,' the guru protested. 'It's esoteric.'

'Is that another word for bloody boring?' asked Jessie. 'Look, just gie Kathy his address. And put yer wee phone number oan the back, so that she doesnae havtae bother wi' a' that code nonsense, then ye can go an' sit in the car, son. She'll want tae let him know his Da's deid.'

'Brother Peter won't want to know,' Harry replied, reluctantly writing his precious mobile number on the front of one of his be-spidered cards. He turned it over and wrote down Peter's address in California. 'The cult doesn't recognise family ties.'

'Well, in that case,' Kathy said, 'he's been in it since he was born. He worked damn hard a' the years that Ah knew him tryin' no' tae recognise any o' us!' She looked at the address. 'What's that they call theirsels?'

'The Higher Seekers,' Harry said glumly.

'Is that no' wanna they bands?' Jessie asked, and Kathy laughed. 'Were they no' aroond at the same time as the Beatles? Sang kinda folk songs?'

'No, Mother,' Harry replied shortly. 'You're thinking of something else entirely.'

'That's us done noo,' said Jessie. 'When he calls me "Mother", ye know he's really annoyed, an' that buggers his aura tae hell for hours at a time!' She looked at her son. 'Away an' take Kathy's bags an' put them in the car noo, son,' she said kindly. 'We'll be doon in a minute. An' try tae stop lookin' as if somebody's made ye suck a lemon. Sure you know we're just havin' a wee joke wi' ye.'

When he'd gone she turned her attention to the forthcoming ambush of Father McCabe. 'Right, get yer things,' she said. 'We're off!'

'Dae ye no' want tae lay doon a few ground rules first?' Kathy asked.

'Ah've been plannin' this for years,' Jessie said with relish. 'Ah don't need tae work oot the tactics, Ah've been working oan it since the day Ah came hame early frae school an' heard Mammy an' Daddy talkin', hen! Get yer coat an' let's get this show oan the road!'

The Glenfinnan Monument: A memorial not to Prince Charles Edward Stuart, but to the Highlanders who fought in the 1745 Rebellion, and I defy anyone to look at it without wanting to tear off their clothes, run to the top of Ben Nevis and sing 'Bonnie Scotland I Adore Thee' at the top of their voice. The sentimental fool who had it built knew just what he was doing, the beauty of the place and the link to a hopeless cause, how the Scots love both!

12

Kathy had only been living in Glenfinnan for a month or so when Rory Macdonald arrived to see his mother. He'd been working in Argentina when his father's letter, telling him of Bunty's accident, had eventually found its way to him. She had been expecting, or perhaps she had just been hoping for, a younger version of Angus, a calm, pleasant, benign man of adventure, but he took her unawares. He was an inch or two taller than his father, with the same solid build only more muscular, probably, she thought, because of the physical work he did, and he had brown, curly hair and deep-set blue eyes in a square, tanned face; a handsome man, she decided. Bunty introduced her.

'This is Kathy,' she said, 'and Macdonald and me couldnae manage without her. She's come from Glasgow.'

A bored look crossed Rory Macdonald's face. 'Another Sassenach that thinks she belongs in the Highlands!' he sighed, looking away as he put his hand out unenthusiastically to shake hers.

Kathy was stung. 'I *am not* English!' she protested. 'I'm from Glasgow!'

Rory sighed. 'Ignorant, too, like all the rest,' he muttered. He looked at her, and she noticed that his eyes were the same shade as Bunty's. 'A Sassenach is a Lowlander,' he said, with exaggerated patience. 'The English are the extreme end of Lowlanders, I'll grant you, but everyone who isnae a Highlander is a Sassenach too, and it strikes me that you're no Highlander.'

'And it strikes me,' said Kathy defiantly, 'that you're one of the worst mannered people I've ever met!'

'Possibly,' he replied, turning away and looking out of the window over the loch. 'But it's not something I'll have to worry about. You won't last six months up here. Your sort never do.'

'My sort? What exactly is "my sort"?'

He turned again, looked her up and down, laughed quietly without replying, then turned back to the view. 'You know, Mother,' he said gently, 'wherever I go, this is the picture I carry in my mind. I see it last thing at night when I close my eyes and first thing in the morning when I open them again.'

Furious at being ignored, Kathy looked from Bunty to Angus and back again, but neither of them seemed to be in the least surprised at their son's behaviour. She had been prepared to make him account for his rudeness and his hasty, unfair assessment of her, but what could she do when the fight was entirely one-sided? How could she argue with someone who did not argue, but simply let the matter drop and die? Instead she marched from the room, then she waited outside for a moment to eavesdrop on their conversation and hear what they might say about her when she wasn't there. But the only remarks between them were about the happenings in Glenfinnan since his last visit some years before; they didn't even notice that she'd gone. She had adored Bunty and Angus from the first moment, but now she thought they must be as odd as their son. He had returned to home, hearth and family after an absence of years, yet as he'd walked in they had all greeted each other as though he'd only been gone a few minutes. Standing outside in the corridor, listening in vain for some remark about herself, Kathy went over Rory's arrival in her mind.

'It's yourself then, Rory,' Bunty had said, with a happy smile, admittedly, and Angus had looked up from his knitting and smiled warmly too.

'Aye, Father,' Rory had greeted his father. 'How's the leg, Mother?'

'Fine, fine,' Bunty had replied. 'Have you had something to eat?'

Rory nodded. 'And you're all right yourself, then, Father?'

'Aye,' Angus smiled, 'I'm fine, Rory, and you're looking well yourself.'

'The knitting looks good,' Rory remarked, sitting down at the table by the window across from Angus and looking out of the window. And that was it; no delighted yells, ferocious hugs, or tears of joy. With the minimum of greetings and no fuss whatsoever, the Macdonalds slotted effortlessly in to each other's company as though they had never been apart. The only one in the house to show any emotion had been Kathy, but her excited anticipation had quickly been turned to anger. She'd heard a great deal about Rory, and the fact that there were no family photos anywhere in the house – Angus felt such things were unnecessary conventions – had allowed her to build up a picture in her mind of a swashbuckling wild rover. Faced with the reality she had felt like slapping him. He had the bedroom across from hers at the front of the house, and every morning they would pass each other in total silence. She would look at him expecting some sort of greeting, 'Hello' would have done, even 'Buzz off' would've been something, but not a word passed Rory's lips, and she had the feeling that if she'd spoken first he would've ignored her, so she didn't. Kathy put up with it for nearly two weeks, the pressure of her anger building with each snub. She didn't care if he liked her, she just wanted a reaction. Everyone she had ever known had reacted to her, that was the basis of the way people talked about her as 'that Kathy Kelly'. Their impressions were often wrong, they saw her as brimming with confidence, for instance, though inside her head she always felt shy and awkward, others decided she went through life looking for an argument, and that wasn't true either, it was just that she didn't let things pass, she had opinions. She didn't really mind if the likes of Miss Smith, or Nigel Dewar and his cohort, the besotted Ida, loathed her for her less than deferential attitude. She had long ago accepted that, apart from her mother, Lily, and her cousin, Harry, her entire family and Father McCabe spent all their time in a rage against her, at least they knew she was alive. If there was one thing she could not stand it was being ignored, being treated like a non-person, and Rory Macdonald did just that. He looked straight through her without the slightest effort, he regarded her as unworthy of the briefest amount of attention, civil or otherwise. Finally she could stand it no more and found herself looking for an opportunity to have a go. It didn't take long to appear. She had been in the kitchen arranging tea and biscuits for Bunty and Angus, and Rory had strode in, picked up a cup and poured himself tea out of the pot she had just prepared, then he had departed in silence. Kathy picked up the tray and pursued him into the reading room, where Bunty and Angus were happily arguing.

'I told you at the outset, Macdonald,' Bunty was saying, 'I do not want a Fair Isle cardy, and I won't have one!'

'Did anybody offer to make you one then?' Angus replied, calmly knitting.

'But I know you, don't you think I don't! I can see that you've been knitting that thing hanging on they needles there, in my favourite colours! You don't fool me, Macdonald, you can put it on one of the hill beasts, but you're not putting it on me!'

'It would look better on one of the hill beasts than on you,' Angus replied. 'Yon black lass that's about to calve any minute, she'd set it off with more style than you ever would, that's for sure.'

'Well, you'll be the expert on cows,' Bunty replied sweetly, 'seeing as you're always running after them in the bars of Fort William!'

'I keep telling you, woman,' Angus said happily. 'They run after me, there's nothing I can do about it, it's this natural attraction I have.'

'Like dung has for dung beetles!'

Into this came the tray-bearing Kathy, her feet almost screeching along the corridor in Rory's wake. 'Here you!' she called furiously after him.

Rory turned round in the middle of the room and looked at her with his easy, calm stare.

'Is there something you want?' he asked, so casually that she felt like throwing the full tray at him.

'You could've asked if there was enough tea to go round before you poured yourself a cup!'

'And was there?'

'Aye, but –'

'So you didnae have to go down the hill to the well and haul up a bucket of water, then hike back up again and boil another pot because I'd poured a cup of tea in my own home?' he asked sarcastically.

'You know fine well –'

Rory shrugged his shoulders and sat down by the window; conversation over.

'I don't think I've ever met anybody as ignorant as you!' Kathy protested. 'Do you know the meaning of civility?'

'Why?' he asked, without looking up. 'Don't you? You'll find it in one of the dictionaries on the shelf there.'

'That's what I mean!' Kathy exploded. 'Never a polite word when a nasty crack will do!'

Rory made no reply. He sat sipping his tea and turning the pages of a newspaper on the table in front of him. The silence stretched.

'Well?' Kathy demanded, marching close up to him.

He looked up. 'Well what?' he asked, totally unfazed.

'Have you nothing to say?'

'No,' he said, and turned his attention once again to the news-paper. 'I see,' he said to his father, 'that Lochaber are doing well at the shinty.'

'Aye, they had a bad patch for a while there, but they're coming away fine again. I saw them rattle a few past Kingussie the other week, and I was thinking to myself that it was the best I'd seen them for a good few seasons.'

Kathy looked across at Bunty, who was doing a crossword puzzle by the fire as though nothing had happened. She couldn't believe it. Her attack on Rory was all but an invitation to see him outside, and not only did no one seem upset, but they hadn't even noticed. Placing the tray on the table she left the room and sat in the kitchen, listening to the amiable chatter coming along the corridor as the Macdonalds finished their tea. After a time she heard Rory's footsteps coming towards the kitchen and she made a dash for the sink so that she would appear to be doing some urgent cleaning instead of stoking her wrath. She heard the tray being placed on the kitchen table and then he left without a word. She tried, she really tried, but she had to say *something*. 'So why have you nothing to say?' she asked.

Rory stopped at the door and turned to look at her. 'Why have you such a need to be spoken to?' he asked.

'I don't! I just think that if people are living in the same space they can at least be polite to each other!' Where was this coming from, she wondered? It was the exact opposite of the way she had lived her entire life. She decided not to think about that now.

'I don't have anything to say,' he replied calmly, holding his hands out at his sides, palms upwards. 'Are you saying I have to make small talk with you even though I haven't a word I want to say? Would it make you feel better if I commented on the weather?'

Kathy felt she'd been manoeuvred into a corner.

'Maybe,' he continued calmly and quietly, 'that's what really annoys you, the fact that there isn't anything I want to say to you?'

'Don't flatter yourself, chum!'

'Och, well,' he replied with a slight smile as he turned to go, 'I don't suppose I could've expected anything more original than that from you, could I?'

She couldn't explain why he irritated her so much. Maybe it was because everything in her new life had seemed so perfect, then along he'd come like a big, black cloud and spoiled it. Or perhaps it was because he had effortlessly usurped her role as annoyer-in-chief. That was what she had done all her life, so she should know how to handle this situation, but she couldn't; with Rory Macdonald she was always that one vital step behind. Not that it mattered much, because the situation was soon brought to an end. Rory walked in to the kitchen one day and said to Bunty, 'That's me off now, Mother.'

'Fine, fine,' Bunty replied, scarcely looking up from the pastry she was rolling. 'Have you seen Macdonald?'

'Aye, he's driving me to the station.'

'Well, then, keep in touch!' Bunty replied, still rolling her pastry.

Kathy was washing up at the sink and looked up as he left, but he didn't say a word or return her glance.

'Where's he going?' she asked Bunty, thinking that it couldn't be what she thought it was.

'Och,' said Bunty, looking up, 'isn't that daft of me? Do you know, I forgot to ask! It'll be somewhere,' she said decidedly.

'You mean that's him gone away? He's not just going down to Fort William? He's *gone*?'

'Aye,' Bunty smiled gently. 'He's gone back. Where was it he was before he came home? Argentina was it? Maybe that's where he's gone then.'

'Just like that?' Kathy asked.

'Well, what would you expect?' Bunty laughed. 'How else would he go?'

'Did you know he was going?' Kathy persisted.

'Well, not in so many words,' Bunty said cheerily. 'I had a kind of feeling he'd be away soon.' She looked up at Kathy. 'You'll miss him, won't you?'

Kathy didn't know what to say. She put her head down at the sink and ran the water. 'No' if Ah had a hatchet in ma hand, Ah wouldnae!' she muttered under her breath.

'I was pleased that you two got along so well!' Bunty continued, as Kathy looked up at her sideways to see if she was joking. 'He doesnae take to many people the way he took to you.'

'*Dear God!*' Kathy thought. '*Whit's he like if he really hates somebody?*'

'He's that like Macdonald when he was young!' Bunty continued.

'I didnae think he was anything like Angus!' Kathy said, almost unable to control herself.

'Och, but he is! He's like him in every way, even if he has got my eyes. That same friendly nature when he likes somebody, but nobody has ever crossed our Rory twice, not even when he was a laddie. And he looks like his father too. You didnae know

Macdonald when he was young. Oh, but he was a handsome brute! I'd watch him from the kitchen as I was working, and he'd be outside there, chopping wood or digging a tree root up, and the sight of him stripped to the waist, the sweat on his back so that you could see every muscle, those broad, broad shoulders!' Bunty had stopped rolling her pastry and was gazing into the distance, a happy smile on her face. 'I'm telling you,' she said with a sudden laugh, 'there were times I had to lock myself in to stop from rushing out there and ravishing him!'

'Bunty!' Kathy laughed, slightly taken aback.

'What?' Bunty asked. 'Just because we're a pair of decrepit old creatures doesnae mean we havnae had our times, I can tell you that! He could keep going all night in his prime, and all day too, and so could I for that matter! Many's the time we did!'

Kathy gasped. 'I don't think I want to hear this!' she laughed, not altogether in jest.

'Och, you don't know you're living till you've been lying out in the heather together, going at it like knives! I'm telling you, Kathy, Cromwell's army coming up the hill there couldnae have stopped us once we'd started!'

'Bunty!' Kathy said, brandishing a washing cloth, 'if you don't stop it this minute, I'll let you have this wet cloth across the face!'

Bunty giggled. 'Aye, well,' she said wistfully. 'The memories are still there, that's all I'm saying, and Angus and me have more than most folk! Angus did what he always did, he learned everything there was to know about sex, and by God, he put it to good use!'

'Maybe I'd better run the cold tap on this cloth before I throw it!' Kathy threatened, as Bunty turned once more to her pastry, giggling delightedly.

Later that day Angus came back from taking his son to the station and started moving things from the upstairs bedroom he shared with Bunty before her accident, to the downstairs room where she had been sleeping to save her climbing stairs.

'I'm being forced to move in to her bed,' he said to no one in particular. 'I'll be dead in a week, the woman's insatiable!'

Bunty was cutting the pie she had made earlier, Kathy holding a plate by her side.

'I know that!' Kathy murmured, nudging Bunty with her elbow. 'I've heard all the gory details, no need to tell me!'

Bunty leaned against her, shaking with laughter. 'Not all of them,' she giggled. 'There were times I could tell you about would make your hair fall out, never mind put a curl in it!'

'Well, *don't you dare!*' Kathy scolded her, and the two women stood together giggling.

'I won't get a minute's sleep tonight,' Angus muttered in mock complaint as he passed. 'Whatever you're making for the tea tonight, you could maybe do me a favour to save my life. Could you put in a wee nip of bromide, do you think?' and he winked at Bunty.

Kathy looked at the two of them and the obvious adoration that passed between them. Rory like Angus? Never!

The years she spent with Bunty and Angus were the happiest of Kathy Kelly's life, that would always be her view. Though Bunty recovered from her broken hip it had weakened her, and she and Angus never moved out of their bedroom in exile, it became a permanent fixture. Bunty was still fit and agile, though judging from Angus's attitude, she wasn't as she had been before. Between them Kathy and Bunty kept the house running smoothly, and Angus had someone there, just in case. His enthusiasms absorbed him and took up his time as they always had, but he wasn't a selfish man, he was thinking of Bunty all along. If he'd changed his lifestyle to care for her she would've known it was because of her failing health and she would probably have failed faster, but this way he knew she was being looked after without sending the message to her that her usefulness was over. She was still his wife, she cooked for him, baked for him, washed, mended and argued, but Kathy did the legwork and the fetching and carrying. After two years she went to them and asked them to stop paying her. Bunty and Angus exchanged a look. She was happy with them, she argued, she was part of the family, they had given her a home, she didn't feel like an employee. Bunty and

Angus exchanged another look. 'It's only money,' Angus commented with a shrug.

'I know,' Kathy replied, 'but I don't need it. I'm so well looked after here, what do I have to spend it on?'

Angus shrugged again.

'But you're a young lassie,' Bunty said kindly, 'stuck here with us old fogeys when you could be out there having a good time. Of course we should pay you for looking after us so well.'

'Bunty,' Kathy said quietly, 'my mother died years ago, I grew up with a drunken father who had to be lifted off the floor and put to bed every night. I didn't know what a family was till I came here. *You're* my family, I don't know what would've happened to me if I hadnae found you. I should be paying you!'

Bunty put her arms round her and hugged her. 'All right then,' she said, wiping her eyes, 'have it your own way, but you're a daft lassie!'

Angus looked at the two of them, hugging each other and crying. 'Women!' he muttered. 'Never happy unless they can have a good greet!' and shaking his head he wandered off.

But she did get out, of course, sometimes she met Seona and Kirsty in Fort William for a drink and a gossip, and very soon the trio expanded to include the women in the National Trust's Tourist Centre below the house, it coming as no surprise that Mavis, the manager, was Seona's sister and Kirsty's mother. Mavis had been a History teacher at Lochaber High School until the form-filling got on her nerves, and now she was the local authority on the '45 rebellion. On their nights out she and Kathy would sit over a drink in the bar of the Nevis Bank Hotel, arguing about Bonnie Prince Charlie, neither one ever giving ground, even on this night, the occasion of Kirsty's hen party. In two days' time she would marry Kenny, the chef from the Glenfinnan House Hotel just beyond the monument, but before the fun could begin Kathy and Mavis had to discuss the Young Pretender, or 'that bloody liar,' as Kathy called him. 'He was a chancer!' was her opinion. 'He came over here, got a lot of poor people involved, then scarpered back across the Channel, leaving them to deal with the aftermath. That's not what I call a leader, you wouldnae find me being loyal to a weak creature like him!'

'Aye, well, I used to think that too,' Mavis answered as always, 'but he must've had something about him. Think of those months hiking through the Highlands with a huge bounty on his head, yet he was never given away. And there he was, sleeping in caves to avoid the Redcoats, never warm or dry or safe, and no matter what you think of him, he did it, he stuck it out.'

'Only till he could get to hell out of it to safety!' Kathy responded. 'He didnae exactly hang around to face the consequences, did he? But the Highlanders had no choice.'

'No, no, no,' Mavis insisted. 'He had something about him!'

'Should've been a rope about his neck!' Kathy replied.

'Oh, bugger Prince Charlie!' Seona said. 'Who cares? It's just part of business, he's just another version of the Loch Ness Monster, and as long as the tourists keep coming, who cares?'

'Are you saying you don't believe in the Loch Ness Monster?' Kathy demanded. 'That's treason!'

'And you do?' Seona asked.

'Of course I do! Haven't I met and lived in the same house as one of her offspring, the monstrous Rory Macdonald?'

The women all laughed. 'I can't believe you hated him!' Seona said.

'Aye, but you had a terrible crush on him all the way through school!' Mavis said to her sister.

'I did not!'

'You bloody well did! It was embarrassing the way you used to drool when he was about!'

'Well you had lousy taste!' Kathy said to the giggling Seona. 'I've never met a more unpleasant, pig-ignorant sod in my life!'

'Yet you get on with Angus,' Seona spluttered, 'and everybody says Rory's like him.'

'Everybody's wrong! Angus is gorgeous!' Kathy protested. 'If I'd been older or he'd been younger, me and Bunty would've been mortal enemies, I'll tell you that!'

'You must be in need of a father figure, that's what it is,' Seona said, and suddenly Kathy was quiet. 'You could say that,' she replied.

The wedding was at the church of St Mary and St Finnan's, beside the hotel on the lochside. The parish priest, Father O'Neill, was a friend of Angus's and a regular visitor to the house up the hill. The first time he and Kathy met he had made the mistake of thinking he knew her religion, and she had quickly disabused him of the notion.

'I just assumed because of the name,' smiled the priest.

'Aye, your sort always do assume!' Kathy responded. 'You should get an operation for it, that might cure you.'

'I do apologise, no offence intended. It's just that I've never met a Kelly who wasn't one of ours.'

'Well you have now,' Kathy growled.

Beside her Angus had chuckled. 'I think I see a kindred spirit!' he beamed. Angus liked Father O'Neill, he played chess with him, went to shinty matches with him, argued with him and poured him drams, but thought he was insane. Angus had studied every religion that had ever existed and had long ago decided that anyone who believed any of it was insane.

'I really do apologise,' said Father O'Neill again, his Irish accent annoying Kathy even more than his assumption.

'Maybe I should assume that you're an atheist like me,' Kathy persisted, 'given that we've got this great thing in common, Irish surnames?'

'Wonderful!' Angus said. 'Right, you poor, pathetic, weak little man,' he said amiably to his friend, 'answer that, why don't you?'

'I don't think I will!' Father O'Neill said. 'I sense more than animosity here!'

'Too bloody true!' Kathy said darkly. 'Enough animosity to rip your throat out with my teeth if you assume anything else about me!' She marched into the kitchen, where Bunty was at work. 'I hate priests!' she said. 'They're cruel to horses you know!'

'What?' Bunty asked. 'All of them?'

Kathy grinned sheepishly, knowing how she must've sounded. 'Aye!' she said. '*All* horses!'

Bunty laughed. 'Now that I didnae know!' she said.

Standing at the altar behind Kirsty she kept a mental distance between herself and the surroundings while staring Father O'Neill firmly in the eye. Kirsty was her friend, she had been delighted to be her bridesmaid, but she was only there for her, not to be involved in Father O'Neill's rituals. She had to admit, though, that she looked quite stunning. She wore a deep turquoise, Empire line gown, the bodice made entirely of cotton lace flowers. The heavy satin skirt was scattered with single lace flowers, and more had been woven into her reddish hair which had been plaited high off her face. She had never worn anything like this, never looked anything like this, and staring at her reflection in the mirror she had hardly recognised the poised young woman of twenty-three staring back at her. She wished Lily had been there to see her, but Bunty was, and Lily could've had no better deputy. Rory Macdonald was back for his first visit in three years; there had to be one fly in the ointment.

'Don't you think Kathy looks just beautiful?' Bunty asked him, her eyes shining.

Rory looked up from the fishing fly he was working on. 'Aye,' he said simply, then looked away again.

Kathy waited till Bunty, leaning ever more heavily on her stick, had left the room to get herself ready for the wedding. 'That was as much as you could manage, was it?' she demanded.

Rory looked up again, a blank expression in his eyes. 'What are you complaining about now?' he asked quietly.

'I think your mother was looking for a bit more than "Aye", that's all. She's been really excited about this bridesmaid thing, you could've dredged up something better for her sake, surely?'

'I know my mother better than you do and she knows me. Is it not,' he said in his slow way, 'that you were hoping for more yourself?'

'No, it's not! Christ! I've never met a man more full of himself!'

'Because,' Rory continued evenly, 'you've already looked in the mirror more than once and you know perfectly well what you look like, so why would my opinion matter more than your own?'

'Your opinion doesnae matter as *much* as my own!' Kathy seethed. 'I was thinking of your mother!'

'Aye,' Rory muttered, not even glancing up from what he was doing. 'You said.'

'Do you get on this well with everybody you meet?' Kathy demanded sarcastically.

'I get on pretty much with everybody I meet,' Rory replied absently, holding the fly up against the light of the window and squinting at it.

'Well you don't get on with me!'

'Well, maybe,' he said, picking up a pair of pliers and adjusting the hook, 'that has something to do with you. As they say in some parts, YP.'

'YP?'

'Aye,' he smiled happily at the completed fly before looking up at her solemnly. 'YP. Your problem.'

Kirsty and Kenny's wedding lasted at the hotel from Friday afternoon till Sunday evening, with different bands taking over when one fell exhausted and the guests attending in shifts. Angus was the only man Kathy knew who wore the kilt every day, but it was trotted out on special occasions like weddings in a way that offended Angus. It reduced the garb to fancy dress, he said, when so many men who didn't normally wear it did so at social functions, and you could always tell them too, because they wore it so badly. But the sight of so many unusually bare male legs made an increasing impression on the women as the time wore on and the drink flowed freely. At the reception, Mavis, the mother of the bride, was sitting at a table with Kathy, Seona, and a group of women who worked in the tourist office beside the monument. She was a small, plump, dark-haired woman with brown eyes that were permanently screwed up to protect them from her own cigarette smoke; Kathy, and everyone else who knew Mavis, had never seen her without a lit cigarette in her hand, though she rarely seemed to smoke them, she was always too busy ordering people about. That night, with her daughter safely married, Mavis was feeling merry. Her screwed-up eyes fell upon the hapless and specially bekilted form of the local carpenter, Lachie Stuart, who just happened to be coming through the door at that moment.

'Lachie Stuart,' she called out. 'Are you a real Scotsman?'

Lachie Stuart's hands flew down to his kilt. 'Of course I'm Scottish!' he laughed.

'You know bloody well what I mean!' Mavis said, advancing on him somewhat unsteadily.

'As I'm in a good mood I'll give you another chance. Are you, Lachie Stuart, a *real* Scotsman?'

The other women had by now followed Mavis and were forming a circle around Lachie and, before it was completed, he tried to make a dash for freedom through the remaining gap, only to be felled by the mother-of-the-bride's rugby tackle.

'Now, Lachie,' she said reasonably, lying at full stretch on the floor and hanging on to the unfortunate Lachie's legs and her habitual cigarette with equal determination, 'we think you're telling fibs. You've left us with no alternative, we'll have to check!'

Lachie gave a scream as he disappeared under a pile of struggling, giggling women. Eventually an arm emerged from the scrum, proudly waving a pair of tartan Y-fronts and a loud cheer erupted as Lachie's knickers were thrown aloft to land on the ceiling fan, where they lazily began to spin round for all the world to see. Lachie, knowing when he was beaten, shrugged his shoulders and took off at speed towards the bar. The women resumed their seats until the next man entered wearing a kilt, to be greeted by the challenge, 'Are you a true Scotsman?' and then assaulted. By the end of the third night the overhead fan was spinning slowly, its progress hampered slightly by dozens of pairs of knickers in every colour and design that had been forcibly removed from 'false' Scotsmen. At one point Rory Macdonald walked in. 'Why,' demanded Mavis, 'are you not wearing the garb?'

'Why?' Rory asked. 'Because I know what Highland women are like when they've had a few, that's why!'

'I wouldnae worry,' Kathy said sourly. 'I wouldnae think many women would want to remove your drawers.'

'So you've obviously given the matter some thought, then, to come to that considered opinion,' Rory remarked as he passed, and all the women laughed.

Another highlight was the seeming non-appearance of the bride's cousin, a noted Irish dancer who was appearing in a show in Edinburgh, though it was hoped that she would arrive before the three-day event was over. In the meantime several of the men were only too happy to fill in, performing with commendable gusto, if impaired balance, their very own, very unique version of an Irish jig. Legs were flying in every direction, arms held strictly to their sides, which was just as well, given that they had recently been initiated as 'true' Scotsmen, and there was almost a touch of regret in the air when the diva herself arrived in full costume, ready to delight the audience. Unfortunately, as she kicked out in the very precise manner of the true professional that she was, she accidentally kicked someone in the front row on the chin. Watching from the sidelines were the earlier dancers, who had only reluctantly vacated the floor and had been indulging in a few discreet catcalls, feeling slightly resentful that the efforts of the latecomer were, till that moment, receiving more appreciation than their own flawless and artistic performance had drawn. As her kick felled the guest one said loudly, 'Look at that! Was that not awful? Now, *we* didnae do that, did we?'

As ever with weddings, the talk among the women turned to who was next. They were all feeling no pain, though Kathy, ultra-cautious because of Old Con, had never tried anything more powerful than Babycham.

'Hands up,' said Mavis, 'them that think the next one will be Kathy!'

A roar of approval went up, though they were in that merry state where the announcement of an imminent tidal wave would've been cheered just as enthusiastically.

'It won't be me!' she said with feeling.

'Och, we all said that!' a slightly tipsy Seona laughed. 'When I couldnae have Rory Macdonald there, I said I'd never marry, but I did. It comes to us all.'

'With taste like yours I'm just surprised you ended up with a normal human being,' Kathy retorted.

'I'd take him now!' Seona announced, in that peculiarly over-precise manner that the slightly tipsy always think will convince the world that they are not. All the women around the table laughed. 'I'm telling you!' she protested. 'If that Rory Macdonald tipped me the wink my drawers would be up on the ceiling as well!'

Mavis stood up and shouted. 'Rory! Rory Macdonald! Where is he?' and from the crowd Rory appeared. 'My sister,' Mavis announced very carefully, 'would have carnal knowledge of you forthwith! How about it?'

Rory shook his head. 'Highland women and booze,' he said.

'Aye, I know,' Kathy said icily. 'I've just been saying the same thing myself. Doesnae just rob them of their inhibitions, but their normal good taste as well!'

Later, lying in her bed, her head slightly muzzy, she went over the conversation. Marry? Forget it! Jamie Crawford had inoculated her against men for life. She remembered the times she had slept with him, though slept was wrong, their couplings having consisted of taking the chance when either of their houses might be empty, while she hoped each time they wouldn't be. She had hated it. The awkwardness, the embarrassed, silent fumbling; it turned her stomach just to think of it. Even that first time, when it hurt and she bled, he had said nothing, it was women's business. He would lie on top of her, sweating slightly with excitement, his eyes closed as he worked away, and she hated him for that. She would lie there watching him, desperately hoping it would end that second, her mind full of furious anger thinking, '*He doesnae even know it's me!*' Then, within a couple of minutes it was blessedly over. And she hated cleaning herself up afterwards too, the whole messy, smelly, stickiness of it. At least it never lasted long, though too long for her, but even so, she always wondered what he could've got out of such a brief encounter. Physical release? Well, any tension was entirely one-sided, so she would have to pass on that one. Was the status of having done it the most important thing, she wondered? Was it a means of putting his brand on her, so that he could look at her at any time and think '*Ah've had her*'? And they never talked; was it perverted to think there should be a few words of polite conversation? Beforehand there was the rush to do it, on his part at least, then the brief, joyless act, followed by more silence. It was as though nothing had happened, they might as well have shared a dual sneeze. He didn't ever ask if she had enjoyed it, it hadn't even entered his head that she should. He didn't ask if she was all right or, more importantly, if she was on the Pill. He assumed she was, because that was women's business too; they were the ones who could get pregnant, so it was understood that preventing it was their responsibility alone, and it didn't even occur to him to want to know. The Swinging Sixties had brought universal free love, or so everyone on TV said, the old stigmas and conventions had been swept away, and every female was rampantly sexually active and on the Pill. Yet there they had been at the start of the seventies in the East End of Glasgow, the only place in the world the sixties had somehow swung past without stopping. Following on from that, a natural consequence you might say, had been the horror of what had happened in the Moncur Street bathroom one Saturday night, and the baby she had failed to keep alive. The whole thing made her feel sick, it wasn't anything she would ever try again, and any man who approached her was, and always would be, given short shrift. She thought again of Kirsty's wedding reception and the chatter about Seona's lifelong lust for Rory. OK, they were all tipsy and having a laugh, but even talking about it reminded her of sex with Jamie. She got up from her bed and rushed down the corridor to the bathroom where she was copiously sick. As she made her way back to her room she could hear the distant sounds from across the loch as the next shift arrived at the wedding reception. Rory was standing at the top of the stairs on his way to his own room as she came out of the bathroom. He shook his head as she passed, feeling like death.

'I see Sassenach women don't hold their drink any better than Highland women,' he said mildly.

But Kathy wasn't in the mood for witty repartee. 'Oh shutup, you arse!' she replied, shutting her door. She heard him laughing but she hadn't the strength to argue just then; she'd get him back for it later, she promised herself, as she fell asleep.

Rory left a week later and life settled down again. She was glad to see the back of him, the man irritated her so much that he actually affected her happiness. She couldn't find the key to whatever personality he had, that was what bothered her, and the fact that it bothered her bothered her even more. Bunty was becoming gradually frailer, she had never recovered her old vitality after breaking her hip a few years before, and as they both neared eighty Angus was showing signs of slowing down too, in that his obsessions were becoming less physical, though he did fit in a spell of Geology before concentrating on cerebral topics. He would set off with a little hammer and a cloth bag and return after hours spent tramping the hills, carrying various treasures. The house overflowed with different pieces of rock and quartz that he arranged and labelled, but much of it could be done through reading too. His Fair Isle period had, as Bunty had predicted, resulted in various sumptuous garments taking up residence with all the other products of his knowledge-seeking, among all the other items that were 'just things'. These days, some four years after Kathy's arrival in Glenfinnan, he was more interested in projects he could work on without moving about too much, and languages fitted the bill. In no time at all he was fluent not only in living languages, but in dead ones as well, though Kathy was never sure which category Esperanto fitted into. He was concentrating on Sanskrit when Rory came home again, announcing quietly that his wandering days were over, this time it was for good. Kathy almost burst into tears of dismay and unhappiness.

'He can't!' she protested to Bunty as they worked together in the kitchen.

Bunty laughed, misunderstanding Kathy's alarm. 'Och, I know!' she said. 'He loves to travel, I can hardly believe myself that he's giving it all up. I have this picture in my mind of him when he was much younger, you know the way you do? Then I look at him and I think to mysel' that he's nearly forty years old, he's not a wild laddie any longer, maybe he feels it's time he settled down.'

Kathy was glumly silent. If he was intent on settling down, couldn't he do it just as well in darkest Peru?

'And I think it'll be good for Angus too, you know, he's getting on a bit.'

Kathy smiled at the thought of Bunty, who was eternally seventeen inside, conceding that Angus might just be 'getting on a bit'. But Rory's imminent arrival bothered her so much that she began for the first time to think of leaving the home she had found. Was there any point, she wondered, in staying around just to be in a constant state of irritation, with all the joy taken out of life in the house?

'Maybe it's time for me to go,' she suggested to Bunty.

Bunty looked shocked, as though someone had hit her. 'But why?' she whispered.

'Well, I came here to help you about the place, and with Rory coming home, maybe you won't need extra help.'

'But Rory will help Angus!' Bunty protested. 'You and me, we're a good team about the house, I couldnae run it without you, Kathy. No, no, this is your home, Angus and me couldnae think of you not being here, and Rory would be so upset too, you know how much he likes you!'

'*Aye, right!*' Kathy thought. 'Look, we'll see how it goes then. But if you think I'm getting in the way once he comes back, if you don't need me as much as you thought you would, just tell me.'

Bunty looked as though she might be about to cry and Kathy, feeling guilty, put her arms around her. 'I don't want to go,' she lied. 'I'm just thinking ahead, giving you the option.'

'Well, *don't!*' Bunty chided her. 'We'll hear no more about it. Is that understood?'

Rory's homecoming was as low-key as those before had been. He arrived one afternoon, quietly announced he was home and then put his bags in his room upstairs. She never got over their lack of excitement; it seemed to Kathy that the Macdonalds accorded each other total acceptance, never taking offence no matter the length of absence or silence. They seemed to have an ability to drop into and out of each other's lives without losing their closeness, and when they next saw each other it was as if they had been apart for only a few hours. And that, Kathy had to admit, was how she felt about Rory's visits, though she came at the problem from a vastly different angle; however long it had been since he'd gone, his return always came too soon for her. But Bunty was right about him spending more time with Angus, even if the fact of his being there felt like having an itch she could never quite scratch. They went everywhere together, Rory doing the driving, which was a relief to everyone in the area, given Angus's disregard for the highway code. He bought a boat with an outboard motor for Angus to do his fishing from, so that he wouldn't have to row himself back and forth, and later the Mini went before it fell to pieces on the road, and a van arrived, with plenty of room in the back for shopping, fishing tackle and whatever Angus needed. Over the months and years the two men worked together about the house. They installed central heating for the first time, oilfired, because there was no way gas would be brought that far north, even if they were taking it from the North Sea fields on the other side of the country and piping it all the way down to London, which was considerably further away than Glenfinnan. Rory measured all the windows and ordered double-glazed units, an innovation in the Highlands at the time; he replaced doors throughout the house, so that suddenly, with the gaps blocked, they could appreciate how many draughts they had been used to living with up till then. He even laid a proper driveway from the main road, up the hill to the house, one that didn't wash away in heavy rain, leaving them negotiating something like the surface of the moon. It was a curious sight to see Angus gradually taking the back seat, and more curious still to watch Rory subtly deferring to his father in things he obviously knew more about. Over the years Angus had kept the house from falling down with the odd repair here and there when necessary, but his endless search for knowledge had taken precedence over major work, and that's what Rory concentrated on once he came home. If she hadn't hated him so much she might've liked him for his gentle treatment of his father.

Then it happened, as it had to. The day had started like any other. Kathy had been down in Glasgow, called there by the first crisis of Old Con's illness, though she hadn't told anyone the real reason for her visit to the city, her first in nearly fifteen years. It was business, she had said, something she had to attend to, and she'd be back in a few days, which she was, wrestling with her changed perception of her cousin, Hari the guru, friend of spiders everywhere, and cursing herself for keeping in vague touch with him, but enough for him to find her. It was September, the trees were turning a million shades of green, yellow and orange and the rowan trees were heavy with berries. Rory had taken Angus down to the loch that morning in the van and watched him move across the water to his usual fishing spot. She looked out of the window and smiled, watching Angus propping up his latest language book – Urdu she thought it was – in front of him, casting his line then sitting down. It was good to be home again, even Rory couldn't spoil that, though it had to be said that they had rubbed along together better these ten years or so than she could ever have imagined. They were both older, of course, maybe they'd mellowed, or maybe it was just a tacit understanding that Bunty and Angus wanted them both there, and neither wanted to upset them. Later that morning she looked out again, and Angus was still there; everything was as it should be in the universe. Bunty was sitting by the fire in the reading room doing a crossword as usual. She felt the cold more these days; even with the central heating on and the house like a furnace, she had to have a fire on too. Well, she was in her eighties now, why not? She deserved a bit of comfort. Rory was by the window, reading, as Kathy brought in a tray with tea and biscuits. He had his binoculars up to his eyes, occasionally scanning the loch as he always did.

'I'll be back in a minute,' he said, and disappeared.

'Aye, fine, Rory,' Bunty smiled from beside the fire, barely looking up from her crossword.

Kathy had no idea what caused that tight feeling in her throat. Maybe it was the wheels of the van spinning more than usual as he drove off; he wasn't like his father, he drove well. She picked up the discarded binoculars and sat by the window, spinning the focus adjustment till Angus's boat came sharply into view. He was still there, like a rock. Then she moved slightly to where Rory was launching the old rowing boat and pulling hard towards Angus, and somewhere, somehow, she knew. Time stood still as she watched Rory tie his boat to his father's and jump aboard. Holding her breath she watched him bend over Angus and touch his shoulder, his face inclined towards the sitting figure. She saw Rory's head drop, a gesture so heavy with meaning that she had to bite her lip to stop from crying out, then he knelt in front of Angus and put his arms around him.

'I've got this one wrong,' Bunty said behind her. 'Damn the thing to hell! Why does no one ever help a senile old woman with these crosswords?'

'Because,' said Kathy from a long, long way away, 'you curse us all if we offer suggestions.'

She was wondering what to do next, thoughts rushing frantically about her mind. Rory was on his own out there, he would need some help.

'That's only because you get them all wrong,' Bunty said. 'Macdonald himself puts you up to it, I know that fine, he bribes the lot of you to give me bum steers.' She looked up at Kathy and smiled. 'What is it you're watching this long time?' she asked.

'Oh, the loch, you know,' Kathy said brightly. 'I think it's being away from it that makes it look so perfect when you come back again that you can't stop looking at it.'

'Aye, Rory used to say the same every time he came back,' she said, returning to curse her crossword once more.

Kathy raised the binoculars to her eyes once more. She could hear her own breathing and heartbeat so loud in her ears that she wondered if Bunty could hear them too and tried to calm them. Rory was still kneeling in the boat holding his father; she would have to *do* something. Just then the phone rang and she got up as slowly as she could and went to the kitchen to answer it.

'It's Father O'Neill here,' said a voice. 'I was wondering if Angus was on for a game tonight?'

'Father! Thank God!' Kathy whispered.

'Now that can't be you, Kathy Kelly,' he chuckled.

'Father, shutup and listen –'

'Ah, now that's more like it!'

'Father, this is serious! Angus is out on the water, but something's wrong. Rory's with him, but he'll need help bringing him in. I can't leave Bunty, she doesn't know. Get your boat and go out and help him.'

She replaced the phone and went back into the reading room. 'It was Father O'Neill,' she said brightly. 'He's after another drubbing at chess, I told him to call back later.'

Bunty nodded. 'You know, I think I'll have a lie down,' she said. 'I can't seem to get heated up at all, maybe I need my rest a wee bit early today.'

Later, Kathy would go over that remark and wonder if Bunty already knew, if some sixth sense had alerted her. She helped Bunty to bed and put her electric blanket on.

'Now, you're sure this is safe?' Bunty demanded. 'I'm never sure if you're in cahoots with Macdonald. Maybe he has put you up to this for a cut of the insurance money, frying a helpless old woman in her bed!'

'A helpless old woman!' Kathy scoffed. 'Listen to you, you're more lethal now than you ever were! And yes, it is safe to have it on these days, move with the times, woman!'

By the time she got back to the window and lifted the binoculars to her eyes the three boats had reached shore, Father O'Neill's tied to Rory's and trailing behind Angus's as the priest sat at the back, steering homewards, and Rory still holding his father. She watched as Rory jumped from the boat and made for the van, leaving Father O'Neill to hold Angus, then between them they lifted him gently into the back of the van. As they brought him up the hill Kathy opened the front door.

'My father's dead,' Rory said.

'I know.'

'Where's my mother?'

'She went for a rest, she's probably asleep now.'

'Good. We'll take him into the reading room. Call the doctor.'

She nodded, but as she turned she caught sight of the lifeless figure in the back of the van and, feeling all the strength suddenly going from her legs, she steadied herself by holding on to the door for a moment. She couldn't take it in, it couldn't be happening.

Rory looked at her sharply. 'I don't need this!' he said angrily. 'Pull yourself together and stop indulging yourself, there are things we have to do!'

A retort stuck in her throat, though she had no idea what it would have been.

'Move!' hissed Rory. '*Now!*' and he pushed her roughly inside the house.

It seemed that Angus had been having heart trouble for years. When he first found out he wrote to Rory, and Rory had immediately come home. Many of those trips Rory had taken him on were for checkups; he could've gone any time, but he'd lasted years longer than the doctors had predicted. He had told only Rory, he had even kept it from Bunty. When she woke from her sleep that autumn day the doctor had already signed Angus's death certificate, but he decided to stay on in case Bunty needed him. Rory went into the room alone and told her of Angus's death. Kathy never knew what words he used, but when she went in afterwards, Bunty was suddenly years older than she had been two hours before. Kathy sat on the bed beside her, the two of them wordlessly holding hands. What was there to say when they were beyond grief?

There was no undue ceremony. Angus was placed in the coffin he had carved all those years ago just as he was, wearing the garb he wore every day of his life, and arrangements were made to take him for cremation in Inverness, some seventy miles away.

Bunty asked for a few moments alone with him before they left the house. 'So, Macdonald,' Kathy heard her say as she closed the door behind her. 'You've done it again, have you, you blaggard, gone away and left me behind here again?'

Kathy began weeping quietly, and Rory immediately grabbed her arm and held it hard.

'Stop that right now!' he said sternly. 'My mother needs you, stop thinking of yourself!'

She hated him so much that she could've put her hands round his neck and choked him to death. Who did he think he was, the emotionless pig? She loved Angus, she worshipped him, which he obviously didn't, who was he to tell her not to cry? 'Have you any feelings at all?' she demanded. 'Because it seems to me that I care more about your father than *you* do!'

'That's enough!' he said. 'This is neither the time nor the place!'

Bunty was too frail to go with Angus to Inverness the next day but she demanded her right to do so anyway, and all the way there she kept repeating, 'This isn't how it was meant to be! I was supposed to go first!' It was frightening how childlike she had become in little over twenty-four hours, looking to Rory and Kathy for reassurance on every detail, and much as she hated him, Kathy was secretly relieved that Rory was there. Had she been left to cope with this on her own she didn't think she could've done it. At the crowded crematorium Father O'Neill gave a speech that was entirely non-religious. He spoke as Angus's friend, not as a priest, and told some of the old stories, of the legendary bareknuckle fights with the old Major, of his endless quest to learn as much as he could about every subject, of how he had no time for 'things', religion or religious people, except to beat them at chess. There were murmurs of laughter, but Kathy couldn't join in. She could only think of how impossible life would be without Angus, not only for Bunty, but for her too. And somehow her mother was mixed up in the event too, it was almost like reliving the day they'd buried Lily in St Kentigern's all those years ago. '*It's me,*' she thought miserably. '*Everybody I love dies, it must be something about me.*'

When they returned from Inverness Kathy had expected Angus's ashes to be scattered, but Rory shook his head. 'Why?' she asked.

'Because I say so,' he replied.

'But I *know* that's what he would've wanted!' she protested. 'He would've hated being kept in an urn like some bloody icon! Why are you doing this to him?'

Rory stared out of the window silently.

'Why won't you answer me?' she demanded angrily. 'You're the most ignorant bastard I've ever met, but you could at least have the decency to explain this! I knew Angus, I loved him, I know he wouldnae have wanted this!'

'Control yourself!' he said, his voice full of contempt. 'You're behaving like a fishwife. Maybe that's what you are, but *I* know he wouldnae have wanted this kind of behaviour in his house, on this day of all days, with his widow in the other room!'

The following week felt as though it had lasted a year. Bunty had withdrawn into herself, not leaving her bed and barely eating and, even then, only to please Kathy or Rory. Most of the time she slept and they could hear her calling for Angus in her sleep. Kathy came downstairs one morning just after eight o'clock and headed for the kitchen, thinking what she could make for Bunty's breakfast that might tempt her to eat. As she passed the reading room she heard Rory's voice. He was sitting at the table by the window.

'Did you say something?' she asked.

'I said don't bother.'

'Rory, we've got to get her to eat again.'

'She's gone,' he replied. 'She died in her sleep. I heard her call for my father about four o'clock and when I came down she was dead.'

'Why didn't you call me?' she demanded.

'And what exactly do you think you could've done?' he asked. 'You're good at resurrection, are you?'

Kathy stood by the window, looking out over the loch, her mind in turmoil once again.

'Thank God she's dead, it's over,' Rory muttered.

She gasped. Suddenly all the anger she had been holding in check, about losing Angus, losing Bunty and her happy home here, about Rory Macdonald himself, boiled up, and she slapped him hard across the face. He put a hand up to grab her wrist and fixed her with a cold stare.

'Don't you understand anything? She couldnae have lived without him, you stupid bitch!' he said sternly. 'It's a blessing for my mother that she didnae have to go on too long. And I'll give you that one slap, but you ever try it again and you'll be leaving here in a hearse yourself!' Still holding her wrist, he shook her so hard that she felt the pain in her shoulder. 'Understand?' he asked, then he let go of her abruptly and left the room.

She looked at her wrist, the white patches left by his fingers were taking a long time to turn pink again, but more than that, she realised that she had been frightened. For a split second there as he held her gaze, she had been scared of him, and she couldn't figure out why. She had been battling people all her life, she had been facing them down and scaring them, yet with a few stern words and the look in his eyes he had terrified her so much that goose pimples were standing out over her entire body.

So there they were, just over a week later, returning to Inverness with the other carved coffin. They spent the journey there and back in silence, as they had the days since Bunty's death, but when they arrived back at Glenfinnan Rory appeared in the kitchen doorway.

'Come on,' he said, and she followed wordlessly as he led the way to the hill outside. It was now October, dusk was falling and the wind was rustling the trees. Rory set the two urns on a flat rock, poured the contents of one into the other, then threw them into the air. They stood for a few moments, then he left her, returning to the house in silence. So that was why he hadn't scattered Angus's ashes. He had known from the start that Bunty wouldn't survive long and he had wanted them to be together. She made her way back to the house. 'Why didn't you tell me when I asked you?' she asked.

'Why should I?' he replied calmly, but it wasn't really a question.

They lived in the house for a few days more, passing each other in silence and making sure they didn't have to meet, at least Kathy did, knowing Rory wasn't bothered one way or the other. Within a week her entire world had changed and she couldn't quite work out what she should do next. There were phone calls for her about Con, as the doctors in the Southern General tried to work out what had caused his sudden paralysis, but she couldn't have cared less. She knew they thought she was heartless, but she didn't care about that either, she had something else on her mind, a numbing grief that had paralysed her just as surely as Con's drinking had paralysed him. Then gradually she began to see a little more clearly. She would leave here, she told Rory, she couldn't stay any longer.

'Why?' he asked.

'This is *your* home,' she shrugged. 'I was brought here to look after Bunty, and now Bunty's gone.'

'My father left a will,' he said. 'It'll be a while before it's sorted out, but he told me what was in it. The house and the grounds were to be left to both of us once my mother had died.'

'What?'

'Which of those words did you have trouble understanding?' he asked.

'But I don't want it! This is *your* house, not mine!'

Rory shrugged. 'I don't know what you're making such a fuss about,' he said quietly. 'It doesn't matter a damn to me, it's only a thing, after all.'

'But it doesnae make any sense!' she protested. 'I canny take your house! Honestly, Rory, I swear I didn't put him up to this!'

He sighed. 'Why is it that you have this need for melodrama?' he asked. 'It's simple enough, surely? Why must we have these hysterics at every turn?'

'I'm not hyster –'

'And it says a helluva lot for your knowledge of my father after all these years if you think *you* could've influenced him about anything!' he said scathingly. 'He was his own man till the day he died.'

She sat down in Bunty's chair by the fireside and, looking up, noticed that he was watching her. 'I'm sorry!' she said, jumping up. 'I shouldnae have sat there!'

'Christ Almighty!' he said, getting up from the table and throwing the chair back so hard that it fell on to the floor. 'Here we go again! Everything always has to be a drama with you! It's only a bloody seat, woman, my mother's not sitting there you know, you havnae sat on top of her!' And with that he stormed out of the room. She had never seen him genuinely angry before these last few days. Mostly he said little to her or quietly ignored her, so his sudden rage added to the general sense of the world being out of control. Two more days passed in mutual avoidance before she tried to talk to him again, and she resolved to be as calm as she could. 'We need to talk,' she said, standing beside him as he read a newspaper in his usual place.

He folded the paper. 'As long as we can do it without the Oscar-winning performance,' he said without looking at her.

She sat as far across the room from him as she could. 'About Angus's will. It doesnae matter what he wanted, I don't want this house.'

'You've only got a half share,' he said.

'Stop it, Rory,' she said quietly. 'Who's acting up now?'

He didn't answer.

'And I'll have to leave, we canny stay here together like this. You know how people talk.'

'Is your mind that narrow that you'd care about that?'

'Aye, it is.'

'So where will you go?'

'I was thinking. The wee cottage down the road at Drumsallie, your father said it was yours.'

He looked up in surprise. 'Old Edith's place?' he asked.

'I don't know. Is it?'

He laughed. 'Aye, it is. But you wouldnae want that, it hasnae had any work done on it for years now, I've just let it go.' He sat in silence, looking at her. 'It would take a while to do it up, mind.'

'Who was she? Edith?'

He laughed again. 'She was a spinster lady of these parts!' he said. 'She was never married, but as they say, she was never neglected either! She dyed her hair orange, smoked fags, drank whisky and entertained many men.'

'She was an old slapper, then?'

'No, she was not!' he said sternly. 'No money changed hands, there's a subtle difference. Edith just lived life as she wanted and didnae give a damn about what people thought. I used to drop in on my way back from school, got her messages, lit her fire, made sure she was all right. There was a lot of gossip about it at the time, she was seen as a bad influence on a growing boy. People even took it upon themselves to talk to Angus about it.' He gave another burst of laughter.

'What did Angus say?'

'He just laughed at them! You know that way he had, you didnae so much hear it as see it in his eyes?'

Her eyes watered and she looked away.

'Edith left me the cottage when she died. I was abroad at the time, I only found out when I came back years later. You havnae even seen inside it. You're sure you want it?'

Kathy nodded. 'I'll pay you rent.'

'Here we go again!' he said. 'I knew we couldnae get through this without the melodrama!'

'What is it about you?' she shouted. 'Do you actually feel anything? I'm upset because two people I loved have died, and all you can do is make cracks!'

'Just because I don't carry a vale of tears around on my back doesnae mean I don't feel anything!' he shouted back. 'They were in their eighties, they'd both had a good innings and as far as I'm concerned, they went when they were ready! What is your problem with that?'

'My problem is that I loved them both and I miss them, why are you so threatened by feelings?'

'I'm not threatened by feelings!' he yelled back. 'Where do you get this stuff? Do you believe everything you read in my father's psychology books? I'm not like you, I don't parade my feelings, I don't go about with a bleeding heart on my sleeve. One of us going about the house like a wet rag is more than enough!'

'You know,' she shouted back, standing beside him with her fists clenched at her sides, 'your mother used to say you were like Angus, but she was wrong. Angus was ten times the man you'll ever be!'

'So now you're taking it on yourself to tell me what my father was like, are you? He was the best man I ever knew, the best man you'll ever meet, and you havnae even the intelligence to begin understanding that!' He looked at her fists. 'So,' he said, his angry tone suddenly changing. 'You're thinking of hitting me again, are you? Think about it. What would you give for your chances, really?'

'And you thought we could go on living together in this house, did you?' she asked.

'And you thought the only danger was your virtue being impuned,' he shot back calmly. 'Well, let me reassure you on that score at least!' With that he turned back to his newspaper, leaving her and her anger with nowhere to go.

In the kitchen she picked up the phone and dialled the monument tourist office's number. 'Mavis? It's Kathy. Listen, I canny explain now, but can I stay with you for a few days till I can get something sorted out?'

'Aye, aye, of course you can. It's a big flat and only me in it, and Donnie too if you want to count him. I'd be glad of the company. Are you OK? Is there anything wrong?'

'I'm fine,' she said. 'But if I don't get out of this house now there'll be another funeral, and I'm not sure if it'll be mine or his!'

Mavis, being the manager, lived in a flat above the Tourist Centre with her husband, Donnie, and this was the beginning of the slack period. For six months from the end of September to early April the Centre closed, though Mavis still had off-season work to do. An extension was being built to house a tearoom in the Centre and she was overseeing the efforts of the workmen, all of them local, which was just as well. No one and nothing escaped Mavis's attention, she enjoyed ordering people about and could never understand why anyone should take umbrage at being questioned, supervised or dragooned into helping her. If a box of leaflets or postcards arrived she would look around to see who was available to take the package from where it was to where she wanted it to be. And it didn't matter whether or not they were employed by the National Trust, to Mavis any idle pair of hands was at her disposal. The only person who seemed to have worked out how to cope with this was her husband of many years, Donnie, a retired railwayman who now worked on *The Jacobite*, a preserved steam locomotive that ran on the West Highland Line during the summer months. Donnie was a good-natured man who, it was believed locally, was henpecked, though in that he was hardly alone, because Mavis's enthusiastic ordering and opinion-giving stretched far beyond her domain. But Donnie had his ways of evening the score denied to others. Under the influence of a dram he sang his own specially composed version of the old song, 'Bonnie Mary of Argyll'. Instead of 'I have heard the mavis singing/Its love song to the morn', Donnie's version started off 'I have heard the mavis singing/And it sounded like a crow.' Thereafter it descended in to innuendo and, if he was allowed to get that far, well beyond and, though Mavis pretended to join in the joke, everyone knew that she hated it. At every gathering Donnie was sure to be asked to sing his song and, at their daughter Kirsty's wedding, he had sung it several times till his wife threatened to knock him down. This was viewed as a blow for all humanity on the West Coast, and a great cheer had gone up. His other ploy was to sound *The Jacobite*'s steam whistle every time the loco passed the Tourist Centre. To the delight of those present, Mavis repeatedly looked at her watch as the train times neared, and shut her eyes and ground her teeth as the cheerful greeting from her affectionate husband rang out. He did this to say 'Hello', if you listened to Donnie, to drive Mavis mad according to everyone else, Mavis especially.

Now that Kirsty had her own home, Mavis and Donnie 'rattled

about', as she put it, inside the three-bedroomed flat, so Kathy was welcome to stay with them as long as she wanted. There were bound to be chores Mavis wanted carried out and she certainly wanted to hear everything that had led to the present impasse between Kathy and Rory, which would in turn lead to her own opinions on the matter and the giving of advice to be carried out to the letter. She wasn't long in entering the fray; Kathy had still to put her hastily-packed suitcase in her bedroom when Mavis instructed her, with an impatiently waved hand, to put it down forthwith.

'Right,' she said, pushing Kathy into the armchair opposite her, and quickly lighting a cigarette. 'What's been going on?' She looked across the lounge at Donnie, who was happily sprawled in front of the TV. 'And, Donnie!' she called, 'you can take yourself out of this! This isnae for your ears!'

'Right you are, my little dove,' Donnie replied lazily, making a great show of shuffling his feet and moving about in his chair without actually moving from it, and as Mavis turned her attention to Kathy, Donnie settled back as he was.

'There's nothing been going on,' Kathy replied. 'He's just the way he is. He canny say anything pleasant, every word that comes out of his mouth is some kind of crack. It was bad enough when Bunty and Angus were there, but now?' she shrugged.

'You know,' Mavis said, taking a puff at her cigarette, 'you could do worse than Rory Macdonald.'

'What do you mean?' Kathy asked, shocked to the core.

'Well, he's what? In his forties now? And you're no spring chicken.'

'I'm thirty-five!' Kathy gasped, confused about which insult to tackle first.

'And,' Mavis continued unabashed, 'he's a fine-looking man. Our Seona's not the only one sweet on him – Donnie! Are you still here? Go and do something useful, make us a cuppa, Kathy and me need to talk!'

'Absolutely, my cherub,' Donnie replied, not moving from his chair. 'Going this very minute, so I am.'

'Aye, he's a fine-looking man,' Mavis recapped, 'but he must be getting desperate at his age.'

'What the hell do you mean?' Kathy demanded again. 'You think that's all I'm good for then? Taking on some sod who's too old to bother finding himself a wife and is getting desperate?'

'Well you must be getting worried yourself,' Mavis said amiably. 'I'm not saying you're Doris Karloff exactly, but let's face it, you're not in your first flush either, Kathy.'

'Hang on a minute!' Kathy blustered. 'We'll leave the exact level of my flush to one side for the minute, but has it not struck you that I've never wanted a man and weans?'

'Ach,' Mavis replied dismissively, 'away to hell!'

'Feminism has passed you right by, hasn't it?' Kathy demanded.

'Aye,' Mavis replied. 'I live in the real world, where women's choice ends up the same every time.' She looked across at Donnie. 'That's the reality,' she said cheerfully. 'That thing sitting in the chair there, listening to every word *and letting on that he isnae*!'

'That's a lie!' Donnie said without looking up.

'That's what feminism amounts to in these parts! And you,' she shouted at Donnie, 'have you got that kettle on yet?'

'Aye, and the biscuits are on the plate ready too,' Donnie lied. 'Tea will be served in a minute, so it will.'

'Mavis,' Kathy said, trying not to sound as exasperated as she felt, 'you obviously don't understand. I hate Rory Macdonald, and he hates me. We canny say a word to each other without it ending in a fight. Hatred isnae attraction.'

'Of course it is!' Mavis laughed, leaning forward to stub out the remains of her cigarette and, in the same movement, reaching for another. 'You don't know anything, do you? Every happy marriage thrives on mutual loathing! Isn't that right, Donnie?'

'Havnae a clue, cherry blossom,' he called back. 'Havnae been listening to a word, as directed.'

'No, Mavis,' Kathy said. 'This isnae like you and Donnie, honest. I really don't like Rory, we don't like each other. And I'm telling you the truth, I've never wanted to get married and have kids. Never.'

'I don't believe that,' Mavis replied with utter conviction.

'Therefore,' came Donnie's voice, 'it cannot be!'

'Are you listening to us?' Mavis demanded severely.

'No,' Donnie lied.

'Have you made the tea?'

'Aye,' he lied again.

'I don't mind seeing you moving from that chair!' she accused.

'That's because I'm like greased lightning, my love,' he smiled, his eyes never leaving the TV screen. 'The most you could expect to see was a blur from the corner of your eye!'

Kathy was feeling uncomfortable. 'Mavis, I don't want you going about saying there's something between me and him,' she said. 'It's the last thing I want to be going around. Please, don't say things like that to anybody else.'

'Please yourself!' Mavis replied, flicking ash off her knees. 'But everybody had the two of you matched up for years, folk have been taking bets on when. My money's on any day now. Now that his mother's gone he'll need somebody to look after him, and you're available!'

'Have you any idea how insulting that is? And on so many different levels that I don't know where to start!'

'Oh come on, Kathy! You don't believe in all that hearts and flowers nonsense, do you? People get together because it suits their needs, not because they're struck by Cupid's dart! You're far too old to be thinking like that! If you annoy each other at least it's a reaction, think what it would be like to spend all that time with somebody who didnae get on your nerves – you'd die of boredom! Isn't that right, Donnie?'

'Aye, well, not that I'm suggesting I have an opinion of my own, you understand,' he smiled sweetly, 'but what the hell would I do with real wedded bliss?'

'Y'see?' Mavis said triumphantly. 'And I was thinking. You know this tearoom we're opening? You must've learned a lot from old Bunty, you could run that, couldn't you? Make a few buns and things?'

Kathy opened her mouth to protest, she had been thinking of doing something else entirely, but Mavis rushed on.

'You'll need a job anyway, and what else are you good for apart from looking after old folk? I don't mind doing you a favour, and you can stay here.' She slapped her knees as though sealing a bargain. 'I'm really looking forward to having some female company about the place again,' she said happily, then she looked across at Donnie. 'It'll be good to have some sensible conversation.'

'But I'll have you bored senseless,' Kathy said tartly, 'seeing as I'm only fit to cope with geriatrics.'

'Och, don't worry about it, we'll put up with you fine!' she said, and set off to make the long-awaited tea.

From the other side of the sitting room Donnie looked across and smiled. 'Nice try,' he said slyly, 'but you'll need to do better than that, Kathy! She has the hide of a rhinoceros, that one!'

The next day she kept an eye out for Rory Macdonald, and when she saw him heading towards Fort William in the van, she walked up the hill to the house, collected the rest of her belongings and brought them back to her room in the flat. So that was it, then; the thing was done. It was hard to believe that her life had changed so much in such a short time. Two short weeks, that's all it had taken, and now she had no idea which direction she would take or what would become of her. Still, no point in sitting around getting depressed, she decided, and at least she had a job and a temporary place to call home. Mavis was arguing with the workers who were building the new tearoom extension, you could hear her long before you could see her, but being locals they were taking little notice. She broke off when Kathy entered, pulling her from one spot to another, pointing out where the counter would be, where the tables and chairs would go. 'And,' she said excitedly, 'I have news for you!' She turned to Lachie Stuart, the carpenter who had been so memorably inducted into the ranks of real Scotsmen at Kirsty's wedding. 'Tell her, Donnie!' she ordered.

'Old Edith's house is being done up,' he said.

Kathy shrugged and looked at Mavis quizzically.

'Tell her *right*!' Mavis ordered.

'There's nothing else to tell,' Lachie protested. 'Rory Macdonald asked me to give him a hand with it, that's all.'

'And *why* do you think it's being done up?' Mavis demanded, looking excitedly from Kathy to Lachie.

'How the hell should I know, Mavis?' Lachie grinned.

'Are you saying you never asked?'

'Course I didnae! What business is it of mine? Either he's doing it up to sell it or somebody's moving in. Maybe Rory himself. The house up the hill will be too big for him now.'

Mavis drew him an exasperated look. 'Men!' she said, reaching for a cigarette. 'Do you know what he's up to, Kathy?'

'How would I know?' she asked. 'When was the last time he and I spoke?'

Over the coming months there was much talk about how the work on Edith's house was progressing. It was double glazed, they said, central heating had been installed, a new kitchen and bathroom too, but Rory explained his plans to no one. There was a great deal of speculation locally, but Kathy said nothing, even if she did daydream. Then one day he phoned down to the flat. He would, he said, be waiting outside in the van for Kathy in five minutes, then the line went dead. She climbed in beside him as quickly as she could, hoping Mavis was too busy hounding the men working on the extension to have noticed, and the van sped off to Edith's house.

'If you still want to live there you'd better see what it's like,' Rory said, the first words he'd spoken since putting the phone down. 'If you've changed your mind I have other plans for it.'

'What plans?'

'I could sell the big house and live here myself —'

'You couldnae do that!'

'— or I could sell both and go abroad,' he finished.

Edith's house had two bedrooms, but it was small and compact enough for her needs. She remembered her arrival at Glenfinnan fifteen years before, with Angus driving in his usual bat-out-of-hell fashion. All she had had was a glimpse of the cottage as the battered Mini zoomed past, but she'd liked it from that first brief look. Rory had stayed outside and she watched from the window as he went down to the shore and walked about. She didn't know how to

227

handle this development. With anyone else she could express her feelings, say how delighted and grateful she was, but not with him, not with the way things were between them; it would have to be kept on a strictly business footing. And yet she *was* delighted, she *was* grateful. How was she to handle this? She walked down to the shore, where he was sitting on a rock, looking out over Loch Shiel. He looked up at the sound of her feet sinking into the shingle.

'How much rent do you want?' she asked.

'What?' He looked annoyed. 'I don't want any rent!' he said quietly, his voice showing his irritation.

Was there anything she could say that didn't provoke his annoyance?

'It wouldnae be right if I didnae pay rent.'

He stood up and threw a handful of pebbles into the loch. 'What the hell is it with you?' he demanded angrily. 'Why is it so very important to protect this virtue of yours? You're a grown woman, for God's sake, not some innocent virgin! Why do you care what people might say?'

She didn't reply.

'How will anyone else know what the arrangement is between us if neither one of us tells them? And even if they did find out, do you really think they've got nothing better to do than wonder what, and why?'

'It's not for other people,' she said quietly. 'It's for me.'

'Then what's wrong with you?' he asked, running his hand over his hair. 'I'm not giving you something, you're not a charity case, you own half of the house and the land.'

'*I don't want it!*' she said angrily. 'How many times do I have to tell you that? Angus shouldnae have done it! It's not my house, I won't take any part of it!'

'You're such an ungrateful bitch!' he shouted at her. 'Have you any idea how hurt he'd be if he heard you saying that?'

She felt tears prickling her eyes. 'I'm grateful,' she said formally, 'to you for showing me the cottage. If we can come to some arrangement about the rent, I'd be happy to move in. Otherwise, maybe you'd be better to sell it.'

'Suit yourself,' he said. 'I've done everything I can.'

'As they turned to go back to the van Rory stopped. 'Can you hear that?' he asked, inclining his head.

'What?'

'Ssh! Listen!'

There was a faint cry. 'It's a bird,' she said.

'It's not a bird!' he replied. 'Listen.' He looked around the shingle and then picked up a cloth bag lying at the base of a tree by the water's edge. He set it down on a rock, took out his knife and cut the string tying it at the top. 'Somebody's tried to drown kittens!' he said. 'Bastards!'

He took out two tiny, lifeless things. 'The other one's barely alive,' he said. 'It's hardly breathing!' He handed it to her, taking off his jacket.

'What am I supposed to do?' she asked helplessly, a disturbing feeling of having been here before filling her.

'Get something to dry it off, get it up to the cottage!'

She pushed it back at him. 'I canny,' she said. 'You do it. I don't know how to.'

He glared at her. 'It's a living creature,' he said. 'Do you want it to die?'

'I'm no good at helping things to live,' she protested, feeling the panic rising. 'Even plants die when I have to look after them.'

'For God's sake!' he said. 'Next you'll be telling me you've got the kiss of death!' As he was shouting at her he was taking his sweater off and wrapping it around the kitten. 'So, tell me,' he said sarcastically. 'How many small, innocent creatures have you killed, then?'

Kathy stared at him in horror. It was as if he knew and was tormenting her with it. She tried to stifle the cry in her throat, so that when it came out of her mouth it sounded like someone in pain, as she turned and ran awkwardly, her feet slipping on the shingle, back to the safety of the van.

On the way back to Glenfinnan the barely-alive kitten lay on Kathy's lap, and not a word passed between her and Rory. He was no longer angry, it had evaporated the instant he saw her reaction and, like her, he seemed to want to get the episode over with as soon as possible. He stopped outside the Tourist Centre. 'Leave the kitten on the seat,' he said. 'He'll be all right there till I can get him home.' She got out of the van and laid the kitten gently on the passenger seat. Rory leaned across without looking at her and closed the door, then he drove on up the hill. She went straight to her bedroom and lay on the bed, shaking with a cold so raw that it seemed to come from deep inside her bones, and froze every tissue in her body. It felt like being back in Moncur Street all those years ago. The tiny, weak creature in desperate trouble, wrapping it in what was available, holding it close for safety, for warmth and, above all, the feeling of helplessness, of uselessness. *Well, Kathy Kelly? How many small, innocent creatures have you killed, then?*

The following day Rory left an envelope at the flat for her. Inside were the keys to the cottage and a brief note. 'It seems,' he had written, 'that we can't talk without getting angry and fighting, so I thought I'd write instead. Take the cottage. We can work out the details later. We'll need to talk at some stage, we have things to resolve, but the cottage is yours if you want it.' He had signed it 'RM'. What he had no way of knowing was that she had spent the night before locked in nightmares, and all the fight had already gone out of her. At lunchtime she asked Lachie Stuart to run her the short distance to the cottage in his van, but, as they pulled away from Glenfinnan, she looked up at the house on the hill and saw the shadowy outline of Rory standing at the window, watching. She asked Lachie to stop, went back inside and called Rory. 'Thank you for the cottage,' she said. 'I canny fight any more. If you want to come down this afternoon we can discuss whatever you need to discuss.'

He arrived at three o'clock, knocking on the door and looking unsure of himself for the first time that she could ever remember. Once inside they were awkward with each other from trying not to be. He looked very big in the cottage, his broad frame blocking the light from the window as he sat on the deep ledge, speaking very quietly and deliberately, as though he had been practising in front of a mirror.

'Kathy, I don't know what I said the other day, but I know I hit a nerve. You looked like you'd seen a ghost.'

She smiled wryly. A ghost; he'd got that right.

'I'm sorry,' he said, 'whatever it was. But I'm tired of fighting too, we've got to find a way of talking that doesnae end up like a battle.'

She nodded.

'About the house. I had no objection to my father leaving it to both of us, but if you really don't want it, I have a suggestion. Have the cottage instead. Sign your part of the house away if you like, if that would make you feel better, and we'll make it a condition of the deal that the cottage is yours.'

She nodded again. 'I would just feel that it would look as though I had got him to do it,' she said. 'Do you see?'

'No. I told you, no one could ever get him to do anything, you know that, everybody knows that. But it doesnae matter what I think, it doesn't matter what other people think either, though I know you don't believe that. I have to get his affairs settled, do you understand? I'm not trying to trick you, or annoy you, I just need it all to be finished.'

Well, there was a meeting place she had never expected. She had always thought finishing things was her fetish alone. There was silence, then he held out his hand. 'Angus left this for you.' It was a bank book. 'He said it was your wages, that you hadnae collected them in a long time, so he had opened up a bank account with them.'

She laughed and raised her eyes to the ceiling. 'I wish I'd been born at the same time as him, or he'd been born at the same time as me!' she said. 'I feel that I missed the love of my life by fifty years! I really loved your father, you know.'

'Aye, I know,' he laughed back. 'Do we have a truce?'

'Aye,' she smiled. 'Would you like some tea?'

As she made the tea, the first time she had done so as mistress of her own home, he sat in an armchair by the fire and she was surprised how relaxed he seemed; they might have been friends.

'Tell me something,' she said, sitting opposite him. 'Have you ever wanted to be married?'

'Is that a proposal?' he grinned. 'No, the answer is that I never felt the need to be married. I've always been happy on my own, I never wanted to have someone else around permanently. Folks hereabouts think that's unnatural, but that's just tough. How about you?'

Kathy shook her head. 'Me neither. Even when I was wee it never occurred to me. It was as if it was OK for everybody else, but not for me. I only ask because it seems that everybody for miles around has been pairing us off for years.'

'Och, I've always known that,' he smiled. 'They'll see the van outside now and be putting up the banns. It's a convenience thing. They think everybody should be married, that everybody wants to be married, and here we are, loose ends that they can tie up in a neat parcel. But I think we'd end up killing each other, that's the truth.'

'Is that why you were so bloody horrible to me from the first day?'

'No,' he replied thoughtfully, 'that was just me, my honest reaction. For some reason you've always managed to annoy me. I'm pretty easy-going, canny recall losing my temper more than a couple of times in my life, but there have been times when I've been so mad that I didn't know whether to strangle you, or climb to the top of the hill and throw myself off to get away from the constant arguments.'

Kathy laughed. 'When I heard you were coming back for good I almost left,' she said. 'Your mother stopped me.' It seemed odd that they were telling each other of their mutual dislike in such friendly tones.

'Maybe,' he mused, 'we'll get on better apart. What do you think?'

'It's possible,' she said. 'Can I ask something?'

He looked at her.

'Can I come up to the house to get a book sometimes?'

He looked suddenly serious again. 'You see, that's what I mean. You know perfectly well you can, yet you go out of your way to make it sound like a favour to a servant!'

'And,' she continued, 'could I have Angus's typewriter?'

'A slightly bizarre keepsake, but take it if you want it.'

'And –'

'Dear God! First I canny get you to take what's yours, now you're asking for more!'

'The wee kitten,' she said. 'Is he OK?'

'Aye, he's fine. Do you want him?' he asked, surprised.

'Aye, I do. That should convince them all that we'll never make a match of it. We'll stay here together, the old spinster and her cat!'

He brought the typewriter and the kitten down the following day and, as he handed over the kitten, it lashed out at Kathy with a screech and scratched her arm. 'Maybe I should call it Rory,' she smiled.

13

Father Frank McCabe had been waiting for them. He had a look of bravado on his face as Kathy and Jessie were shown into the chapel house by his housekeeper. Kathy looked from him to Jessie and back again. Dear God! Why hadn't she made that connection before? The eyes definitely had it; both father and daughter were wearing the exact same bags, like rimless skin spectacles, around their slightly bulging eyes. Kathy wanted to grab the little priest by the throat and demand Con's cash, but she held herself in check, watching Jessie settling herself into the sofa and taking the hankie away from her mouth and nose. She was full of admiration for her aunt at that moment, knowing how much strength and determination it had taken for her to drop the safety props her life depended on. Jessie stared at Frank McCabe and held her hand out to Kathy, who placed a piece of paper in her palm as they had arranged earlier. Jessie's hand didn't even waver. What a woman the old whore was!

'The money,' Jessie said, waving the paper as a bluff, 'that's whit we're here for. Just hand it ower an' me an' Kathy here will be oan oor way.'

'What money?' the priest asked innocently.

'Noo, don't play silly buggers!' Jessie smiled calmly. 'You know bloody fine whit money!'

'If you're referring to the money donated to the Church by the late Cornelius Kelly, then I have to tell you that donations are rarely refundable, and certainly not to anyone other than the donor,' he smiled.

'Well, wee man,' Kathy said quietly. 'It seems that Ah was the donor, only Ah didnae know, an' the reason Ah didnae know was that you got it away frae Con before I found oot aboot it.'

'It was your father's view that the money would be put to better use by the Church,' he smiled. 'And you didn't miss it, Kathy Kelly, did you? You managed perfectly well without it, so your father was right.'

'An' how dae you know how Ah managed?' she demanded. 'Ah was fifteen, Ah hadtae leave school the followin' year an' go to work tae feed and clothe masel'. If Ah'd had that money Ah could mibbe've stayed oan at school, gone tae university even. That was whit the money was for, wasn't it? Tae help the dependents o' the people who died?'

'No,' he smiled smugly. 'It was for whatever the recipient wanted it to be for. Cornelius was the recipient, and Cornelius wanted it to be used for the good of the Church.'

Kathy and Jessie looked at each other. 'Well, let's stop beatin' aboot the bush – an' Ah know ye've beat aboot wan bush in yer time,' Jessie said, as Kathy tried to stifle a giggle. 'Bein' reasonable people, me an' Kathy here were quite prepared tae dae this the easy way, but ye've changed the entire nature o' the negotiations. Put it this way. Hand ower the cash or Ah'll make sure everybody knows that ye got yer leg ower Auld Aggie, an' while she was married tae the Orangeman at that, an' furthermore, that you're ma Daddy!' She stared him straight in the eye. 'Noo, whit's it tae be, Daddy dearest?'

'There is not,' he said eventually, 'the slightest shred of truth in that monstrous allegation!'

'Aw, gie it a rest!' Jessie said dismissively. 'Ah know it a'! Ah've known it since Ah was a wean! Mind the time you an' Aggie were discussin' ma confirmation name? Was it tae be Frances or Francesca, an' you were shit scared somebody might suspect somethin'?'

The look on the priest's face said it all.

'Aye, Ah see ye *dae* remember *that!* Ah was listenin' ootside the door, as it happens. An' tae put the tin lid oan it, Auld Aggie tellt Kathy the full story, ya dirty wee bugger, the day before she died!'

235

Kathy nodded firmly. 'An' helluva shocked Ah was tae!' she said solemnly.

'There's ways o' provin' monstrous allegations these days tae,' Jessie said. 'First ye go tae the papers,' she looked across at Kathy and laughed. 'They'd pay a packet for this story,' she said. 'Ah didnae thinka that! Imagine me missin' an angle!' Then she turned back to Frank McCabe. 'An' when you deny it, Ah then say "Gie's wanna they DNA tests, pronto," an' Ah'm sure ye'd be only too keen tae gie a sample o' some kind, tae prove ye're innocent, like. It'd make a great story, no' think so? Yer daughter's wanna the East End's best, an' Ah don't use the term lightly, whores, an' yer grandson, son o' a gangster, is as mad as a hatter an' turns his ain kinda tricks puttin' folk in touch wi' the occult. For a wee consideration, of course! Ah don't think ye'd have much chance o' bein' made Pope efter that lot came oot. Whit dae ye think yersel', like?'

Frank McCabe got up, went over to a desk in the corner of the room and took from it a chequebook and pen. 'Christ, Kathy,' Jessie said in a stage whisper, 'he's gonny get a gun an' shoot us!'

'I never intended keeping the money indefinitely,' he said, in a voice straining with dignity. 'I only took it into safekeeping to stop Con misusing it. It was always my intention to hand it back to the family.'

'When ye were found oot, that is!' Jessie said calmly.

He wrote a cheque and held it to Jessie. Kathy held her breath, wondering if Jessie dared take it from him, even with a cotton glove to protect her. There was a moment's hesitation, then Jessie smiled sweetly. 'Thanks, Da!' she said, looking at the cheque. 'Helluva gooda ye! An' this is the amount Con gave ye, is it?'

'It is.'

'Well, in that case, we'll accept this as a down payment, an' the morra Ah'll get ma accountant tae calculate the interest due ower the last thirty years, ya cheatin' wee bastard. Ah'll let ye know how much merr ye owe us. We don't need it, ye understand, baith me an' Kathy here has a bob or two put by, we just want it.'

It had been too easy for Kathy. She had wanted a battle, she had wanted to be on the TV news, holding Frank McCabe hostage in his chapel house and making him confess all before the cameras, but Jessie, fine businesswoman that she was, had handled the matter perfectly. As they left, Kathy could contain herself no longer, she needed to get at least one blow in, she was due it. 'An' don't you forget, wee man,' she hissed at him, 'Ah was there when ye wanted tae murder that horse!'

Jessie handed her the cheque, then with slow, deliberate grace she led the way from the room, holding her hankie again to her nose and mouth with shaking hands. Once safely outside in the waiting Mercedes, Jessie asked furiously, 'Whit the hell was that aboot him murderin' a horse?'

'It was when Ah was a wean,' Kathy replied, feeling her cheeks redden. 'A horse fell ootside wee Maggie's fruit stall an' he wanted tae get it shot. Wee Maggie got it up by giein' it sugar an' apples.'

'For God's sake, Kathy!' Jessie exploded. 'Thank Christ Ah didnae let ye get a word in edgewise in there, ye havnae the heid for negotiations at a'! Bloody murdered horses!' She shook her head in disapproval. 'There Ah was, knockin' ma pan in there, an' you're oan aboot bloody murdered horses?'

'Ah hadtae say somethin'!' Kathy protested. 'You got your blows in, Ah was left standin' there like a dummy! It, well, it just seemed tae me that it needed finishing aff, like!'

As she spoke, Jessie was retrieving an antiseptic wipe from her bag and carefully cleaning both hands, then a fresh pair of gloves was produced, the 'soiled' ones being put in the plastic bag that the fresh ones had come in. Kathy wondered where it stopped. Was the inside of the bag routinely disinfected to prevent germs from being transferred from 'soiled' items to clean ones? And what about the outside of the bag? Was there a point at which the germs invaded the inside, and where exactly in Jessie's mind was that point? And, come to that, how did she reconcile the possible cross-contamination caused by the packaging her various bits and pieces came in? 'Look,' said Jessie, 'Ah'll needtae get hame an' lie doon, this's knocked hell oota me. Drive us hame, Harry, son.

Ye'll needtae spend the night at oor hoose, Kathy, hen, an' Hari-Kari here'll run ye tae the station in the mornin'.'

She couldn't remember the interior of Jessie's house. The only time she had ever seen it before was on a fleeting visit with her mother when she was a child, and the overwhelming impression of the outside had been of neat gardens and respectable, net-curtained windows. Going inside was like entering a fairy grotto, with glass animals all over the place, obviously an obsession of Jessie's, and china figurines of women in long dresses, with names like Rose-mary and Daisy. She'd seen them in the display cabinets of numer-ous china shops, dainty, brightly coloured figures, flying kites, sitting on swings, skating, all with beautifully pure, wholesome smiles on their delicate, polished faces. Each new one on the market had a long waiting list of customers anxious to add it to their collection and, by the look of the place, Jessie hadn't missed one. The house smelt of polish and disinfectant, and nothing was out of place. Kathy could imagine it remaining just like this for ever, the various ornament collections being moved only to dust underneath and then replaced on the same spot, at the exact angle that Jessie had predetermined God knew how many years ago. The colour scheme was predominantly white and pink through-out. Pristine and clean, that was the only way to describe it, and unlived in somehow, a bit like a showhouse. In the sitting room, cushions had been arranged just so on the plastic-covered deep-pink sofa and two armchairs, which in turn had also been arranged just so on the deep-pink-carpeted floor. The effect was so perfect that it seemed an affront to enter the room, never mind sit on the chairs. The TV was hidden behind the double doors of a mock-Regency cabinet, and the shell-pink vertical blinds at the windows, like every other window in the house, were accom-panied by shell-pink nets, as a backup, Kathy mused, just in case some passer-by should develop the ability to look through the gaps in the blinds. The kitchen had a distinct 1950s feel, the units were all white, the floor white-tiled with tiny black diamonds where the corners of the tiles met. Here and there about the room were touches of red-and-white gingham, giving the illusion of pink, and nothing looked as though it had ever been used. The downstairs bathroom, she was told on arrival, was Jessie's alone; she couldn't use a bathroom anyone else used. It too was pink and had undoubtedly been installed straight from the factory. Just in case she should be caught short while upstairs, she had an identical en suite bathroom in her bedroom. Kathy was free to use the big upstairs bathroom, but she must not use the others; that was Jessie's absolute rule. Kathy wondered what catastrophe would befall Jessie's sanitised universe if she did. She would sleep in the bedroom that had belonged to Claire, her beautiful, thick cousin, but first she would be required to remove her shoes and leave them at the front door. This was said by Jessie with some distaste, as though she had fully expected Kathy to have known this and was now justifiably upset that it had had to be mentioned. A new pair of sock slippers, pink, were produced from a cellophane packet and given to her for the duration of her stay, after which, she surmised, they would be ritually burned in the back garden.

Sitting on the sofa in the sitting room was more of a challenge than Kathy could have anticipated, because she slid all over the plastic covers. She looked across at Jessie in one of the armchairs, seemingly at ease, and guessed it must be something to do with the fact that she weighed about as much as a tea leaf. There was nothing of her; she looked like an animated skeleton, and once again there was that curious attempt not to exist by twisting her legs around each other till they almost seemed to merge. Her thin arms were crossed tightly over her chest, another attempt to take up as little space as possible, or maybe to ensure that she touched as little of the surrounding environment as possible, and one gloved hand reached up bearing the ubiquitous hankie over her nose and mouth. No wonder Harry had gone quietly insane, she thought, living in this mausoleum, with this mentally disturbed woman who would not allow contact with an endless list of dangerous items that existed only in her own head. How would he know if he had transgressed and therefore exposed his mother to murderous bacteria, if he didn't know what was and wasn't on her highly personal list? The only way he would know, Kathy realised, was to himself become as demented as Jessie. Was that, she wondered sadly, why he had lost all his early promise and why he had retreated into his mystic world? Maybe it would've been better if Claire had been the one left behind to care for Jessie, because Claire had neither imagination nor intelligence, whereas Harry had been blessed with both, so where was there for him to go in this insane situation but into a slightly insane state of his own?

'So,' said the voice behind the hankie – she must keep an enormous supply of new hankies about the place – 'ye say ye don't need the cash. Whit dae ye dae, like,' a bony hand reached out in a vague motion, 'up there?'

'Ah work in the Tourist Centre,' Kathy replied. 'Started off in the tearoom, then moved on tae bein' a guide.'

'An' ye *like* that?' Jessie asked, bemused.

'Aye, it's good fun,' Kathy said.

'It canny bring ye in that much, though, surely?'

'Well, Ah, um.' How was she to say it? 'I write a bit as well.'

'*Write*?' Such was Jessie's amazement that Kathy wondered if she had inadvertently told her she water-skied naked behind an elephant. 'Whit dae ye mean *write*?'

'Stories an' things,' Kathy said uncertainly.

'*Stories an' things?*' Clearly she had muddied the waters still further. 'An' there's money in that, is there?' Jessie asked.

'Aye,' Kathy replied, feeling about an inch tall.

'Well, whit kinda thing dae ye write aboot?'

God, couldn't she just let it drop? 'I write wee stories for women's magazines,' she explained, 'and Ah write romantic books.'

'Like Mills & Boon?' Jessie demanded. 'That kinda thing?'

'Aye,' Kathy smiled. 'That kinda thing.'

There was a silence while Jessie mulled this over. 'Whit name dae ye write under?' she asked eventually.

'Lillian –'

'No' Lillian Bryson?' Jessie interrupted.

'Aye, that's right! How did ye know that?'

'You're Lillian Bryson?' Jessie laughed. She leapt from her plastic-covered chair, went over to a bureau in the corner, pulled open a drawer and took from it a pile of slim booklets, each one encased in its own plastic cover. '*That* Lillian Bryson?' she demanded, holding one aloft.

'Aye,' Kathy replied quietly, recognising one of her romantic adventures.

The two women stared at each other, shocked by the revelations. Kathy *was* Lillian Bryson, Jessie *read* Lillian Bryson!

'Ah read these a' the time!' Jessie said excitedly. 'You wrote these?'

Kathy nodded. 'Aye,' she said again.

'But these are good!' Jessie said. 'Ah love these! But why did ye call yersel' Lillian Bryson, well?'

'Ah just liked the idea o' my mother's name on the covers,' she laughed, 'an' the publisher thought Lillian was merr high-class soundin' than Lily.'

'Oh, that's great, hen!' Jessie said breathlessly. 'Yer mammy woulda loved that!'

Watching Jessie's excitement, Kathy found herself close to tears. She wrote stories for lonely women, tales of romantic love that always triumphed, of beautiful heroines from good families, living blameless lives and being pursued by handsome heroes with chiselled features and fine intentions. Innocent fantasy, that was what she produced, not literature, fairy tales for those who yearned for romance. Somehow the fact that Jessie the whore, who lived in a sterile, pink-and-white house and spent her life trying to fend off the dirt that she felt polluted the world, that deep down Jessie wanted the true love story that she had said she had given up long ago, filled her with pity and sadness. Not for the first time either. There was that other woman, the one who wrote to her about the fictitious men in her books as though they really existed, the one who had become her penpal without knowing who it was she was writing to. That had taught her a lesson too.

She had wanted to write all her life, that was her fantasy and, when Angus died, Rory had let her have his typewriter. She still had it, though it had long ago given way to a computer that frightened the life out of her. If Rory, who was frightened of nothing and no one, hadn't more or less stood over her, mentally if not always physically, she would dump the computer even now and go back to doing her writing on Angus's old typewriter. It wasn't writing of course, not real writing; she didn't have the confidence to try, so she had – what was it Rory called it? Frittered away whatever ability she had, that was it, because she was too afraid to take the risk of finding out if she had any. But that was Rory, he said what he thought. Angus and Bunty had, he said, raised him with the knowledge that there was nothing he couldn't do, nowhere he couldn't go, and so he didn't understand how it was with other people who hadn't had them as parents. The old Major, he said, had recognised in the young Angus a ferocious intelligence cheated of the kind of education it needed, and so, being a decent kind of man, he had made it possible for Angus to expand his mind. If it hadn't been for that old Sassenach Angus Macdonald might easily have gone to the bad, because with all legitimate avenues to learning blocked, all that intelligence would have taken him in some other direction. So Angus got the house and the land, with the beasts to bring in the money, and a wife who had known him well enough and long enough to understand that he had to go wherever his mind took him. And he had passed his beliefs and his vision on to his son, only the two had very different characters; that had been the flaw in Angus's grand design. He had, himself, a naturally kind and gentle personality that saw the differences in others and made allowances for them, while his son saw the same traits and regarded them as failings. Regarded them and announced them loudly. Rory was his father's son, but he wasn't his father. He was talking of Angus's philosophy of personal freedom one day, sitting by the fireside in the cottage, when Kathy had remarked that he really didn't understand, that not everyone had a father like Angus.

'Dear God, don't!' he said.

'Don't what?' Kathy asked.

'Don't tell me a sob story about what a hard life you had growing up in the streets of Glasgow, being beaten by a cruel father and all that!'

'You really are an insensitive pig!' she said. 'Ever thought of applying to become a Samaritan?'

Rory didn't mean to be insensitive, but he was, and he couldn't understand why others took offence. He had no time for small talk or social niceties, he had been raised to be honest and he expected others to be just as honest as he was himself, whereas Angus had taken care not to hurt people's feelings. And Rory's honest opinion of her writing was that she lacked courage. He was the only one, apart from Kathy herself and her publisher, who knew she was Lillian Bryson, and he openly disparaged her for it, finding it impossible to understand why she wasted her time on 'this trash', as he called it. Wouldn't it be better to try, even if she failed, than to go on churning out this lightweight drivel? Her head knew he was right, but she had never listened to her head, and there were compensations, little incidents that bolstered her position, if only temporarily. Like her penpal, Ishbel Smith. Miss Smith had been a lady of more than seventy when their correspondence began, right back at the emergence of Lillian. Miss Smith had been manageress at William Hodge's, a Glasgow printing firm where calendars were produced in great numbers, she even sent Lillian one as a sample, though it was by then many years out of date. Kathy hadn't expected to see those damned white Scotties in tartan tammies ever again. Miss Smith, or Ishbel, as she had gradually become, had a staff of many women and girls under her control and, now that she was older and wiser, she knew that she had often been hard on them. She hadn't realised it at the time and she greatly regretted it in later years, but it was too late to make amends. The reason and, furthermore, a reason she had never divulged to another living soul outside her family and friends of the time, was that she had lost Bruce, her one true love, in the Second World War. Ishbel had been eighteen and Bruce twenty-two, and they had intended marrying when he came home on leave after Dunkirk, only Bruce didn't come back from Dunkirk. It had taken her a long time to stop waiting for him, to let her dreams of the life they would share vanish in the cold light of day. The shock had caused her hair to fall out, it seemed, and it had never regrown, so even had she felt like loving again, who would've taken her? It had made her bitter, Ishbel confessed, seeing all those other women marrying and having children, and then their children doing the same and, she was ashamed to say, she had taken it out on them. '*There you are, Kathy Kelly,*' Lillian said to her. '*You never considered that, did you? You never stopped to wonder how the auld biddy had got like that, did you?*' She recalled the day she had walked out of Hodge's for the last time, having emptied a pot of thick, brown glue over Miss Smith. She had watched her reach up to protect her always neat hair and was shocked, but not displeased, when it came away in the older woman's hands. Until that moment she hadn't suspected that Miss Smith wore a wig, and even when she found out, she had felt no pity. Miss Smith had goaded and abused her, as she had done all the other women who'd worked in Hodge's, but poor old Miss Smith had her reasons after all. It was Kathy's penance to keep up the correspondence without letting Miss Smith know who she really was, and how could the old woman ever have suspected? This Lillian Bryson she wrote to had some psychic connection with her and her Bruce, because all the heroes in Lillian's books were Bruce to the life. It brought their romance back so vividly that it was almost like seeing him again, she wrote, and she would always be grateful to Lillian for that.

And it wasn't just Miss Smith. As Lillian, Kathy supplied the romance that was missing from the lives of a certain slice of ordinary women everywhere. They married men who wanted to be looked after in every possible way and, in return for all the washing, ironing, cleaning and caring, they wanted a little spark that proved they weren't being taken for granted, even though they knew they were. A smouldering look across a crowded room, a hand holding theirs, the caress of a finger against a cheek, a single red rose, all totally out of the question as far as the men they had married were concerned. Such things never occurred to them and, even if they had, would have been labelled 'soft'. Lillian Bryson provided that missing spark, and let the intellectuals scoff, because if it made a difference, if it lightened the lives of those women

244

for even an hour, well, that was worth doing. She wouldn't have been in the least surprised if Angela Crawford turned to Lillian in moments of extreme stress, of which there must be many in her life in Moodiesburn, and the truth was that it filled a gap in her own life too. You could keep the sex. She had tried that and the very thought of it thereafter had made her feel sick, but romance was something else, something Lillian Bryson brought to Kathy Kelly's life too. But, that apart, Rory was right, though she would never admit it to him. The longer she was Lillian the less chance there was that she might take a chance and try to write beyond chiselled-featured, impossible heroes.

Her correspondence with Ishbel set her thinking of other loose ends in her early life, of her other adversary, Nigel Dewar, and his acolyte, Ida, in Govan. Con was three years into his illness when the chance came to find out what had become of the corduroy-loving pharmacist. He would've taken over Wilson's by now, he might even have bought it out and be strutting about, white goatee bristling with pomposity, master of the little he surveyed. She had been called to Glasgow because Con was ill with another infection that he wasn't supposed to recover from, only, of course, he did, and she took the opportunity to stroll down memory lane. The chemist shop across from Fairfield's Shipyard had gone, as had Fairfield's, but it didn't take much searching to find a shopping centre nearby in which was housed an updated Wilson's. They were everywhere. Had she been asked what changes she noticed in her native city, she would've said Glasgow had turned into one giant shopping centre made up of countless smaller shopping centres. She went into the shop and asked the woman behind the counter if she might have a word with Mr Dewar, receiving in reply a strange look. Well, could she then see the duty pharmacist, Kathy suggested, in her best English. Out came a white-coated woman in her thirties. Lillian came smoothly to her aid with a plot.

'I was looking for Nigel Dewar,' she smiled. 'He was a colleague of mine many years ago. We lost touch when I left the country.' '*Ahem*,' said her conscience, but she ignored it. 'I just thought it would be nice to meet up again.' But what, she wondered, would she say if a silver-haired Nigel was produced from somewhere? She would cross that bridge, she decided, if and when she came to it.

'Oh, that was a bad one!' said the pharmacist quietly, beckoning her, as she was a fellow pill-counter and therefore of impeccable character, into the pharmacy. 'You wouldn't have heard about it, seeing as you were out of the country, but I understand it caused quite a fuss at the time, though there's no one here now who was there then.'

Nigel, it transpired, had been accosted in the old shop by two men, relatives of a woman who claimed Nigel had deliberately tried to make a sale, instead of giving her sound advice about the urgency of her child's condition. If an unknown lady doctor hadn't been there at the time, the woman claimed, her baby could've died, and her relatives wished to have a word with Mr Dewar about the incident. There had been what the Glasgow Courts liked to call 'a fracas', and the police had been called to eject the men, but an hour later Mr Dewar had dropped dead of a heart attack in the pharmacy. There were so many thoughts going through his 'ex-colleague's' mind at that moment. There was 'Hooray!' and 'Damn it to hell, Ah shoulda been here tae see it!' She desperately wanted to ask if Ida had been dragged off in a straitjacket, foaming at the mouth, for some reason, about letting Fenians in to Govan chemist's shops. But uppermost in her mind was the need to keep a straight face and mouth words of shock and a few platitudes, difficult though this was to accomplish. Thanks to the enthusiasms of youth she was now carrying Ishbel Smith on her conscience and, of course, you should never speak ill of the dead, even if you spoke exceedingly ill of them when they were alive and they had richly deserved it. Some you win and some you lose, but still, amid the philosophy there had to be room for a slight snigger or two as well, surely?

'So when did you last see Mr Dewar?' the pharmacist asked.

'Must've been just before Easter 1973. That's when I went abroad,' Kathy replied thoughtfully.

'I'm sure it was about then that it happened. It was definitely around Easter, but I can't say for sure which year.'

'*Ah can!*' Kathy thought, but she shook her head in an acceptably mournful manner and tut-tutted, as tradition required.

'I've often wondered, actually,' the pharmacist said, 'who the lady doctor was. I know Mr Dewar was a friend of yours, and we're all human, we all make mistakes after all. There but for the grace of God and all that, but by all accounts he did make a bit of a mistake. The doctor called for an ambulance to take the baby to hospital and apparently it wasn't a minute too soon, she saved the child's life.'

'And there was another pharmacist working with Nigel at that time, as I recall,' Kathy said, 'a Mr Riddell was it? Tall, quiet, losing his hair, but he'll be long gone now too.'

'You mean Mr Liddell?' the pharmacist said.

'Yes, that was it, Liddell. I suppose he'll be dead now too.'

'No, no he's not!' replied the pharmacist. 'He's nearly eighty now but you'd never think it to look at him. He spends all his time sailing his boat, bright as a button and fit as a fiddle.'

It was like a fairytale, it had such symmetry, such justice, somehow. 'Well,' said a delighted Kathy, 'if you should see him, could you please pass on to him Kathleen Kelly's very best good wishes, and tell him that there is a God after all? He'll know what that means.'

'I will indeed! But isn't life strange? Poor Mr Dewar!'

'Mmm,' Kathy said sadly. 'As you say, poor Nigel!', and she would've sworn that she sounded as if she meant it.

14

So, finally she was on her way home. As she sat in the train she had visions of Jessie's house being scrubbed out by a team of white-suited individuals wearing masks and rubber gloves, cleansing the abode of all outside contamination. But was there another, more specialised team, waiting in the wings, she wondered, to scrub the pink-and-white mausoleum clean of the pollution brought in by the first one, and perhaps another after that? She had called Rory the night before to tell him what time she would be arriving at Glenfinnan, and as she was talking she suddenly realised that she was trying to keep the conversation as brief as possible, in order to restrict the contamination she would be leaving behind on Jessie's phone. It got to you, she thought, it really got to you, and once again she thought of Harry living in Jessie's strange little world all these years and almost forgave him for disappointing her ambitions for him.

Whenever she had been in Glasgow at the behest of Con's various illnesses, Rory had been instructed to make sure the cottage was kept heated and Cat kept fed. She had never got round to finding a name for the kitten he had rescued from the murderous intent of whoever had drowned the rest of the litter, and Cat he had remained. He wasn't the brightest of felines or perhaps he had suffered oxygen starvation before Rory had hauled him out and revived him. He seemed to hold Kathy personally responsible for the entire episode, and no matter how well she cared for him, whenever he got within striking distance he would lash out with his claws and screech at her. Rory, though, Cat adored, climbing on his knees when he visited the cottage, twisting himself around his legs, purring loud enough to lift the roof, and occasionally he would disappear and be found at Rory's door, having walked the couple of miles from Drumsallie to Glenfinnan.

'How come he hates me and loves you?' Kathy asked, nursing yet another scratch. 'Doesn't the daft thing know I saved his life?'

'No you didnae,' Rory replied calmly. 'I did. As I remember it, you stood there shaking, it was me warmed him up.'

'Aye, well,' she conceded, 'I was there, and I gave him a home, yet he lives just to attack me. He sinks those claws in even when I'm putting out food for him, for God's sake. Now that's not natural behaviour for a cat, is it? How d'you explain that?'

'Och, well,' Rory replied, staring into the fire and petting the besotted feline, 'it's a well-known fact that cats are good judges of character.'

She had lost count of her visits to Glasgow and resented every one. Having graduated from running the tearoom to being a guide, she had embraced the history of the Jacobites enthusiastically, while managing to keep her personal opinion of Bonnie Prince Charlie to herself. The Tourist Centre had expanded in recent years to include another extension, this time housing a small exhibition of the charming Prince's little adventure. It was decided that two fibreglass models would be commissioned, one of the Prince as he had arrived in Scotland, wearing a clerk's black suit as a disguise, and the other of a Highlander of the day. When the chosen artist arrived to discuss the commission, Kathy was away affronting Con's doctors and nurses with her refusal to give up her life and devote it to what was left of his. She was away, too, when the figures were delivered and arranged in the exhibition. When she arrived back, anxious to see the results, Mavis and the others were almost dancing with excitement, happy, she had thought, at how well it had all turned out. The first figure, of the Prince, had been placed at a table by the entrance, and then there were various information points, maps etc., and finally, turning to the right, was the figure of the 1745 Highlander, complete with kilt, philabeg and drawn broadsword. The others had gone back to work, leaving her to browse over their handiwork at her leisure, or so she thought till she examined the figure more carefully, and looked at his face. It was Rory! 'Oh, my God!' she shrieked, and Mavis and the others rushed in, all of them helpless with laughter.

'How? Who?' she stuttered, shocked to her toes.

'We thought it would be a nice surprise!' Mavis giggled.

'A nice surprise?' Kathy repeated. 'But it's . . . it's . . .'

'Aye, it's Rory!' Once again everyone collapsed in heaps of laughter.

Kathy was furious that they should all find it so funny. 'Why is it Rory?' she demanded.

'The artist guy wanted a typical West Coast male,' Mavis replied, dabbing at her eyes, 'and he saw Rory putting his boat out on the loch. He went after him before we could stop him!'

'And you're telling me that you *tried* to stop him, are you?' Kathy asked, and once again the assembled company collapsed in a communal howl.

'Not really,' Mavis admitted eventually. 'I mean, who were we to argue with an artist?'

'You should've dragged him away, shown him Donnie, or Lachie even, shown him the nearest German tourist!' She looked around her colleagues, her friends, as they held on to each other for support in their mirth. 'And why is it that you all find everything I say so bloody hilarious?'

'Shown him Donnie?' Mavis screeched. 'You mean you'd rather I had to live with a thing that looked like him even when I'm working?'

'And you think this *thing* is going to be any easier to have around?'

'Well, it's a damned sight easier than Donnie anyway, at least I can trust it not to burst into one of his songs!'

'I'd prefer it to be Donnie, songs and all! Rory Macdonald is rarely a bundle of laughs, but this is like having him staring at you in his worst mood!'

'Aye, I know!' Mavis chuckled. 'He wasnae too happy about posing, but he did it under protest. We made him promise not to tell you, so that it wouldnae spoil the surprise!'

'This object is here under my protest,' Kathy replied sourly. 'Look at the eyes, they follow you around!'

'I know! The cleaner refuses to be in here on her own because it's so lifelike!'

'So why are you laughing? Can we not get it changed?'

'Course we canny!' Mavis replied. 'The money's been spent. What d'you expect us to say to Head Office? That the cleaner's scared of it and Kathy Kelly says it's too like the man the artist chose to model it on?'

'But it's . . . it's *horrible!*'

The others danced around with renewed glee. 'I know! I know!' Mavis giggled. 'And you havnae seen the best of it yet, wait till the next tourist bus comes in!'

So they all waited excitedly until a busload of German tourists arrived and were encouraged in to the exhibition. The leading group reached the figure of the Prince and, thinking he was real, tried to pay him an entrance fee. The dedicated staff tried to stifle guffaws. 'They all do that!' Mavis whispered to Kathy. Then they found their way to Rory Mark II, and one by one they looked around to see if they were being observed. Staff eyes were averted and hands busied themselves with nothing, and thus reassured each tourist carefully picked up Rory's kilt and looked underneath.

Kathy gasped and the others danced around holding each other and giggling. 'They all do *that* as well!' Mavis shrieked. As she clapped her hands the ever-present cigarette fell from between her fingers and burned her thumb. 'Ouch!' she shouted.

'Serves you right!' Kathy said happily.

'Know what I think we should do?' Mavis asked, struggling to regain control of her cigarette.

'I'm scared to ask!' Kathy replied.

'Well, we could get a fan put in under him there, and we could put in a coin-operated machine to work it –'

'*Don't!*' Kathy screeched, covering her ears.

'And every time the tourists wanted to check him out underneath, they would have to put fifty pence in the machine, and up would go the kilt! It'd be like that Marilyn photo, you know the one? With the white dress up round about her ears!'

'Mavis, you're bloody *warped!*'

'Well, it's just an idea,' she giggled. 'Could be a great wee private money-spinner for us, a perk of the job if you like!'

Kathy looked at the statue again. The artist chap had captured Rory to the life, he'd even given him that scowl he had when he was too displeased to bother telling you so. And somehow he'd managed to reproduce the authentic wry expression in Rory's deep-set blue eyes that made you want to slap him. No wonder, she thought, the cleaner was too spooked to work alone in the extension, she'd be none too happy about it herself.

'We could try putting a bag over its head,' she offered.

'What's the point of that?' Mavis asked. 'We'd know it was still Rory, wouldn't we?'

'So tell me,' Kathy asked her. 'Is he a *real* Scotsman then?'

'Well, we had a talk about that,' Mavis said, rubbing her burnt thumb, 'and we've decided not to tell you. If you want to find that out, Kathy, you'll have to do what everybody else does – lift up his kilt and look!'

She had never told anyone why or where she was going when she went to Glasgow, only that she would be away on business, and her recent visit, the longest and, as it turned out, final one, happened during winter when the Centre was closed. Rory had insisted on driving her to Glasgow; he was, he said, going on his annual shopping expedition anyway.

'So,' he said, 'why are you actually going to Glasgow?'

She was surprised, because he had never questioned her previous absences. 'My father's dying,' she replied.

'I didn't know you had one,' he said.

She looked wryly at him. 'Well, Rory,' she said, 'there's a lot of people have said the same thing about you over the years, even the ones who knew your father!'

He grinned, stopping the van where she asked, at Glasgow Cross. 'Why am I dropping you here?' he asked. 'It would be easier to take you right to where he lives.'

'Not for me,' she replied curtly.

'Don't you want me to know where you come from?' he asked, smiling. 'Is it that bad?'

'I didnae say that, did I?' she demanded. 'It's a while since I was last here, I fancy a walk through the old neighbourhood, I'm a nostalgic kind of creature. OK?'

'In a pig's ear you are!' he scoffed, driving off and leaving her.

She waited till he was out of sight before walking along London Road. He was right, of course, she didn't want him to take her right to Con's door. If he did there would be a connection in her mind between the West Coast and the East End of Glasgow, and she didn't want that; the two places were completely separate, both geographically and emotionally, even if they did have a connecting door. And now that door was closed for ever, never the twain ever would meet. Sitting on the train, watching familiar station names flash past, Crianlarich, Tyndrum, Rannoch, Corrour, there was quiet satisfaction about finally being finished with the life she had been born into. She went over in her mind everything that had happened, from Con's interminable, lingering death, the funeral, meeting poor, repressed Angela Crawford, forcing Frank McCabe to cough up the loot and to face up to his worst nightmare, that the knowledge of his little transgression hadn't died with Aggie after all, and the news about her brother Peter, or Brother Peter as he apparently preferred to be known these days. That had been a high point, she had to admit, the thought of Peter, who spent his entire life criticising other people and instructing them in how to live their lives, was now being told how to live his life. That, she knew, was what cults did, they laid down their own rules, those of a highly individualistic mind set couldn't be prime material. So what could've happened to him to make him surrender his opinions, she wondered. All Peter had ever wanted was to get the best of everything, and he had never cared how he did so or who he stood on, put down or abandoned in the process either. If she had ever been asked to venture a guess on who in her family would have reached the top and be living the good life, she would instinctively have chosen her brother, even before Harry, or at least, the Harry she thought she knew. Harry, she always thought, would be successful and happy, but still there; Peter would've gone elsewhere, indeed Peter had, but this wasn't how she could ever have imagined him spending his life. And Harry had mentioned his client, Peter's mother-in-law of all things, and her concern over her daughter's wellbeing. There had been no communication, she said, all letters were ignored and attempts to contact her by phone were blocked. Well, cults did that too, everyone knew that. The way to control every thought and action of the adherents was to be the only influence in their lives, and that was done by slowly but surely cutting them off from past ties. She had read newspaper reports of desperate families trying to convince relatives, usually sons or daughters caught in cult webs, that they were being controlled, and those operating the cult turned this against them. Your family are the ones trying to control you, they'd say, if they really loved you they would understand and accept that you're happy, that you belong here, therefore if they are trying to take you away, they don't love you and are trying to harm you. It was standard brainwashing procedure, well documented and often described. Kathy had never understood how anyone could be taken in by it, but she had always assumed that the ones who were must be young, weak and vulnerable. Her brother was in his fifties now, and by all accounts he had been involved with the Higher Seekers for years. It made no sense. Not that she was concerned about Peter; why should she be? He had never been concerned about her, about any of the family for that matter. He hadn't even attended his mother's funeral, citing 'important business' as his excuse. She remembered her grandmother, Old Aggie, opining that Peter had avoided Lily's funeral because he was 'too sensitive' to face his grief, and how she had attacked Aggie for it. Presumably 'important business' was, then, basic cult code for refusing to relax the ban on family contact. It made sense that a family crisis, like the death of a close relative, would've been a danger point for the cult's control, presumably, given that at such times entire families would meet, thereby intensifying the strength of feelings, however latent, feelings the cult had worked hard to eradicate. So she didn't care one way or another about Peter, he had made his choice and it was no business of hers, it was just that she was curious about how someone as self-centred as him could've become entangled in a cult. It couldn't have happened to a better person, she decided, poetic justice, hoist by his own petard, whatever a petard was, and she laughed every time she thought of it. She was curious, that was all, she'd just like to know.

Everything was as it should be at the cottage. Rory had kept it heated so that even in December there was no hint of dampness, and the frequent rain in the Western Highlands ensured dampness at the best of times. Tourists often remarked on the full burns and rivers, and they stopped to film the many waterfalls cascading off the hills when it rained, all rushing to the sea through lush greenery. As visitors were only there for a couple of weeks, it seemed churlish to point out that the high rainfall causing all those photo opportunities also made for a general dampness that could seep into your soul during winter. Cat was as cantankerous as ever with her, as affectionate towards Rory, and given Rory's lamentably low level of interest in local gossip, she knew she would have to wait till she saw Mavis to be brought up to date. He did have one piece of news, though, Mavis and Donnie were now grandparents; Kirsty and Kenny the chef had produced their first child during her absence. 'Boy or girl?' she asked. 'Aye, one or the other,' he replied. Over the years the easy approach to relationships of the Macdonalds had taken them over. During her days at the house up the hill, she had been constantly amazed at how years could pass between Rory's visits home, but he walked in the door as though he'd been in Fort William for a couple of hours, and his parents treated him the same way. They slipped into whatever groove they had been in when they had last met, there was no awkwardness, no getting to know you again strangeness, and these days Kathy and Rory were the same. He didn't ask if her father had died; he assumed that as she had gone to Glasgow because he was dying, the fact that she had now returned meant that he *had* died. He asked no questions about the events, if she wanted to tell him he knew she would, and if she didn't, well that was fine too. Once she had mistaken the Macdonald way as uncaring, which sat uneasily with her knowledge of and affection for Angus and Bunty, but she understood it now for what it was, a total acceptance that went beyond emotional ups and downs or, in the case of her own family, explosions. Having been thinking about the fate of her brother recently, she remembered how her mother had described her two children. 'The same,' Lily had said about Kathy and Peter, 'but different', and it struck her that over the years she and Rory had become like that too, but unlike the situation between her and her brother, they were comfortable with each other like that. Life, she thought contentedly, was strange.

It was the dreams that did it, that stabbed through her contentedness. That the child cried and would go on doing so from time to time, she had long ago accepted, but another twist had now been added. The child cried and, as always, she chased through the streets she had left behind long ago looking for it, but instead of being unable to find it, she now did. She would follow the sound of the plaintive screams from one long gone East End street to another, with the child always just beyond her reach, sure that around the next corner she would finally be able to hold it and console it, telling it how sorry she was that she had failed it, that she would do anything, *anything* for another chance. Only now she would see the child and pick it up, its cries mixing with her own sobs of relief and joy, but when she looked into its face she would find Peter staring back at her. The horror of the usual dreams was bad enough, she thought, but now it had become positively bizarre! And what was worse, there were other dreams, entirely non-threatening, where she would be happily going about her normal business and would then be arrested by the sound of someone whistling 'Pedro the Fisherman'. It had been Peter's tune, the one he whistled as he came up the stairs of the old Moncur Street tenement, and she couldn't remember how many decades it had been since she had last heard it. It was a whistle, that was all, but each time she would awake as though being pursued by the hounds of Hell. She tried to rationalise it. It was only natural, she told herself, that family memories should surface in the wake of Con's death, she had, after all, laid her background to rest when Con had been cremated, and like it or not, and she never had, Peter was part of that background. Maybe the death of your last parent was like drowning, she mused, maybe it made all your life pass before your subconscious. But it would stop soon, as long as she didn't dwell on it and make more of it than there was. It would pass in a while. In a longer while, then.

It was January and she wouldn't start work at the Centre again until the end of March. These winter breaks were usually welcome because they meant she could become Lillian again, but this time she couldn't settle. Thanks to Rory's persistence she had a smattering of computer knowledge, and if she didn't exactly surf the net, at least she could dip a toe in it now and again. After a few defeats she managed to find some information about the Higher Seekers, just to satisfy her curiosity. They were an elite little organization, they believed in salvation through culture, and they didn't just accept any passing refugee from the days of Flower Power. No standing at bus stations picking up lost teenagers with suspect promises for the Higher Seekers, they accepted only university graduates. Brain power mattered to the Higher Seekers, because they were 'the chosen' whatever that meant, and therefore no mongrels would be entertained, only pedigree stock. She wondered if some escapees from the Third Reich might have started it. Their headquarters was a commune in the middle of the Mojave Desert that they called Gabriel's Gateway. She wondered why the Angel Wally hadn't called it after himself, but maybe even he had spotted the consumer difficulty of putting that above the door. Behind the gate the Higher Seekers bought and sold international art collections and, in their spare time, meditated with 'teachers' until they too reached the status of angels. She had to admit that that was quite an eye-catching offer, it beat the Reader's Digest selling techniques into a cocked hat, no problem! Other cults waited to be beamed up by some passing spacecraft and transported to Nirvana, but she'd never heard of one that promised each follower their own pair of wings! Other, lesser mortals, collected stamps, ran marathons or followed football teams, but not the Higher Seekers, they thought themselves towards personal means of flight! True, there was only one to date, dear old Wally who'd thought the wheeze up, but if the others were good, he had decreed, if they studied with their gurus and worked hard to rid themselves of outside influences, especially family and friends, one day they too would become angels. Not could, but would. Kathy kept thinking that for Peter the Messiah this would be a bit of a comedown, but still, he would look fetching in feathers. The group was self-sufficient and self-protective, and those who were permitted to join the so far solitary celestial ranks underwent a long apprenticeship, being sent to hellholes all over the world, but hellholes carefully and strictly controlled by the cult. She remembered odd reports of Peter being seen in various countries, Canada, Alaska, though no one ever knew what he actually did for a living, even those who had encountered him in these unlikely locations couldn't say, because Peter had managed not to fully answer their questions. Well, cult orders could certainly explain his globetrotting. And there were those postcards that arrived less and less often, much prized by Old Aggie as proof that her grandson was special, was somebody. There had been something about that too on the Internet, something written by an ex-Higher Seeker. She clicked on the 'back' symbol, and there it was. In the first three years contact with family and former lives was scaled down to the minimum, but after five years there was a rule that it must stop completely. If they survived this weeding process they were excused duty in the far-flung cult spots of the globe and taken to Gabriel's Gateway, which sounded like Heaven, Valhalla and Utopia rolled into one. There were strict rules governing how many pictures could be put on walls, and what sort; pop art was strictly banned. The only approved music was classical and, of course, the staple of all dictatorial regimes, newspapers, magazines and books were banned, as were radio and TV, and marriages were only permitted from inside the cult. It was very difficult to see what possible attraction any of this held for anyone and, inevitably, there were some who did escape, poor, disillusioned souls, still partly brainwashed, who were pursued and told in writing that they would die horrible deaths.

When Harry had first told her about Peter's life in California,

Kathy had laughed at the thought of him being involved in anything so bizarre, but the more she learned, the more uncomfortable she felt. There must be an angle, she decided. Peter couldn't have fallen for anything like this unless he was making something out of it, unless he was the first and only angel, for instance, reaping the rewards as the drones laboured in the vineyards. Still, it would be nice to know. Swallowing her pride she called one or two religious organizations and, bit by bit, was put in touch with groups that kept tabs on cults. The chap on the other end of the phone was kind and patient as she told her story. She explained what Peter was like, said it had to be a mistake, and finally the chap sighed wearily at the end of the phone.

'Please,' he said, 'don't tell me he's the last person you'd expect to join something like this. That's what every relative in your position says.'

'But, honestly,' she protested, 'Peter has a very strong character, he had big ideas, he was going places.'

'I know what you're thinking,' he said sympathetically, 'that he's perhaps being held against his will. Every relative thinks that too. But the fact is that it's the strong characters who get caught up in these things. They're the ones who have high expectations of life, high ideals, and they're on the lookout for *something*, for an alternative outlook on life, even if they don't know what it is. Often they're caught at a vulnerable time in their lives, a turning point of some sort. Along comes this nice person, usually attractive, articulate, persuasive, and that's that. If there's one thing I've learned working in this area, it's that we don't know people as well as we think we do, even if we're close to them they can do things that astound us.'

'So, you're saying, "Never say 'Never'"', are you?' Kathy asked.

'I suppose I am,' he said. 'There have been times when I've said about my own family that he or she would never do this or say that, but these days I stop myself, because I know better. Believe me, nobody really knows anybody, very few of us even know ourselves come to that, and I'm not being philosophical, I'm being realistic. I've done and said bizarre things in my life that I've looked back on years later and thought how out of character they were. I'm sure you've done just the same.'

At her end of the phone Kathy nodded; the man spoke no lies. She thought back to a conversation she had had with her aunt. Jessie, who missed nothing, had remarked approvingly that there had never been any gossip about her niece's morals, that Kathy had been too smart to give anyone grounds to question her good name. What might Jessie say if she knew about her out-of-character stupidity with Jamie Crawford, and the contents of Lily's red box? And Kathy was sure Jessie didn't know, because if she had, she would have said so. A whore Jessie might once have been, indeed there was no doubt about it, a whore she had been, yet Jessie Bryson was the most honest and strangely moral individual Kathy had ever known, her only regret was that it had taken so long to get to know her. And add to that all the other people she'd got wrong in her life, and how many people had got her wrong. When you really thought about it, human beings, unlike cats, were generally rotten judges of character.

'And there's something else you should consider,' the cult chap broke into her thoughts. 'It may seem incredible to you, you may think your brother's been hoodwinked and brainwashed, and he probably has, because groups that take over complete control of other people's lives and minds, down to telling them what they can read, have to be suspect. But perhaps this cult suits your brother, perhaps he's actually happy.'

'I never thought of that,' she admitted. 'I haven't managed to get past the disbelief yet.'

'That takes time,' he said. 'Relatives find it hard to come to terms with losing someone, because that's often what it's like, a death in the family. Often that's how it will remain. We usually advise families to keep writing letters, to maintain one-sided contact if that's what it turns out to be. Even if they get no replies it reminds those inside cults that there is a life outside, and even if they seem to have rejected it, it does still exist. But from what you've told me, your brother's been with the Higher Seekers for a very long time. My honest advice to you would be to settle for the death-in-the-family approach.'

What she hadn't told the helpful, sympathetic chap was that she was still quite likely to collapse with laughter at the thought of it. There was a part of her that thought if it had to happen to someone, then it couldn't have happened to a better bloke than Peter Kelly. It was so ironic; Peter Kelly who knew everything better than anyone, everyone else, even about their own lives, was now living a regimented life and being ordered about himself. But gradually she laughed less and wondered more; there *had* to be something wrong. She had examined Harry's business card many times, looked at the telephone, then looked away again. It was in the early hours of one morning, with the ghostly strains of 'Pedro the Fisherman' having once again roused her from her sleep that she finally dialled Harry's mobile number. He answered on the first ring.

'Ah hope ye wernae asleep?' she asked.

'No,' Harry replied mystically. 'I was pondering a client's problem. I never sleep until the answer has been revealed to me by the forces.'

'*For God's sake shut it, Harry,*' she thought. 'Harry, son,' she said kindly. 'This client o' yours, the wan that's Peter's mother-in-law, I need ye tae put me in touch wi' her.'

There was a sharp intake of breath at the other end of the phone. 'I can't do that!' he replied, aghast.

'Course ye can!' she said encouragingly. 'Look, it's simple, son. Tell her the forces brought me tae you, the same forces that brought *her* tae you. It's the forces that want us tae meet. See whit Ah mean?'

From the silence at the end of the phone she guessed that she had half-convinced him. 'We won't tell her that we're related, or that you're related to Peter, see? It'll be, um –'

'Irrelevant,' he offered helpfully.

'Exactly! An' it's true, isn't it, Harry? Somethin' higher than oorsels must've preordained this.' She closed her eyes and cringed. 'Ah mean, there's her, worried aboot her lassie, an' here's me, worried aboot ma brother, an' we're baith in touch wi' you, the wan person that knows where they are an' whit they're daein'. Noo,

261

if there's no' mystic forces involved in that, well, Ah don't know!'

'I could give her your number and tell her that you've come to me with similar concerns, and that I think you could help each other through me,' he mused. 'But I can't see that she needs to know that we're cousins, it might make it sound as if there's some kind of collusion.'

'An',' Kathy continued the thought, 'we know it's they mystic forces, daen't we?'

'OK, I can do that!' he announced.

Kathy put the phone down. 'Just as well, son,' she muttered. 'Ma next move was to threaten tae tell yer Mammy!'

It was two days before Margery Nairn called from Bearsden. She sounded like her name, and she sounded like Bearsden, a no nonsense lady of means from a respectable suburb of Glasgow. Kathy's number had been passed to her by 'Hari' – there was a subtle difference in the pronunciation, a kind of breathless note. Kathy assumed her best polite accent.

'I believe that you and I may be related in a way,' she said. 'My brother Peter is, if I understand Hari –' ye gods! – 'correctly, married to your daughter Rose?'

'Yes! Isn't Hari wonderful? How does he know these things?'

'*You should see him with Find the Lady, sweetheart!*' Kathy thought. 'I know what you mean!' she lied in her affected voice. 'And there are some people who refuse to accept there's anything in what he does, that he's a crank. Would you believe that?'

'I know, I know!' said Margery Nairn. 'But they're in denial, the thought that he's in touch with powers beyond the normal is too much for their closed minds to take in, that's how I think of it!'

'Could I perhaps come and see you, Mrs Nairn?'

'Margery, please.' She was talking to a fellow believer, after all.

'Margery,' Kathy beamed down the phone, hoping the aura would arrive undimmed at the other end. 'I have concerns too, perhaps we can help each other now that Hari has acted as our conduit?'

'Absolutely! You and I are fellow travellers, Miss Kelly.'

'Oh, please, Kathy!'

'Kathy, then. With Hari's help I know we can get to where the forces want us to be!'

'My thinking precisely, Margery!' she said. 'Kathy Kelly, ye're a right bloody liar!' she said to herself as she laid the receiver down again. 'An' ye wondered where "Hari" got it frae?'

When she told Rory she was going away again, he greeted the news with a look. She needed to finalise matters arising from her father's death, she said, and he nodded, though she knew he didn't really believe her. But would he, she wondered, believe the real story if she told it to him? Brother Peter? Sister Rose? Mystic Hari? Margery Nairn's house was very similar to Jessie's, though neither would've accepted that, given the traditional and never-ending antipathy that existed between those who lived on Glasgow's South and West sides. There might be no visible dividing wall running down the city, but it was there. Margery was a tall, thin woman in her late sixties, with pale, lined skin and huge glasses covering a fair part of her face. She was neat and ladylike in a grey skirt and pale blue twin set. Her hair had been dyed a discreet blonde and carefully coiffed in an immaculate French roll at the back of her head. Looking at her, Kathy doubted if Margery had financed the buying of her house in quite the same way as Jessie had hers, and it came as no surprise that she had once been a teacher, as had her husband, though she had been a widow for almost twenty years now. Was that, Kathy wondered, the beginning of her interest in the likes of her daft cousin, a turning point of loneliness and grief in her life? Still, better mad Hari than some winged wonder, surely? Her only child, Rose, a student of archaeology, had been on an exchange year at a Californian University in 1967. There she had met a psychology lecturer, Peter Kelly, and after a very short courtship Rose had called to say they had been married. Naturally, Margery had been concerned about this. Rose was barely nineteen and away from home, while Peter was an experienced twenty-five-year-old whom Margery had never met, so to satisfy herself she had gone out to meet her new son-in-law. For her part, Kathy was shattered. He had been home in the mid-sixties, just before Lily died in 1968, so Peter was a married man by then. Margery had been reassured, apparently. She had been afraid that Rose had married some weird American, but Peter was Scottish and, what was more, he was an intelligent, ambitious young man. 'He was very charismatic, very much the toast of the campus, always surrounded by students, and very young to be in the position he was in,' Margery smiled. Kathy could see that; it was definitely her brother they were talking about. He and Rose looked to have a good future ahead of them, and at first they had travelled, taking part in unspecified 'projects' in universities across America. Gradually their travels had taken them outside the United States, and there had been reasonable enough contact, given their busy, nomadic life, until some years ago. Letters from Rose and Peter had become fewer, less frequent, and those that did arrive never seemed to tally with the letters Margery had sent, as requested, to a PO Box number. Questions she had asked in her letters remained unanswered, and her growing concerns unaddressed. 'The letters seemed to me,' Margery said, 'like the sort of thing some people send out with Christmas cards. You know the kind of thing, newsletters rather than personal letters to your own mother.' So Margery had consulted Hari, knowing that his mystic powers were legendary, and he had been able to tell her that the PO Box number she had been given was the address of some group calling themselves the Higher Seekers. Intrigued, she had tried to find out who or what this was. She had contacted some of Rose's old university friends at home, and was shocked to find out that in the intervening years, her daughter and son-in-law had been back in Scotland several times, often on lengthy stays, and she had known nothing about it. The friends too had concerns, they felt Rose's behaviour towards them had been vaguely odd, though they couldn't say why, it was hard to put a finger on. At a recent university reunion a number of her old friends had got together and were swapping gossip, and when they related their individual tales of her odd behaviour they realised it hadn't been personal, that it was common to all of them. But they didn't know what any of it meant, and even if they did, what could they do? All they had was an uneasy feeling that things weren't quite, well, right. What did they have any right to do? She was a grown woman who had made her own choices just like the rest of them, what right did they have to nosey into her life and ask her to explain herself? The Higher Seekers had never been mentioned to any of them, but some of them had formed the impression that Rose was involved in 'something'. And that, Margery Nairn said, was as far as she'd got, though dear Hari had told her that her daughter was content and happy and, of course, she believed him. But still.

Kathy then revealed her own information. She left out her brother's earlier existence, but told Margery Nairn that she hadn't seen or heard of her brother in many years. He hadn't come home for his mother's funeral in 1968, citing 'important business', and as far as she knew, no one in the family had heard of his marriage to Rose until Harry – sorry, Hari – had told her in recent weeks. However, their father had died recently and she hadn't known of any way to contact him and, of course, there were matters arising that needed Peter's input. Margery looked shocked. Rose, it transpired, hadn't attended her father's funeral either. A very formal-sounding letter had arrived some weeks later, saying that she and Peter had been away on 'important business', and had only heard of her father's death when they had returned. By then, of course, it had been too late. Margery had been disturbed about it, she had felt hurt and let down, she supposed, but she assumed her daughter would come home to console her as soon as possible, only she didn't. Kathy didn't tell her Old Aggie's opinion of Peter's absence when Lily died, or her own explosive reaction; she was dealing with a refined lady, after all. Sitting listening to Margery's worries she felt angry. She had never minded Peter disappearing, not for herself anyway, they had, as she was the first to admit, never been close. But Margery Nairn, for all her alien upper-crust ways, had obviously been a good mother to Rose. She had brought her up in a good home, given her a decent education and yet she had been cast aside by her daughter because she had no further use for her. The cult of wannabe angels had decreed that families, especially close, supportive families, were obsolete. If someone felt the need for wings that was certainly their business, she thought, but those who had been discarded should at least have been accorded the decency of an explanation, especially from offspring who had benefited from being part of a family, as Rose had. Instead Margery, and doubtless many others just like her, had been left to worry and fret over missing relatives, fearing the worst but unable to get through the brick wall the cult had erected to keep them out, unable to find out what had happened to people they loved. It wasn't right; it was arrogant and elitist. Those who had been discarded had a right to be told why, to be told to sod off, she decided. Peter and Rose should've had the decency to at least say, 'Look, we're involved in something, we're happy with it, but it doesn't include you. We want you to consider us unrelated from now on, and if you try to contact us we won't reply.' That at least would have been clear; even if the likes of Margery didn't like it, they would've been saved the anxiety of wondering if their relatives were in some kind of trouble and needed help. In Kathy's mind it became a quest, a search for justice, and anyway, she dearly wanted to face Peter the Messiah and tell him what a prat he was, but she'd keep that to herself for the moment. The big question was, could she keep a straight face while she was delivering her telling-off in the middle of the Mojave Desert?

There was a brief return to her cottage at Drumsallie while her passport was sorted out, then Kathy told Rory she was off again.

'I knew it,' he replied calmly.

'You knew what?' Kathy asked.

'I knew as soon as you spent any time in the city again you'd want to go back for good.'

'Don't be stupid!' she protested. 'If you must know, I have a brother in California and over the years we've lost touch. Now I have to find him to tie up the loose ends after my father dying.'

'Hmm,' Rory muttered. 'First I find out you have a father, now it's a brother! Seems to me that whenever you need an excuse to get away from the West Coast you invent a long-forgotten relative!'

'Oh, listen to the man!' she said. 'Rory Macdonald, you used to accuse *me* of being melodramatic, have you listened to yourself?'

'Och, I always said it anyway,' he said with a grin. 'I always said you'd never last up here, your sort never do!'

'As I recall, you said I'd be gone within six months – that was twenty years ago!'

'Aye, well, six months or twenty years, what's the difference?'

'What's the difference?' she shouted at him. 'I've been living here at least as long as I ever lived in Glasgow!' But he'd turned his back and was walking off, with Cat following happily behind.

15

The further away from home she got the less sure she became about what she was doing. It made no sense to go chasing after her long-lost brother like this, especially when he didn't want to be found. She hadn't been able to stop thinking about him, though, and she couldn't explain that either. It wasn't as if they had ever been close, or even liked each other for that matter, but ever since Con's death she had lain awake in the wee small hours calling Peter to mind. She remembered his determination that he knew what was best for everyone, and how they had accepted it; she could never fathom that one out, even when it was happening before her very eyes. He had seemed so strong and confident, so sure of himself, but just occasionally she had wondered about that, even when she was a child. Their natures were similar, she had always been aware of that, though wild horses wouldn't have dragged it out of her. People talked about her as 'that Kathy Kelly', who always stood her ground, who said what she thought, who took no prisoners, yet she had never felt strong, not deep inside. She remembered someone once saying to her, 'It's all right for you, you've got a lot of confidence,' and she had been astounded. She had never felt confident, she felt as though she had lurched from one crisis in her life to the next, making decisions on the hoof and desperately hoping they were the right ones. She had no capacity for seeing through the mist to the core of whatever problem appeared on the horizon, her survival instinct had provoked certain reactions that to outsiders looked like confidence, that was all. But still, she was pleased that she had come across as though she knew exactly what she was doing, even if it had all been a trick of the light. She was Harry in another form, she thought, laughing to herself, her whole life had been a conjuring act, the illusionist's art ran in the family after all. So what if Peter's life had been the same, she mused? What if Peter's strong, dominant personality was a front to disguise the extent of his weaknesses? It was something that had crossed her mind before. There was that time when he had lashed out verbally at her because, he had said, her interests were insular, they proved she was incapable of engaging with people. And even as he ranted on, she had suddenly realised that, despite being older and supposedly superior, he was jealous of his younger sister. She had demonstrated a talent and he had been threatened by it; a truly strong, confident nature wasn't threatened by the success of others, surely? And there were times, too, when he was pontificating on other people's lives and problems, decreeing from on high that they were all idiots, and she had caught a glance from the corner of his eye, a swift look to see if she had swallowed it. She never did, of course, that was partly why they had never got on, Peter needed to be acknowledged as the one and only authority on everyone and everything, and it annoyed him that his younger sister refused to join the adoring masses. But why had it mattered to him, she wondered? She was nearly eleven years younger than him, he was adored by his family and everyone around him, so why was he so afraid that she had seen through him? Was it because he had seen through himself and, sensing that they were so alike, suspected that she had too? Thinking about it annoyed her. She didn't want to think about Peter, she hadn't given him more than a passing thought in more than twenty years, he was out of her life and she was out of his. Yet here she was, almost feeling something for him, though she couldn't make up her mind what it was. Empathy? Dear God, please, not that! Understanding, forgiveness? 'Oh, gie's a break!' she muttered, but despite that she was on her way to find him; it made no sense.

'If you look out of the windows on the left-hand side of the aircraft,' said the co-pilot over the intercom, 'you'll be able to see Las Vegas.'

Kathy looked down at the bright spot of light in the darkness, the excess of electrical power that was Las Vegas. At least she could say she had seen it, she thought, for what that was worth. In a few minutes the plane would be landing at Los Angeles airport, the furthest from home she had ever been. Even from the sky Los Angeles looked like what it was, a shrine to the car, with multi-laned roads stretching in every direction, crammed with automobiles. From the air it looked as though they were crawling along, like spaghetti studded with flies, she thought, and just as unappetising. The specially tailored deal she had made with the travel agent included a driver to take her to Gabriel's Gateway, but first of all she had to get away from the unbearable heat that had hit her like a blast furnace as she stepped outside the airport, and she needed to get some sleep too. The driver could pick her up the next day, and luckily he knew where he was going, because she wasn't at all sure that she could say 'Gabriel's Gateway' without collapsing in a heap of laughter in front of him. She had decided not to tell the aspirant angels that she was about to descend on them, suspecting that they might not be terribly welcoming, especially to family members, and forewarning them would give them time to man the barricades against her. She would, she decided, simply turn up and ask to see Brother Peter. She had waited a long time for this, nearly a lifetime in fact, and she could hardly wait to see his face when she confronted him.

She had started compiling a hate list immediately she heard the first 'Have a nice day!' She hated LA, she decided, the noise, the heat, the sunshine that hurt your eyes; it was hard to believe that people not only lived here, but chose to do so. As soon as she could get this business over with she would be on the first flight home again. She was annoyed about everything, at herself for being here, mainly. After picking her up the next day the taxi driver tried valiantly to open up a conversation, but he soon gave up when her replies refused to move beyond one repeated syllable. Was she on holiday? No. Was she thinking of joining the commune in the desert? No. Was she planning to stay long, because he could provide very competitive rates if she wanted a conducted tour? No. Did she like LA? No. In Glenfinnan she dealt with tourists all day, so she refused to be treated like one. Did she like

LA, indeed! She would never have thought of asking a tourist the same thing about Scotland, it was so crass! The journey took three long, mostly silent hours, at the end of which she had discovered something else she hated: air conditioning. She would've died without it, but it was unnatural. She thought of the freshness of a West Coast morning, with the cool, clean mist still capping the hills and creeping across the loch, as the deer grazed on the grass along the shoreline. She felt a stab of homesickness and yearned to be back, wondering again what the hell she was doing here. 'If Ah ever get back,' she promised no one in particular, 'Ah'll never complain about the rain ever again!'

Her first sight of Gabriel's Gateway reminded her of every picture she had seen of prison compounds. The high walls contained the area owned by the cult, screening those inside from the gaze of the world, and vice versa, she mused. She had once heard a deluded Communist trying to explain the rationale behind the erection of the Berlin Wall. It wasn't, he said, to keep those inside from escaping to the West, perish the thought, but to keep Westerners from gatecrashing and partaking of the delights of the East. She thought the High Seekers would probably say the same about their wall, and they would probably believe it too. At the entrance were two huge, wrought-iron gates, predictably representing angels and carefully painted in purple and gold. She got out of the car and yelled through the security intercom that she wished to see Brother Peter Kelly. There was a pause.

'Have you an appointment, ma'am?' a voice drawled politely.

'No,' Kathy replied.

'Well, ma'am, admittance here is strictly by appointment only. I suggest you go back and call this number –'

'Look, chum,' Kathy said wearily, 'I've travelled several thousand miles to get here. I suggest you let me in to see my brother, my *actual* brother, because I'm not going anywhere.'

'Your "actual brother", ma'am?'

'As in, we inhabited the same womb, were fertilised by the same sperm source, God help us. Peter Kelly, married to one Rose Nairn. Do you know who I'm talking about?'

'Oh, yes, ma'am, I know them,' the voice said carefully. 'I just don't know if they'll be at home to visitors is all.'

'Is there a local newspaper around here?' Kathy asked. 'Radio stations, TV stations? You wouldn't have their numbers, would you?'

There was another silence. She imagined furious celestial discussions going on somewhere behind the gold and purple gates. 'Grieving sister turned away from Gabriel's Gateway, that's what the headlines will say,' Kathy said into the intercom. 'Screaming very loudly and telling of her disgraceful treatment in the desert.'

The gates opened. 'Please drive through, ma'am,' said the voice. 'Follow the road till you come to our reception area. Brother Peter will be summoned there to meet with you.'

'Thank you,' she said sweetly, hopping back in to the nasty, blessed air conditioning, sweat covering every part of her body.

It was like following the yellow brick road and entering Oz, none of it felt or looked real. Here they were in the middle of this ghastly, burning hot desert, the sand as far as the eye could see shimmering with a silvery heat haze, yet inside the gates was a land of greenery, with fountains, well laid-out and tended gardens and giant palm trees. It looked like a garden centre that had been delivered to the wrong address, only it had been too much trouble to take it away again, so here it had remained, out of place and wrong somehow. All around were people clad in purple. These, she surmised, must be the apprentices; if she saw a solitary creature wearing wings she would know she had encountered Wally, the one and only angel she was ever likely to see in her life, or after it, come to that. The car drew up outside a tall, white building. It had been constructed of glass and concrete, but whoever had designed it had a classical Greek theme in mind that didn't quite come off in modern materials. Wasn't that just like the Americans? All that cash and application, and they still couldn't get European concepts right. Aristotle would've been horrified.

She took a deep breath before bolting out of the car; going into that merciless heat was like going under water, you needed something in reserve till you reached safety. There was a committee of one waiting for her in the reception area, another purple-clad clone who looked so cool and relaxed that she hated him on the spot; another one for her list of hates. He extended a cool hand and shook her proffered hot, sweaty one weakly, with obvious distaste. If she would take a seat, he told her, Brother Peter would be here momentarily. Why didn't they speak properly? 'In a minute', 'soon'; what was wrong with that? He extended a graceful arm, indicating a row of seats with a long, low table in front, and on the table was a glass and a jug of water, the outside of the jug dulled by the cold temperature of the icy water inside. The thought crossed her mind that the liquid could be spiked, she could wake up tomorrow and find herself in the custody of a white slaver somewhere in Arabia, a son of the desert with a burnoose and a mouthful of gold teeth, but she didn't care. It was hard gulping down an entire jug of cold water with gorgeous, beautiful ice cubes floating around inside, in a ladylike manner, so she didn't bother trying. The annoying cool purple clone stepped forward and wordlessly refilled the jug from a standard American, upturned-flagon, water dispenser in the corner, and brought it back to her. Then he retreated behind a desk on the other side of the wide stone-tiled floor. She would've given anything to take her shoes off and walk barefoot over those cool-looking tiles, but she decided against it; with her luck Brother Peter would appear at that very moment, and nothing would lose her the higher ground faster than being barefoot. She looked around. You couldn't call this a room, it looked like a cross between a cathedral and an aircraft hangar, as though the architect, the same one, presumably, who hadn't got the outside quite right, had found it just as difficult to make up his mind about the inside. Various purple clones passed back and forth, and there was nothing particularly alluring about the one approaching the cool one at the desk. There was a short conversation before the figure turned round to face her. 'Dear God!' she muttered under her breath. 'Did Ah no' have him burnt in the Linn a few weeks ago?' She didn't recognise him as Peter, but had she seen him in a street anywhere in the universe she would've recognised him as Con. Like all the others he was wearing a shirt of some coarsely woven material, with a mandarin collar and long sleeves, and a pair of wide, baggy trousers in the same material and colour. On his feet he had thong sandals; Harry was right, he would be perfectly at home here, she thought. There was a long moment of eye-contact as he walked to where she was sitting. She stood up.

'I'm –'

'I know who you are,' he said, in a strong American accent. 'You look exactly like your mother.'

Not *my* mother, she noticed, not even *our* mother, but *your* mother. She passed the ball. 'And you look exactly like your father.'

Peter smiled slightly, a strange smile, polite but distantly cold. Then she looked into his eyes and was suddenly horrified by what she saw, or didn't see, there. She had come here full of righteous indignation, ready and anxious to face her brother, determined to make him account for himself, to rub his nose in it. And not just about his cult either, it went deeper than that. She wanted to attack him for the way he had always behaved towards her, then she would leave here and feel vindicated, feel that she had got her revenge. But all that died the instant she looked into his eyes. He wasn't there, that was the problem, no one was there. It was as if he was inhabiting an empty space, but there was something else. What? There was no feeling of connection, it was as if they were looking at each other, talking, thinking, but behind a screen.

'Peter, is there somewhere we could talk?' she asked, aware of being watched.

'You'd better come to our cabin,' he said. 'But first we will have to wait for my Teacher to join us.'

'Your *what?*' she asked.

'All discourse with outsiders has to be conducted in the presence of a Teacher. We shouldn't really have started the conversation without him.'

'*Conversation? What conversation?*' she wondered.

'Virgil will be here any moment,' he said, falling silent. There was no expression in his voice, but she got the feeling that she was being snubbed, politely, but snubbed.

A few minutes later a tall, thin man arrived, swathed in purple. He smiled at Peter, but there was a feeling that it wasn't a pleasant smile, there was a hint of censure there too, presumably he would be held to account for causing the arrival of this unbeliever who had forced her way into the hallowed premises. She wondered if Peter's wings were already under construction, if so he would be deducted three feathers for the transgression. As they went outside Kathy looked at the car and driver waiting in the sun. 'Your driver can wait in the reception area,' Virgil said, 'until you're ready to leave.' There was no mistaking the message; she would not be staying here long. In her mind she retorted, '*Ah've been thrown oota better places, pal!*', but she made no reply.

The cabin Peter and Rose lived in was identical to many others laid out among the palms and gardens, with the vineyards rolling off into the distance, down a valley to the side. Peter moved easily through the hot sunshine; he had obviously become accustomed to it over the years. It had become her enemy in the short time she had been here; having left a Scottish winter two days before she was suffering badly. Looking around the cabin she was struck by the austerity. There were three prints on the walls, all classical subjects, just as she had learned, but no personal touches; she would've laid money on every other cabin being exactly the same. '*Little boxes,*' she thought, '*on a hillside, little boxes in a row,*' recalling the lines of an old Pete Seeger song, and just as he had warbled, they did indeed all look 'made out of ticky-tacky'. There was no pink one, green one or blue one, far less a yellow one, though, they were built of the same wooden construction, arranged around each other like the chambers in a honeycomb, homes fit for drones, or purple clones. Peter indicated a chair on her right then he and Virgil sat beside each other at a basic table as far from her as they could, and again there was that identical, strange, polite distance about their behaviour. Peter smiled slightly again, his right elbow on the table at his side, the hand cupping his chin and the fingers spread across his mouth, as though to protect against an unguarded word slipping out. He waited for her to talk, holding her at bay behind the screen by atmosphere and attitude rather than words.

They were brother and sister, they hadn't seen each other in twenty-five years or more, there was a generation of news from home he hadn't heard, but there was no excitement or recognition, not even a shred of curiosity on his part. And it wasn't just a hangover from those long-ago days when they had never much liked each other, it was, well, *something*. This wasn't like the Macdonalds' way of meeting up again after years apart, there was no underlying warmth, no low-key pleasure in the greeting, Peter was just coldly polite.

'I wanted to see you to let you know Con had died recently,' she said, following the script she had prepared. 'There was a sum of money left, money he got when my mother died in 1968 that had been put in the bank.'

Nothing.

'Even though you haven't been in contact for a long time,' she continued in her stilted, pre-rehearsed manner, 'you're still his son and entitled to a say in what happens to the money.'

He looked at Virgil, then 'I have no need of it,' he said quietly. Virgil gave a slight nod.

'Fine,' she said. 'Neither have I. I thought we could donate it to some charity, Save the Children perhaps. Would that be OK with you?'

Peter nodded and the silence stretched.

'Peter,' she started, deviating from the script, 'this place. Are you happy here?'

He nodded again.

'I think what Brother Peter is trying to say –' Virgil announced.

'Who asked you?' Kathy shot at him.

Virgil fell silent, but she could hear another couple of feathers hit the deck.

'Do you see yourself ever coming back to Scotland again?'

This time he shook his head. 'There's nothing for me there,' he said.

'Brother Peter does not regard Scotland as somewhere to return to,' Virgil tried again.

Kathy looked directly at Peter and jerked her head towards Virgil. 'Who is this joker?' she demanded.

'Virgil is my Teacher,' Peter replied. 'As I explained, we cannot have conversations with outsiders without our Teachers being present.'

'Well he's no' *ma* bloody Teacher!' Kathy said in broadest Glaswegian. 'An' mibbe ye'd better tell him that where we come frae, articles like him don't get too many chances before they get a slap on the kisser!'

Virgil looked from Peter to Kathy and back again, he clearly hadn't understood a word.

'You must realise,' said Peter, 'that we have certain rules here, and you're on our territory, so you must obey our rules.'

'So whit ye're sayin' is that ye're that feeble ye canny risk talkin' tae yer ain sister withoot this numpty talkin' for ye?' Kathy demanded in a furious whisper. She turned to Virgil before Peter could reply. 'Listen, pal,' she said reasonably. 'Now you may very well be my brother's keeper, but you're not mine. This is a private, personal conversation, and I object to having you here even listening to it, never mind trying to take part. I've compromised, I've let you stay, but one more interruption and you'll be picking fingernails out of the back of your throat for a month after I've gone. OK, pal?'

Virgil clearly did. She heard the clunk of a whole wing hitting the floor. He leaned forward, a smile so tolerant and beatific on his face that she had trouble not fulfilling her threat without further warning. 'You have to understand,' he said, 'that we can't have our community upset. That is why I am here.'

'And you'd better understand that there's more chance of it being upset if you don't sling your hook and leave me to talk to my brother. Please believe, Thingmy,' she said, using the Glasgow putdown, 'I am a nasty bitch, the sooner you let me say what I've come to say, the sooner I'll bugger off and leave you to whatever it is you do here.'

There was a hurried, whispered conversation between Virgil and Peter, resulting in Virgil walking out of the door, taking care to leave it ajar.

'That's fine, pal,' Kathy called after him. 'You'll hear me trying to put him into a big sack and cart him off over my shoulder from there.' She turned her attention to her brother. 'Look, I can't explain this, but since Con died you've been on my mind. I think I just need to know what's happened to you before I can get on with my life. The last time I saw you was at home –'

'That depends where you call home,' he said.

'Well, the East End, where you were born, where you were raised. Let's for argument's sake call that "home", OK?' She was floundering. She could make the same claims for herself, yet she no longer lived in the East End either.

'None of that matters,' he said. 'This is where I belong.'

'But your family . . .'

'The only family I have are the people here, and I don't want those I'm involved with now to know of my original background.'

She looked at him, looked at the dead eyes. If this was what it was like to discover your own Heaven, Valhalla and Utopia rolled into one, she thought, you could keep it. There was no happiness in those eyes, just a vast, empty sadness, and that feeling she still couldn't pin down.

'Peter, how did this happen?' she asked, in a kinder tone than she could ever have imagined using to her brother. 'I don't understand. You were always an arrogant bloody know-it-all, you ordered everybody around. Now look at you!'

He said nothing.

She tried again. 'I'm not here to try to drag you away, I just want to understand.'

Peter sighed. 'I don't think you can,' he smiled.

'Well, that's more like the Peter Kelly I know,' she replied coolly. 'You *can* understand, but *I* can't.'

'I mean that you and I are different, that's why you won't understand.' He fell silent.

She sat looking at him, wondering again why she was here, why she was wasting her time being baked alive in this God-forsaken dump of a place. Then she thought that as she was here, she'd get part of what she came for or die in the attempt. 'Try me,' she said.

'I never liked the East End,' he said. 'No, it was stronger than that; I hated it. From as far back as I can remember I was repulsed by the place, repulsed by the people too. When you arrived it was obvious that you fitted it, and that made it worse somehow.'

'What was there to repulse you?'

'Everything. The fact that we had ice inside the windows in winter, that we slept with coats instead of blankets over us in bed, the fact, too, that everyone accepted it was how it should be. I hated the way they all scrabbled about for a few shillings, that they didn't try to improve themselves. That existence, it was sleazy, dirty,' he gave a little shiver of disgust. 'I never felt I belonged there, never felt I was one of them, all I wanted was to get out.' He stopped and thought. 'You remember the smell of rotten fruit as you passed the market stalls?'

Kathy nodded, smiling, Maggie, saver of horses, immediately springing to mind.

'It made me sick,' Peter said sourly. 'And the smell of old clothes, and the way they yelled at the crowds and the way the crowds were all jammed together, all that noise and –'

'Don't tell me,' Kathy said tightly, 'the smell of them.'

He nodded. 'Exactly.'

And yet, she thought, they had all adored him, these people he had so despised.

'But I got away, I made something of my life when I came to America,' he continued. 'It wasn't enough though, I still carried that place, that background, around inside, I couldn't get rid of the memories. And no matter how much money I made and how well I lived, I knew I still wasn't living how I wanted, with the people I wanted to live among. I felt, dissatisfied somehow, nothing was ever enough. I felt I might be going mad. Then I met someone, and he told me about the Higher Seekers.' He shrugged his shoulders. 'That was it really. It was like finding the place where I should've been born, the people I should've been born among. When you come here everything before is cancelled, your life begins here. We're interested in learning, in the Arts, in being the best that we can be.'

So the cult sleuth had been right, then. What Peter had just described was that 'vulnerable moment' scenario, when, coincidentally, along had come a Higher Seeker with all the answers to his unhappiness and a once-in-a-lifetime offer to forgive him for his poor background and wipe it out for ever. It wasn't too different from Frank McCabe hearing confessions and handing out absolution, when you thought about it. Peter had stumbled across these people, this higher caste than existed in the East End he hated so much, that he was clearly too good for, and instead of a few Hail Marys he had only had to hand over his mind for the rest of his life. Who could resist that? Well, she was pretty sure *she* could, but as she had always maintained, no matter how alike she and Peter were, they were different too.

'But Peter,' she said, 'you always had opinions, free will for God's sake. Here you're told what to do, you live behind a high wall with a locked gate. You can't even speak to anyone without being monitored!'

He shook his head. 'I said you wouldn't understand. Here we think alike, we don't need to have our own opinions, we have a collective opinion. It's like finding a world of identical beings, they're all just like me. We have evolved together into a higher consciousness. And Virgil isn't monitoring me, he's here to help me, to make sure I don't stray into old ways and misguided loyalties. Free contact with outsiders contaminates the communal thoughts we all have here, we all understand and accept that it would undo years of meditation and work. As it is, this will take some work after you've gone.'

'But, Peter, you say you belong here, but you don't look as though you're enjoying life.'

'We have so many gifts here, we are evolving to higher levels than ordinary people, why should that come cheaply? Just because something is difficult, doesn't mean we should give it up,' he smiled. 'Life here can be hard, anything worth achieving can never be easy after all. Enjoyment, happiness comes from knowing that we have endured, because by doing so we evolve more.'

'And you really believe the guy who founded this is an *angel?*' she asked. 'And the rest of you will become angels too?'

He smiled, and she realized that the questions she was asking had been asked before. They were logical, so of course others had raised them and, listening to Peter, she heard the Higher Seekers' stock answers. 'Yes,' he said simply. 'It doesn't mean we'll all fly around on wings, but we'll have the consciousness of angels.'

She wanted to ask how they could be sure of what the consciousness of angels was, but then she remembered that they already had one, Wally himself, so of course they were sure. It was like asking if the chicken came first or the egg, the answers went round and round, as they were designed to do.

Still, the prospect of flying around on wings had been the only attractive part of the deal, as far as Kathy had been concerned, and now that had gone. What was the point of being an angel without wings, for God's sake?

She couldn't think of anything to say, or rather, there was so much to say that she didn't know where to start. Besides, she knew none of it would actually reach him behind the invisible barrier where he lived. But a world peopled entirely by Peter Kellys, wingless ones at that, she thought, now there was something to think about. She decided to change the subject. 'I hear you're married,' she said.

He nodded wordlessly. There seemed no way of conversing with him in a normal manner.

'And your wife, she believes in this too?' Kathy persisted.

'At first she wasn't as sure as me,' he admitted, 'but she's my wife.'

Kathy wanted to shout 'So bloody what?' but she didn't. 'Peter, look, I've spoken to your wife's mother, Harry put us in touch. You remember our cousin, Harry Nicholson?'

'Family relationships mean nothing,' Peter said. 'But Harry and I always had a special connection, we would've had that without the blood link. Like always recognises like.'

Kathy smiled. There it was again; Peter wasn't as deep and spiritual as he thought, he'd been caught out just like all the rest. He too had mistaken Harry's blandness for 'a special connection', even enlightened, highly-evolved Peter here couldn't tell a numpty when he grew up with one. 'Well, Margery Nairn's really worried about Rose. Can I meet her, so that I can at least tell her mother that she's alive and well?'

There was a pause while Peter thought, the strain of making a decision without the guidance of Virgil obviously showing in his worried expression. Finally he nodded again, then, to her shock, he walked into an adjoining room, spoke quietly, and returned with a woman. 'This is Sister Rose,' he said, making no attempt to introduce Rose to Kathy.

Kathy almost felt the hair stand up on her neck. All that time when they had been not quite conversing, Rose had been sitting in the other room, and if Kathy hadn't asked about her, she would never have been summoned to join them. She too was dressed in a purple shirt that covered her arms, and she was wearing a skirt that reached to the floor. She had grey hair caught untidily at the back of her head, and she was pale, painfully, sickly pale. Her eyes had no discernible colour, but there was that identical expression in them, that dead, sad look. What was it? Disillusionment? Disconnection? Kathy couldn't find the right word. She decided to push her luck. She put her hand out to her sister-in-law, but Rose ignored the gesture apart from a slight movement backwards.

'We don't,' Peter said. 'Not with outsiders.'

Rose retreated into a corner, making it clear that she would take no part in the conversation. Kathy turned her attention to Peter again.

'Did you never wonder what happened to Lily?' she asked.

Peter shook his head. 'I told you, past relationships are meaningless here,' he said. 'These connections are from a time we had no control over, therefore we have no allegiance to them.'

Kathy was shocked by that. His own mother and he had never wondered how or why she had died so young. Lily had given birth to him, raised him as best she could, cared for him, defended him against Kathy's frequent verbal onslaughts, and yet she was no more than a 'past relationship' to him. How could that be? She tried again. 'Old Aggie is dead now,' she said conversationally.

He looked at her quizzically. 'Aggie?' he asked.

'Your grandmother,' Kathy said, not sure if he was joking, then realised with a feeling of bewilderment that he wasn't. Old Aggie, who had kept his rare, non-communicative postcards till they fell apart with age and fond handling, unaware that they represented the final throes of his 'connection' with his family, Aggie included, and Peter couldn't remember her. She had had no great love for Aggie, but the old harridan was due more than that from someone *she'd* loved. She wanted to tell him what a rotten sod she thought he was, but it would've been a waste of emotion, Peter wasn't there to be offended. Even so, she struggled to keep the tone of her voice light. 'And all the old characters from the Barras are gone now too,' she waffled on brightly. 'The Pearsons still have businesses in Moncur Street, but they're the third generation now.'

Silence. He wasn't pretending; it was as though familiar people and places from his past had been wiped from his mind. Every time she tried to jog his memory an occasional, puzzled expression would flit across his eyes, only to disappear as quickly as it had come, leaving behind only blankness.

'Glickman's is still there, but Frances, Anne and Max are long gone.' Her voice sounded very loud in the silence. Peter didn't remember any of them, she could see that, but more than that, she realised, he didn't want to remember them either. That's when it hit her; it was called brainwashing. How many times had she heard that description and assumed she understood it? Only she hadn't, not really, not till now. He had gone, Peter no longer existed, and with him had been banished all his memories of his family, except for Lily, because Kathy looked like her. The place where he grew up, his background, they had all been erased. He'd told her this, of course, he'd said he didn't want anyone in this strange place to know of his background, because he had reinvented himself. 'Look,' she said, 'I'll be going back to Scotland tomorrow night. Why don't you meet me in LA in the morning or the afternoon, and we can have a proper chat?' She took a piece of paper from her bag and wrote on it the address and telephone number of her hotel, then placed it on the table in front of him. Peter didn't look at it or attempt to pick it up, nor did he make any reply. 'I'll wait for you to call me,' she said brightly, but she knew that she wouldn't hear from him.

On the long drive back from Gabriel's Gateway she frantically tried to marshal her thoughts. It should have been the showdown of the century, her revenge, the outpouring of the anger that had been simmering against him all these years, about the way he had always treated her, about his non-appearance at Lily's funeral and his total lack of concern afterwards. About being so bloody loved for no bloody reason! But there had been nothing there to fight against, it would've been like punching marshmallow. Whoever that weird, purple-clad creature was, and however much he resembled Con, he wasn't her brother. She had seen only pictures of Rose before, and the woman she had met without exchanging a word was as dead as Peter. He would now be in his mid-fifties, which meant Rose herself was barely fifty, but they both looked much older, and Rose looked ill; she had the look of someone in the latter stages of a terminal disease, and maybe she was. Yet she and Peter also looked so alike, as if they were related by blood rather than marriage. She had an overpowering impression that they weren't happy, but they were caught, trapped where they were and had been for many years, and there was no turning back. She knew that even if she'd said, 'Peter, Rose, I can get you out of this place,' neither one of them would've accepted; they had gone too far down the road they were on to turn back. She couldn't believe it, the tragedy of it. Peter was always going to make it big, Peter, as Jessie had said, couldn't wait to shake the dust of the East End off his shoes, he was going places, and yet he had ended up like *this!* It was such a waste, such a tragedy, somehow. Even now that she had seen him and talked to him, in a fashion, she still found it hard to believe; every now and then she'd stop and think '*It* can't *be!*' She thought back to her conversation with the pleasant chap from the organization that kept watch on cults. She had tried to explain what Peter was like, that it wasn't possible for him to be a follower of anything but the Cult of Peter, and the chap had replied wearily, 'Please don't tell me he's the last person you'd expect to join something like this. That's what every relative in your position says. But the fact is that it's the strong personalities who get caught up in these things. They're the ones who have high expectations and ideals, that's what leads them to look for something more than ordinary life.' Well, he'd been spot-on with his analysis, even his 'vulnerable moment' prediction had proved to be true. But what could she do about it anyway? Sneak back through the golden gates at dead of night and rescue Brother Peter and Sister Rose? People did that, of course, kidnapped their brainwashed relatives from the clutches of cults and tried to remove the brainwashing then repro-gram them back into normality, into who they had been. But she could see there was no possibility of that. Peter and Rose would never be able to live in the normal world again, they were stranded in this bizarre life that they had freely chosen, and they would never leave, could never leave.

When she got back to the hotel she immediately arranged her flight back for the following evening. If Peter called and they met again before she left, she would tell him about her life, about where she was and what she was doing now, she decided, let him know, as the nice chap had suggested, that the normal world was still out there. She felt like a child telling herself reassuring fairy tales. 'And they all lived happily ever after?' she asked herself wryly. That night she went over it all in her mind, trying to make whatever sense there was of it. All the things she had liked, he had hated. Her bad memories of the East End were to do with Con and his drinking, and the rest of her mixed-up family, too, of course, because, let's face it, Old Aggie was hardly an asset. But she had never blamed the other people she grew up amongst for that, they couldn't be held accountable for the sins of her family circumstances. It was hard to believe that Peter had found it all so disgusting. The familiar smell of the Barras that to her had meant safety and security, he had loathed, even the way the people struggled to survive marked them as almost degenerates in his eyes. To Kathy they had been heroic. She admired the fact that they never went under, that however hard it got they managed to get through it, to get their families through it. They didn't have the time or the opportunity to 'evolve', that was a dream they had for the next generation. The women her mother worked with in Stern's, most of them were doing it to support children through university. They had given up on the dream of a better education and a better life for themselves, but they knew it was there and it would happen for their children and their grandchildren. And they were still involved with each other, they all had the usual problems of working-class life, but they had time for each other too. She remembered the anger of the women at Stern's when Nancy tried to pretend her handicapped granddaughter was 'a wee bit slow', and how they had felt her anguish so much that they'd occasionally attack her for deliberately fooling herself and prolonging the agony. What was that but fellow feeling for one of them in pain? She had known people like that all her life, had instinctively recognised their situations and their feelings; why hadn't Peter seen it too? He had even held their poverty against them, condemning them for living through cold winters in poor housing as though they had caused it. How could you blame people for being poor? They were all good people, decent, hard-working, kind – well, OK, *most* of them were, you couldn't include the usual suspects – yet he had been disgusted. How dare he! She had worked herself into a rage, almost ashamed of herself for not telling him all of this, telling him exactly what she thought of his pathetic, self-absorbed attitude. Then she thought of how he had looked and her anger evaporated. He had achieved his ideal life among ideal people, he said, higher beings just like himself, but there was no happiness there. She would go home tomorrow and she would never see him again, but the memory she would carry with her would be of his utter sadness. Inexplicably, great sobs broke from her throat and floods of tears ran down her cheeks. 'Why dae *you* care?' she demanded of herself angrily, blowing her nose and trying to stem the tears, and the truth was that she didn't know why, just that she did care. He was Lily's son, she reasoned, Lily would've wanted her to try to reach him, to make sure he was OK, and though he wasn't, there was nothing she could do about it. And, of course, there was her natural instinct to finish things, to tie up the loose ends, but it was more than that. They were all that was left of Lily and Con, they had common beginnings, common memories, not many of them good, but still. She was feeling her way towards it. He had been unfinished business; somewhere in her mind, though she hadn't consciously thought about him for decades, somehow she hadn't really believed that she would never see him again. Unfinished business then, was that it? Maybe. They should – what? – know each other? No, it was more than that. It came to her, not with the flash of a thunderbolt, but with a slow, soft, sadness that gradually came into focus till she saw it clearly: she had wanted him to be her brother, that's what it was. After all these years she had wanted his approval, to have him look at her and admit that he'd been wrong, that she was OK after all, that she'd made something of herself. Maybe she'd wanted a big argument, a clearing of the air, then for him to hug her and, what? – to *love* her? She laughed harshly and blew her nose again. 'Ah think that's takin' things a bit far, Kathy!' she scolded herself.

Just as she had expected, he didn't call by the time she left the next day, and she knew with absolute certainty that she would never see him again. Now it was over, and yet he remained a loose end and always would. It went against the grain, but maybe growing up was accepting that sometimes you couldn't tie off every one. She had spent her entire life doing just that, thinking each time that she would be able to get on with her life after the next one was dealt with, but the truth was that there was always one more, then another. That was a fact, and the only way to avoid that was to do as Peter had done, retire behind a big wall and never again talk to 'outsiders'. She remembered the time he had accused her of having no interest in other people, well now she understood that he had in fact identified his own greatest fault. He had looked at his very similar sister and seen the greatest difference between them reflected in the mirror, only instead of facing up to it he had shifted the blame on to her. On the plane back to Heathrow she couldn't stop thinking about their cold, emotionless meeting. There had been no great reunion, no resolution even of their old differences, no 'Well, cheerio, mind and keep in touch,' even if neither side meant it. All she had was confirmation of how things had been, how they were and how they always would be. Peter had gone from her life for ever; it was almost, as that nice chap had said, as though he was dead. But what was it about men, she wondered, that sent them scurrying off into fantasy if they didn't like the reality they had? Con had retreated into drink and Irish martyrdom, her mad cousin, Harry, had taken to his insane, though highly lucrative, world of mystical forces, spiders and conjuring tricks with gusto, rarely visiting Planet Earth. Even the old Orangeman she'd never met needed his sash and his marching bands to get by, and Angus, much as she loved him, had run up the white flag as he and Bunty were approaching the ends of their lives, making sure he wouldn't be the one left behind to cope alone. But Peter, poor Peter – now there was an odd concept! – was the saddest of all, condemned to spend what was left of his life among the waving palms of the tragic purple land of Oz. He, like all the others, had found the harsh realities of his true background and early existence so unbearable that he had abandoned Peter Kelly from Moncur Street, and become reborn as Brother Peter, and in the process of running away from the East End he'd become trapped in Never-Never Land. Yet the women coped no matter how hard life was, they had no option because the men were all escaping to their boltholes. Lily coped with Con, as Kathy had herself, she had even been there at the end, with bad grace, it was true, because she hadn't wanted to be there. And Jamie Crawford, living in his nice semi in Moodiesburn in his fantasy respectable world, his one of each children, and his repressed wife sacrificing herself and her dreams to keep it together for him, because she had to, she was a female after all. Even horrible Old Aggie had been left with the forbidden fruits of Frank McCabe's loins, raising his child and letting him get on, unscathed and unimpeded, with the strange life he wanted to live, keeping their secret till the end, or near enough. And poor old Jessie the whore, who Kathy had despised all those years. Well, she had made the best of the bad breaks life had dealt her after the men in her life escaped too. Big Eddie Harris had tried to live out his big-time gangster fantasy and been dispensed with for being a nuisance, leaving Jessie with his child. Then Sammy Nicholson had taken a header down his own stairs, and OK, maybe he was only stupid, but Jessie was still left to cope. Even thick Claire's unknown father had walked off, scot-free, as had all the other men Jessie had had through her hands, not to mention other parts of her anatomy. She had provided them with a few hours of fantasy and, once the money had changed hands, they had walked back to better lives than she had ever had, doubtless underpinned by wives too busy to lead them around on all fours like dogs, telling them what naughty boys they were and occasionally slapping their arses. And now she lived in an obsessive, anxious world, terrified of germs, beset by rashes and weeping flesh, paying more than her customers ever did for the way she'd coped, for being a woman. Dear God, with all those men standing by in the wings, it had even been left to the diminutive Maggie to save the collapsed horse the day Frank McCabe wanted to murder it! Rory was the only man she had ever met who dealt with life as it was, but then, Rory was Rory, the fabled exception that always proved the rule.

She thought of Margery Nairn, sitting in her nice, neat Bearsden villa, waiting for Kathy to bring news of her missing daughter. What was she to tell Margery, who'd probably done no one any harm in her life? She'd tell her that Rose was indeed part of a cult, that she'd had a long talk with her and Peter and there was nothing anyone could do, because they were happy and content. That was it; she'd lie. Margery would be heartbroken enough with that, but she'd cope, because she was a woman, she had no choice. Then she thought of herself, of her secret dead child lying with Lily and the other Kelly women all these years in St Kentigern's, and of her flight to the West Coast. Wasn't she living in a fantasy world as well? No, she damned well wasn't, she wasn't the one who needed a high wall to protect her from being contaminated by the rest of humanity! She had found a life that suited her, but she hadn't turned her back on the East End. She could've, of course, she could've told the doctors treating

Con at the outset not to contact her again, that she wasn't interested. But she hadn't, she had kept in touch, interrupted her life, her *real* life, and gone back to Glasgow when she had to, and in those last three months she had nursed him. She'd hated it, she'd objected loudly and often, but she'd still done it. What had happened was that she had outgrown her background, she had moved on from the poverty and the pain of her childhood and found something better, but she had never been ashamed of the East End. She was, and always would be, 'that Kathy Kelly', and even if she'd walked away, she had always come back when necessary, just as she would when Jessie's time came, though where they'd find a coffin antiseptic enough for her to lie down in was anybody's guess. All the men she knew, on the other hand, had *run* away, and chosen to inhabit their individual fantasy worlds rather than reality. Peter had as much responsibility for their father as she had and, as everyone knew, had been worshipped and adored in return for his blatant negligence; Peter had cut and run without a thought. In his need not to be who he was, he had become someone else, a poor, sad, brainwashed, wannabe if wingless angel, exiled in a land he could never leave. She had always thought he was the survivor because he'd managed to travel far enough to stay out of reach of Con's demands and needs, while she had struggled to stay afloat. But she *had* stayed afloat, that was the point, when the dust had settled *she* was the survivor, not Peter, Peter had sunk without trace. She felt tears welling up again; maybe growing up meant admitting to feelings for people who probably didn't deserve them, she thought. 'Next thing ye know, ye'll be greetin' for Con!' she chided herself, then added, 'Naw, ye're takin' things too far again, Kathy!' She determinedly diverted her mind to going home. This time tomorrow she would be back in Drumsallie, sitting with Rory by the fire he'd set in the cottage, and Cat would be waiting to pounce on her and rake her with his claws again. It would be cold, there would be snow on the ground and she'd have to wrap up to keep warm, though it would never be as warm as it had been in the furnace of LA. Cold winter, numb toes, chapped lips, now *there* was something to look forward to, she thought happily. In a couple of months she would be back at work in Glenfinnan, spreading the word to the tourist hordes about Bonnie Prince Charlie, chancer that he was, watching them lift Rory Mark II's kilt to see, as Mavis loved to say, if there was anything worn underneath. This winter her alter ego, Lillian, had done no work at all, she'd been placed in mothballs for the duration. Maybe this was an opportunity to try something new as Kathy Kelly, though of course she wouldn't tell Rory, not till it was finished and she was satisfied with it. If she did it, that was. She wondered if there would be a letter waiting for Lillian from Ishbel Smith, and how her greatest fan would take it if Lillian disappeared and wrote no more of heroic Bruces.

The picture of Peter pushed its way into her mind again. As she'd left Gabriel's Gateway she had turned to look at her brother for what she knew in her heart would be the last time. He was standing looking back at her with his dead eyes, looking, but probably not registering. She wondered what Lily's reaction would've been had she lived to see her only son like that. Disbelief, sorrow and hurt, no doubt. Maybe there were some things, she thought, it was better for Lily not to have known about. What was it Lily used to say about them? 'The same, but different,' that was it, and Kathy used to protest 'But a helluva lot different, well!' And she'd been right, but she still felt unutterably sad. Kathy Kelly who always insisted on having the last word, even, as dear old Jessie had said, if it was a daft word, had had to accept that sometimes there is no last word, daft or sensible. Then she remembered the hideous outfit Peter had been wearing, the purple shirt with the stand-up mandarin collar, the thong sandals, and the baggy purple trousers. Even feeling as sorry for him as she did, she couldn't help laughing. At the end of the day he was still arrogant, better-than-everyone-else Peter Kelly, wasn't he? '*What an arse he looked*!' she thought, chuckling to herself. '*What an* arse!'

16

Getting from London to Glenfinnan took longer than getting from LA to London. She had only just made the six o'clock evening train from Queen Street Station, and when she finally arrived at a quarter to eleven at night, Rory was waiting for her. As usual there was little ceremony, he just nodded as she got off the train and followed him to his van.

'So,' he said, starting up the engine. 'Are you planning to stay this time, or have you come up with a few more imaginary relatives to get you away from the place?'

'I'm staying, you daft sod,' she replied.

'Charming as ever,' he grinned quietly.

'I'm too tired to be charming,' she protested. 'I've travelled halfway across the world, you know!'

'Aye, and you canny expect anybody up here to know anything about foreign travel,' he said. 'It's not as if any of us have ever moved out of the place, is it?'

'What I meant,' she said, 'was that you of all people should understand!'

'Well, sounds to me as if you're maybe angry because you're regretting being back. Is that not the case?'

'I have never met anyone in my entire life who could twist things the way you do, Rory Macdonald!' she shouted at him. 'You know fine what I mean!'

A fresh fall of snow had coated the familiar landscape, making it glow in the dark, and in the silence the van tyres creaked through the snow. The headlights picked out the startled eyes of deer by the roadside, forced down from the hills by the cold to find food on lower ground. Beside her Rory grinned silently, pleased with himself for provoking a reaction from her. She looked at him, smiling, too, despite herself. She had disliked this annoying man at first sight and the years hadn't changed him; no one could ever mistake Rory for an angel, winged or otherwise. He was just as annoying today as he had been way back then, yet somehow he had become inextricably linked with everything she thought of as 'home'. She couldn't explain how or why he had become so much a part of her life. He just had, that was all.

Part of the exhibition in the National Trust's Glenfinnan Visitor's Centre, showing 'A Highlander of the '45.' I know better though, it's really Rory Macdonald . . .